W9-BIL-850

"I adored *A Short History of a Small Place* and I am sure it will have a long history in a lot of places. Rich in character and strong of plot, Tom Pearson's first novel is a glorious accomplishment. Even better, it's fun to read."

Rita Mae Brown

"T. R. Pearson's charming, undauntable first novel is about human decency: the unrecognized variety that cures insomnia and occasionally ensures a ticket to heaven.... There's an archaic, heartfelt element to *A Short History*— disarmingly kind and unabashedly funny—that rings of the essence of the Southern tradition of literature.... But then the people of the town don't die, they 'succumb'; they have relations instead of sex, and they 'hold silent counsel' when a less complicated soul would just sit and think a spell. It is this charming deference to language—to regional homilies and, consequently, to truth—that gives the novel its freedom and compassion: the sense of lying on a hot porch in the afternoon and listening to someone special and very, very wise. There are less levelheaded educations to be had in the world than sitting captive at this father's knee."

The Boston Globe

"Tom Pearson has dealt a magnificent literary full house. What a voice! What a view! The whole book is a sort of austere riot. I loved it!"

Barry Hannah

(more...)

A
SHORT
HISTORY
OF A
SMALL
PLACE

T. R. PEARSON

BALLANTINE BOOKS • NEW YORK

For
Momma and Daddy
and
Beezy Boo

A portion of this book appeared previously in the *Virginia Quarterly Review*.

Library of Congress Catalog Card Number: 84-29720

ISBN 0-345-33263-6

This edition published by arrangement with Simon & Schuster, Inc.

Printed in Canada

First Ballantine Books Edition: June 1986
Eleventh Printing: October 1989

Daddy

DADDY SAID it was a bedsheet, a fitted bedsheet, and he said she was wearing it up on her shoulders like a cape with two of the corners knotted around her neck. She was standing barefoot on an oak stump, he said, standing on the one nearest the front walk where there was ordinarily a clay pot of geraniums, and he said her hair was mostly braided and bunned up in the back but for some few squirrel-colored strands of it that had worked their way loose and hung kind of wild and scraggly down across her forehead and almost to her nose. She was talking, he said. Then he stopped himself and creased the newspaper twice and put it in his lap, and he changed it to ranting, full-fledged bad-planking-in-the-attic ranting. It was something about Creon, he said, something about Creon and the stink of corpses.

Momma came from out of the kitchen and stood there in the doorway of what Daddy called the sitting room where he had his chair, his magazine hamper and his RCA television, and where Momma kept her drop-leaf maple table which none of us had ever eaten from, not even at Christmas, and which was cluttered up with three shoe boxes, Grandma Yount's crystal punch bowl, an assortment of odd-sized fliers from the A&P and the Big Apple, and a set of decorative scales that had mysteriously struck a balance between the one pan full of rubber grapes and waxed bananas and the other containing a forty-watt light bulb, eight cents in pennies, and three unrelated buttons. Momma crossed her arms over her apron bib and worked the small of her back against the edge of the doorframe. Daddy drew a Tareyton out of the pack in his shirtpocket and looked straight at me and talked straight at Momma and said, "Madness."

Daddy was afflicted by what Momma called an involvement with tobacco, which seemed to mean that he was always either smoking, had just smoked, or was preparing to smoke a Tareyton. Momma considered smoking to be a grave liability and she tried to purge Daddy of the habit along with the rest of his vices, and even though she was greatly successful in preventing him from saying "goddam" on Sunday, the best she could do with his passion for Tareytons was to negotiate an agreement which prevented Daddy from carrying any means of making fire. So as he lay the filter end of the cigarette on his bottom lip with one hand, he searched between the arm and the cushion of his chair with two fingers of the other and shortly brought out a perfectly good pack of safety matches. Momma just kept scratching her back on the doorframe and didn't even bother to sour up her face. Sheer and uncompromising necessity had made Daddy a wizard of a sort and she had seen him produce books and boxes of matches from most every seam and niche not just in our house but all over town, and more than once I myself had watched him turn over a rock at Tadlock's pond and pluck a full, unweathered matchbox out from among the ants and the nightcrawlers. As a courtesy to Momma, Daddy blew the smoke mostly across his chin and onto his shirtfront. He dropped the spent match into his cigarette pack.

He said Everet Little, the jailor's boy, was riding the iron gate in and out of the yard and half the town was standing up snug against the fence watching her jig on the lawn and cut capers on the oak stump where the geraniums should have been. Aunt Willa Bristow was up on the porch, he said, but she never came down to retrieve her, never even came out from the shadows hard up against the house, and he said she danced as tireless and light as a child all across the yard and up onto the stump and off again, and she brought the hem of the bedsheet up under her nose and played out what Daddy called the siege of Thebes, taking all of the voices herself and making the likes of a swordfight by beating together a hickory branch and a piece of a staub. Folks were quiet, he said, and polite and they leaned up easy against the fence with their forearms through the palings and their faces drained of most every expression except for an unexcited and slightly critical strain of curiosity like they were seeing something they'd expected, maybe even paid for.

He said every so often she'd break off whatever she was in the middle of, be it swordplay or some puffed up oration on the agony of kingliness, and she'd work her arms up and down, quivering them in the air, and say, "Putrefaction, putrefaction, sniff it on the breeze, ripeness and death," and Daddy said her voice was all shaky and inhuman. It sounded ghostly, he said, and a little ominous too, so people obliged her by sniffing and snorting and got for their trouble the stink of the Dan River Paper Mill, which Daddy said was slightly more potent than a pile of carcasses.

He stopped himself short, got up and loosened the window screen, and launched his cigarette butt into the sideyard; Momma did not allow them to linger in the house. And before he could come away from the window and sit back down, she grabbed up the one ashtray we owned—an oversized scallop shell with "Graveyard of the Atlantic" painted across the bowl of it in bold black letters—and took it off to the kitchen where she rinsed it out and washed the ashes down the drain. Daddy had to fetch it back himself, part of Momma's unspoken and utterly unsuccessful policy. We heard him snatch it out from the dish drainer and he began to whistle the first few phrases of "Mona Lisa" as he toweled it off. Momma just stiffened some and Daddy wasn't hardly back down in the chairseat before he started fumbling at his shirtpocket and scratching around beneath the cushion.

He said that animal of hers was pawing at the screen door to get out and setting up a fierce racket with all of his screeching and chattering, and he said Aunt Willa would give the siding by the doorframe a ferocious wallop with the heel of her shoe and that would shut him up for minutes at a time, but then he would set in to slapping at the screen again and hooting worse than ever. Daddy didn't know when Aunt Willa first started talking. He said he just picked her voice out from the general uproar behind the screen door and on the stump, and he said it wasn't much more than a voice since Aunt Willa, who is an inky color anyway, stayed lost in the shadows underneath the porch awning.

"Come on h'yer, Miss Pettigrew," she said. "Come on back to the house." And Daddy said it was altogether the most weary and bloodless tone he'd ever heard from a human. He said that animal chattered and slapped at the screen and Miss Pettigrew wailed and fluttered on the lawn and Aunt Willa just talked in a flat, dogged, openly hopeless voice. "Come on h'yer, Miss Pettigrew," she said. "Come on back to the house." And Daddy said all the folks along the fence picked up their faces and tried to find Aunt Willa in the shadows on the porch and Everet Little dragged his foot and stopped the gate to look and that creature beat the screen door with all ten knuckles but Miss Pettigrew just flapped her bedsheet and kept on ranting, he called it.

Daddy said he didn't imagine anybody sent after Sheriff Burton but that he had probably seen the crowd from his courthouse window and had come nosing in on his own. He was a man who was fond of paraphernalia, Daddy said, and as he edged his way toward the gate he used his arms to clear out a berth for his pistol butt and the shaft of his nightstick. He had a badge on his hat and a badge on his shirtpocket and a badge in a wallet on his left hip, and Daddy said he was dripping with bullets, festooned with them, he said.

Daddy said Sheriff Burton's first official act was to tell Everet Little gates weren't made to be swung on, and Daddy said that cowed Everet some and he stepped down onto the sidewalk where he made out to be enchanted with the workings of the latch. Miss Pettigrew was fresh off her stump, he said, and had just recently set out on a high-stepping tour of the front lawn which Daddy imagined was meant to serve as a kind of airy distraction from the ponderous and dismal goings on at Thebes. Sheriff Burton went after her, he said, chased her down along the sideyard, across the front of the house, up the walkway, and then back along the fence where Daddy said folks watched the two of them go by with the same sort of detached and curious expressions as before except for the hint of merriment, and he said the good money was on Miss Pettigrew who was pulling away from the sheriff with her bedsheet sailing and popping behind her.

Aside from being naturally soft and mealy, Daddy said Sheriff Burton was probably a little too much encumbered with the implements of law enforcement to have the chance of being nimble. He couldn't take half a step without the leather creaking and the metal jangling, and when he tried to run, Daddy said he was extremely musical and put himself in some peril what with all of his free-swinging attachments threatening to beat him senseless. So he drew up short alongside of the fence, Daddy said, and took hold of his knees while he waited for Miss Pettigrew to sprint back around to him. This was an unpopular tactic with the crowd who considered it shameful enough for their sheriff to have been beaten in a footrace by a woman nearly twice his age and saw no call for him to become unsporting in defeat and humiliate himself further. So when he latched onto Miss Pettigrew's arm as she tried to dash by him, Sheriff Burton had to suffer what Daddy called public ignominy.

Daddy said he'd never seen anything wither and shrivel away like Miss Pettigrew's spirit when she felt Sheriff Burton's hand on her arm. Every bit of liveliness shrunk off from her, he said, and she deflated right there on the spot. He said the exhilaration had put some blush in her cheeks and her vigor had seemed to flesh her out some, but Daddy said when the sheriff touched her she became all tallowy again, and frail and slight and painfully ancient looking.

The sheriff nudged her a little and said, "Let's you and me go to the house, Miss Pettigrew," and Daddy said she made a feeble noise in her throat and let him take her wherever he would. He helped her up the steps and onto the porch and Daddy said when that creature saw them coming he screeched and chattered most wildly and gave the screen door a ferocious beating with the leathery sides of both hands. The sheriff didn't offer Aunt Willa charge of Miss Pettigrew as far as Daddy could tell. He took it upon himself to see her into the house, and Daddy said when he opened the screen door, that monkey bolted for the front lawn and would have been out and gone toward Africa if Aunt Willa hadn't cut him off at the lip of the porch and scooped him up in both arms. And that was a sight, Daddy said, to see Aunt Willa there on the edge of the sunlight in her smock and with her usual grim expression lurking underneath the brim of what used to be Mr. Bristow's fedora and her arms full of Miss Pettigrew's monkey who had a hat of his own, a porkpie with a chin strap, and a plaid sportcoat, and a toothy ape face that was altogether as sour and unpleasant as Aunt Willa's.

Daddy said Sheriff Burton came out directly and as he passed Aunt Willa on his way off the porch he touched the brim of his hat and said, "Earn your money, Miss Willa," and Daddy said Aunt Willa just looked at him with no more expression than a doorknob and that monkey lifted his porkpie a half foot straight up and then let the chin strap snap it back onto his head.

Sheriff Burton drew out his nightstick, Daddy said, and opened up his arms as if to herd everybody back toward their own business, but Daddy said there were few people there with any business earnest enough to call them away, so most everybody lingered by the fence and watched Sheriff Burton try to send them home. Daddy said he waggled his nightstick under folks' noses and said, "The show's over. Get along home now. The show's over." But people just looked at the sheriff and looked at the end of his nightstick and nobody went much of anywhere. And Daddy said he stalked up and back the length of the fence, all the while slapping the shaft into his palm and saying, "Don't you folks have homes to go to? Don't you have something you need to be doing?" But the same forearms dangled through the palings and the same shameless faces followed the sheriff back and forth across the lawn. "Am I gonna have to run you all in?" he wanted to know. Daddy thought Sheriff Burton had been watching entirely too much *Dragnet*, and when he finally did leave he said, "Suit yourselves," and went storming off in the direction of the courthouse, Daddy said, like maybe he was going after a firehose or a load of mace.

Daddy said folks watched him up the courthouse steps and out of sight and then turned back to Aunt Willa who was still standing in the band of sunlight on the edge of the porch. She had set the monkey beside her on the planking and had snatched up a handful of sportcoat collar to keep him there. Daddy said the creature curled his lips and screeched once or twice and Aunt Willa just stood for several minutes facing the fence and the people canted up against it and the people behind them but not really looking at anything or anybody. Then she plucked the monkey up into her arms and went inside, Daddy said, and shut the heavy front door behind her. And he said folks looked at the door and looked at the windows hung with chintz curtains and studied the bushes across the front of the house and considered both halves of the lawn and the sidewalk in between and pondered the stump where the geraniums should have been and then watched Everet Little climb back up onto the gate and ride it in and out of the yard.

Daddy fished a Tareyton out of his shirtpocket and Momma eased herself against the edge of the doorframe and looked up to where the wall met the ceiling.

"She was so elegant in her day," Momma said.

Daddy grunted and brought out a matchbook from the depths of the magazine hamper.

"She was such a fine lady," Momma said.

And Daddy cupped his hands over the lit match and told her, "Well, seems she's gone bats."

"Louis Benfield!" And I knew by the way Momma said it she wasn't talking to me. She gave Daddy an icy once-over and he just shook the match out and looked right back at her with his cigarette hanging out of the corner of his mouth in the way Momma said made him look like a hoodlum. "That's no way to speak of a woman of her position," Momma told him, and when he never did say anything back, she went off shoulders first to the kitchen and left a kind of chill hanging behind her.

We could hear the water running and the sound of Momma loading the sink up with dishes, probably clean ones since she'd washed the dinner dishes already and we'd yet to have supper. But that didn't matter to Momma; she just needed her hands in the suds. There's a window over Momma's sink that looks out into the spiny branches of an apricot tree and, beyond them, onto the tin roof of our carshed which is flaked with rust and shot through all over with holes, and whenever Momma washes dishes, she looks out into those limbs and onto that carshed roof like she's never seen them before. After we buried Grandma Yount Momma came straight home to the kitchen and put an apron on over her funeral dress. She took a stack of plates out of the cabinet, ran the sink full of water, and scoured each dish until the drainer was piled high with them; then she dumped them back into the sink and started over. I remember climbing up onto the countertop and watching Momma handle those plates without ever bothering to see them and I remember watching her look out the window and I remember looking out the window myself and finding the same old apricot tree, the same weathered roofing, and just a glimpse of the sunset, a puny jagged edge of it off beyond the far wall of the carshed. And I remember drawing away from the window and saying, "What do you see, Momma?" and when she didn't answer me I tugged on her apron and said, "What do you see, Momma?" and she dropped her plate on the linoleum, where it pretty much exploded in all directions.

I surely would have gone off the countertop backwards if Daddy hadn't grabbed me from behind. He took me off to his and Momma's bedroom and set me on the edge of the bed, and he said, "Louis, you can't do that to your Momma."

And I said, "Yes sir."

And Daddy said, "When your Momma's washing dishes, she's always somewhere else." He waited until I looked at him and he looked directly at me and said, "Do you see what I mean?"

And I said, "Yes sir."

So Daddy uncreased his afternoon paper and I sat on the floor beside his chair and listened to the sound of Momma rattling dishes in the kitchen. Then there came a particularly long spell of silence and Daddy lit a fresh Tareyton off the butt of an old one, blew a plume of smoke straight out into the room, and winked at me over the top of it.

ii

*T*HAT WAS the day Miss Pettigrew stopped being just peculiar. She'd been peculiar ever since I'd heard tell of her and ever since I'd known what being peculiar meant, but now when folks spoke of her they would say she was Not Right, which was an advancement of a sort. The town of Neely had seen a blue million peculiarities in its history, but those among its citizenry who were genuinely not right were rare and cherished. In my day alone I'd seen any number of oddballs but less than a handful of the truly unbalanced, and three of them were from the same family. They were the Epperson sisters, and they had distinguished themselves in the minds of the Neelyites by going from reasonably normal to unquestionably insane without ever pausing at peculiar.

The Epperson sisters had lived across the street from us in a huge clapboard house that went entirely uncared for from the moment their father died to the day the roof collapsed and the fire department decided to burn what was left for practice. Daddy told me Mr. Epperson had been in commodities but had done so poorly at it that he had to take a job at the FCX on the side where he was given a pick-up truck and was employed delivering salt licks to the surrounding farms. He died three years before I was born. Daddy said he was nailing a shutter tight against the siding when he was taken by a stroke.

I don't ever remember seeing Mrs. Epperson except when they carried her out of the parlor all bedecked with flowers and greenery and loaded her into the back of the hearse, and I couldn't see her then. Momma said she was a mousy woman. Daddy said he'd always suspected she was mute, but Momma told me that wasn't so. Momma and Daddy both agreed that she was nobody's pretty child, and I didn't need anybody to tell me that her daughters were three of the homeliest women I'd ever laid eyes on. They looked like old photographs of sodbusters' wives—shapeless figures, plain, manly faces, and heads full of thin brown hair drawn back tight into buns.

When their mother died, they were all three still fairly young women. Eustace was near forty, which was a good seven or eight years older than Cora and Annie whose ages were indistinguishable from each other since sometimes Cora looked older than Annie and sometimes Annie looked older than Cora depending on the light. I'd usually see one or the other of them a couple of times a week pulling a metal shopping cart off to the Big Apple, and whichever one of them it was would always say, "Hello little Louis Benfield."

And I'd say, "Hello Miss Epperson."

And she'd come back with, "It's wonderful to be out of doors, isn't it?" which Mrs. Epperson must have taught all three of them to say since they all three said it and which they probably would have still insisted on saying even if it were raining hot lead.

And I'd always answer, "Yes ma'm, it is nice to be outside."

And whichever Epperson it was would unfailingly leave her regards to my Momma and Daddy which I would usually deliver at the supper table. "An Epperson said hello," I would say.

We never suspected that the Eppersons would ever be anything but kindly spinster women, so all of us were a little shocked when Annie got married, or anyway when she ran off with a man. He wasn't from Neely but somewhere else, had to be from somewhere else since there wasn't a man in Neely desperate enough to take up with an Epperson. He'd been in the area three or four days before he got down to our end of town. He was selling rhyming dictionaries, which came in a handsome two-volume set and for a very slight charge the owner could have his name tooled in gold across the front of each volume. When he arrived at our house, Momma had to field him since Daddy always refused to do that sort of thing, and she said he was a handsome enough gentleman and that he had entertained her by talking in couplets. She said he promised to make us all more poetical than we ever dreamed we could be, but Momma said she told him Daddy was an actuary and had no desire to be poetical, and as for herself she was too busy a homemaker to engage in such frivolity, and her son, God bless him, suffered from a brain deficiency which left him with no hopes of ever being an accomplished rhymer. Momma said he told her he was extremely sorry about my condition, and Momma told Daddy that made her feel mean and low. Daddy said better mean and low than poetical.

The Epperson sisters bought three sets of dictionaries. For almost a week solid we saw the salesman come and go from their house, and we assumed that he was merely working out the details and delivering the merchandise. But on a Friday evening when he left for the last time, he took Annie with him. Eustace and Cora acted like there'd never been anything but the two of them, and Annie was gone for the better part of a month before she came back to town one afternoon on a bus from Martinsville Virginia. She walked all the way home from the bus station carrying her suitcase and a paper sack, and I stood on the end of the sidewalk and watched her come from way off down the opposite side of the street.

When she got abreast of me she said, "Hello little Louis Benfield."

And I said, "Hello Miss Epperson."

And she said, "It's wonderful to be out of doors, isn't it?"

And I said, "Yes ma'm, it is nice to be outside."

Daddy imagined that salesman thought Miss Annie rich,

resourceful, or potentially beautiful and then discovered she was just an Epperson.

That summer the Epperson sisters would sit out on their porch in the evenings and one of them would read interesting bits out of the Neely *Chronicle* to the other two. Then autumn set in, and winter, and they shut themselves up in the house until spring. Something happened to the Epperson sisters that winter, and Daddy said it was probably Eustace's idea and that it must have just stewed there with the three of them all closed up together. He called it a certifiable case of simultaneous insanity, which he said was certainly rare and probably unheard of.

They had decided they were triplets.

One morning in early April when it was still a little cool and breezy, a hired car pulled up in front of the Epperson house and Eustace and Cora and Annie came parading out the door and down the sidewalk, each one of them dressed in the same identical sky-blue frock, and the same black heels, and the same elbow-length gloves, and the same little white hats the shape of an aspirin tablet, and each one of them carrying the same black patent clutch purse. They were gone for most of the afternoon and the news of where they'd gone to and what they'd gone to do got back almost before they did. They had traveled to the county seat of Eden, which was just a few miles down the road, and had paid a visit to the county clerk there, a Mr. Woodley. Carl Browner was sheriff of Neely then and he said Mr. Woodley called him along about midafternoon sounding decidedly agitated and distraught. He said there were three Neely Eppersons in his office who had come to declare themselves triplets. Sheriff Browner told him he was surprised to learn the Epperson sisters were triplets, and Mr. Woodley replied that they didn't appear to be triplets as far as he could tell, that they didn't even appear to be the same age. Sheriff Browner said no, he didn't believe they were, and Mr. Woodley said that Eustace—he called her the mature one—wanted him to search the records and draw up a document certifying their triplethood, and he wanted to know from Sheriff Browner just what he was to do about that.

"Search the records, I guess," Sheriff Browner told him.

The sheriff dismissed the hired car when he got to Eden and he said he found Mr. Woodley at his desk neck-deep in official papers with Eustace and Annie and Cora Epperson hovering over him from behind. Mr. Woodley was tracing the Epperson migration from the banks of the French Broad River to the east and then to the north towards Neely. He was still a hundred years and over two hundred and fifty miles out of the county when the sheriff arrived, so Sheriff Browner suggested the Epperson sisters give Mr. Woodley a little time to do his work on the matter, which the three of them thought altogether reasonable, and they made an appointment for the following week. The sheriff said he feared Mr. Woodley might leap up from his desk and kiss him.

Once he got them in the car, Sheriff Browner turned to Eustace who had taken the front seat and told her he had no idea the three of them were triplets.

He said she bristled a little and drew her purse up tight against her chest. "We have discovered that we are," she said.

When Mr. and Mrs. Epperson moved to Neely they came complete with three more or less full-blown daughters, so we only had our suspicions about the attachments from Epperson to Epperson and were probably more surprised at what Mr. Woodley dug up than Eustace, Annie, and Cora were. The Epperson sisters weren't triplets; one of them wasn't even an Epperson. That was Cora and she was her Momma's brother's child, which made her a Greene. Mr. Epperson had taken her in after Mrs. Epperson's sister-in-law had died and Mrs. Epperson's brother had turned out to be no count. Cora must have known all this at one time, since she was five when it happened, and Eustace certainly knew it, but Cora told Mr. Woodley it was a baldfaced lie and Eustace said yes indeed it was a baldfaced lie and Annie said it absolutely had to be a baldfaced lie. Sheriff Browner, who had driven the three of them to Eden, said it was a sad sight to see those women, all of them in identical scarlet dresses, wailing and moaning at poor Mr. Woodley who the sheriff said looked as if he might be willing to strike up a compromise and recognize Annie and Cora as twins in exchange for some peace and quiet. He said the news had put all three Eppersons in a kind of indignant but still moderately polite rage, since they were respectable ladies after all, and the sheriff said he was so pained by their predicament that he suddenly suffered a massive lapse in good judgement. In an effort to offer some sort of comfort the sheriff told them he would consider recognizing them as triplets if they were able to get fifty adults in Neely to sign a petition verifying their claim. It was a tremendous mistake. The sheriff said he had temporarily forgotten what people were like.

They collected the names on an ordinary sheet of lined white paper, and for three mornings only at nine o'clock they came out of their house and set out towards town. On the first and the third day they wore their blue frocks and on the middle day they wore their scarlet outfits which were quite a hit with the ladies of Neely and got them no end of comment. Eustace always carried the paper in her purse and when they visited homes and shops and stopped folks on the street, the three of them would take turns explaining their situation. People said they were gracious and altogether levelheaded, and I suppose with nothing more than their manners and show of good sense they managed to inspire among the citizenry of Neely the general impression that they had been victimized by some sort of terrible prenatal injustice. Nobody who was asked didn't sign. The three church deacons signed. The ladies of the garden club signed. All of the icehouse employees signed. Every shopkeeper on the boulevard signed. The mayor signed and the mayor's wife signed and the mayor's ninety-three-year-old blind and bedridden aunt signed. Miss Pettigrew signed and Miss Willa Bristow made her mark. And Mr. and Mrs. Pendzinski, who were passing through on their vacation from Ohio with a carful of little Pendzinskies and who qualified by virtue of being adults in Neely, signed and then took turns having their pictures made with the Epperson sisters.

Cora carried a dainty gold pen that she produced from her purse as Eustace drew the petition out of hers. Annie made her back available for a writing table if one wasn't handy. Always before she handed over the paper, Eustace would clear her throat and read the terms of the proposal which the three of them had devised and one of them had scrawled across the top of the page:

> By order of Sheriff Carlton Benjamin Browner and as testified to by these fifty below written people, Eustace Joy Epperson, Cora Simpson Epperson, and Annie May Epperson are hereby officially and forevermore recognized as the three triplets they are and always have been ever since they were born into it.

Then Eustace would determine whether or not the prospective signee understood the terms of the document and Cora would offer the pen to whoever it might be signing, and whoever it was surely must have looked up to take the pen and seen Cora and Annie side by side before him, the two of them related more by pure homeliness than anything else, and then Eustace, off a little to herself, and a half dozen years older than the both of them and already beset with long iron-colored strands of hair laying in with the brown, and whoever it might be would take hold of the gold pen, which was so slight and delicate as to be almost impossible to get a grip on, and he would sign anyway, probably not because he saw any advantage in being triplets over being just sisters or over being just two sisters and one cousin, but because he couldn't see any harm in it either.

By the afternoon of the third day the Epperson sisters had filled the fifty slots and we all thought they'd bolt directly for the courthouse while the ink was still clammy on that last name. But Eustace put the paper away in her purse and Cora put the pen away in hers and the three of them strolled home very leisurely and shut themselves up in the house for the better part of two hours. It seems they had gone to change and freshen up. Me and Momma stood at the front window and watched them when they finally did come out away from the porch and into the late afternoon sunlight. Momma said they were dazzling, just dazzling. It wasn't blue frocks this time or scarlet ones but three awesomely elaborate ivory white dresses, and three pairs of long ivory gloves, and three lacy ivory hats garnished on the backside with peacock feathers. We thought a car might call for them, but they walked all the way to the courthouse and all gages of people fell in behind them as they went so that the crowd of us spilled out of Sheriff Browner's office into the corridor and partway down the marble courthouse steps.

Somehow Sheriff Browner didn't seem at all surprised to find himself host to half of Neely. He just sat a little uneasily at his desk not quite looking at anybody, which was his way, while Eustace removed the petition from a pearl-laden purse dangling from her forearm and flattened it out on the desktop in front of him. He picked up a pencil from the blotter and began to check off the names, which resulted in the document being momentarily voided when it was discovered that Daddy had signed it twice. But the sheriff, a sensible man, just scratched out one of Daddy's signatures and put his own in place of it. The jubilation was general and immediate. Eustace, Cora, and Annie accepted our congratulations with extreme modesty and thankfulness, and a courthouse clerk along with Mr. Singletary from the five and dime helped Eustace up onto a chair from which she delivered a brief speech directed mostly towards Sheriff Browner without whose assistance, she said, none of this would have been possible. That unleashed a fearsome ovation in the sheriff's honor and he moved away from his desk, still refusing to look entirely at anybody, and made his way out of the room without ever offering to say a word.

Three days later, in the fat part of the morning, two men in a state-licensed station wagon followed the sheriff to the Epperson house. I suppose we knew they would come or that somebody like them would come since we all knew that the state would not allow two sisters and a cousin to parade around as triplets. Sheriff Browner assured us they were kind men, gentle and competent men. He promised they would treat the Eppersons with respect and dignity, and we were satisfied. Me and Momma watched them bring Eustace and Cora and Annie out from the house and load them and their luggage into the car, and it struck Momma as an odd thing to see. She said everybody was a little too happy, a little too quick to laugh, everybody but Sheriff Browner who just looked all around himself at the treetops and the sidewalk and the hubcaps on the state-licensed station wagon. His coloring was funny, Momma said, and he was slightly more hunch-shouldered than usual. She thought he might be ill and I thought he looked it myself, but then we'd never seen shame on Sheriff Browner before so there was no call for us to recognize it.

The Epperson sisters were taken to the Dix Hill mental facility in Raleigh where they were tested for traces of sanity. We heard nothing from or about them for nearly a month until a very brief article appeared on the Statenews page of the Neely *Chronicle*. A committee of two doctors and a clinical psychologist had concluded that the Epperson sisters were "disoriented as to reality." It seems they were a little more afflicted than we had imagined since the doctors judged them disoriented enough to have all three of them committed and their belongings auctioned off and their house put up for sale when a statewide search produced no heir. But nobody would buy the Epperson house. The realtor couldn't even get anybody to look at it, and it was boarded up and sat empty for a year and a half. Then the roof collapsed in November, and people said it was a good thing the Epperson sisters had become triplets; otherwise they probably would have been crushed and mangled. In December the fire department burnt the remains in a training exercise and put on a less than encouraging show of firefighting; they managed to save the concrete footings.

It got to Sheriff Browner, at least that's what people would say when they would talk about him after he was gone, and they would hardly ever talk about him, but when they did, they would say it was the Epperson sisters that started it. Momma didn't think so, and Daddy said no, it wasn't them exactly. It was more than them, he said. I was seven years old when the Epperson sisters decided they were triplets. I was nine and a half when we got word of their transfer, which was the last we heard of them and which came to us in the form of a banner headline across the front of the *Chronicle*:

TRIPLETS FIND HOME AT BUTNER

Momma wrote them letters and sent them cards but left off the practice when they began to return to her unopened. So by the time I was eleven we had not heard much worth hearing from the Epperson sisters in over three years, and Momma said it wasn't them, and Daddy said no it wasn't them exactly. He said three and a half years was a long time. Momma said it was a very long time.

I was only midway through my eleventh year when Sheriff Browner killed himself. Momma said the shock of it was in not knowing it was going to happen, was in not even suspecting that it might. But Daddy said we should have known, we should have suspected. Sheriff Browner had always been different. We would have called him peculiar except that he was sheriff and we couldn't put our faith in a man who suffered from peculiarities, so we said he was different and left it at that. Momma said he was a painfully shy man, but Daddy just called it pensive, and when we found out he was dead Momma said something must have snapped, but Daddy said no that wasn't it exactly. He said when the sheriff went to the well he drank too deep, and Daddy said the world became so burdensome for him that he eventually went down under the weight of it.

I don't recall that Sheriff Browner ever shot a man. I don't remember ever hearing of him firing his revolver except one Fourth of July when it was raining and the town councilmen couldn't get the fireworks lit. I don't think he ever clubbed anyone with his nightstick; I don't think he ever used it except to crack walnuts. And I'm sure he never hit anybody with his fists, though I imagine he spent half his life wanting to. Mostly Sheriff Browner whittled, carved on hunks of oak and beechwood, spat occasionally, and pondered, I suppose. There's never been much crime in Neely. Sometimes men get drunk and beat up their wives or try to beat up their friends. Sometimes people get their t.v. stolen or their grandmama's silver or a little money they were too lazy or ignorant to put in the bank. And every now and again a vagrant will break into the laundromat to keep warm, but from week to week that's about all we ever get. Then there's the less frequent sensational cases that rate a quarter column on the inside of the Greensboro *Daily News*. Sheriff Browner had two of those right near the end and Momma said they were the straws that broke the camel's back. Daddy said yes, he imagined that was pretty much the truth of it.

We had not had a murder in Neely in well over four years when the widow Mrs. Doris Lancaster was beaten to death with a chairleg on a Tuesday evening. She lived outside of town on the 48 highway in a house her husband had drawn up and built himself during their courtship. It was stuck back off the road in a maple grove and was separated from the nearest neighbor by a sprawling kudzu thicket that had once been a regular wood but was since reduced to mostly vines and rotting treetrunks. Nobody missed her for nearly a week until Mrs. Spencer came from the other side of the thicket and failed to get anybody to the door. She called Sheriff Browner who jimmied his way in and found Mrs. Lancaster in a heap on the livingroom throw rug.

When they heard in Greensboro that something grisly had happened in Neely, the *Daily News* dispatched a correspondent, who caught up with Sheriff Browner in his office and asked for a few details of the murder. The sheriff told him it wasn't a murder; it was a slaughter.

And the correspondent made a few notes and said, "Yes sir."

And Sheriff Browner asked the correspondent if he knew what he meant.

And the correspondent said, "Yes sir, it was a savage murder."

And Sheriff Browner told him it was no murder at all; it was a slaughter and slaughter is what happens to a cow when the man puts its head on a block and breaks it open with a sledgehammer.

And the correspondent thought that was extremely clever and said, "Can I use that?"

Sheriff Burton was deputy then and he's the one that told everybody how, as near as they could reconstruct it, the victim had been surprised by the assailant in her bedroom, had struggled with him across the bedroom floor and out into the hallway, and had finally been subdued in the livingroom where the assailant wrenched loose one of the legs from an old ladderback chair and proceeded to render the victim unconscious with repeated blows to the frontal portion of the skull. He said the wounds sustained by the victim proved to be fatal and that the condition of the interior of the victim's house suggested robbery as a probable motive. But Daddy said the thievery was just a sidelight. He said pure meanness was certainly the motive.

In the several weeks that followed the murder, Deputy Burton kept talking about tips, and leads, and hunches, and lights at the end of the tunnel, but Sheriff Browner didn't have anything on anybody, not anything at all. Then, in what appeared an episode of unrelated violence, two rail bums got into a knife fight out back by the loading dock of the Bright Leaf tobacco warehouse. The second shift was packing up a boxcar for Richmond when the two of them came out from around the backside of it already kicking and swearing at each other. The activity drained most everybody out from the warehouse and they collected on the dock where they watched those bums claw and spit and roll around in the high weeds of the right of way. Then they said one of them pulled a knife out from his trouser pocket. It wasn't anything but a little hinged Barlow, they said, with about three and a half inches worth of blade and the point of that broken off, but they said he waved it around like it was a saber and swore the other fellow a blue streak. And they said the other one reached inside his coat and brought out a hunk of steel nearly a foot long that had been rubbed down to a point at one end. Then they commenced to circling each other, they said, and swearing ferociously and eyeing each other out from under the ridge of their foreheads. And then they said they ran together like two old bulls and fell to slicing at each other as best they could. And they said in the first encounter alone the one with the little Barlow got his leg gashed and lost the most of his left ear and the other one had his cheek laid open from his eye all the way to his chin. Then they drew apart, they said, and circled some more until they came together again in a clench, and they said the one with the steel blade was clearly getting the best of it this time. The other one tried to break away, they said, and fell over backwards, and the one with the blade jumped on him and laid into him, and they said from up on the loading dock it sounded like he was sticking a plump melon.

Then somebody went after the sheriff. The one with the little Barlow was long dead when he got there, and the other one was too cut and beat up himself to have the strength to run off. Deputy Burton took him away to the doctor's and had him stitched up and fumigated before he locked him in the holding cell in the basement of the courthouse. Sheriff Browner stayed with the dead one, and what few men were left on the loading dock said the sheriff started going through that bum's pockets and pulled out a handful of string, a few pennies, some foil, and one of Mrs. Doris Lancaster's good silver forks. They said the sheriff fell back onto his haunches there in the high weeds and with that corpse stretched out in front of him, and they said he studied that fork for what seemed a quarter hour, just looked at it, they said. And then they said he put it down beside him and looked off beneath the carriage of the boxcar to the other side of the tracks and the weeds over there, and then back at that bum, and then at Mrs. Doris Lancaster's fork where he'd set it next to him on the dirt.

Daddy said since Sheriff Browner was quiet and private anyway nobody noticed when he became more quiet and more private, and that's why Momma says we were shocked and couldn't have known, but Daddy says we were just caught up in the glamor of violence and murder and weren't paying any attention. Poor Mrs. Browner, who was as plain and normal as a bar of soap, didn't see it coming and never forgave herself for it, but Daddy says she probably saw less of the sheriff than we did what with the reporters and the newsmen and that one fellow from a national crime magazine who wouldn't let off hounding him until he got an interview. And Mrs. Browner said he just came in one night for supper after not coming home hardly at all since the stabbing, and she told him she'd cook him up a quarter chicken with potatoes and green beans, which he was very fond of, and she said he went off to the bathroom and drew himself a tub full of water while she boiled the potatoes and the beans and started the chicken baking. And she said she got it on the table and called him to eat but he didn't answer. And she said she called him again and he didn't answer again. And she said she went to get him herself and found him slouched over the edge of the bathtub with his head entirely under water and nothing in the world to hold him there, Daddy said, except his own desperation.

That was in November just before Thanksgiving and on the day we buried Sheriff Browner it was threatening to sleet and the sky was close and dark. The pastor talked very generally about death and the everlasting, and Deputy Burton said a few words in praise of what he called the sheriff's professional integrity. Then we all sang "On Christ a Solid Rock I Stand" and Mrs. Browner had to be helped from the sanctuary. It began to rain as we were on our way to the cemetery, and some people didn't bother to get out of their cars for the graveside service. Mrs. Browner and a half dozen of her and the sheriff's kin sat under a green canopy with the coffin, and the members of the sheriff's legion post stood in rank by the grave and recited a prayer in unison. Another preacher from another church committed Sheriff Browner to the earth, and Mrs. Browner, as she was being taken away, reached out and gently patted the top of the casket twice.

Momma washed every dish in the house when Sheriff Browner was laid to rest. She stood at the window over the sink for hours and gazed out through the limbs of the apricot tree to the carshed roof where the raindrops and pellets of sleet were rebounding into the air. Daddy said it took a bold man to end his own life, to perish in an act of will, but Momma didn't say anything; she just cried and cried and watched the rainwater run off the carshed roof and drip from the limbs of the apricot tree.

Daddy put it this way. He said that sanity had been a scarce commodity among the Epperson sisters and that's why their madness had seemed such a jolly affair, but that Sheriff Browner was plagued with sanity in spadefuls, loaded down with it, and Daddy said the weight had put the sheriff on a kind of slow burn. He called it thinking man's madness and said there was never a thing giddy about it. But folks forget, Daddy said. I was eleven when Sheriff Browner died and it wasn't until I was fifteen and a half, near sixteen, that Miss Pettigrew wrapped herself up in a bedsheet and took to her frontyard, so we'd enjoyed a spell of levelheadedness in Neely, and I imagine most people were anxious for a little relief from it.

iii

WHEN DADDY leaned his face down towards mine there in the sitting room and looked directly at me and talked directly at Momma and said, "Madness," I was somewhat confused since I didn't see any reason for people like Miss Pettigrew to go mad, but Momma was openly dismayed and deflated. Miss Pettigrew had been beautiful until she got old and wasn't beautiful anymore and then she had become merely elegant. That's where she was when she took the pot of geraniums off the stump and climbed up onto it herself, and Momma and all the women of Neely suffered a kind of defeat that afternoon because they themselves were not elegant, did not lead elegant lives, and required for their own satisfaction that Miss Pettigrew do it for them. And that's why Momma stormed off to the kitchen and to her sink of dishes and her window. I didn't really understand it then, but something had passed on that day and Momma was obliged to mourn for it.

Miss Pettigrew was the wealthiest woman I'd ever come across, but Daddy said it hadn't always been that way. Miss Pettigrew's daddy had arrived in Neely in relative poverty and had proceeded to become successful and rich, which was cause of both pride and resentment among native Neelyites, who would boast of the Pettigrew fortune to strangers but who generally had either come into the world with little to speak of

themselves and had failed to make any noticeable advancement
or had been born into considerable resources and had managed
to backslide into insolvency. It's not that the people of Neely
are unusually idle, it's just that they are not particularly lucky
like Mr. Pettigrew was lucky, or shrewd like Mr. Pettigrew
was shrewd, or willing like Mr. Pettigrew was willing.

Mr. Pettigrew was what most people call enterprising. He
made his money speculating in construction, and since nobody
in Neely had ever speculated himself into a fortune before,
people were a little suspicious of Mr. Pettigrew's success and
imagined his money was somehow indecently gotten. He had
arrived in town directly from New York State with nothing
more than a valise, a sizeable carpetbag, and a Mrs. Pettigrew
(née Bennet, Daddy said), and Daddy said he immediately hired
himself out as a carpenter's apprentice without really knowing
which end of the hammer drove the nail. He worked for three
different carpenters in Neely and one in Eden before leaving
off the occupation altogether and getting on with the McKinney
brothers, who were brick masons, and he hauled brick and
slopped mortar for them for nearly a year. Then he took up
with a plasterer for a spell, then a house painter, and afterwards
got himself on as an electrician at the power plant before finally
apprenticing to one of the first plumbers Neely ever had call
for.

Along about 1904 the railroad decided to hook Neely into
the Southern Crescent route, which swung south out of West
Virginia all the way to New Orleans. That meant laying new
track through the north end of town and building a new passenger depot to go with it. The railroad dispatched two men
out of Danville and the one in charge of getting the track laid
collected himself a work crew made up mostly of negroes and
hard luck whites. But the other one needed skill and, not being
from Neely, he didn't know exactly where to get it. Daddy said
that's when Mr. Pettigrew's career as a speculator got off the
ground. Daddy didn't call it contractor, he called it liaison,
and he said the railroad man just put it down as coordinator
and then sat back and let Mr. Pettigrew coordinate.

All they gave him was a budget and a blueprint, and Mr.
Pettigrew hired out the carpenters and the masons and the
plasterer and the painter and the electrician and the plumber
and built himself a train station without ever striking a lick.

The railroad man collected his salary for doing little or nothing and was satisfied. The carpenters and the masons and the plasterer and the painter and the electrician and the plumber all earned steady wages and were happy to get them. And when the depot was finished and the expenses were all paid up, Mr. Pettigrew took what was left and discovered that he was already nearly rich. That was when Mr. Pettigrew became a contractor, Daddy said, the minute he walked out of the train station for the last time with that railroad voucher in his pocket. He set up an office in the garage of the house he was renting and advertised himself as a builder with one depot to his credit already, and then it was a depot and a bank, and then it was a depot and a bank and two private residences, and then he left off advertising entirely. There was no need to anymore since everybody in Neely who built for a living built for Mr. Pettigrew.

Sometime along about when he became established and saw that he would probably remain a wealthy man, Mr. Pettigrew must have decided it was advisable to build himself a homeplace and have himself an heir. He saw to the homeplace, that being in his line, and he bought a parcel of land right there in the heart of Neely where municipal square runs into the boulevard. There was the shell of a guest house and the remains of an old harness shop on the property when he bought it, and he hired out a crew of men to raze the both of them and level off the lot with picks and shovels. Then he proceeded to put himself up a mansion, Daddy called it. It was the biggest, most sprawling, most elaborate house Neely had ever seen. Daddy said it was built on the plan of one of the churches of Rome with half of it running north-south and half of it running east-west and the two wings meeting towards the tip of one and towards the middle of the other. Daddy said it was meant to look something like a cross, but it looked more like an airplane or maybe some kind of ship what with the porch coming off the front end in a half-circle and a balustrade running the length of the roof like the rail on a flying bridge.

Most of the town watched it go up and people were in general agreement that it was an ambitious, grand, and awesome structure. Daddy said Mr. Pettigrew built it with an eye towards eternity and maybe had hopes of hosting the last judgement in the front parlor. To avoid rot and deterioration, he had the siding done in cedar clapboard and the roof laid with orange terra cotta tiles brought in from Georgia. A furniture builder in Eden custom made the window sashes and doors out of clear blond oak and hand carved each newel post for the main stairway from a hunk of mahogany. Mr. Pettigrew ordered his iron fence direct from a foundry in Newcastle, England, and it arrived in eight separate crates on the bed of a truck out of Norfolk. As a finishing touch he had a load of shrubbery, mostly boxwoods and camellia bushes, brought in from a nursery in Albermarle down near Charlotte, and he sowed the frontyard himself in a hardy strain of rye. Daddy said folks were generally indifferent to what came from where, but he said that most anybody old enough to recollect the building of the Pettigrew house would tell how for a week solid when the carpenters were sawing and nailing up the cedar siding, all of downtown Neely smelled like the inside of a hope chest.

Mrs. Pettigrew saw to the heir, that being in her line, and she hit it right off with a son that Mr. Pettigrew named Wallace Amory after himself. Two years later in March of 1911 Mrs. Pettigrew had another baby, this one a little girl that Mr. Pettigrew named Myra Angelique after nobody anyone could ever determine. Daddy said that second birth gave Mrs. Pettigrew all grades of trouble and she was hardly ever out of a nightgown from there on out. Then in the winter of 1914 she went onto the front porch in her robe to hear the Baptist choir sing Christmas songs and caught a chill that came to be pneumonia and caused her to succumb, Momma said, in February. Daddy said he'd always suspected the Baptist choir was deadly.

Momma said Mr. Pettigrew didn't have much of a way with children and hired a negro woman to raise them up until they were old enough for him to ship off to a private school in Virginia where Wallace Amory Pettigrew jr. was educated and Miss Myra Angelique Pettigrew refined. And Daddy said they were still off at school in 1925 when Mr. Pettigrew climbed up onto a slapdash scaffold two of his carpenters had thrown together and the whole business collapsed out from under him. It nearly killed him. The impact fractured an arm and cracked several ribs, and a ten-foot section of 2 × 8 planking fell edge-first onto his left hip and shattered it. I guess they thought he was dead—the carpenters and the electrician and the masons and their mortar boy—when they all came tearing around the house and found Mr. Pettigrew in a heap with a plank athwart him. One of the carpenters leaned over him and patted him on the cheek and said, "Mr. Pettigrew. Mr. Pettigrew. Say something, Mr. Pettigrew."

And Daddy said Mr. Pettigrew popped straight up from the waist and said, "You no count sons-of-bitches," and he picked up a handy scrap of board, Daddy said, and clubbed that carpenter on the crown of the head with it. Then he flung it at the rest of them, and scooped up some dirt and threw that, and picked up some rocks and threw them and Daddy said he was so unbelievably accurate that the whole bunch of them—the remaining carpenter and the electrician and the mason and the mortar boy—all went tearing back around the house. And Daddy said Mr. Pettigrew took hold of the collar of that man he'd clubbed on the head and shook him awake so he could tell him what a jackass he was.

That episode was Mr. Pettigrew's last hurrah, Daddy said. His arm and ribs mended fine, but the doctors couldn't do much of anything for his hip, and the same negro woman who'd raised his children was engaged to take care of him. Daddy said Mr. Pettigrew bought himself a fine wicker-bottomed wheelchair, and his hired woman, Mrs. Broadnax, would wrap him in an afghan and wheel him up and down the sidewalks of Neely. But he wasn't right anymore and when folks would meet him out on the walkway he'd grab any part of them he could get hold of and look at them all wild and fiery-eyed, and sometimes he'd say, "Them sons-of-bitches nearly killed me," and sometimes he wouldn't say anything at all.

After Mr. Pettigrew had wasted away sufficiently, he contracted a virulent infection, Momma said, and succumbed also. Mr. Wallace Amory Pettigrew jr. and Miss Myra Angelique Pettigrew returned to Neely for the services and were said to have blossomed into an extremely handsome and graceful couple, and although they were in town for only a week before they returned to school, their show of culture and refinement inspired among the ladies of Neely the frenzied conviction that the town could not possibly thrive and flourish without a finishing school of its own. The ladies organized and held conferences and debates and handed out fliers on the steps of the courthouse and went door-to-door for donations, but they couldn't seem to stir up any sort of widespread cultural anxiety.

So when a gentleman who claimed to hail from New York but was actually from Winston-Salem arrived in Neely and opened up a tapdancing school in the basement of the hardware store, the ladies counted themselves victorious, having decided that even if tapdancing was not exactly culture it wasn't very far from it. A kind of refinement for the feet, Daddy said.

Momma said it was the fall of 1935 when Wallace Amory and Myra Angelique Pettigrew came home to Neely for good. The care of the Pettigrew mansion had been left to Mr. and Mrs. Broadnax, who saw to the upkeep of the house and grounds for two years after Mr. Pettigrew's death up until July 4, 1927, when they were dismissed from their duties after Sheriff Browner, who was Deputy Browner then, investigated a complaint from a neighbor and discovered the Broadnaxes and twenty-seven of their negro friends sprawled throughout Mr. Pettigrew's parlor waiting for some sort of creature to finish roasting in the fireplace. Daddy said it was very possibly a goat. So the Pettigrew house had been closed up for a little over eight years when Wallace Amory jr. and his sister moved back into it, and Momma said they revived it entirely. Wallace Amory had the exterior of the house painted a sparkling white and Miss Myra Angelique planted a blue million trumpet flowers in among the shrubbery and along all four runs of the iron fence. The Rescue Mission hauled off two truckloads of old chairs, sofas, endtables and the like, and Momma said new furnishings arrived in a boxcar from New York, including a countless number of Turkish rugs and a pair of cement cupids for the flower beds.

The Pettigrews gave their first ball at Christmastime and Momma said it was lavish, just lavish. They hired out a chamber ensemble from Greensboro and a caterer from there also, and the engraved invitations were brought around from house to house by a local negro who had been given a black suit and gloves for the occasion. Of course all the good Baptists of Neely sent their automatic theological regrets since, as far as they were concerned, the only place you could dance to was Hell, but most everybody else would have attended or had to die first. The women made themselves dresses and the men had their funeral suits cleaned and pressed, and couples gathered in front of radios all over Neely and practiced the three-step, which very few of them could maintain for more than a half-minute at a time without misfiring and banging together. Even the younger, more agile Neelyites were clumsy waltzers though most of them could tapdance up a storm.

Momma said it was a smashing success. Momma was only seven then and wasn't invited herself, but she said her Momma and Daddy went and left her with a babysitter and that she and the babysitter snuck out the back door while Grandma and Granddaddy Yount were going out the front one. It seems that most everybody who was not in attendance on the dance floor was in attendance at the imported iron fence in front of the Pettigrews' house, and Momma said there was such a crowd of people that she couldn't hardly see anything until Deacon Furches picked her up and set her on his shoulder. She said the windows were hung with sheer draperies which gave the ballroom a soft, dreamy look and Momma said what music came out from the house sounded very far-off and magical. She and the deacon both agreed that it was a glorious affair and they decided that Miss Pettigrew looked especially handsome and comely in her pale-yellow gown and that Mr. Wallace Amory jr., in his formal black suit and with his mother's dark features, was pretty in the way that antique princes and kings were pretty. Momma said Grandma Yount came home all flushed and lightheaded and complained that she'd done too much dancing, but Granddaddy said she'd just washed down too many finger sandwiches with too much champagne punch and he packed her off to bed. Momma told him she imagined it had been a glorious affair, simply glorious, and she said Granddaddy Yount thought for a minute and then responded that no, it had not been glorious exactly but had seemed to him very much like musical wrestling.

Daddy said it was a good thing Wallace Amory could dance and look pretty because he was hardly able to do anything else. One of the underlings had taken charge of the business upon Mr. Pettigrew's death and Wallace Amory left him to run the construction end of it while he hired a bookkeeper to take charge of the payroll and the supply expenses. Daddy said Wallace Amory took charge of the profits on his own. He had no other responsibilities as far as anyone could tell. He didn't rise in the morning and head out to his daddy's office and he rarely showed up at construction sites except for groundbreakings when there would be a photographer from the *Chronicle* handy.

Daddy said Wallace Amory had a garden spade he'd painted gold on the blade and the grip, and he said about every half year you could open the *Chronicle* and find a picture of him stomping his gold shovel into the ground to mark the commencement of some sort of construction in Neely, but Daddy said he had no more of a hand in the completion of the building than the man who rings the bell at the track has in the outcome of the race.

Daddy said Wallace Amory jr. was an accomplished piddler. He could engage himself for days on end in the sorts of chores an average man could dispatch with in an afternoon. And he was not ashamed to piddle, Daddy said, but made himself conspicuous at it. He said Wallace Amory could squat on his lawn grubbing weeds for three days running, or drag a mattock and a shovel out of his cellar and tell every passerby how he was digging a drainage ditch off from the house, or announce to his carpenters how he planned to help them hang doors or lay shingles. And Daddy said his lawn was always as ragged with weeds as it ever was, and he said a little ground might get cut up but the ditch was never dug, and the carpenters told how Mr. Pettigrew would get him a hammer and a nail apron and then occasionally finger a door hinge and sometimes set foot on the roof. But he waltzed divinely, Mòmma said, and made delightful conversation. And Daddy said it was a good thing.

Then the war came and everything stopped. Daddy was twenty in 1941 and he wanted to be an air cadet, but he said when he was standing outside the induction center in Texas, he saw a fighter plane and a B-17 collide over the airstrip and fall to the ground in a fiery heap. So when the sergeant called him in and said, "Air corps?" Daddy said, "No sir. Infantry," and Daddy said that's how he got to tour Europe clinging onto the outside of a tank. He saw action in France and Belgium and got wounded in Paris when a buddy dropped his rifle and it went off and creased Daddy's calf. Daddy loved to tell that story and he would just cackle, but Momma lost a cousin at Corregidor and a neighbor of hers got drowned coming off a troop transport at Sicily, so she never laughed when Daddy talked about the war.

Momma said that in the war years Neely was full of little boys and granddaddies and old worn-out women and young

worn-out women, and she said there was nothing in the world
to do but wait for the mailman to come and pray that he wouldn't.
Momma said the postmen in Neely had never worn neckties
until the war, had never worn their grey wool uniforms with
stripes down the trouser legs, had never worn their postal issue
caps, had never been so severe and proper until the war came
along to make them extraordinarily significant. They would
knock on doors, Momma said, and out would come mothers
and wives and sisters already on the raw edge of agony, and
the postman would extend the notice towards them and he
would not say, "I'm sorry," or "Forgive me," or "If there's
anything I can do," but simply "Ma'm." And Momma said
nobody who got one ever opened it right off, but clutched it
and bent it and worked it through their fingers and never neglected to say, "Thank you." Kissing the axe, Daddy called it.

Daddy said Wallace Amory jr. didn't go to war but went
only as far as Georgia where he got attached to the personal
staff of a colonel at Fort Benning. He was charged with the
responsibility of being handsome and diverting at formal functions, and Daddy said Mr. Pettigrew built himself a reputation
as a man with a rarified knowledge of the intricacies of the
German mind. But after the war was over and everybody had
either come home for good or not come home at all, Mr.
Pettigrew told Daddy that everything he knew about Germany
he had gotten from a man he'd once shared a table with in a
restaurant, including the only two sentences he could utter in
the language: "The weather is pleasant though cool" and "Bis-
marck was a remarkable fellow."

Momma said he came home to Neely about once every six
weeks, and he and Myra Angelique (Sister, he called her) would
stroll arm in arm down the boulevard, Wallace Amory in his
snappy dress uniform and Miss Pettigrew done up in a simple
frock and hair ribbons so as to seem, Momma said, almost
inadvertently lovely. They would chat with people on the sidewalk and stop into the shops and businesses, and Momma said
Mr. Pettigrew would talk in the most lighthearted and careless
way about "our little European engagement," or "our little
continental flare-up," or just "our little skirmish." And he was
jolly, Momma said, offhanded, and seemed always to assume
that everyone was as untouched and unscathed by the war as
he was. She said he gave pain to some folks, especially to

those men and women who had lost a son or a brother or a
husband and who had not quite gotten out of the habit of
listening for troop trains and watching for that familiar scrawl
in the letterbox. They didn't want to hear about skirmishes and
flare-ups, but they let Mr. Pettigrew tell them and they let him
laugh and be casual about the war, probably, Daddy said, because
he was Mr. Pettigrew of the Pettigrew fortune and the Pettigrew
mansion and the Pettigrew heritage, all of which assured him
of the sort of respectability that he would sometimes fail to
live up to.

But Daddy said Mr. Pettigrew made up for his indiscretions
once the war ended. Daddy said we needed him then, Neely
needed him because folks were weary and fairly down-trodden
and it would take a Mr. Pettigrew to pick them up again. So
Daddy said the citizens of Neely did the only thing they could
do: they made him mayor. There was no campaigning, there
was not even an election. It was all very proper and fitting to
the occasion and the candidate, Daddy said. The town council
invited Mr. Pettigrew to become mayor and he accepted their
invitation. Daddy said Buddy MacElrath was mayor of Neely
at the end of the war and was very contented with his position,
but he gave it up, Daddy said, gave it up without a whimper
because he saw that it wasn't a matter of politics but a matter
of morale, of what Daddy called spiritual necessity. Neely
didn't need a mayor in 1945. It needed a beacon, Daddy said.
And Mr. Pettigrew, with his fortune and his mansion and his
heritage, was more than prominent enough for the citizens of
Neely to take a heading from. Daddy said Wallace Amory jr.
stunk of his daddy's success and his daddy's money and his
daddy's ambition, and he said it gave the people of Neely a
healthy kick in the pants to point to Mayor Pettigrew and say,
"That man represents us."

Consequently it didn't matter that Mayor Pettigrew was a
piddler since there was really nothing a mayor did that couldn't
be piddled through, except maybe presiding over commence-
ments and openings, and Daddy said folks figured that if Mayor
Pettigrew could handle a golden shovel he could manage well
enough with a pair of scissors and a ribbon. So people couldn't
have known what they started when they invited Wallace Amory
Pettigrew to become mayor. They couldn't even have suspected
that the job would catch fire with him. Momma said they were

all surprised. Daddy said they were astounded and that he'd never seen a man so ripe with zeal, he called it.

There was a time in Neely when the mayor was treated to a swearing-in dance at legion hall #33, but Wallace Amory jr. changed all of that. He and Miss Pettigrew gave an inaugural ball at the Pettigrew mansion where they served exotic canapés and authentic French champagne in crystal glasses. Momma and Daddy went and Momma said it was exceedingly glorious. Daddy said yes, Mayor Pettigrew did indeed dance divinely and did indeed make delightful conversation. A photographer from the *Chronicle* was present, and a half dozen of his pictures appeared on the "Social Sidelights" page of the Sunday edition. There was one of all the councilmen and their wives. One of the Presbyterian minister Mr. Holroyd with his mouth full of pâté. Two of the dance floor taken from up on the balcony. One of the mayor shaking hands with a man who was obliterated from the knees up by what Momma said was the knobby part of her shoulder. And one of Wallace Amory jr. and Miss Myra Angelique waltzing which carried the caption "Mayor and Sister cut the shine."

Daddy said this was the sort of thing we wanted from our new mayor—idle pleasure, extravagance, simply something to point towards. But he said the office had a horrible and unexpected effect upon Wallace Amory jr.: it made him a politician. According to Daddy, nobody had imagined there was a politician inside of Wallace Amory waiting to get out. But there was, Daddy said. And it got out, Daddy said. He said the mayor made two speeches right off that seemed to put his career on the wing, one to the Ladies Garden Society and the other to the Neely chapter of the D.A.R. Each address was received with a riotous ovation which the mayor attributed to his political bravado, but Momma said the ladies were most likely applauding his beauty, his grace, and his fine tailored suit. She imagined very few of them had even heard the mayor. It seems he had been talking water bonds.

And that's the way it went, Daddy said. Wallace Amory would give a politician's speech and get a Pettigrew's reception. He got up before the Methodist Men's Association, and the Neely Cotillion, and the Rotary Club, and the Businessmen's Council and was uniformly met with wild enthusiasm, which Daddy said was nothing more than overblown courtesy but which the mayor took to calling his "endorsement by the good people of this fine community." And Daddy said Wallace Amory jr. became almost entirely unbearable. He said Neely wanted a mayor who made delightful conversation and danced divinely, not a political advocate. But Wallace Amory was burning to be an advocate, Daddy said, and he did not want to be delightful or divine, just earnest, deadly earnest. Daddy said it got to where the mayor would not talk anything but what he called Brass Tacks. Folks just have to tighten their belts, he would say. We have to take the good with the bad, he would say. The little man can't hardly make it, he would say. Prosperity is just around the corner, he would say. Daddy said the mayor had grown particularly fond of this last one and could make it ring most impressively.

So he went off to Raleigh and represented us at conferences and political gatherings of every sort, and Daddy said the *Chronicle* would frequently run photographs of the mayor holding forth on taxes or leash laws or what Daddy called the general proximity of prosperity. And sometimes him and Momma would discover Wallace Amory jr. and Miss Pettigrew on the inside of the Greensboro *Daily News* where they had been caught posing at a fund-raising dinner or taking the dance floor at a political ball. Momma said Miss Pettigrew made a radiant picture, but the mayor always looked a little bothered. Daddy called that Wallace Amory's camera face. He said it wasn't exactly "bothered" the mayor was after but something more like "upstanding" or "concerned." Daddy said it was just the mayor's way of wearing his civic conscience between his ears so as to get it into the picture.

Of course we elected him to a second term of office. Momma said it was the decent thing to do, and Daddy said it was merely a serving up of justice, the only proper answer to the mayor having campaigned so untiringly throughout the four years of his first term; according to Daddy the natives of Neely are blessed with a keen sense of this sort of evenhandedness. So the mayor got his second endorsement by the good people of this fine community and Daddy said he did a remarkable thing, probably by way of celebration: he bought Miss Myra Angelique a monkey. Momma said she didn't know Miss Pettigrew was lonesome for a pet and she didn't imagine Miss Myra Angelique had ever expressed a desire for a monkey, but Daddy said it could have happened one evening when the mayor came home to the supper table after a long day of belt tightening and taking the good with the bad. He supposed Miss Pettigrew might have leaned over the sugar bowl and said, "Mayor," which Daddy said was all she ever called him anymore, "I'd be pleased to have a chimpanzee." And Daddy supposed the mayor frumped himself up a little and muddied his expression some and said, "Sister darling, your chimpanzee is just around the corner."

"Louis!" Momma said. Daddy was hardly ever a very big hit with Momma.

We had never had a monkey in Neely before Miss Pettigrew got hers and the only one we had after was a fit-in-the-palm-of-your-hand monkey that Jimmy Roach and two of his brothers ordered out of the back of a comic book, and it wasn't but two days and about four dozen palms later when that one gave up the ghost and had to be buried in a legal envelope in the Roaches' backyard. Miss Pettigrew's was a legitimate monkey-sized monkey right from the start and Daddy said it arrived in the front seat of a station wagon, uncaged and diapered. The mayor had a flagpole erected on his front lawn for it to climb on and hard by the sidewalk he staked a tether that would allow that creature to wander most anywhere inside the iron fence. Daddy said at first they called it Junious after a cousin of theirs, but later on, when they'd bought it a blazer and a plaid sportcoat and a porkpie hat and had discovered it had no love for trousers, they called it Mr. Britches since they were the only things it was without.

Daddy said most folks in Neely had never seen a monkey before, so anytime the mayor or Miss Pettigrew turned it out of the house, an audience would collect against the fence. Of course, Daddy said, you always got the mayor along with the monkey, and the one of them would squat on the knob atop the flagpole and pick at himself while the other paced the lawn and talked issues. That was just the price of curiosity, Daddy said.

Politically, Miss Pettigrew's monkey turned out to be quite an asset for the mayor. He was no longer very engaging on his own, but Mr. Britches made him a human interest story and he got his picture in scores of newspapers and a couple of national magazines, which Daddy said was somewhat unfor-

tunate for Neely since the mayor always looked a little foolish
with his troubled expression and his arms full of chimpanzee.
But Daddy said all it took was that monkey, and the mayor
became what Daddy called a figure. He got his notoriety on
the coattails of an ape, Daddy would say, and Momma said
where we used to see pictures of the mayor with just Miss
Pettigrew or just Mr. Britches, it got so that he'd show up in
a crowd of senators, or with one arm around the lieutenant
governor, or in the general company of the governor himself.

Then Mr. Nance came into the picture, and I mean actually
into the picture right between Miss Pettigrew and the mayor
and usually with one hand on the back of Miss Pettigrew's
neck and the other latched onto the mayor's shoulder. But it
wasn't that way right off, Momma said. She said her and Daddy
first picked out Mr. Nance in the *Daily News*. He was off to
one side of the governor along with Mayor Pettigrew and the
caption made him out to be a "Notable Democrat." Then he
showed up in the *Chronicle*, just him and the mayor, and
Momma said they were eating sociables and smirking at each
other; the *Chronicle* called this "having a confab." Momma
said after that Miss Pettigrew got in on the act and her and Mr.
Nance would get caught having confabs of their own or taking
a turn on the dance floor or posing with congressmen's wives
or congressmen themselves, and then it was the mayor on one
side, Miss Myra Angelique on the other, and Mr. Nance in
between attached to Miss Pettigrew's neck and to the mayor's
shoulder.

He had been named Alton after his father and Daniel after
his father's brother, and Daddy said what people didn't call
him Mister knew him as A.D. or Addie Nance. He was what
Daddy called a cookie magnate, or anyway his daddy had been
a cookie magnate and he had inherited the rewards of his daddy's
ambition and perseverance, though he personally had no more
of a hand in the manufacture of cookies than did the mayor in
the construction of buildings. Daddy said he used his money
to buy influence and used his influence to tinker with politicians, not dishonestly, Daddy said, since there was no official
who could give him anything he couldn't get for himself, but
just as a means of whiling away the hours. So he helped get
some folks into office and he helped get some folks out of
office and he earned himself the title "Notable Democrat."

Daddy said he was a slimy individual. Momma didn't know about that, but she was convinced he made the best shortbread cakes and cream-filled savannahs she'd ever tasted.

Mr. Alton Nance and rumors of the mayor's candidacy arrived in Neely about the same time. The rumors came on the wind, Daddy said, but Mr. Nance was a little more stylish about it and hit town in a 1928 Ford Deluxe Phaeton with fender skirts. Daddy said it was in the most remarkable condition for a car of that vintage. According to Momma we were supposing governor or at least senator and were a shade disappointed when it turned out that the mayor was after nothing more than a seat in Congress; we'd just assumed he was no longer capable of modesty and caution, Daddy said.

As far as Momma was concerned, Mr. Nance was not a particularly handsome gentleman. She found him too squat and pasty-faced and said he did not look at all rich, just unhealthy. Daddy stuck with slimy, so he was a little more shocked than Momma when Mr. Nance and Miss Pettigrew began keeping company. Actually, it started out with the three of them climbing into Mr. Nance's Phaeton and going to a show in Greensboro or to dinner in Winston-Salem or traveling all the way to Raleigh for some sort of political hubbub or another. Then the mayor merely withdrew his attendance, so it was really more that he left off with his company than they started keeping each other's. But there was talk anyway, Momma said, talk that Miss Pettigrew was finally getting herself a husband who was as wealthy and as prominent as she was if only half as handsome, and talk of the mayor's candidacy for one of the seventh-district seats, which he still had yet to officially announce but for which he had already begun to circulate lapel buttons and fliers.

Daddy said it all looked fine. It all looked proper. However, it was not fine and proper, he said, but rotten underneath like an apple that seems ripe and shiny enough on the outside but turns out to be brown and mealy when you bite into it. Daddy said Mr. Nance did not want to get married; he already was, to a woman who was paid astounding sums of money to remain what Daddy called invisible. That was the first problem, he said. The second was that the mayor alone knew it. Daddy said it was probably the appeal of glory and fame and power, touched with a little of boredom, that did away with the mayor's good judgement, which was no excuse but was certainly a reason. So when Mr. Nance agreed to give the mayor a seat in Congress (which was, after all, what he was doing) and when he made the mistake of supposing that the mayor could give him in return something finally he could not purchase, Daddy said it was somewhat understandable that the mayor made the mistake of supposing so too.

And it was a mistake, Daddy said, a tremendous miscalculation on the mayor's part, and it ruined him, ruined him altogether. The mayor's end of the bargain came due on a very warm, still night in Neely, and Momma said half the town was out in shirtsleeves making aimless excursions along the boulevard or lounging on porches in the dark. She said the silence was amazing and had a kind of hum to it, and Momma imagined that if a town can seem secure and contented then that's what Neely seemed. Daddy said both wings of the Pettigrew house were all lit up and Mr. Nance's car was parked alongside the curbing out front, which Daddy said was natural and reassuring, him being considered a suitor and the object of Miss Pettigrew's happiness. And he said folks were wandering back and forth in front of the Pettigrew house with some regularity, a few of them pausing to admire the inside of Mr. Nance's car but the better part of them just lingering along the fence and seeing what they could of luxury and grandeur through the Pettigrews' milky window sheers.

Then Miss Myra Angelique screamed, Daddy said, and the people on the sidewalk out front of the Pettigrew house gaped at each other and the people on nearby avenues and porches caught up their breath and looked out into the darkness. And then Miss Pettigrew screamed again. Daddy said it was not the sort of wild and frantic screeching you'd expect from a woman but more along the lines of a high-pitched moan. It was wordless, he said, and brief and despairing. Momma said folks dashed for the boulevard from all over Neely since even those who hadn't heard the outcry firsthand had already heard about it, and she imagined there were two or three dozen in attendance along the fence when Miss Pettigrew said, "I will not!" in a voice that was still highpitched and somewhat mournful but a little more wild and a little more frantic. Daddy said the mayor tried to calm her down, or anyway that's what people supposed since they could hear the drone of the mayor's voice but could not exactly decipher any sense from it. Then Miss Pettigrew said, "NO!" and she was howling, Daddy said, and he said the mayor's voice came in again right behind hers, not soothing now but what Daddy called plaintive and more than a little frantic itself. But the mayor left off, Daddy said, when Miss Pettigrew broke in and wailed at him, "NO NO NO NO NO!" in a most frightful and wholly uncontained way.

That's when Mr. Nance snuck away, Momma said, or at least that's when folks first noticed him coming out from around the backside of the house and making for his car. Momma said he didn't speak to anyone, didn't even look anybody in the face, but just slipped into the frontseat and drove off. She said he was nearly four blocks from the house before he finally cut the headlights on. And then the Pettigrews' front door flew open, Daddy said, and the mayor came backing out onto the porch with his forearms drawn up in front of his face and Miss Myra Angelique flailing and slapping at him with her open hands and driving him across the planking and onto the concrete steps. She was sobbing, Daddy said, and making noises like words but not words themselves, and he said that Mr. Britches came through the doorway behind them, turned his gums pink-side out, hooted once, and then bolted across the porch on his knuckles, cleared the bannister, and slipped off into the night.

Then Miss Myra Angelique went back inside, shut the door, and latched it behind her, and Daddy said the mayor stood on the walkway with his hands in his pockets and looked up at the stars and at a little piece of moon overhead. Daddy didn't imagine the mayor knew he'd collected a regular gallery against the fence, but he said Wallace Amory didn't even twitch when somebody called out from the crowd and said, "Mayor, your monkey's done run off."

The mayor just looked at the moon and the stars and he rattled a set of keys in his pocket and said, "Oh?"

Momma said that was the beginning of the end. Daddy said that was the end. And I suppose Daddy was onto it this time since nothing much else came along to advance the drama any. Miss Pettigrew, of course, did not marry Mr. Nance and, to the best of Momma's knowledge, did not ever speak of him again—not even in derision. The mayor, of course, did not run for Congress and, to the best of Daddy's knowledge, did not ever again speak of having intended to run—not even to folks wearing his likeness on lapel buttons. And Mr. Britches, of course, did not know enough about chickens to stay out of a henhouse and the chickens did not care to know enough about a sportcoated monkey to tolerate the visit agreeably, so he was thrilled to be rescued and returned home.

Momma said the mayor had been guilty of indelicacy with Miss Pettigrew's emotions. Daddy said he had simply tried to farm her out and had failed at it. They both agreed the whole episode was sad and unnecessary since the mayor did not need Mr. Nance to win his seat in Congress and certainly could not have lost it without him. And although Momma would not admit it, Daddy said Miss Pettigrew herself became somewhat tainted on account of the circumstances, not that she had engaged in anything unseemly but because her brother had supposed that she might. So when the Pettigrews became what Momma called retiring, Neely let loose of them and watched them fade almost completely from sight. The mayor took to walking only in the dusk of the day and rarely was Miss Myra Angelique at his elbow anymore. Momma said she had become the victim of sick headaches which were so severe as to send her to her bed for days at a time. The mayor hired Aunt Willa Bristow to see to his sister and she would sit at Miss Pettigrew's bedside and do nothing but steep Miss Myra Angelique's lace hand-kerchiefs in a bowl of vinegar and apply them to her forehead. Charge of Mr. Britches also fell to Aunt Willa, and Daddy said anymore when folks stopped at the fence to watch him scuttle up his flagpole and squat on the knob at the top of it, they got just the monkey, or maybe just the monkey and the amusement of seeing Aunt Willa fetch it in by yanking stiffly on the tether and saying, "Come on h'yer you ape" until Mr. Britches relented since she never would. And Momma said there was nothing sadder than to watch the lights in both wings of the Pettigrew house go out one by one early on in the evening while the rest of Neely was still lively and bright.

Then the mayor up and went on a cruise, or anyway Daddy said it seemed that he up and went since nobody knew he was leaving until he left or got wind of where he was going until he had already come back. He took a train out of Greensboro for Miami and from there he embarked on a ship called the *Island Beauty* which was scheduled for a stop at the Yucatan peninsula before heading on to points in the Caribbean. According to the ship's captain, the mayor had been having a wonderful time of it, and he enclosed in his letter a snapshot of Wallace Amory jr. in the company of an Inca chief which, in a scrawled note on the back, was said to have been taken at a sacred burial ground at a cost to the mayor of one dollar and seventy-five cents. They had tried, the captain said, they had all tried to dislodge the radish from the mayor's throat—the ship's doctor had even attempted a tracheotomy with a carving knife—but he had suffocated anyway and the captain was very sorry, very sorry, and would see to the transportation of the body himself as soon as the ship redocked in Miami, which was nine days off when the mayor died and still six days off when Miss Pettigrew got the captain's letter by way of a company representative.

In the meantime the mayor was put in the meatlocker for safekeeping and Daddy said the freezer was either too cold or not cold enough and caused Wallace Amory jr. to turn an unspeakable color. So there was no viewing, no family hours at the funeral home, and by Miss Pettigrew's request, the service was brief and private, so private in fact that she herself did not attend, leaving the preacher to carry on with God as his witness and under the passing scrutiny of a couple of funeral parlor attendants who wandered into the chapel to discover what in the world was going on there. When the mayor was finally laid to rest with his head at his daddy's feet, Momma said that was in fact the end, but Daddy said that Wallace Amory had been more or less dead for a considerable spell already and this was just the official confirmation.

So Miss Pettigrew was left alone in the world except for her monkey and her negro woman, and Momma said she closed herself up in her daddy's house and did not interrupt her solitude but twice—once of a Sunday prior to Christmas of 1962 when she attended the Methodist Church, and once in the summer of 1970 when she gave a July 4th luncheon out of the clear blue and distributed little colonial flags as favors. Otherwise she confined herself to her bedroom and her parlor while Aunt Willa cleaned for her and cooked for her and tended to her monkey for her and generally allowed Miss Myra Angelique to become an old woman in the privacy of her family home. It was no wonder then, Daddy said, that Neely was electrified by the appearance of Miss Pettigrew in her frontyard after nearly a decade of just a monkey on a flagpole and a sullen negro woman in the shadows under the porch awning. And ranting no less, and wearing a fitted bedsheet up on her shoulders for a cape. And though Momma assured us that it was probably good linen, maybe even Irish, Daddy said it was still madness and that was all that mattered.

iv

M ISS PETTIGREW first jigged on her lawn in the middle of a Tuesday afternoon and Daddy said folks lingered and dallied along the fence well on into twilight and were out early Wednesday morning so that they might happen by the Pettigrew house before midday came when they would commit themselves to casing it in earnest. But the doors stayed closed up and the yard remained vacant throughout the day, even to the top of the flagpole, and on Thursday only the most tenacious and otherwise unoccupied citizens of Neely haunted the Pettigrew end of the boulevard until they eventually went home unrewarded.

Then Friday came and nobody expected anything at all from Miss Pettigrew in the way of entertainment, so just the few folks with genuine business in the area saw her strike out from the house and turn south on the walkway in the direction of downtown. She was in the company of Mr. Britches, who, aside from his usual blazer and porkpie hat, was wearing black sneakers for the occasion; Miss Pettigrew kept him in check on a jewel-studded dog lead. Momma said Miss Myra Angelique was rather stylishly dressed for a woman who had hardly seen sunlight in almost a decade. She was wearing a navy skirt and matching jacket along with a white ruffly blouse and some sort of neckerchief that Momma said was certainly silk. Miss Pettigrew's gloves buttoned at the wrist and were as startlingly white as her clutch purse, which was extremely elegant and sheathed in pearls. Momma had her reservations only as to Miss Pettigrew's choice of hats. The one she had decided on set up on her head like a jarlid and was not quite as purely white as her gloves or her purse. It had put forth feathers in the back and was hung in front with a partial veil that stopped just short of Miss Myra Angelique's eyebrows. Momma considered this sort of headwear a bit severe for a weekday afternoon. Otherwise, though, she said Miss Pettigrew was at the height of fashion and taste; Daddy said she had just managed to leave the bedsheets on the bed.

Daddy called it outright gawking. He said the mere sight of Miss Pettigrew on the street blasted folks into a kind of instant idiocy and faces fell slack and people went silent wherever she passed. Mr. Britches didn't get the least little attention, not even when he climbed up atop a parking meter and relieved himself onto the curbing out front of the Guilford Dairy Bar. Daddy said you'd have thought the gutters of Neely were intended to run with monkey urine. Nobody greeted Miss Pettigrew, he said, and nobody was greeted by her, though she looked pleasant enough and did not seem to be in any sort of hurry. And the only people who showed any noticeable signs of consciousness in the presence of her and her monkey were two salesmen in the doorway of the Ford dealership. One of them howled and pounded the jamb with his fist while the other just leered at him; he was dressed for all the world exactly like Mr. Britches except for the sneakers.

Miss Pettigrew and her monkey walked all the way from the Pettigrew house at municipal square, through town, past the cotton mill, and didn't stop until they arrived at what is known as Southend, where people who can't afford to live anywhere else live. Southerners are generally not exceptionally trashy, just poor. According to Daddy they are fairly proud, reasonably well-scrubbed people, and when Miss Pettigrew showed up in their part of town, everybody who knew what a Miss Pettigrew was (which was almost everybody) took her visit to be proof that Southend had finally arrived. Housewives mostly eased themselves out onto their front porches and then down to the street, where they collected in spirited little bands along the sidewalk and studied Miss Pettigrew's progress, which was fairly steady and unswerving and took her dead towards Southend's only park, a small plot of land that dwindles to a point where the boulevard and the Burlington highway run up on each other from more or less the same direction.

There isn't much in the way of recreation in the Southend park since the center of the property is occupied by a concrete slab that supports the Neely water tower. Daddy has always said that the Neely tower is a gem of its breed since it is not of the usual variety with legs and a basin atop but is instead a steel cylinder which rises about one hundred and fifty feet into the air and, according to Daddy, can be seen by motorists a good mile or mile and a half outside of town. The outer shell fairly much bristles with rivets, and at regular five-year intervals the city council comes to terms with the most daring paint crew it can run up on and the exterior gets silvered over afresh. Nobody remembers precisely how but somehow two faithful reproductions of the Lucky Strike emblem found their way onto the upper quarter of what are more or less the east and west faces. It is the general consensus that the American Tobacco Company, which lies midway between Neely and Danville, paid for the privilege of permanent advertisement by funding the construction of the tower, and only old Mr. Nettles ever objected to the theory: before he passed on he swore up and down that the likeness of a jar of brilliantine had once been located partway up the Burlington side. But then Mr. Nettles didn't ever recollect his dead wife's name the same way twice, so it was probably the case that the Lucky Strike emblems had always been where they were and would still be there when the steel finally gave way and the water ran out on the ground.

Mr. Raymond Small told Sheriff Burton he was weighing a woman's apples by the fruit bin out front of his grocery when he noticed Miss Pettigrew in the park across the street. He said he didn't know her right off, since it would have been twenty-seven years in August that he had last seen her, but the monkey gave her away. He reported how he asked the woman beside him, "Isn't that Miss Pettigrew there?" and he said she recognized the monkey too. Then all the women in the market came outside and Mr. Small said there were about a half dozen of them altogether and they watched Miss Pettigrew and Mr. Britches go in among the shrubbery at the base of the water tower.

The Ladies Garden Society of Neely had seen to the planting of several rosebushes around the concrete slab and had supplied a few sections of splitrail fence for them to cling to, but they had never flourished and taken hold like the ones along the borders of the sewage plant, which were said to have produced some truly incredible blossoms, so Miss Pettigrew had to poke around for awhile before she came up with any rose worth having. Mr. Small said she finally decided on two, a red one and a white one, and she broke them off from the vines and put them into her purse. Then she pulled a bread sack out from her jacket pocket, he said, and dropped her purse into that before leading Mr. Britches around to the access ladder and sending him up it ahead of her.

Mr. Small said he was astounded by her agility, and as far as he was concerned that monkey had nothing on her, though Mr. Small was obliged to add that Mr. Britches was slightly handicapped by his sneakers which were giving him fits. He said she climbed steadily, nudging the monkey on ahead of her when she caught up with him, and the two of them didn't stop until they were along about as high as the Lucky Strike emblems, not so far up as the words "Lucky Strike," he said, but pretty much on a line with "It's toasted." And even then she didn't take a breath, he said, but set in tying the neck of the breadsack to a ladder rung. And she never looked down, as far as Mr. Small could recollect, and he said she never jumped at all, just let go and fell over backwards. He said the ladies screamed and hid their faces but he just watched the hem of her skirt flap in the wind and never even blinked when she splintered a section of splitrail fence and landed in the scraggly heart of a rose bush. Mr. Small said the most miraculous part of the whole business was that her hat never came off, never even got batted askew.

Me and Momma didn't know a thing about it, didn't hear the sirens trailing off Southend way, didn't get a word by phone or otherwise, just didn't know anything at all until Daddy came home to tell us, and you'd have thought he would come sailing down the sidewalk screaming blood and murder, but it wasn't like that, not in the least. He simply appeared, not on the walkway or the front porch, but inside the house, right there in the sitting room where I was lolling in his chair with my legs over the armrest. I never heard him coming and I don't know how long he'd been standing beside me when I saw him, but I must have yelped like death. Anyway, Momma said that's what brought her out of the kitchen, and she took one look at Daddy and said, "Louis?"

He didn't have any color to speak of or much of any expression on his face, and without ever seeming to move at all he dropped his suitcoat, his satchel, his lunchbag, and his afternoon paper in a pile on the floor.

"Louis, are you alright?" Momma asked him. But Daddy just looked over her head to the far wall or maybe on into the kitchen and Momma reached out and touched his forearm with the tipends of her fingers.

Momma

DADDY SAID it was better than the madhouse. He recalled how he'd been to a madhouse once to see his mother's brother, Uncle Warren Lanier, and he said anything at all was better than the madhouse. Daddy was twenty-five then and Uncle Warren was already an old man who had failed to marry, who had failed to settle into an occupation, and whose own mother held him directly accountable for Great-granddaddy Lanier's untimely death at the age of fifty-seven. She said he had been galled into an early grave. However, Daddy said Great-granddaddy Lanier had died of angina complicated by regular and ungentlemanly drafts of the local mash; acute disappointment had nothing to do with it. According to Daddy that was Great-grandmomma Lanier's affliction. She was ravenous for grandbabies, he said, and she was convinced that Uncle Warren's bachelorhood was at the least inexcusably inconsiderate and otherwise very possibly unlawful. Daddy supposed Great-grandmomma Lanier would have taken Uncle Warren into litigation if she'd thought she could get a favorable judgement by it. But since there were no laws on the books specifically against bachelorhood or celibacy, Daddy called it, she vented herself by raging at Uncle Warren when he was at hand and just generally despising him in his absence. Daddy said she talked about him like maybe he'd helped the Romans crucify Christ, like maybe she thought he'd driven a nail or two. Yes, Daddy said, Uncle Warren was the one that was committed.

Daddy did not hold Great-grandmomma Lanier exclusively

responsible for Uncle Warren's deterioration; he imagined she merely contributed to it and hurried it along some. It seems Uncle Warren had always been a solitary individual who sought out no one's company and was never sought out himself. He lived in a room over a signpainter's shop and worked as a paper carrier for the Greensboro *Daily News*, an occupation which took him out into the world only two times a day and one of them before dawn. Daddy said the nature of Uncle Warren's employment probably afforded him the great leisure insanity requires and he imagined Uncle Warren had spent the better part of his life losing his mind. He never went violently or dangerously crazy, Daddy said, just noticeably so, but according to Daddy there was no reason to suppose that Uncle Warren would have ever been committed if not for the combination of his particular brand of madness with Great-grandmomma Lanier's affliction. They simply did not mix.

Somehow Uncle Warren had decided he was the rightful king of Prussia, and Daddy said he was fairly modest as far as kings go. He did not demand any knee bending or ring kissing, just an occasional "your highness" or "by your leave." And Daddy said the coronation had even brought him out some and done him a bit of good, but when Great-grandmomma Lanier heard that her Warren had made himself king of Prussia she went into absolute fits. Daddy said it was difficult enough for her to abide missing out on a regular grandbaby; she could hardly stand being denied a regal one.

So it was Great-grandmomma Lanier that had Uncle Warren packed off to the madhouse in Raleigh and he had been there nearly twelve years when Daddy visited him in the fall of 1946. A nurse let him into the ward and showed him to Uncle Warren's bed, and Daddy said since he'd never been to a mental hospital before he half expected the patients to be swinging from the light fixtures and hanging upside down on the bedsteads. But it wasn't like that at all, he said. Only a very few of them twitched and rolled under the bedclothes, and some one of them on the farthest side of the ward sang sweetly to himself in a high soprano voice. Daddy said all of the rest were as still as death.

Uncle Warren didn't know him right off, leastways he didn't let on that he did. Daddy said he just sat on the edge of the bed with his hands on his knees and looked out beyond his

headboard through a window covered over with wire mesh that
gave onto the corner of a little barren courtyard and the backside
of an adjacent building. Uncle Warren was a huge man with
big fleshy ears and rangy limbs, and Daddy said the orderlies
had stuffed him into a nightdress that didn't hardly cover him
down to the thighs. He said it was awfully sad to see, awfully
pathetic. When he started talking, Daddy steered clear of anything to do with Hitler and the allied effort and he said he
mostly talked family to Uncle Warren and told him how folks
asked after him regularly. Daddy supposed he was still chattering away when Uncle Warren finally looked at him. He was
already crying, Daddy said, and the tears were rolling freely
down his cheeks and some of them were running into his mouth
and some of them were dripping from his chin. Daddy said
he'd never seen a man cry before and didn't know what in the
world to do, so he put as much of his arm around Uncle
Warren's shoulder as he could manage and he said Uncle Warren
laid his head on his chest and sobbed into his shirt.

"My kingdom," he said. "My people."

It seems a doctor had told him there wasn't a Prussia anymore so there wasn't any use for a king of Prussia anymore.
He called it therapy.

Daddy always had a special attachment for Uncle Warren
after that, and I remember how right after Sheriff Browner died
a reporter from the Raleigh *News and Observer* showed up in
Neely with the theory that something in town was driving
people crazy; he suspected fluoridated water. I think he was
hoping for front-page news, so he diligently scratched around
in our past and dug up the Epperson sisters along with Uncle
Warren. He also tried to tell us how a Mr. Harry Gunn had
"desperately thrown himself in the path of the 4:15 out of
Danville," and he was convinced as well that Shep Bristow,
Aunt Willa's husband, had "sought to end his travails at the
bottom of a millpond." But that's where his theory fell apart
because Mr. Harry Gunn had never done anything desperately
but drink; he had simply managed to pass out in the wrong
place. And Shep Bristow discovered the pondbottom when he
slipped off the end of a fishing dock and swam like granite for
a quarter hour. We thought that would be the end of it, but the
reporter merely lightened up his tone a little and his editors
moved his story from the front page to the inside of the Sunday

travel section. The Epperson sisters became "zany," Uncle Warren got knocked down to "just another local lunatic," and the whole of the state was warned against long stopovers in Neely since life there tended to "bore folks to distraction." When Daddy saw the article he goddammed that reporter up one side and down the other and, Sunday afternoon or not, there wasn't a thing Momma could do about it.

So Daddy said it was better than the madhouse, but then he had always had a soft spot for suicide. When I was little and Daddy would put me to bed with a story, I think Momma supposed he was giving me knights and princesses and faeries and ogres and the occasional scaly beast, but Daddy told me how the Greeks were always drinking hemlock or throwing themselves off bluffs into the Aegean, and he said when things got tough for the Romans they fell on the pointy ends of their swords, and according to Daddy hardly a day went by in England when you couldn't pick up a paper and read how lord somebody or another had been discovered dead in his study with a brace of pistols in his lap. Most people supposed you had to be weak and cowardly to take your own life; Daddy said you had to be brave. He didn't see any other way for a man to bugger fate except by his own hand, and I always got the feeling Daddy would have tried it himself if he didn't have to die from it. The idea was really all he was warm to.

Momma did not ever allow Daddy to speak of death in her presence, which I guess is why he told me all about the Greeks and Romans; he had to tell somebody. Of course Momma had her reasons and it was when I came home from the second grade one afternoon and asked why my Momma and Daddy were older than everybody else's that Daddy took me off to the breakfast room and showed me a picture of a little girl he said was my sister who got run over and died; Daddy said that had scared Momma off from children for a while. She was named Margaret after Grandma Yount, and Momma could never ever bring herself to say the least little thing about her. So it was only when Daddy put me to bed that he got the chance to talk of fate and courage and the trials of existence. Momma could not bear to hear of them. Daddy said she had probably never imagined life could be so sad.

That's why Momma sat down on the rug, dropped right down on the floor of the sitting room alongside of where Daddy's belongings lay all in a heap. She did not speak and had not spoken except to ask, "Who? What?" when Daddy came in with his collar all full of sweat and his face bleached and drained of color. "The old girl jumped," Daddy had said, and Momma asked him, "Who? What?" and then it just seemed that her legs left her, crumpled underneath her, and she sat right down on top of them. "From the tower," Daddy said. "From up near the top of the tower." And Momma did not speak and Daddy did not speak again until I asked him, "Daddy, who jumped off the tower," because I truly didn't know. And Daddy looked directly at Momma. "Why, Miss Pettigrew," he said. "Miss Pettigrew." Then Momma took a breath in stages and shuddered most violently. Even after everything she'd seen and everything she'd been pressed to suffer, there was no heartbreak, no calamity that did not come to her as a fearful surprise.

The news of Miss Pettigrew's death made Momma quite ill. She drew the shades in her and Daddy's bedroom and wrapped herself up in the covers and tried to sleep. Daddy changed out of his suit and me and him went off towards Southend to see what we could find out. Daddy was not ill in the least; he was utterly astounded and about half pleased. "You know," he said to me, "I didn't think the old girl had it in her." I told him, no sir, I didn't think so either. And after we'd stopped off at Mr. Gibbons's mailbox so Daddy could get a light, he said to me, "You know, I never even suspected she had it in her," and he kind of looked off into the sky and away. Daddy was considerably proud of Miss Pettigrew.

Sheriff Burton had thrown up a barricade around the water tower. It was not a proper barricade but was put together mostly with sawbucks and rope and a few folding chairs filched from Mr. Small's grocery across the street. All variety of people were wandering around outside of it and as many were wandering around inside of it, regardless of the efforts of the sheriff's three regular deputies along with his auxiliary force—two bankers, a municipal employee, and a druggist who had been sworn in for the occasion. By the time me and Daddy arrived the body had long since been hauled off in an ambulance so there was nothing much left to see except where it fell from and where it landed, but we could no more determine exactly which rung Miss Pettigrew had launched herself off of than we could tell which rosebush she had ended up in since there was one on either side of the broken section of fence and they both appeared beaten back and naturally unsightly.

So Daddy and I didn't know just what to think until we ran up on Mr. Russell Newberry, a gentleman who had been retired from barbering by glaucoma and who was friendly enough with Daddy to light his cigarettes for him without him having to ask. He took us off to where Mr. Small had perched himself on the hood of one of the sheriff's patrol cars. Mr. Small was a very slight man and although Daddy said he was not a public speaker by disposition, he surely gave a fine accounting of himself in this instance and in front of a sizeable audience. Sheer repetition had pretty much refined his story by the time we heard it, and Mr. Small heightened the effect some with pauses and asides and a sprinkling of dramatic gestures. Several of the lady customers who had been party to the event verified certain details of Mr. Small's version and elaborated on others, but they had to yield completely to Mr. Small when the story arrived at Miss Pettigrew's departure from the access ladder since the ladies had left off watching at that point. Daddy called this part of the narrative Mr. Small's soliloquy and Daddy thought it was just splendid. He said it was enough to make the bard cry.

Mr. Small pointed up to the rung of the ladder from which Miss Pettigrew's breadsack still dangled and he counted down four rungs from that one and said, "There. That's where she stood." Then he indicated the rung above the one with the breadsack on it and said, "There. That's where she held on." He was not so precise with Mr. Britches and his "There" took in about a fifteen-foot section of ladder. "That's where that monkey hung from," he said, "sometimes headfirst and gripping with his feet." Then Mr. Small told how Miss Pettigrew did not pitch herself off from the ladder but simply let go and fell over backwards, and he said she did not for a moment tend towards tumbling but remained in the horizontal all the way to the ground. Mr. Small said she almost gave the impression of flight, an observation which caused Daddy and Mr. Newberry to look at each other and say more or less at the same time, "Flight?"

Mr. Small was emphatic about Miss Pettigrew's line of descent and he traced it for us with his finger from the breadsack down through the railing and into the rosebush, choosing not to respond to Daddy's question concerning crosswinds. Miss Pettigrew's encounter with the section of fence was given a full reckoning by Mr. Small. He told exactly how she hit it and which pieces she caused to fly up and which pieces she caused to fly out and which pieces she caused to fly down, and then he made a very harsh, unpleasant noise in his throat and said, "There. That's what it sounded like when she landed in the rosebush," which prompted one of the lady customers to pipe in and say yes, she had heard it just that way, precisely that way. Then Mr. Small told how he bolted across the street and discovered that Miss Pettigrew, although noticeably dead, did not appear disfigured or brutalized at all except for the scratches from the rose thorns, and he said it was next to miraculous to him how Miss Pettigrew's hat had managed to remain in its proper place atop her head. "All in all," Mr. Small assured us, "she looked very presentable."

Daddy and Mr. Newberry agreed that Mr. Small's version of what Daddy called Miss Pettigrew's departure from this life was the most satisfying to be had. We heard several afterwards, all of which were secondhand and delivered by men who Daddy said had sat at the feet of Mr. Small, and pretty soon it got to the point that you couldn't turn around without seeing somebody's raised finger caught up in the business of tracing Miss Pettigrew's path to glory. However, no matter how lively and colorful the various accounts we sampled, Daddy and Mr. Newberry stuck by Mr. Small's version. The others did not differ considerably from the original except in authority, but Daddy said that makes a world of difference in this sort of thing.

Sheriff Burton was not altogether pleased with the way his deputies were controlling the crowd, and he took it upon himself to encourage us towards the outside of the barricade, but folks generally resisted him or ignored him altogether and the sheriff was only successful in removing Mr. Small from the hood of his patrol car. "Car hoods aren't made to be stood on," he told him.

When we came up on the sheriff Daddy asked him right out what harm there was in folks poking around the water tower, and Sheriff Burton sort of drew himself up and said there was a very good chance that every last shred of evidence would be trampled underfoot. But Mr. Newberry told the sheriff not to worry about his evidence and then he put his mouth up close to the sheriff's ear and whispered to him, "I think I know who did it," which caused Daddy to hoot and stomp but hardly got a rise out of Sheriff Burton. He just spat and said a very vile thing.

Mr. Newberry was about half blind since his operations, and the lenses in his glasses were so thick that you could hardly see his eyes through them unless the light was just right. As it was with me and him and Daddy sitting on a sawbuck and facing pretty much to where the sun was flat out in the west, I couldn't see his eyes at all for the glare, so it appeared to me that Mr. Newberry was not looking at anything in particular but maybe just ruminating or pondering over some weighty notion or another. Him and Daddy didn't exchange a word for what seemed a quarter hour but just sat on the sawbuck and smoked Daddy's cigarettes courtesy of Mr. Newberry's matches, which is all Mrs. Newberry would allow him to carry. They were hard smokers the two of them and went about the business of inhaling with a kind of undue ferocity, and just about as soon as Daddy could draw his cigarette down to ash Mr. Newberry was right along with him and they would each have another one. So I suppose Mr. Newberry was only partway pondering and partway caught up in the joys of tobacco, but anyway he showed he was paying at least some consideration to Miss Pettigrew when he eventually said, "Funny thing, I don't think I've laid eyes on that woman in maybe fourteen or fifteen years."

"What woman?" Daddy said.

"For Godsakes, Louis, Miss Pettigrew. I say I don't think I've seen her, up close anyway, in what I know is ten years and maybe fifteen."

"When was that?" Daddy wanted to know.

"The spring of the year as I recall," Mr. Newberry said. "Yes, the spring of the year in nineteen and sixty-four. She came to church, up and came to church and brought that niggerwoman with her. I think it was for Easter services."

"Maybe it was," Daddy said, "but seems to me it was earlier than that. Maybe along about 1960."

"How in the hell would you know?" Mr. Newberry asked him. "You ain't never set foot in a sanctuary."

"I don't need to," Daddy said. "Inez comes home and tells me every little thing that goes on, and she as good as sprinted into the livingroom that day. And I don't think it was in the spring, Russell. As I remember it was in the late fall, right around Thanksgiving I think."

"Maybe it was," Mr. Newberry said, "but I seem to recall it was along about the time Momma Newberry passed on and that would put it in April of nineteen and sixty-four."

"Maybe it was," Daddy said. "I don't know."

And Mr. Newberry said, "Well, I don't know either. Maybe so." Then him and Daddy lit fresh cigarettes and thoroughly engaged themselves in smoking them.

ii

THEY WERE both wrong. It was Christmas of 1962 and I got that from Momma who never forgets a date. She said Miss Pettigrew had hardly shown herself since the evening the mayor and Mr. Nance contrived to make her what Daddy called a paramour. That was late in the summer of 1949 and Momma said Miss Pettigrew did not actually venture into town in broad daylight until the spring of 1952 when the shipping company representative arrived in Neely to tell her the sad news of how the mayor had managed to stopper up his windpipe with a radish. Momma got the story from our neighbor Mrs. Phillip J. King who got it from her cleaning woman, who had gotten it from a cousin of Aunt Willa's who had gotten it from Aunt Willa herself. It seems the gentleman was left waiting in the outer hallway for the best part of a quarter hour, long enough anyway for Mr. Britches to back him up between the hatrack and the umbrella jug, and by the time Miss Pettigrew descended the stairs that fellow had established a toehold on the lip of the baseboard and appeared set to scale the wall if necessary.

He told Miss Pettigrew he'd always had a fondness for monkeys and he patted Mr. Britches on the belly without actually touching him.

"What is it you want, sir?" Miss Pettigrew asked.

And the gentleman recollected himself in time to be appropriately somber and grave. "It's bad news, ma'm," he said. "You might want to take a chair."

"What is it?" Miss Pettigrew did not show any desire to sit down.

"Your brother, ma'm."

"Mr. Pettigrew has died I suppose." And Momma said she let it out just like that, like maybe she was supposing the weather would change or that she should wear a green dress instead of a blue one.

"Yes ma'm," the gentleman said, "Mr. Pettigrew passed on at sea."

"Was he buried there?" she wanted to know.

"No ma'm." He produced the captain's letter from the inner pocket of his coat and gave an account of the particulars of the mayor's case, including storage and arrangements. He bore with him personal condolences from the president of the shipping line, and he assured Miss Pettigrew that her brother's last hours had been happy ones. He said that Mr. Pettigrew and his partner had just taken ribbons in the foxtrot immediately prior to the mayor's encounter with the vegetable platter.

Miss Myra Angelique said, "I see," and she did not thank him and did not formally excuse herself but yelled out down the hallway, "Aunt Willa, get my purse," which Aunt Willa got and which Miss Pettigrew took with her as she stepped out into the sunlight of an April afternoon.

Momma did not imagine more than a half dozen people actually laid eyes on Miss Pettigrew, a fact she attributed not so much to surprise and chance as to Miss Myra Angelique's carriage. Daddy has always said Miss Pettigrew walked like she was being hauled in on a winch, and Momma supposed the mixture of purpose and sheer velocity was what got her from her front door to Commander Tuttle's Heavenly Rest pretty much unnoticed. The commander ran his operation out of a monstrous Victorian house with a slate roof and a cupola and a wrap-around porch protected from the weather by green canvas awnings. Of course he was not a legitimate commander but had gotten the title from his daddy who was not a legitimate commander either but who had gotten the title from his daddy who all the Tuttles swore was a bona fide war hero and duly commissioned ship's captain, but Daddy said he was no more legitimate than the rest of them no matter what any Tuttle claimed, and it seemed they hardly ever shut up about it. Commander III, who would be Commander Jack Tuttle, carried in his fob pocket a steel rivet which he said his daddy, Commander Douglas Tuttle, had carried before him and which his grand-daddy, Commander Rupert Tuttle, had introduced into the Tuttle lineage sometime directly after the war between the states. Daddy said Commander Jack had a great fondness for the Tuttle rivet and could not be kept from extracting it from his fob pocket and holding it aloft between his thumb and forefinger. "This here's a piece of history," he would say, and then he would elaborate by way of recounting the development of naval knowhow beginning with the Phoenecians and carrying on through to the confederacy, which had seen Rupert Tuttle miraculously advance from port gunner to ship's captain on a vessel Commander Jack called the ironclad *Virginia*, otherwise the *Merrimac*.

The commander was understandably vague as to the precise circumstances of his granddaddy's promotion and he pretty much held to his daddy's version of the story, which had the original captain of the ship sometimes shot and sometimes temporarily blinded by a powder blast and sometimes just generally incapacitated, any one of which opened the door for the crew to simultaneously insist that port gunner Rupert Tuttle be given command of the vessel, which he unaccountably was— due to his peerless bravery, Commander Jack would say, due to his matchless nautical wisdom. Displaying his rivet prominently, Commander Jack would go on to tell how his grand-daddy's ship sank a pair of Union frigates in the mouth of the Chesapeake Bay and then engaged the *Monitor* for two days solid before routing her into the open sea where she foundered and was lost.

"Yes sir," the commander would say, studying his rivet, "this here's a piece of history. My granddaddy took it from the belly of the *Virginia* just as she was to be scuttled."

But Daddy insisted it was not a piece of history at all. He said either Commander Douglas or Commander Jack had probably pried it off the water tower one moonless night.

Commander Jack had had dealings with Miss Pettigrew prior to April of 1952 when she arrived in the grand hallway of the Heavenly Rest with news of the mayor's misfortune at sea. As apprentice to Commander Douglas, he had helped tend to the burial of Mrs. Pettigrew in 1914 along with that of Mr. Wallace Amory sr. in the winter of 1926. Commander Jack had buried

Commander Douglas in 1934 and had run the business with no additional Tuttles until 1951 when he was joined by his son, who was only nineteen at the time so was just plain Avery but would become Commander Avery when he reached his majority in October of 1953. Commander Jack told how he was not shocked by the news of the mayor's death but was certainly saddened by it, and he said Miss Pettigrew did not at all dally on her instructions but kept them extremely brief and to the point.

"Bury him," she said.

Of course there were no particulars; there was not even a corpse as of yet. And the commander told how Miss Pettigrew did not seem disposed to select a casket at the moment, did not seem disposed to have anything at all to do with her brother's burial besides the commissioning of it. But even if Miss Pettigrew did not care to chat, Commander Jack had never been caught at a loss for words, even in the face of the most acute bereavement, so he carried on well enough for the both of them. As Commander Avery recollected it, his daddy got underway by explaining to Miss Pettigrew his theory of the evil magnetism of birthdays which he illustrated by way of a desk calendar that provided what Commander Jack called graphic proof of the tendency in people to succumb hard by and sometimes directly on the date of their birth. He called it a phenomenon and said it was most mysterious and unaccountable. Then he asked Miss Pettigrew just when the mayor had come into the world.

"December," she said.

The commander told her he had been a July baby himself.

Daddy said of course the commander talked about the rivet, had to talk about the rivet since Miss Pettigrew provided him an ear he had not bent in that direction before. But she brought it upon herself in part, Daddy said, having made the mistake of saying "ship" and having made the mistake of saying "ocean." And Commander Avery said yes, his daddy did produce the Tuttle rivet from out of his fob pocket, and did hold it up between his thumb and forefinger so Miss Pettigrew could get an eyeful of it, and did go on to tell her how it was a piece of history. Daddy said that's a scene he always wished he had a picture of, just the least little snapshot of Miss Pettigrew there in the grand hallway of the Heavenly

Rest as near to the front door as she could get without being out it and still an extremely handsome woman, still elegant and fine Momma would say, and more or less courageously suffering the Tuttle rivet beneath her nose as displayed between the fingers of Commander Jack who, looking generally like a Tuttle, seemed convincingly incapable of any sort of dauntlessness and who, out of the entire Tuttle clan, was the one most framed like a melon, the one most hairless, the one most eternally short of breath.

Daddy said he simply wanted a picture of it and maybe to go along with that one a companion shot of the commander's face taken sometime after his elaborate and painstaking explanation of the Tuttle honorific, probably taken along about when Miss Pettigrew said, "Good day" and nothing more whatsoever.

Commander Jack did not see Miss Pettigrew again on the business of the mayor's interment, most likely did not ever lay eyes on Miss Pettigrew again since he was already two years in the grave before she bothered to set foot outside once more. He got all his instructions over the telephone and even then only once. That was after the body had arrived and his men had fetched it over from the train station. He called for a funeral suit, but she did not see the need to provide one and told the commander to take something appropriate from the mayor's luggage.

The Commander reported that the mayor did not arrive with any luggage.

So Miss Pettigrew told him to bury the mayor in whatever he had on.

"He's wearing a white dinner jacket," the Commander said.

"That'll do fine," she replied and hung up.

The Commander had the mayor's jacket cleaned and his trousers pressed while the head mortician attempted to do something about the mayor's color, which had gone from its usual ruddiness way past pallor and down to blue-black, due primarily, the mortician said, to freezer burns and general mistreatment. But when he could find no remedy short of housepaint, him and the Commander agreed to screw down the coffin lid, which sat well with the both of them since the mayor looked pretty much like a minstrel and since the cleaners had been unable to remove the swallow-tailed blue ribbon that had sort of glued itself to the mayor's lapel, a ribbon lettered in bold, white characters that spelled out TOP FOXTROTTER diagonally. So the mayor was sent to his reward in a closed coffin and with a private ceremony that no one attended except for the preacher and, briefly, Avery Tuttle and an apprentice embalmer who entered the chapel out of sheer curiosity and joined in with the reverend on two verses of "The Old Rugged Cross" so he wouldn't have to sing alone.

Momma said ten years and eight months, almost eleven years, and Momma never forgets a date. Momma did not suspect Miss Pettigrew as much as put her nose to a windowscreen from the April of the mayor's death to Christmastime of 1962, and she imagined most everybody in Neely had supposed Miss Myra Angelique would not ever again depart from the Pettigrew mansion except in the horizontal. But, along with Aunt Willa, Miss Pettigrew presented herself at the Methodist church on the evening of the children's nativity play after over a decade of pure invisibility, and Momma said it just went to show how the only thing you could know about Miss Pettigrew was that you could never know anything about her.

Of course Miss Pettigrew was not a Methodist. Momma did not figure she held by any strict affiliation but at best retained loose ties with the Presbyterians since she had received her schooling at a Presbyterian institution. Mrs. Pettigrew had been raised in a Catholic household, but Momma said she surrendered her faith when she married Wallace Amory sr. who would not sit still for Catholicism, who would really not sit still for any sort of organized spirit mongering. Daddy said Mr. Wallace Amory sr. might have been the first practicing heathen ever to make his home in Neely. The mayor attended a kind of military academy with vague attachments to a peculiar strain of Virginia Baptists, but Daddy did not recall the mayor ever mentioning anything about religious training except indirectly when he once told how his education had been overseen by the sort of men who probably thought the Spanish Inquisition was a fine thing. As far as anybody could tell, Mayor Pettigrew was pretty much his daddy's son, and he only showed himself in local sanctuaries during his post-appointment mayoral campaign when he worked on the assumption that God-fearing people would not vote an openly faithless man into office.

Momma said it had not been the children's nativity play that brought Miss Pettigrew to the Methodist church, though she did add that the Methodists had a reputation for putting on a truly inspiring Christmas pageant. But as Momma heard it from Mrs. Phillip J. King who got it from her cleaning woman who got it from Aunt Willa's cousin who had not exactly gotten it from Aunt Willa but who had speculated and deducted on her own, which was her right as a relative, and had then broadcast more or less the same version throughout town, one species of which Mrs. Phillip J. King's cleaning woman picked up and relayed to Mrs. King who relayed it to Momma who said the children's nativity play had not lured Miss Pettigrew to the Methodist church; she had come to pray for Aunt Willa's gums and to meditate and seek consultation upon the whole shabby business of Aunt Willa's dentures.

Momma said Aunt Willa had always been cursed with a mouthful of bad teeth and when it got to the point where she could hardly chew meat she set her mind on a pair of plates and immediately began to accumulate whatever money she could so as to prevent herself from becoming a vegetarian. Of course Aunt Willa could not afford a regular dentist, which caused her to fall in with an old disreputable negro named Janks Alison that folks called Mr. Janks who owned a covered truck and made his money driving mostly other negroes to and from a roadside dental clinic in Sumter, South Carolina. Momma said Mr. Janks got away with anywhere from twelve to twenty dollars a head, depending on the desperation of the client. His customers did not ever know exactly when they would be leaving for Sumter since Mr. Janks refused to travel without a full load of seventeen—fifteen in the truckbed and two in the cab along with Mr. Janks himself. So Aunt Willa stayed on standby for several weeks, Momma said, while Mr. Janks drummed up business throughout the county, all of which was his territory. Momma said he had attained to a kind of slick and accomplished salesmanship which was part sheer deception, part threat, all of it helped along by means of a pair of uppers and lowers that Mr. Janks carried in his coatpocket and produced from time to time for effect. As for himself, Momma said, Mr. Janks had retained all of his original teeth.

Aunt Willa finally made the trip to Sumter sometime along about the first week of December, 1962. All of Mr. Janks' customers collected in the middle of the night at the icehouse where Mr. Janks picked them up, timing himself so as to arrive at the clinic with the morning. As Aunt Willa told it, the patients were as much as herded into a common room equipped with four dentist's chairs, one hygienist, and two dentists—Dr. Hathcock and Dr. Ursone—who Daddy said had probably never quite evolved into respectable human beings. Aunt Willa said they started in on the first four right off, yanking teeth and dropping them into metal pails between the chairs, and she told how each of them took two patients and alternated from mouth to mouth working so feverishly as to keep the incisors and molars and bicuspids ringing against the sides of the buckets like hailstones. The hygienist took molds for the plates before the gums had time to swell, or anyway before they had time to swell much, and the remainder of her duties consisted of providing the patients with cubes of ice to suck on which she distributed directly out of freezer trays. According to Aunt Willa, Mr. Janks stopped at the state line on the return trip for what he said was the standard complimentary dinner, but since nobody was willing to chew just then he had to eat alone.

The trouble with Aunt Willa's teeth was that they never did fit properly, not even after she'd fought off two infections and her gums had shrunk down to their regular size. The uppers would not stay up and the lowers would not stay down, which turned out to be the general complaint among Mr. Janks' customers who would collect on occasion at a negro dance hall and trade plates in hopes of finding a snugger fit. But Aunt Willa did not come up on any dentures that rattled around in her mouth any less than her own, so she just experimented with what she had and discovered that if she wore her uppers where her lowers should be and her lowers where her uppers should be she could chew passably well and without much worry of either plate dropping onto the table. Of course Aunt Willa's dentures were not especially attractive upside-down. Daddy said they made her look like some sort of flesh-tearing creature and he imagined Aunt Willa and her dentures could make a home for themselves in any jungle of the world.

According to Mrs. Phillip J. King, who told Momma she had studied the matter from every conceivable angle, Aunt Willa and Miss Pettigrew probably decided to apply themselves in prayer directed towards the gums instead of the teeth because Miss Pettigrew had concluded that while the size of the teeth was pretty much set, the gums might be somehow divinely manipulated. Momma told Mrs. King yes, she supposed so, but actually Momma did not at all hold with the view that Aunt Willa's dental troubles could draw Miss Pettigrew out of her daddy's house after ten years of unbroken solitude. Momma said Aunt Willa's gums were not good enough reason to send Miss Pettigrew to church but served as a fair excuse for getting her there, and Momma had her own theory as to why Miss Pettigrew might trade her daddy's parlor for the Methodist sanctuary if only on one evening out of a decade's worth of evenings. Momma's theory did not reflect poorly on Miss Pettigrew's faculties, did not reflect poorly on Miss Pettigrew at all, but then Daddy said Momma always thought better of Miss Pettigrew than most everybody else did.

iii

WINTERS IN Neely can be most forlorn and desolate. By the time November arrives the trees have all gone bare and what leaves were not raked into ditches and burned lie under shrubbery and against the backsides of houses where they blacken and rot. There is always a particular day no closer to Halloween than Thanksgiving when Daddy sends me into the backyard with a rake and has me clean the last of the leaves and the rubbish out from the row of mock orange bushes that marks the far line of our lot. I've never tangled with anything so aggravating as a mock orange bush in November, and I suppose I lost all patience with them the first time I was big enough to hold a rake and Daddy turned me out into the backyard alone. Later Momma told me how he watched me from one of the windows of the breakfast room and just grinned. She said that was a golden day for Daddy; she said the mock orange bushes was why he wanted a son.

Of course you can't hardly get leaves and rubbish out from a mock orange bush, but I didn't know that then. And of course Daddy did not expect me to be any more effective at it than he had been, but I didn't know that then either. Confronting the mock orange bushes had simply become what Daddy called a point of honor, a sort of obligation he had seen through until I could inherit it. So once a year in November I wake up on a Saturday with the sort of feeling that must come over birds just before they migrate, and I get straight out of bed into my playclothes and put on my carcoat and my workgloves and my green corduroy hat with the earflaps and I fetch the rake out of our cellar and set out for the bottom of the back lot, where I am condemned to thrash at the mock orange bushes for the balance of the day. And that is when it usually happens, not while I'm still trying to extract from the mock oranges everything that has blown or fallen into them in the course of the year, but after I have left off from the struggle for a spell and have sat down on the grass where I pluck at the rakehead to make the tines sing, and I listen to the sound of the sprung metal dying away sometimes mixed with the cry of a hound or the low, indecipherable noise of a voice on the air, and suddenly I am aware of the sort of chill I haven't known in a year and I notice that the sky is very high and tufted and the color of ash in a grate, which is the color of my breath, which is the color of the afternoon, which is the color of the season; and I know it isn't autumn anymore.

In our household we have never kept the seasons by a calendar. Spring commences with the buds on the apricot tree. When Momma lets me go barefoot it's summer. The first chill night after Labor Day means autumn. And I bring winter in myself when I return the rake to the cellar and meet Momma in the breakfast room where I find her gazing out the back window. "My my, Louis," she always tells me, "those mock oranges look a hundred percent better." Daddy says that's her part in the ritual.

Winter in Neely is a monotonous time of year and nothing much can really break the spell of the season except for a healthy snowfall, which tends to drive the good sense out of most people since very few of the natives have seen enough snow to have become indifferent to it. We are accustomed to sleet and to the sort of rain that freezes in treetops and downs powerlines, so even the rumor of flurries makes people's eyes bright. I don't suppose there is anyone in all of Neely or in the farthest reaches of the outlying areas around it who could not be called upon to tell how on the evening of January ninth,

1957, a storm set in which raged and blew for a day and a half and left behind it a six and three-quarter inch accumulation not counting drifts, a record for the area. According to Daddy, that was a time of general lunacy in Neely, but then Daddy has always said there's nothing like a good snowfall to bring out the feeble-mindedness in people.

There is a tendency among Neelyites to panic in the face of poor weather, and the reaction to snow is no less frantic, just a little more lightheaded. Before the first few flakes have had time to settle in and melt, every school in the county closes down and any merchant who does not specifically deal in provisions, what are usually called groceries, has locked up his shop and gone home. When we children arrive from school, the mothers and housewives of Neely begin to expect the worst and busy themselves making shopping lists for such indispensable items as dishpowder and confectioner's sugar and institutional-sized cans of ravioli, just the sorts of things no family can be snowbound without. Since it is us children who will make the trip to the store, we set ourselves to rooting around in the bottoms of the closets looking for boots, which most of us usually find only one of and that one made to go on last year's foot. About the only citizens of Neely with boots that fit are the garbage men, who have to stomp trash all day and who, of course, don't work when it snows. So we settle for Baggies over our sneakers, and while our mothers finish up their grocery lists, we go into the cellar after our sleds which have usually had a full year to rust and deteriorate but which require only a little candle wax on the runners to be operational again. I don't imagine very many of us ever get away without the sort of sendoff that is a mixture of warnings, instructions, and outright threats and that, Daddy says, is probably just the kind of thing Commander Scott heard from his mother before he weighed anchor for the antarctic. Momma usually tells me not to dally unless I want to catch pneumonia or get frostbite or become disoriented in the snow and lose my way, which would be a sheer impossibility since most everybody under voting age is either going to or coming from the Big Apple and making enough racket for ten people in dragging their sleds over pavement that is considerably wetted down but far from icy. Daddy says the idiocy falls with the snow and sometimes Momma manages to avoid it and sometimes she doesn't.

On the evening after a two or three inch snowfall Daddy and me take our supper in the breakfast room where we can look out the window to where the floodlights shine through the limbs of our apricot and our elm and play off the peaks and drifts against the carshed and just generally make a spectacle of even our backyard. Of course by dinnertime Momma has been cooking in vatfuls all afternoon and has amassed an ambitious selection of stews and sauces and puddings along with a gracious plenty of garbage, which she insists has to go to the can in the yard before the night is out. So me and Daddy eye each other gravely since even the least little errand has become an expedition, and then Daddy usually bows out to me saying something like, "You take it admiral, I'm faint of heart." And I go after my Baggies and my coat and when I get to the door with two armfuls of trash, Daddy sometimes toasts me with his coffee cup. "Safe return," he says.

Sometime after midnight and before sunrise it is not at all uncommon for the clouds to blow off leaving the moon to break through and put a glow on things. Daddy says because the light is extraordinary and unnatural, it inflicts a kind of madness on some people while they sleep and they wake up in the morning wanting to drive their cars. Daddy says he cannot explain it otherwise since there's no reason at all for a townful of people with absolutely nowhere to go to wheel their Buicks and Pontiacs and oversized Fords out into the streets of Neely where they pass the day veering off into ditches or phone poles or just running up onto the fenders of people going nowhere in the opposite direction. Folks only learn enough to use chains about the time the snow has begun to seep off into the ground and slush up in the gutters, and for at least an afternoon and most of an evening Neely sounds for all the world like a town under armored attack. Daddy holds with the notion that there's nothing for a sane man to do on the day after a snowfall but plant himself in the northeast corner of his cellar and hope for the best. He's always said that if Washington had kept company with Southerners at Valley Forge the whole group of them could have passed the winter making snow angels and igloos and generally having a high time of it.

But a hardy blizzard is a rarity in Neely and cannot be

expected to arrive with any sort of regularity, cannot even be counted on for a yearly showing. Winters in Neely are mostly sadly predictable and barren and colorless and genuinely forlorn. Momma is the one of us who tends to suffer most through the season. She holds up well enough until Christmas and on into the New Year, but by the first week in February Momma is a lost woman. On February afternoons Momma turns on all the lamps in the house and sits in the livingroom in one of Grandma Yount's burgundy boudoir chairs where she applies herself to the same novel she has been reading off and on for six years now, the one that starts out "Save when it happened to rain Vanderbank always walked home." From year to year Momma forgets where she left off, so she sets in at page one and makes a kind of erratic go of it until March. Momma tells me she keeps expecting it to get lively and is annually disappointed. Daddy has tried that book himself; he says Momma is a woman of infinite hope.

But no matter the lamps and the distractions, the last two weeks in February tend to take Momma under and occasionally she frets and cries and tells Daddy how she has to get away from Neely, how she has to get away from February, how she'd nearly be willing to die for a spring day. And Daddy puts his arms around Momma and rocks with her to hush her up, and sometimes he'll drive us out to the Holiday Inn on the by-pass where he treats Momma to a meal she doesn't have to cook or wash up after, and Daddy talks to the waitresses and talks to the other customers and tells me and Momma how he's been considering pulling up roots and moving to Buffalo where he says Momma can have her own caldron to stew in and I can go to the store with actual ice under my sled runners and Daddy tells how he'll buy us a fleet of Buicks to run off into gullies and just generally slosh around in. Wouldn't that be grand? Daddy says. Wouldn't that be the life? And Momma abides him with a smile.

It was February that gave Momma the chance to think about Miss Pettigrew, and her theory as to why Miss Pettigrew showed up at the Methodist Christmas pageant after nearly ten years of not showing up much of anywhere else was probably born of Momma's long, slow hours in Grandma Yount's boudoir chair where she held the book about Mr. Vanderbank and pondered the somber February afternoons out the side window. Momma did not for a minute think Miss Myra Angelique could bring herself to pray for a set of dentures. But then Momma assumed what very few people in Neely cared to assume: she was of the opinion that Miss Pettigrew might be as human as everybody else. Momma said it must have been the winter or anyway the accumulation of winters that finally drove Miss Pettigrew out of the empty chambers and hallways of her daddy's mansion and into the company of more or less regular people. Momma simply could not believe that a woman like Miss Pettigrew would go to church and pray for the gums of her colored help. That would be madness, and Momma did not think Miss Pettigrew was mad. She thought she was lonely.

Everything Momma could not know herself came by way of Mrs. Phillip J. King and her negro grapevine. Of course Mrs. King kept to her dental perspective and Momma said she spent a solid half hour discussing the sorry state of Aunt Willa's gums and then told how Aunt Willa could not even get down her creamed corn without making faces like she might be working over a mouthful of carpet tacks. Mrs. King said the poor woman was in agony and she wanted a doctor and some pain-killer but Miss Myra Angelique decided they would call on the Almighty instead. Everything else Momma knew for herself, since she never missed a Christmas pageant.

Momma had not started out as a Methodist but was raised a Baptist and converted when she married Daddy whose parents made him join the Methodist church when he was twelve and had forced him to attend Sunday services and revivals until he outgrew Granddaddy Benfield and took it upon himself to lapse into what he calls the ease of sinful living. Every week me and Momma go to the eight o'clock service and Sunday school after, and usually Momma takes me with her Wednesday nights to prayer meeting and ships me off to most every church retreat that comes along. Momma is considerably worrisome and bull-headed about my religious training since she knows I don't have anybody to outgrow but her. She is ever trying to get Daddy on her side, and on Sundays just before lunch Momma tells him how she has prayed that God might reach down His hand from heaven and touch Daddy's soul with His splendor. But Daddy says God knows better.

At Christmastime of 1962 Momma still had a wait of nearly

a year and a half before she'd have me to drag to the sanctuary with her, so she attended the annual pageant in the company of Miss Mattie Gunn, a local spinster woman who Daddy said was normally a High Baptist but took pleasure in seeing what Methodists looked like from year to year. Late in 1961 the regular Methodist preacher, Mr. Miller, got rotated to Mt. Airy and was replaced by the Reverend Mr. Richard Crockett Shelton who was not even a half-dozen years out of divinity school when he took charge of the church. Mr. Miller had been good for nothing in that way that preachers have of being good for nothing, or good for hardly anything anyway, as they seem to figure getting paid to be holy is enough. Mr. Miller could be holy every now and again and could be quite successfully profane every once in awhile too, so naturally people had an affection for him since he seemed entirely capable of as much turpitude as they were.

The Reverend Mr. Richard Crockett Shelton, however, was another case altogether. He stood over six feet tall, was very blond and pure-looking, and did not have any vices to speak of. Momma said he delivered a stirring sermon, but Daddy always said that if religion had done nothing else for Momma it had made her merciful. Daddy had sat through several of the reverend's funeral orations and he said Mr. Shelton distinguished himself by being one of the few preachers he had ever been exposed to who could bore the corpse. Daddy was always hard on preachers and he even slept through the Billy Graham crusades when Momma tried to make him watch them on television. Momma said the majority of the congregation simply did not believe that the Reverend Shelton was advanced enough in years to be at all friendly with God. Folks suspected they'd have to wait until he got a little farther from the seminary and a little closer to the grave before he could tell them anything they didn't already know for themselves. But Daddy did not imagine the passing years would get the Reverend Shelton anything but older. He said Mr. Shelton was merely the sort of preacher who's always beating his wings but can never fly.

Most likely the Methodists tolerated the Reverend Shelton and kept him on at the church not because he showed any promise as a sermonizer but because he took their Christmas pageant to heart. Momma said the quality of the pageant had fallen off considerably under Mr. Miller, who had his own idea of the spirit of the season, and she said it suffered its first cancellation in 1960 when the preacher managed to round up only two wise men and the angel of the Lord came down with the mumps. But the Reverend Shelton changed all of that. He threw himself into the staging of the pageant with the sort of zeal and excitement Mr. Miller had been incapable of, or anyway not inclined to. And even though Mr. Shelton didn't arrive in Neely until nearly the end of 1961, he put on a respectable initial production and vowed better things in the future.

Consequently, work on the 1962 pageant commenced in August of that year with the formation of a Christmas committee and the scheduling of auditions for early September. Mr. Shelton wanted to provide himself with a half dozen wise men, three or four Josephs and angels, and a couple of Virgin Marys so as to protect against any unforeseen occurrences. In the latter part of October the reverend organized a building committee which saw to the construction of the stable and baby Jesus' manger, both of which were made from shipping crates supplied by an appliance store in a shopping center near Draper. By the middle of November Miss Fay Dull had begun rehearsing the choir, and just after Thanksgiving the ladies from the Tuesday Biblettes set in to making costumes for the wise men out of old chair covers. The reverend's schedule provided for two practice runs in December before the actual production on the evening of Sunday the twenty-third, and when Reverend Shelton addressed his congregation on the morning of the sixteenth he told them how the Christmas pageant would be an unforgettable affair. Momma said it surely was.

The animals normally used in the pageant were kept from year to year in the basement of the fellowship hall. They were made out of painted plywood and seemed very lifelike if you didn't look at them anywhere but head-on. But the reverend didn't think his pageant was suited for wooden animals; he thought it called for something a little more grand and spectacular. The Reverend Shelton had actual livestock in mind, livestock which he borrowed from local farmers who agreed to keep quiet about it until after the performance. He got hold of a half-dozen piglets, a pair of goats, three or four chickens, one goose, and Mr. Jip French's old blind pony that his boys chased around the pasture and ran into fences. But when he tried the animals out at a full-dress rehearsal the reverend discovered that he couldn't use the pony because it was given to breaking wind, not very loudly, Momma said, but in near lethal concentrations. So the reverend tried to get another pony but couldn't and had to settle for Mr. Earl Jemison's steely-grey hound, Mayhew, which was probably one of the biggest dogs in the county and which the reverend decided to transform into a camel by means of a couple of pillows and a brown rug.

Mayhew did not come easy, however. Mr. Jemison accounted himself a respectable actor and he bargained relentlessly for the part of the voice of God, a part Mr. Jemison said he had always wanted to play. Mr. Shelton had saved the voice of God for himself and he gave it up to Mr. Jemison with severe misgivings since he did not think God talked at all like Mr. Jemison, whose voice Daddy said could pass for an articulate doorhinge. But the reverend had somehow convinced himself he was desperate for a camel and he wasn't about to lose the services of Mr. Jemison's dog.

Momma said she and Miss Mattie Gunn did not know just what to think when they entered a sanctuary entirely darkened except for three railroad lanterns hung here and there on a fairly legitimate-looking stable up by the altar. And she said neither Miss Mattie nor herself noticed that the reverend had imported actual animals until the both of them caught a whiff of the chickens at about the same time. Unfortunately Miss Mattie suffered from an allergy to feathers and her eyes immediately teared up so that she couldn't see past the pew in front of her and Momma had to tell her just how everything looked. Momma said the reverend and his committees had created a most impressive effect with just a few oven crates, some paint, a couple of bales of hay, a handful of livestock, and the accompanying barnyard aroma. Momma said the reverend had strewn hay across the altar, set the stablefront on top of it, hung a few lanterns, tethered the goats, caught up the piglets and the chickens and the goose together in a wire corral, and left the ammonia to drift where it would. Momma said she could have been out of doors for all she knew and every now and then she wished she was.

Momma did not know exactly when Miss Pettigrew made her entry into the sanctuary since the usher seated her a full two aisles over from Momma, who could hardly make out Miss Mattie as it was. But she suspected Miss Pettigrew arrived just after the reverend had presented himself from a niche beneath the choir loft and come forward onto the altar to greet the congregation. Along about then Momma heard a distinct buzzing off to her left that carried the length of the aisle and she said it was probably the sound of people asking each other if that was indeed Miss Pettigrew or telling each other it was indeed Aunt Willa, not because they could make out her features, not even because they could tell she was colored, but because even in the lanternlight they could detect the radical limp Aunt Willa got from being dropped onto a stone hearth as a baby. And Momma said the usher and Miss Pettigrew and Aunt Willa advanced to the front pew with the noise of their passing advancing just behind them. She said anybody knew whoever was with Aunt Willa had to be Miss Pettigrew.

According to Momma the pageant got underway when the arm of the innkeeper came far enough out of the shadows to direct the Virgin Mary and Joseph to a place where they might bed down for the night. She said the Virgin Mary, as played by Miss Alice Covens, seemed somewhat frightened of the goats and swung excessively wide of them on her way into the stable while Joseph, as played by Mr. Jeffrey Elwood Crawford jr., lingered outside and delivered a little speech on starlight and poverty and the kindness of men. He concluded to a very short burst of applause that lasted only as long at it took for Mrs. Crawford to get hold of her husband's hands. Then Joseph joined the Virgin Mary in the stable and the choir took over with Miss Dull's arrangement of "O Little Town of Bethlehem." Mr. Jemison's big scene followed the music and began with Reverend Shelton playing a flashlight beam onto the angel of the Lord, who was perched a little recklessly on the choir-loft bannister. But nothing happened right away, and Momma said the angel clung onto the railing and waited and the congregation waited and the Reverend Shelton coughed and cleared his throat until finally the voice of God exploded out of the darkness like a train whistle and nearly scared everybody to death. Momma said Mr. Jemison told his angel where to go and what to do when he got there, and then the angel sort of saluted, she said, and threw himself off the bannister, which caused the entire congregation to suck air. But he was harnessed into a system of ropes and pulleys, and after he swooped back into the railing once, he descended more or less without incident to a point just over the stable roof where he could hover and wait for the wise men.

The Reverend Shelton threw a switch that activated a bulb in a Moravian star suspended somewhere above the angel of the Lord and somewhere below the choir loft, and almost simultaneously the three kings from the orient came forward out of the narthex wearing everybody's old upholstery and beards made from cotton swabs and crowns wrapped in aluminum foil. One of them bore frankincense and another one bore both myrrh and gold since the one who was supposed to bear the gold had his hands full with the camel, who did not seem especially interested in witnessing the birth of the Christchild but showed a preference for sniffing shoetops along the aisle. Miss Fay Dull led the choir in four verses of "We Three Kings," which served to carry the gift-bearing wise men on up to the stable but broke off a minute or two before the one with the camel had a chance to make the altar. Only the angel of the Lord seemed at all perturbed by the delay, but then he had just grown somewhat harness-weary and thrashed around in an effort to relieve himself.

The baby Jesus had gotten born in the meantime and as the wise men closed in to adore him, the camel, who was supposed to be tethered up away from the goose and the piglets and the chickens and the goats, got loose into the back of the stable and sprawled on the hay where he licked himself through the better part of Miss Dull's solo performance of "Away in a Manger." Then came time for Reverend Shelton to read a passage from the Book of Matthew, and Momma said that's when the trouble started. When the reverend turned on his pulpit lamp so as to see the Bible, considerable light was thrown onto the front edge of the congregation, and best as Momma could figure it the Virgin Mary, who had the Christchild in her arms and was flanked all around by Joseph and the wise men, looked up long enough to get an eyeful of a colored woman in the front pew, which would have been a rarity in any pew, and then she looked again and saw it was Aunt Willa and since she knew wherever Aunt Willa went Miss Pettigrew might be, she looked off beside Aunt Willa and found Miss Pettigrew herself, who had already become a kind of local spook.

Momma said the sight of Miss Pettigrew must have simply shocked the Virgin Mary and in her agitation she lost her grip on the baby Jesus and dropped him onto the edge of the manger, where his porcelain head got jarred loose from the rest of him and fell onto the hay next to one of the goats, and Momma said the sound of the baby Jesus' head hitting the floor startled the one goat, who bucked into the other one who lunged the length of his tether and jolted one of the lanterns off its peg, and Momma said when it hit the floor the glass chimney broke and the hay caught fire. The wise men bolted off in one direction, Joseph cleared out in the other, and the Virgin Mary crept backwards into the stable with her hands over her mouth until she stepped on the camel's hindquarters, which caused him to jump to his feet and start barking. By this time the angel of the Lord figured things had pretty much fallen to pieces and he set up a fuss to be hauled in right away; he said the harness was making his legs blue. But Momma said he was left to dangle over the stable while two baritones came down out of the choir loft and smothered the flames with their robes before going to the assistance of the Virgin Mary, who had momentarily lost her wits. In a matter of minutes everything was back to order except for the camel who continued to bark and make threatening noises, but he cowed immediately when the voice of God shouted down from the rafters, "Mayhew, shut up!"

Momma said some one of the ushers finally showed the great good sense to turn the sanctuary lights up and everybody along the left aisle leapt bolt upright to see if that was indeed Miss Pettigrew in the company of Aunt Willa in the front row, and when they found out that yes, it was, they told the people beside them who told the people beside them who told the people beside them and the news shot through the sanctuary like electricity. Momma said nobody seemed to care that the reverend's Christmas pageant had nearly burned the church down or that the reverend himself had fallen into a faint behind the pulpit or that the angel of the Lord had commenced to wail and sob and say how doctors would have to cut his legs off with a handsaw if somebody didn't draw him into the choir loft straightaway. She said all people wanted to do was look at Miss Pettigrew since they'd been without the chance to in nearly a decade and didn't know when the opportunity might present itself again. So everybody stood up, she said, and looked. Aunt Willa helped Miss Pettigrew off the pew, and Momma said she tried to lead her on out of the sanctuary but Miss Pettigrew held up and faced the congregation, not seeming at all mysterious or tainted or stern, but just a little wilted and sheepish and fairly human.

Momma said Aunt Willa's cheeks were all puffy and swollen and her gums obviously gave her some pain when she snatched at Miss Pettigrew's elbow and said, "Come on h'yer," but Miss Pettigrew just stood where she was and worked her lips as if she might say something, as if she might say hello. Momma said folks looked at each other and looked at Miss Pettigrew and looked at each other again until Miss Pettigrew finally opened her mouth and said nothing whatsoever.

Then Aunt Willa took her by the elbow. "Come on h'yer Miss Pettigrew," she said. "Come on h'yer to home." And Momma said this time Miss Pettigrew let Aunt Willa have her way and everybody watched them down the aisle, watched them into the narthex, watched them even after the angel of the Lord unhooked himself from the rope and fell through the stable roof.

iv

MISS BAMBI KINCH of Action News Five put Mr. Small on television, and as Mr. Small had never been on television before and did not consider himself dressed for it, Miss Kinch allowed him to dash over to his store and fetch his seersucker jacket. She had arrived in a white van in the company of a cameraman named Larry and Bub, his assistant, who helped Larry get the camera out of the back and then sat sideways in the driver's seat and ate shelled peanuts from a sack. Miss Kinch announced to the crowd of us how she represented the Action News team out of Greensboro, and she said she'd appreciate a few words with whatever witnesses there might be, which I suppose got her anywhere from thirty-five to forty volunteers, most of them graduates of the Small school of witnessing.

That's when Sheriff Burton intervened with Mr. Small himself, who was in his shirtsleeves and a soiled butcher's apron and who would not be committed to film without his seersucker jacket. So as he ran across the street to retrieve it from a peg in the back of the store, Larry and Miss Kinch attempted to set up the shot. Larry was all for having the water tower in the background, but Miss Kinch resisted the idea. She thought it was too big and shiny and might attract far too much attention. And Larry said, "It may be bigger, Bambi, but it's not nearly as sweet," to which Miss Kinch suggested he just point the camera and keep his goddam mouth shut. "Yes, princess," he said, and then him and Miss Kinch snapped and swore at each other for a spell before the two of them threw in together to heap abuse on Bub who, apparently, was entirely no count.

As it turned out Mr. Small did not get to wear his seersucker jacket because it clashed with Miss Kinch's yellow blazer and yellow hair. She told him he had to get hold of something more subdued, and he borrowed a mud-colored sportcoat from one of his followers. But by the time Larry turned on his high-intensity lamp and cranked the camera up, Mr. Small was a defeated man. He had been deprived of his jacket and deprived of his water tower, which was not even in the picture, and every time he tried to turn and point, Miss Kinch wrenched him back around to the camera lens and poked at him with her microphone. Daddy said it was always sad and pathetic when idols tumbled.

After Miss Kinch got done with Mr. Small she grabbed hold of Sheriff Burton's sleeve and brought him into camera range. "Who is the victim sheriff?" she asked him.

"Well, Bambi," the sheriff said and hooked his thumbs in his front beltloops, "the victim is a female caucasian, approximately sixty-five years of age."

"Was she a resident of Neely?"

"Well, Bambi, yes she was an indigenous native."

"Do you suspect foul play, sheriff?"

"Well, Bambi, at this point we think it's a suicide brought on probably by general derangement."

"Did she have a history of this sort of thing?"

"Well, Bambi, not that we know of. She's never done this before."

"And what about the monkey, sheriff?"

"Well, Bambi, he's your basic chimpanzee type monkey, and we suspect we'll have to send a man up after him."

"Thank you, sheriff. This is Bambi Kinch, Action News Five in Neely." Miss Kinch grinned over top of the microphone for a half-minute and then hissed through her teeth, "Pan, Larry, pan to the dirtbags," and Larry swung the camera around to a crowd of people in front of the water tower who studied the lens like most folks look into a fishtank.

Junious

MOMMA HAS always shown a particular fondness for the dusk of the day, and though she has never said so outright, I suspect she is especially taken with the way the world disappears at twilight. Momma naps regularly in the early evenings, or anyway she calls it napping, but I've never yet stuck my head through her doorway and found her asleep. She is always just laying there on the bed with the covers drawn up to her chin and the lights off in the back hallway and in the bedroom itself and the front shade tight against the sill and the side shade only partway down the sash so that the blue wash from the mercury light on the street comes in once the sunset has dwindled away and falls across a quarter of Grandma Yount's chiffonier and touches on a portion of the cedar-lined wardrobe which came to Daddy by way of his Uncle Connelly Benfield, who lived with his second wife in a farmhouse near Draper until he was sent off to the Black Mountain Sanatorium to be treated for the tuberculosis that would eventually kill him. Momma is not the sort to heave and pitch on the bed; she doesn't even rustle the covers. And it is always Momma who sees me before I can separate her from the shadows and patches of mercury light on the bedclothes. "What is it, Louis?" she says and her voice is never rough or broken but rings like it does anywhere else and sort of lurches out from the darkness which is always enough to take my breath at first there with the lights off and house still. So I ask her whatever it is I've come to ask her which is usually nothing worth knowing or at least nothing worth breaking in on her to find out, and Momma tells me what I want to know in that same clear and deliberate voice that never departs entirely from the shadows along the walls and in the corners of the ceiling and is as much a part of the evening as they are.

When me and Daddy were on our way to the tower and stopped at Mr. Gibbons's mailbox so Daddy could use the kitchen matches Mr. Gibbons allowed him to keep there, I happened to turn back towards our house just as the porch light came on. Since it was early in the evening yet I don't suppose that single bulb changed the look of things significantly and I probably wouldn't have noticed it was on if I hadn't happened to be watching the bulb itself when it went from grey to yellow. Daddy didn't see it or anyway didn't make like he did and I don't know as it would have meant much at all to him if he had, but I saw it, saw it as Momma switched it on, and it struck a note with me. And I said to myself without really saying it but just knowing it right off, this is the sort of thing that sets me apart from Daddy and him from me and both of us from everybody else, not simply that I saw the porch light come on and he didn't and nobody else would care anyway, but more that Momma could switch on a single bulb and switch on something in me with it, something of sadness and grief and shot through with the melancholy of twilight, something I could not be sure Daddy would know as I knew it, feel as I felt it. And I told myself how it was probably no more than pure chance and maybe a little grim luck that caused me to turn and look just when I turned and looked, and I said to myself, this won't ever happen just this way again, not even having to say that either but just knowing it and concluding it right off.

Daddy told me how he hadn't even suspected Miss Pettigrew had it in her, and I said I hadn't imagined so either, which must have come along about when Momma put out the lights in the back hallway and set herself to adjusting the shades in the bedroom. And as Daddy smoked he looked up through the limbs of a white oak tree and into the sky, and I turned back to the house one last time, which must have come along about when Momma switched off the bedside lamp and then lay back and pulled the topsheet up to her chin. I couldn't know for certain but I imagined that when she put her head onto the pillow she got the same expression on her face she sometimes gets at the supper table after the dishes have been cleared away and me and her and Daddy sit back in our chairs feeling unnecessary. That's usually when Daddy tells me how he was young once and how him and Momma didn't know what they had, and Momma never talks but to add a detail here and there. Mostly she just looks off beyond Daddy towards the breakfast room window and smiles the slightest, meekest, most sorrowful smile I have ever seen.

Daddy likes to tell how him and Momma lived in a little crackerbox house on Silver Street in Danville. That was when Daddy worked for the railroad and kept an office in the depot downtown where he was charged with timing the trains as they came through and noting on a chart whether they were early, late, or on schedule. Daddy has always said it was simply a riveting occupation. Him and Momma hadn't been married but a little over three years when Daddy got on with the railroad. It was the first salaried job he ever held, and to take it him and Momma had to move down from Lynchburg where Daddy had worked by the hour keeping the books for a furniture dealer and where they had rented the upstairs of a house owned by the Colonel and Mrs. Coggins who slept in separate ends of the downstairs because the Colonel snored like a buzzsaw.

Along about the time of the move Momma must have made a sidetrip to Neely in order to give birth to little Margaret, though she never says as much directly and Daddy does not elaborate himself except to tell how they set off a corner of their Danville bedroom for what he sometimes calls Bumpins. Mostly Daddy talks about the root cellar which had been scooped out from the crawlspace beneath their bedroom and which he could find no use for whatsoever, primarily because every third day or so it would fill up with garden slugs, and according to Daddy they lay so thick on the dirt floor that you couldn't take a step without dispatching a half dozen of them to wherever it is slugs go once they've been spread across the bottom of a shoe. Momma cannot abide a garden slug herself and I imagine she would have preferred sleeping over a nest of crocodiles since crocodiles will never ooze between your toes and are generally too large to crawl up through the ductwork into the house, which is what Momma was afraid the slugs would do. Daddy says he tried to tell her that your regular garden slug would probably not care to trade off the dirt floor of the root cellar for an aluminum heat duct, but Momma did not consider Daddy fully educated in the capabilities of slugs, and anyway she didn't think for a moment that her cellarful was of the regular variety. Daddy says Momma convinced herself that they were a refined strain of slug with the capacity to be conniving and maybe a little vicious too.

So Momma began to live with the idea that the slugs were not just aimlessly slithering around in the root cellar but were scheming down there, and Daddy says it got to the point where Momma would lay in bed at night waiting for the assault and occasionally Daddy would lick the end of his thumb and put it against Momma's bare leg, and he says she would somehow manage to levitate over the mattress until she could land upright on the dresser or light atop the base of Daddy's coatrack without ever having to touch the floor herself. Daddy says he eventually called the exterminator just this side of when Momma might have divorced him or shot him, he didn't know which, and he says the exterminator took one look in the root cellar then sort of grinned at him and said, "I've got just the thing," which turned out to be four boxes of Morton's table salt. "Wonder of wonders," Daddy says. So the exterminator spread the table salt over what slugs were already in the root cellar and left a healthy covering against whatever ones were on their way there, and Daddy says late that same night just after him and Momma had got in bed he heard a distant, extended moan, which he knew right off for a fire whistle, but he hissed at Momma anyway, "Listen!" And Daddy says Momma sat bolt upright in the bed and said, "What is it, Louis?" "I think it's those slugs screaming," he told her, and Momma says she made a swat at Daddy, not knowing exactly where she would catch him but just wanting to catch him somewhere, and she says it was simply by plain unfortunate chance that Daddy rose up just as she came around and put his nose directly in the way of her forearm, all of which Momma says was a little difficult to explain at the hospital.

Daddy says after the slugs were gone and after he got the splints off his nose, things became fairly routine in Danville. In the mornings, Momma would get up first to take care of what Daddy sometimes calls the little one, and then she would pour him a bowl of puffed rice and attempt to brew coffee in the GE percolator Miss Nancy Gant had given them at their wedding. Daddy tells how Momma would measure the coffee out with a tablespoon, toss in a little salt, fill the pot at the tap and plug it in at the counter so it could pop and steam and spew and generally throw the sort of fit that was calculated to produce something drinkable. And Daddy says every morning he would approach the pot carrying with him what he calls fresh resolve along with his cup and he would tilt the percolator and out would come what had been just ten minutes earlier a little coffee, a dash of salt, and plain tapwater now all mixed and transformed through the miracle of electricity into a species of domesticated ditchwash. Daddy says it got so he didn't know what to throw out, the coffee pot or Momma.

Momma doesn't blame the percolator herself; she simply says she didn't know her way around a kitchen back then, probably because Grandma Yount was such a fine cook and got such pleasure from it that she never allowed Momma near the stove, so Momma went off with Daddy to Lynchburg thinking dinner was something you just sat down and ate. Even by the time they got to Danville Momma could hardly operate anything in the kitchen but a skillet and a potato masher, and whatever couldn't be fried or somehow slipped into the mashed potatoes she considered inedible. Daddy says it was along about Danville that Momma discovered Crisco, which she used sort of like gravy and which was more or less responsible for the length of the sofa Momma and Daddy bought for the living room. Daddy insisted it be as long as he was so when he stumbled away from the table he could stretch out on it to let supper work its magic.

Momma usually takes this sort of thing pretty well considering it is coming from a man who has to get out a cookbook to heat water, but when Daddy starts in on how miserable Momma's lunches could be, Momma tends to become somewhat peevish, not because she imagines they were at all tasty but because up until recently Momma thought whatever Daddy had carted off in the morning he had eaten at noon, which Daddy says he could not have done with good conscience what with supper staring him in the face and it and lunch together carrying with them the probability that Momma would be widowed by nightfall. So in the mornings Momma would sack Daddy's lunch for him, usually giving him whatever had survived the previous meal which meant some manner of potatoes and a slice or a slab or a pattie of meat or the occasional salmon cake, which Momma just had to open a can to get at, and Daddy says the sack would sort of lubricate itself there on the kitchen counter so he would have to carry it away from his clothes and ride it on the floorboard of the car to the depot where he was successful in giving it away until word spread and then he had to either leave it on the kitchen counter or, if Momma forced it on him, throw it away in the men's room. For lunch Daddy says he would walk over to Emerson's Fine Foods and eat several hotdogs accompanied by most anything that was not a potato.

According to Momma, though, no matter how sorry the food got at the supper table Daddy never managed to keep his elbow from bending, and Momma says the potatoes and the vegetable oil gravy and the hotdogs at lunchtime all worked together to give Daddy what he likes to call a paunch but what Momma says was more truly just a general swelling up of most every part of Daddy that was inflatable. And Momma says she would tell him, "Louis, you've put on considerable weight," or "Louis, you could stand some exercise," and Momma says Daddy would agree with her entirely as he spooned up a mound of potatoes or cut himself a hunk of boxed cake. Momma supposed Daddy would have inflated himself right out of his wardrobe if him and Momma together hadn't happened to go shopping for a new necktie and if Momma hadn't told the saleslady she wanted something that would pick up the color in Daddy's eyes, to which the saleslady adjusted her glasses and looked hard at Daddy for a half minute before turning back to Momma and saying, "What color are your husband's eyes? I can't see them." Momma says that hit Daddy a broadside in his vanity, which was just what he needed.

So Daddy set out to whip himself into shape, and Momma likes to tell how he'd come out of the bedroom in a T-shirt and a pair of white boxer shorts, which was the closest thing to athletic wear he owned, and stretch out on the living room floor where he would commence with what he called his program which Momma says began as twenty-five sit-ups and became fifteen before falling off to a dozen, all of which Daddy would perform with one hand behind his head and the other holding his fly shut; Momma says Daddy was nothing if not modest. Then Daddy complained that a little bone in the base of his back didn't get along with the hardwood floor and he changed over from sit-ups to push-ups which Momma says started out at eight and got as far as ten before Daddy began to show signs of shiftlessness when Momma says he would rise from the supper table, announce how he was off to suit up for his program, and then disappear into the bedroom where Momma would find him a half hour later sprawled across the bed asleep.

According to Momma, we'd have buried Daddy in a piano case long ago if he hadn't wandered into Sears one Saturday morning and come across a badminton set. Daddy says he had gone after a pound of maple nuts and two white chocolate bars and had to walk through sporting goods to get back out the door, and he says he was not hardly browsing but just carting around with him his thorough dislike for and dread of calisthenics which probably steered him to the badminton set with its aluminum shafted rackets and foreign made shuttlecocks all of which were very lively with color and did not seem in any way dreadful or unpleasant, and Daddy says as he snatched up a box to check the price a salesclerk showed up to tell him it would be a wise investment for a portly gentleman like himself. He bought it anyway. Momma says Daddy did not even come into the house when he got home but went straight into the backyard and strung the net between two poplar trees. Then he called out for Momma to come play with him and she says she tried to but had no talent for the game. Daddy says Momma was as quick as a snake and could swing at the birdie four or five times before it ever hit the ground; she simply could not lay the racket on it except maybe after the bounce when she'd hit it a lick to send it screaming under the net towards Daddy who'd have to double up to avoid it. Daddy says he was reconsidering the push-ups when he happened to look over and see his neighbor just the other side of the property line with his hands in his pockets and the rest of him intent on what Momma and Daddy were calling exercise, and Daddy says he raised the birdie in one hand and his racket in the other and said, "Badminton?"

Momma and Daddy had not become especially friendly with anybody in Danville since they traveled to Neely most every weekend so the relatives could fawn over little Bumpins before she got past precious, and Daddy says what exchanges they'd been party to with the folks next door had come primarily in the shank of the evening with Momma and Daddy on their screen porch and the neighbors across a narrow sideyard on theirs, and Daddy says him and Momma could hear the sound of voices but not the words themselves and could see the fire-coal on what turned out to be the tip of a Tampa Jewel, and Momma says since Daddy was already keeping the Tareyton people in profits, across the way they were probably getting an eye and an earful of pretty much the same thing. And Daddy says every now and again the conversation would fall off first on one porch and then on the other and the crickets would fill up the silence until a voice not much louder than any previously but far clearer and more distinguishable would rise up out of the darkness saying, "Lovely night," and then would come the crickets again until another voice just as soft and pure as the first would rise up out of the darkness answering, "Surely is."

His name was Chick, otherwise Raymond Nathaniel Jarvis, whose Daddy bred trotters outside of Manassas, and she was the former Miss Dickenleigh Fay Warner of Culpepper who went by Dickey and who liked to tell how Chick would come over from Washington and Lee, where he was studying finance, and call for her at Mary Baldwin, where she had hoped to take a degree in social work but got swept up in matrimony after only three years. Momma says Dickey liked to recall how Chick would arrive in his roadster, which Chick himself told Daddy was his Momma's Wyllis-Knight, and take her up onto the ridge for a picnic. And Dickey always told how half a hundred girls would peek out at them from the dormitory windows because everybody on campus thought Chick was simply the limit, which Momma says is the way Dickey Jarvis usually talked. Daddy never says whether Chick was the limit or not, he just generally tells how Chick showed a marked resemblance to Danny Kaye in *White Christmas* except around the eyes. Daddy says Chick's eyes were considerably more bugged out than Danny Kaye's so that he permanently looked like somebody had just jumped out of a closet at him.

Chick and Dickey already had two children when Momma and Daddy moved in next door to them. One of them was a little girl, Melanie Fay, who was diapered up like Bumpins and who had what Chick called the postman's nose and plumber's red hair. Her brother, Ray Jarvis jr., was three years her senior and Momma says he turned out to be spiteful and mean though at first he did not hardly make himself noticeable and she and Daddy mistakenly assumed he was well-mannered, but Daddy says him and Momma simply happened to move to Danville along about when little Ray was convinced that most anybody could breathe through his ears if he only took time to make the effort, so he was ever trying to force breath up into his head and out either side which was not the sort of process that could accommodate much talking. But Momma says soon enough he stopped using his ears for breathing and started back to using his mouth for shouting and his feet for kicking and his head for butting and generally became unbearable for any-body who ran upon him. According to Daddy, Chick didn't have much of a hand in the rearing of his children but left Dickey to see after them on her own, and whenever things got a little dicey around the Jarvis household with little Ray goose-stepping on the coffee table and Melanie Fay howling to be changed and Dickey herself so beat and frazzled down that she didn't know which one to go at first, Daddy says Chick would step out onto the screen porch and begin to sing "Shall We Gather at the River?" in a voice that drowned out and overcame most everything else. Daddy says somehow Chick considered this his contribution to resolving the crisis.

But Momma and Daddy did not know Chick and Dickey until Daddy raised up his racket in one hand and the birdie in the other and said, "Badminton?" to which Chick said, "You bet," and came over directly to take Momma's place and to take Momma's racket, both of which Momma says she was thrilled to give up. They played for the rest of the morning and all the afternoon and on up into the evening until it got too dark to see the birdie, and Momma says in the meantime her and Dickey got up with each other and arranged for a hamburger dinner on Momma and Daddy's back porch which Momma says carried on into the night after Melanie Fay was put in to sleep with little Bumpins and after Ray jr., who had sent his foot through the screen door and bit his sister but otherwise behaved himself, dozed off in mid-rant on Daddy's sofa.

Momma says they played all day Sunday and all the next weekend and the weekend after that, and when the both of them decided they could not get enough of it Daddy brought home a droplight from the train depot and hung it over a limb of one of the poplar trees so him and Chick could play in the evenings after work. Momma says anymore she could hardly get Daddy to sit down at the supper table before he was out the back door to meet Chick and play a match, and she says her and Dickey would sit out in the yard in lawn chairs and talk about little or nothing until the bugs would get too bad for them and Dickey would go to her porch while Momma would go to hers, and Momma says they would chat across the side-yard as the darkness set in.

Daddy likes to tell how that was a glorious summer when him and Chick played badminton on into the night, and even though the rackets stayed sound and the net didn't rot, Daddy says they did not ever play again after those few evenings in that one summer, did not ever mention it between them again according to Daddy since both him and Chick seemed to know it would never be the same again, would always be less glorious. Daddy says in June there is nothing so beautiful and grand as the Virginia night sky, nothing so mild and easeful as the evening air, and he says sometimes he would look up through the treelimbs at the stars and watch the leaves turn over on the slightest breath of the night and would not even discover that he was lost from the world until Chick would say, "Serving," and deliver him into it again. Daddy says the house would be dark except for the light over the kitchen sink, and he says he would know Momma was on the porch with little Bumpins in her lap though he could not see her and could not hear her for all of the ruckus the crickets and the jarflies made. Daddy says Chick would lift the serve high into the air, past the droplight and the moths and down to Daddy who would send it back in the same fashion and wait for Chick to lift it towards him again, and Daddy says the sound of the birdie springing from the racket heads never quite joined with the other sounds of the night but remained distinct and measured and regular like the beating of a heart. And that's usually when Daddy kicks himself back from the table, locks his hands behind his head, and says, "Yes sir, I was a young man once," and Momma looks past him through the breakfast room window and smiles.

So I turned around just as the porch light came on and did not for a minute think Momma simply wanted us to find the keyhole when we got home, did not think anything really but just knew right off where Momma was going and what she was going to do. I saw in my mind the sad way Momma's mouth turns up when Daddy talks about Danville, and then I didn't see anything at all and I didn't think anything at all until something came over me like a fit of blushing that settled into the bottom of my stomach and I thought to myself, This will never happen just this way again. Then I looked at Daddy and at Mr. Gibbons's white oak tree and at the sky above it and I bit my cheek hard between my teeth.

ii

NOBODY WANTED to go after the monkey, so the sheriff asked for volunteers to go after the breadsack, but nobody wanted to go after the breadsack until somebody had gone after the monkey, and nobody wanted to go after the monkey. Part of the trouble was Miss Bambi Kinch had hauled her Action News Five team on back to Greensboro and there wasn't anybody left around the tower who seemed very eager to be glorious only locally, so the sheriff suggested that one of the three regular deputies climb on up and fetch the monkey back but they all three said they would rather not, so the sheriff asked for one of them to outright but they all three said they would not, so the sheriff made an order out of it and they all three tried to hand him their badges. Then the sheriff went to work on the four men he'd deputized to control what he liked to call the throngs, but the two bankers and the druggist just laughed and told him he was the funniest son-of-a-bitch they'd come across lately, and according to Mr. Newberry, who happened to be standing hard by at the time, the sheriff's conversation with the municipal employee earned him an invitation to crawl on up into a place that simply could not accommodate him.

The hook and ladder unit from the Omega firehouse on the boulevard arrived along about nightfall and the driver trained his spotlight onto the upper portion of the tower but Miss Pettigrew's monkey must have been far enough off from the top edge to keep out of the beam so there was nothing to look at except for the breadsack which was nothing much to look at at all from where we were. The fire chief Mr. Pipkin came by in his red station wagon after he'd finished supper. He'd already changed out of his uniform but had remembered himself enough to wear his official fire chief's hat which looked very much like a saucepan and stayed atop Mr. Pipkin's head by grace of his ears each of which he prized up between his head and the hatband so as to make the hat snug. Mr. Pipkin walked completely around the water tower once and then did what he usually did at the scene of an emergency: he sat down on the running board of the firetruck. After he'd settled himself in the firemen sat down with him and the regular deputies distributed themselves along the fenders. Sheriff Burton, who was not given to sitting down on or canting up against anything, moved in to stand facing the bunch of them, and all of us in the throngs—which had not swelled or dwindled considerably, which Daddy said is what throngs are apt to do, but had retained a standard thronglike size—all of us moved in behind the sheriff so we could see what went on.

Except for Mr. Pipkin the firemen were wearing their rubber pants and otherwise just white T-shirts and they passed between them a pack of cigarettes one of the deputies had made the mistake of giving over to them. Mr. Pipkin himself had changed into his bermuda shorts and he sat on the running board with his legs crossed and one hand scratching his ankle while the other ruffled the hairs on his shin. Mr. Newberry told Daddy how Neely's band of firefighters struck him as a sterling example of selfless civil servitude and intrepidation, and Daddy said the bunch of them together probably couldn't put out a pilot light.

So the sheriff stood there in front of Mr. Pipkin all draped and dripping with his usual bullets and shackles and cuffs and badges and whistles, and he caught his thumbs up in his front beltloops, bowed himself out some, and said, "Well?"

Mr. Pipkin did not answer right off but picked at a sore on his leg with his fingernail and then scratched the underside of his nose before he went back to ruffling the hair on his shin, and after about a minute and a half of studying his shoelaces he looked up at the crowd of us there and we looked back at him and then he looked at the sheriff, who sort of glared in his direction, and then he reconsidered his shoelaces and generally pondered his whole shoe before he finally opened his mouth and said, "Well what?"

"We've got a monkey up there on top the water tower," the sheriff told him, "and one of your men is gonna have to go up after it."

Mr. Pipkin looked off over the sheriff's head to where the spotlight shone on the upper section of the water tower; then he looked back at the crowd of us before he made his way to the sheriff again and said, "I don't see no smoke and I don't see no flame and I ain't gonna see none of my men having anything to do with this." Then he reached up with one hand and pushed his hat far enough down on his head so as to make his earlobes stick out into the air and turn bright scarlet like some sort of exotic fruit. "Anyway sheriff," he said, "I don't see no monkey."

And Mr. Pipkin looked hard at Sheriff Burton, who looked hard at Mr. Pipkin in return, and then the sheriff opened his mouth the least little bit and hollered out, "Small!" cutting loose with it so sharply that it came back at us from off the fronts of the houses across the street, and before we could stop hearing it the sheriff hollered out, "Small, where are you?" again moving his mouth just the least little bit and not even twitching otherwise so that from behind you couldn't swear the sheriff was the one doing the screaming.

After that one died off we didn't hear anything right away, not that there was nothing to be heard only that nothing was being bellowed, screeched, or hollered out; it was simply being said and in an insignificant voice from a considerable distance away. The folks on the back edge of the throngs heard it first and they passed it on to the people in the middle who passed it on to us up at the front edge and we all turned around to find Mr. Small off to himself sitting in one of his own folding chairs that the sheriff had appropriated to use for the barricade and which Daddy said was located almost directly over the old eyewitness burial ground. Mr. Small sat a little forward with his hands on his knees and he kept repeating, "Right here, Sheriff, right here, Sheriff" as many times as he thought he needed to to be heard.

Still Sheriff Burton didn't look anywhere but at Mr. Pipkin who didn't look anywhere but at Sheriff Burton and the sheriff opened his mouth the least little bit again and hollered out, "Come 'ere," which brought Mr. Small up off of his seat and directly into the crowd of us there who made way for him. As he walked he took his seersucker sportcoat off his forearm and worked his way into it and by the time he got abreast of the sheriff he'd also finished tucking the folds of his shirt down into his pants. Then he said, "Yes sir?" and when Sheriff Burton who looked nowhere but at Mr. Pipkin who looked nowhere but at Sheriff Burton didn't say anything back, Mr. Small said, "Yes sir?" again. And without ever turning away from Mr. Pipkin and towards Mr. Small, the sheriff opened his mouth the least little bit and said, "Where's that monkey, Small?"

Mr. Small drew himself upright somewhat, flattened his hair with the palm of his hand and generally groomed himself in preparation for his answer, but before he could get past "Well Sheriff" some woman in the back of the crowd started scream-ing and moaning like something wild and then three or four other women set in to screeching with her so that the bunch of them together sounded like a sack of cats until some one of them finally collected herself enough to say, "He's jumped!" which was about all anybody needed to say. Nobody much seemed to feel the desire to look up and see just what had jumped from where; we all took that woman at her word and cleared out as best we could. Some of the people along the back edge of the crowd were lucky enough to make it through the barricade and they kept getting it on out into the street, but there were plenty of people that got tangled up in the rope and the chairs and the sawbucks and they clogged it up for the rest of us so that we had to be content with going down on our bellies in the grass and throwing our arms over our heads for protection. All the firemen including the firechief Mr. Pipkin rolled off the running board under the truck and the sheriff crawled up into the cab while the deputies circled around the back end of the engine and out into the road. Only Mr. Small did not go anywhere, did not even make a motion to go any-where, but remained standing just as he had stood with the sheriff and looked just as he had looked except for the way his chin dangled a little now when it hadn't before.

Then it hit, hit right dead on a bare spot and I said to myself, that surely doesn't sound like a monkey, though I'd never bounced a monkey off a bare spot before to see what it sounded like. And then Daddy raised himself up a little and said to Mr. Newberry, "That was no monkey," and Mr. Newberry said, "No, I don't believe it was," and we got up off the ground along with everybody else and the whole bunch of us sort of closed in and crept up on what Daddy called the impact area. The firemen and Mr. Pipkin slipped out from under the truck and back up onto the running board while the sheriff climbed down out of the cab and ordered his deputies on into the crowd. They came off the road and washed around Mr. Small like water before wading on in to where we had pretty much encircled whatever it was that had sailed off the top of the tower, which the people in front were stooped over and could see fairly well and which the people behind them could probably catch a glimpse of but which me and Daddy and Mr. Newberry could not see at all from where we were until one of the deputies finally broke through to the center where he passed about a half minute looking directly at the ground and about another half minute eyeing the people all around him and then he said, "Shit," bent over at the waist, and came up holding a black sneaker by the laces.

Mr. Small still had gone nowhere and had hardly moved at all except at the chin, which continued to sink away from the rest of his face. Mr. Pipkin went back to sit where he had sat, the sheriff moved in to stand where he had stood, and Mr. Small just stayed where he was, which again put him abreast of the sheriff and facing up to Mr. Pipkin. Once the deputies had cleared the crowd, the one with the sneaker came up alongside Sheriff Burton and held it out for him and the sheriff grabbed at that sneaker like it was the treasure of the pharaohs and the finest thing he'd ever had the honor of taking hold of. Then he grinned and looked straight at Mr. Pipkin who did not look straight back at the sheriff but more towards Mr. Small who himself was staring full at the sheriff, or anyway at the side of the sheriff's head, and Sheriff Burton bent the sneaker double between his hands, then shook the toe of it at Mr. Pipkin and said, "Well?"

Mr. Pipkin brought the calf of one leg up onto the knee of the other and stuck his finger down inside his shoe so as to scratch the underpart of his foot. The fireman closest to him on his right side leaned over to say a few words and Mr. Pipkin met him with his ear, which was all aflame with color by now, and heard the man out before drawing himself upright again. Whatever was said did not seem to register on Mr. Pipkin at all because he continued to poke at the sole of his foot just as he had previously before pulling his finger out of his shoe and rubbing his nose with it. Then he looked full at Mr. Small on his way to reconsidering the crowd of us behind him which had undergone a general overhaul during the uproar and so was worth some new attention, and at last he made his way to the sheriff himself, starting with the rubber toe of the sneaker, which Sheriff Burton was still pointing at him, and eventually working his way up to the sheriff's face so that the two of them might glare at each other for the better part of a minute before Mr. Pipkin finally opened his mouth and said, "Well what?"

iii

IT WASN'T the condition of the ladder any of them objected to, not the firemen or the deputies or the firechief, Mr. Pipkin, or even Sheriff Burton himself, and it wasn't the height of the climb either. It was the monkey, not simply because it was a monkey but because it was that monkey, which was far and away the most peculiar creature any of us had ever come across. Daddy said when Wallace Amory jr. bought it and carried it home to Miss Myra Angelique it did not seem all that exceptional as monkeys go but just scooted up and down the flagpole and ran around the yard smirking and grinning its teeth at everybody, which Daddy said is all anybody could ask of a monkey. Then Mayor Pettigrew and Sister named it and put a suit of clothes on it, and Daddy said that's where the trouble started. According to him, that monkey was not nearly as willing to be civilized as they were to civilize it.

Of course they called it Junious at first after their second cousin on their mother's side. As Mayor Pettigrew gave it to Daddy, his second cousin's mother had possessed all the venom it took to name her son Clyde Junious Bennet for no detectable member of the family in any branch at any time, and the mayor suspected that was just the sort of name his cousin could never quite overcome because he never did quite overcome it as far as the mayor could tell. Daddy said Junious Bennet was already a middle-aged man when Wallace Amory jr. was just a little boy, and Daddy said he lived three quarters of the year in Front Royal, Virginia, where he worked for a lawyer as a legal assistant, what Daddy called a secretary with pants, and then in the summertime him and the lawyer would travel down and set up office at the lawyer's house in Salvo, which I've never been to myself but which Daddy tells me is a godless little sandpit and green-headed fly sanctuary just this side of Cape Hatteras which I've never been to either but which Daddy tells me is a bigger, more notorious sandpit with a grander, more monstrous variety of fly.

The mayor said his momma and daddy would take him and Miss Myra Angelique on vacation once a summer and they would spend three or four days at the lawyer's house in Salvo to visit with cousin Junious. According to the mayor, Junious did not much care for the seashore or the weather there and would only go outdoors on cloudy days and even then wouldn't let himself anywhere near the ocean as the mayor recollected it. He would walk the beach just where the dunes gave way to level sand wearing what the mayor remembered to be crepe-soled shoes and duck pants with a braided rope for a belt. And the mayor said sometimes him and Junious and Miss Myra Angelique would sit down between the dunes among clumps of sea oats, and if Junious found the weather to his liking, which the mayor said meant a sunless sky and a sea breeze that was not particularly salty or fly-infested, he would take his shirt off and stretch out on his frontside, which left his backside partway uncovered to reveal between cousin Junious' shoulders and his waist the bushiest, coarsest, most unbelievably successful crop of hair the mayor could ever recall seeing in his lifetime. And the mayor told Daddy how him and Miss Myra Angelique would take turns touching it with the tips of their fingers because it was the sort of thing you couldn't help but touch. Junious never seemed to mind, the mayor said, not there stretched out in the sand among the sea oats and not in the house after supper when Mrs. Wallace Amory sr. and the lawyer would play scrabble at the dinner table and Mr. Wallace Amory sr. would sleep sitting up in the lawyer's chair with a newspaper over his face and the mayor and cousin Junious and Miss Myra Angelique would sit all three of them together on the floor and talk and laugh while Miss Pettigrew and Wallace Amory jr. took turns combing cousin Junious's back. And the mayor said when Miss Myra Angelique picked up that monkey for the first time and turned it over, the two of them looked at each other and said more or less simultaneously, "Junious," which the mayor told Daddy they intended as a memorial and tribute to their cousin, who had since died somehow though the mayor did not know just how and hadn't found out about any of it until after Junious was already in the ground.

So Junious was what they called it, and Daddy said Miss Myra Angelique decided right off that she would not have a monkey if he weren't decent and maybe just the least bit fashion-conscious, so she rushed him on downtown to Hoopers where Miss Pettigrew figured she could outfit her monkey well enough in the boy's department. But at first the manager wouldn't let her and Junious in the store, not because he absolutely objected to monkeys on the premises but because he had never had a monkey on the premises before and objected to it now out of natural reflex and instinct. He got over it, however, and apologized to Miss Pettigrew who was after all a Pettigrew of the Pettigrew money. According to Daddy, he said he had not been expecting a monkey and had needed several minutes to get used to the arrival of one. But the assistant manager, who headed up the boys' department, did not soften up and give way so readily. He was willing enough to allow the monkey into the store but couldn't see clear to let the creature try on or even touch anything that Miss Pettigrew had not already bought and paid for. Daddy said the assistant manager did not much think his customers would put out good money for clothes a monkey had handled or worn even if only for a few seconds, which Miss Pettigrew said she herself would not be all that eager to do and so agreed to have the assistant manager measure the monkey as best he could and then point her to whatever Junious could most probably wear.

She wanted a couple of sport coats and a few pairs of trousers, and as it turned out the monkey was fairly human in the shoulders so could wear a blazer pretty handsomely, but once that clerk had measured Junious at the waist and inseam he told Miss Pettigrew he could not do much for her monkey in the way of trousers. Daddy said he told her people just weren't made like that and pants weren't either. So Miss Pettigrew said she'd settle for some shirts and maybe a sweater or two and a necktie, but the assistant manager did not especially want to show her shirts and sweaters and neckties, did not especially want to wait on a monkey any longer, and Daddy said he stopped off at a bin full of porkpie hats, pulled one out and handed it to Miss Pettigrew and said, "Ma'm, you can take this on home with our compliments if you'll just take it on home now." Daddy said Miss Pettigrew had most likely not even been considering a hat but, being fairly sharp and polite on top of it, she saw that she could have both it and the salesman's good will all at once and for nothing, so she took the hat and took her monkey and took her monkey's new plaid sportcoat and went home.

Mattie Gunn's sister, Miss Martha Gunn, ended up making the trousers for Miss Pettigrew. Miss Martha had a pretty size-able place down by the ice house and she sewed and took in boarders to earn her way in the world. As best as Daddy could recall it, Miss Martha usually kept her upstairs full of school teachers and would not ever allow alcohol or Republicans across her threshold, but Daddy imagined Miss Martha had not been able to discover anything particularly distasteful in making trousers for a monkey so had made two pair which were not even full trousers anyway but only duck pants, white ones and blue ones, and as a favor to Miss Pettigrew, Miss Martha had sewn an elastic chin strap onto the porkpie hat for the price of materials only.

As Daddy recalled it, Junious had his coming out of a midmorning on a Saturday. The mayor brought him onto the porch, hooked him into his tether, and then turned him out into the yard alone, and Daddy said that monkey went down the front steps and along the sidewalk on his knuckles before he veered off into the grass and made a complete tour of the front lawn that ended up at the base of the flagpole. He did not go up it right away but held on at the bottom and shook himself against it which allowed time for most everybody with business along the Boulevard and in Municipal Square to gather in front of the mayor's house and congregate against the fence. Daddy said when that monkey had collected a considerable audience he shot straight up to the top of the pole and stood there with one foot on the knob and the other gripping onto the shaft itself, and then he struck a noble pose, Daddy said, which brought admiring responses from the audience, and Daddy himself admitted it was quite a display, a mixture of balance and bad taste, but then most people had never had the opportunity to see a monkey up close before, especially a sportcoated duckpantsed, porkpiehatted monkey, so Daddy said it was understandable that folks would be taken with the sight of Junious in such a prominent place and in such a state of monkeyhood, Daddy called it.

According to Daddy the mayor was still too new at politicking to know exactly what to do with an audience so he merely gawked and chitchatted by turns along with everybody else, and Daddy said that monkey scooted up and down the flagpole and around the yard and into the mayor's arms and out again and generally kept the morning rolling along fairly well until he had the accident which Daddy said was not accident at all but certainly intentional on the monkey's part but which everybody called the accident out of politeness and sheer embarrassment. Daddy said the monkey had been skimming across the lawn on his knuckles when he got to the flagpole and climbed on up to the top of it where he stood again with one foot on the knob and the other latched onto the shaft itself, but Daddy said the monkey did not look the same as before because of the expression on his face which had become very serious and thoughtful, Daddy said, like maybe he was reading a menu without really knowing what he wanted to eat. Then the monkey lifted his head a little and Daddy said he looked off beyond the crowd and the treetops and municipal square and on into the distance until it seemed he wasn't looking at anything anymore but just standing there atop his flagpole all lofty and wise and caught up in pondering the general predicament of the world as he knew it. Daddy said it was a most impressive expression to see on the face of a monkey and consequently he did not witness the accident himself since he wasn't looking at that part of the monkey where the accident was occurring, and Daddy said only Mr. Satterwhite down at the end of the fence saw it, or was willing to open his mouth about it anyway, and he didn't even come straight out with it but pointed up at the monkey and said, "Mayor, MAYor," which turned Wallace Amory around who Daddy said studied Junious for a good half minute before his eyebrows stood up and he shouted off towards the house, "Sister, Sister!" which brought Miss Myra Angelique on out into the yard.

Daddy said the mayor flushed some and then declared into the open air and to no one in particular, "I just don't understand this; he was trained on a toilet you know," and he grabbed onto

two prongs of the fence, flushed some more, and smiled a
little, but Daddy said nobody was paying much attention to the
mayor since most everybody was caught up in speculation as
to how Miss Myra Angelique was going to fetch that monkey
down off the flagpole, her being so proper and naturally dainty
and pitched against a creature who had already wet himself
and who looked a little more fiery-eyed, Daddy said, every
time she yanked on the tether. And according to Daddy, Miss
Pettigrew never did coax him down exactly but eventually gave
the tether over to the mayor who pretty much reeled that monkey in against all of the screeching and scrapping and clawing
and flat out holding on that he could manage. Daddy said Miss
Myra Angelique gave that monkey a smart load of scolding as
soon as he touched the ground, which more or less deflated
him on the spot so that he became tame all over again and
stood by while she examined his trousers which had gone to
almost pure navy in the front while the back was still a shade
of royal blue. And Daddy said Miss Pettigrew scooped up
Junious in her arms, accident and all, and set out towards the
house, and he said the mayor, who still had hold of the tether,
which was still attached to the monkey's neck, watched several
loops of it play out of his hands before he looked up briefly
at the crowd of people against the fence, muttered, "'scuse
us," and went off after his sister.

Daddy said Junious Pettigrew's accident atop the Pettigrew
flagpole on the Pettigrew front lawn inspired considerable discussion and argument among the citizens of Neely. He said
even folks who had not been there themselves and who had
yet to get the story straight had a thing or two to say about the
monkey and the monkey's affliction, and according to Daddy
it wasn't until three or four days after the event that the general
buzz and huzzah died down and opinion began to solidify into
several distinct philosophical camps, what Daddy called the
various streams of thought on the urinary problem. He said far
and away the majority of Neelyites started out as Isolationists,
which Daddy defined as those people who thought the monkey
would not wet himself again, who thought that perhaps the fit
of the trousers had provoked him to the first time and, now
that he was somewhat accustomed to pants, would not provoke
him to again. But the monkey himself dealt a severe blow to
the Isolationist cause when he did to his white duck pants the

following Saturday what he'd done to his blue duck pants the previous one, and Daddy said the Isolationists disbanded immediately, modified their views in one direction or another, and allowed themselves to be absorbed into one of the remaining streams.

Daddy said the fallout after the second poletop accident left the Hard Liners in the majority since a sizeable number of former Isolationists had decided to take their humiliation out on the monkey and so joined up with a compatible group who had said all along that any creature who wet himself should have his nose rubbed in his business and then be whipped. And Daddy supposed the Hard Liners remained in the ascendancy for about a week before sentiments began to shift somewhat and the Protectionists commenced to assert themselves and win favor with their more sympathetic notion that a diaper underneath the duck pants would be a suitable and acceptable remedy to the whole nasty predicament. But Daddy said the Protectionists could never quite manage a firm hold over public opinion and were ever having to fend off threats and advances by any number of sects and splinter groups including the followers of Mr. Emmet Moss, amateur astrologer and feed merchant, who were in general agreement that the magnetism of the stars could draw the fluids from any monkey on any flagpole, and the entire congregation of the Pentacostal Holiness Church on Zinnia Drive who Daddy said unanimously apostled themselves to Mrs. Alice Butler of the Oregon Hill Butlers who stood up in church of a Sunday and told the congregation it had come to her in a vision that the monkey was the anti-Christ and should be immolated, Daddy called it, which kicked up the immediate and unquestioning support of the faithful who Daddy said had held Miss Butler in especially high esteem ever since she accurately predicted the eruption of a water main in the winter of 1938. And Daddy said it was while the Protectionists were busy holding off the Mossians and the Butlerites that a relatively small band of liberal-minded citizens saw an opening in the fray and jumped in, and Daddy said for a week and a half, maybe even two weeks, the whole situation was confused and unsettled with everybody claiming to have won and nobody winning and the monkey still making water all over himself until finally all the fuss and furor began to die away and when the dust cleared it was the Free Thinkers who'd landed on their feet, hale and unified, Daddy said, and proclaiming to the world that if a monkey wants to do his business from atop a flagpole then, by God, we should take his trousers off and let him.

Of course Miss Pettigrew had charge of the monkey, and Daddy said in all of Neely only Miss Pettigrew lived far enough out from under public opinion to ignore it altogether. Daddy supposed the mayor might have tracked in a suggestion or two from off the street, but he said there was no call whatsoever for Miss Pettigrew to pay the least mind to any of the mayor's proposals since as far as Daddy could tell the only thing the mayor knew about a monkey was where to get one. So Miss Pettigrew did what she pleased with her chimpanzee and her chimpanzee's affliction, and Daddy said right off she did nothing at all but went on the assumption that the monkey had become a little nervous and excited, what with the crowd and the new clothes, and consequently had done something to himself that he would probably not do again. But when she turned him out the following weekend and the monkey once again did what he had done, Miss Pettigrew was persuaded to change her mind.

Daddy said now Miss Pettigrew figured the second accident, and maybe the first one too, was a sign of rebellion on the monkey's part so she took immediate measures to make life difficult for Junious until he reformed, beginning with the very moment he set his little hairy foot down off the flagpole the second time when Miss Pettigrew was there to tell him what she would and would not stand for before she let him have it in the backside with a rolled up newspaper. And Daddy said the monkey screeched and howled and tried to fight off Miss Pettigrew but was unable to and eventually got himself separated from his duck pants long enough for them to travel from his bottomside to his topside, where Miss Pettigrew draped them around his head and held them there until she thought he'd had enough. And Daddy said the next day when the Pettigrew door opened up around midmorning it was a new monkey that came out onto the porch and went down the steps and along the sidewalk on his knuckles. He was back in the blue pants, Daddy said, but did not at all appear to be the same creature who had relieved himself into them previously. He was a haunted chimpanzee, according to Daddy, and went everywhere looking backwards so as to keep out of the way

of the Neely *Chronicle* if one happened to come at him. Daddy
said he did not go up the flagpole right away but stood cowering
at the base of it all drawn up on himself and skitterish until
Miss Pettigrew showed up on the lip of the porch and said,
"Go on," which was not quite enough to send him scooting up
the pole like before but did start him to creeping towards the
top, still looking behind himself and still seeming altogether
half the size he'd been the day before. But Daddy said something magical happened to that chimpanzee when he finally
made it to the knob and stood up on it; he said Junious sort of
blossomed like a flower, gradually opened up and swelled to
his full size. And Daddy said he looked back at Miss Pettigrew
one last time before he turned his attention to the horizon which
he considered with a very grave and sobering expression as he
soaked himself again.

Miss Pettigrew had Miss Martha Gunn make him some
underwear out of a green bathtowel and she tried them under
the duck pants, but Daddy said Junious put out such a pene-
trating product that the underwear could not effectively prevent
the spot from spreading onto the trousers but could only slow
down its arrival somewhat, so Miss Pettigrew and Miss Martha
Gunn got together again and Miss Gunn made another pair of
underwear out of a white bathtowel this time and she tripled
up on the material and tripled up on the seams so that Daddy
said you'd have been hard pressed to fire a bullet through any
part of them. Miss Pettigrew dispensed with the duck pants,
since the underwear would not fit beneath them anyway, and
turned Junious out into the yard in just his hat and sport coat
and new white terrycloth briefs, which Daddy said was still
fairly exceptional attire for a chimpanzee. And Daddy said the
monkey went directly to the flagpole and scooted up to the top
of it where he struck his pose and looked off beyond the treetops
and on out of town, and Daddy said while the monkey pondered
the horizon Miss Pettigrew and the mayor and all the folks
along the fence pondered the monkey's midsection in anticipation of some activity there, but he said the spot never came
and the monkey shot back down the flagpole and squatted on
the lawn where he picked at himself before running off into
the bushes and back out again and around the yard entirely and
then up to the top of the pole once more. And Daddy said he
stood with one foot on the knob and the other half around the

shaft itself and looked off beyond the courthouse and into the reaches of the county while Miss Pettigrew and the mayor and the crowd of concerned citizens along the fence studied the frontside of his triple-ply bathtowel underwear and waited for the spot to come, but still it didn't, Daddy said, and the monkey climbed down off the flagpole and toured the lawn twice before vanishing momentarily into the shrubbery and then reappearing at the mayor's feet and leaping directly up into his arms. Daddy said the mayor grinned for about two seconds and then let loose of that monkey like he was a firecoal, and he said the monkey tried to jump back up into the mayor's arms but the mayor wouldn't let him so he tried to jump up into Miss Myra Angelique's arms but she wouldn't let him either so he took off down the sidewalk on his knuckles and cut across the lawn and Daddy said first the monkey zipped by the fence and the crowd of people gathered at it and then the aroma came along behind him. Daddy said it was enough to bring tears to your eyes. He said that monkey had become little more than an ammonia pocket with legs.

So he got shed of the underwear, got shed of trousers altogether, and anymore whenever Miss Pettigrew or the mayor turned him out the door and off the porch he arrived on the front lawn wearing a porkpie hat and a plaid sportcoat and only nature's gifts otherwise. And Daddy said just after the monkey had been let outside he would always go up the flagpole straightaway and stand as he had grown accustomed to standing with one foot atop the knob and the toes of the other around the pole itself, and he would gaze out over the treetops as before, Daddy said, and on beyond the courthouse and into the country all the while looking very thoughtful and dignified except for the lack of trousers, and then he would begin to make water, Daddy said, just a little dribble at first but soon enough a regular stream of it, a looping arc of monkey water as thick as your little finger Daddy said. And Daddy said the monkey never much seemed to care where it went but just studied the horizon and left the people on the ground to care where it went for him, which they were more than willing to oblige him in since crowding up against the Pettigrew's fence had become a rather bold and reckless undertaking and since the people of Neely, neither bold nor reckless by nature, always endeavored to be careful instead. So the mayor would turn the monkey out of the house and follow him on down into the yard, and Daddy said as the monkey shot up the flagpole the mayor would lean against the iron fence and say, "Watch yourselves," which would send most everybody into the street.

But Daddy said it got so nobody had to go anywhere when the monkey relieved himself because he turned out to be so extremely though blindly accurate that he hardly ever missed the camellia bush Miss Pettigrew had planted at the corner of the lot where two runs of fence came together, but he said only a few of the shrewdest and most observant spectators first noticed what a reliable marksman the monkey was and made themselves some money on account of it before everybody else caught on. Daddy said the monkey would get himself situated atop his flagpole and just before he could cut loose someone in the crowd would shout out, "I got two dollars says he hits that bush yonder," and several other people would join up with him while most everybody else, who considered that a monkey who didn't look or care where he went certainly couldn't be counted on to hit a single piece of shrubbery, took the wager up in a flash and stood by while Junious emptied himself into the camellia bush. But folks wised up, Daddy said, and soon enough nobody much would take that bet anymore, so the camellia bush was divided into quarters and a complete miss became the long shot which paid off handsomely but was only a popular risk on gusty days.

Daddy said the monkey could be counted on for at least two solid rounds of betting on weekdays and four, sometimes five rounds on Saturdays, and he said Mr. Curtis Amos, who worked at the flour mill and always carried a pad and pencil in his apron pocket, took down the wagers and handled the money and chaired the panel of judges which determined the winning quarter in borderline shots. And Daddy said on account of what the monkey now did regularly into the camellia bush the Pettigrew front lawn attracted a new variety of observer and the crowd against the fence began to show a streak of meanness and poverty running through it, compliments mostly of the icehouse niggers and the night shift at the textile plant, where before the Pettigrew monkey had relieved himself in the company of the idly curious and not much of anybody else. And Daddy said with every passing day the talk grew generally rougher and crowd grew generally iller until it got so the mayor would hardly let Miss Myra Angelique into the yard anymore but attended to the activities himself because, as Daddy put it, the mayor was always one for a good wager even if it was his monkey and his camellia bush.

So the monkey became a regular attraction, Daddy said, and even after the betting had gone on for nearly a month it still had not happened yet though most everyone agreed later that it had been bound and determined to happen all along, that a monkey who was smart enough to liberate himself from two pairs of duck pants and as much underwear was certain to make it happen just exactly when and precisely to whom he wanted to make it happen, but Daddy said for a month it didn't happen and then all of a sudden it did and to about the only person in the entire crowd who could be counted on to raise a colossal stink over it, who could be absolutely expected to. Daddy said it just seemed that the monkey got tired of everybody in the county eyeing his private functions and did what he could to let somebody else put on the sideshow for awhile.

Daddy said it all started on a Thursday in the middle of the afternoon. He said the weather had been especially windy the previous week and consequently the gambling had gone poorly since most everybody wanted to sit with the long shot and nobody much would risk the bush which left the crowd particularly nasty and unsettled until calm weather set back in on Sunday evening and even then, Daddy said, it took almost to Wednesday to get some of the edge off the general temperament. But Thursday dawned bright and windless, Daddy said, and along about two o'clock folks began to gather at the Pettigrew's fence, a little anxious but no iller than usual. It was a sizeable crowd, according to Daddy, with plenty of money to lay down, enough anyway to keep Mr. Amos frantic with his pencil right up until Junious got himself turned out the door and made for the flagpole on his knuckles. The mayor came along behind him and took up his place at the gate while the monkey climbed to the knob and crouched atop it. Daddy said everybody studied the monkey who picked at himself and scratched some and curled his lips inside out, and then when he finally did stand up and erect Daddy said people half-watched the monkey and half-watched the bush until they saw that the creature's face was beginning to draw up into a sort of severe and worldly expression and then nobody at all watched the monkey and everybody watched the bush only.

Daddy said Mr. Amos was nearest to it and almost had his nose in a camellia blossom, which was the sort of close range work his judgeship usually called for. Pinky Throckmorton had moved in next to him and was as tight up to Mr. Amos and the camellia bush as he could get since he had five dollars riding on the lower righthand quarter and wanted to see for himself exactly how things went. Daddy said Mrs. Nell Curtis had managed to get herself up next to Pinky. He said she was not a gambling woman by nature but had come in all the way from Leaksville with her egg money, the entire seventy-five cents of it, and had put it down on the long shot in hopes of taking home some instant capital for Mr. Curtis who was negotiating with his neighbor down the street for a used Studebaker. And Daddy said the farther out over the treetops and the courthouse that monkey looked the closer in folks leaned and edged and crowded until most everybody was up on somebody else's back and had somebody up on his own, and Daddy said most people were staring so hard into the camellia bush that nobody much saw right off what the monkey did but heard it first and couldn't collect themselves to look until he had already delivered the better part of a half pint directly onto the crown of Mr. Amos' straw fedora, which Daddy said was not so unfortunate for Mr. Amos as it might seem since the straw made a particularly effective awning and sent most of the monkey water straight back up into the air. Daddy said half of what bounced off of Mr. Amos' hat splattered harmlessly onto the camellia bush but most of the rest of it found its way to Mr. Pinky Throckmorton's shirtsleeve. And that, Daddy said, was the hell of it.

He said Pinky jumped backwards and hollered, "Shitshitshitshitshit," like a steam engine, and Mr. Amos removed his hat, waved it in front of his face and said, "No, Pinky, I don't believe so," which got quite a rise from the crowd but didn't serve to sooth Pinky any who was having enough trouble of his own trying simultaneously to keep his shirtsleeve off his skin and duck his head away from Mrs. Nell Curtis, who had been all alone on the long shot, the day being fair and windless, and was whooping it up in Pinky's ear. The mayor apologized to Pinky and offered to launder his shirt for him, but Daddy

said Pinky was too hot to talk back right off so just bubbled
and boiled and spewed at the mayor still with a little piece of
his shirtsleeve between his fingers and Mrs. Curtis off his left
flank screeching and yapping about a Studebaker. Then the
mayor told Pinky he'd buy him a new shirt altogether, and
Pinky still didn't respond right off, Daddy said, but he did
manage to get his mouth opened and his head turned along
about the same time and he put his face up next to Mrs. Curtis'
face and screamed at her, *"Hush up!"* which Daddy said went
right through Mrs. Curtis and down to Municipal Square and
back again and sort of let all the air out of her before it died
off completely. Then Pinky looked full at the mayor still with
that little bit of shirtsleeve between his fingers and he said,
"Mayor, you don't have to buy me a new shirt cause it ain't
so much my shirt's been pissed on. It's my dignity, Mayor,
and I'm gone have to clean that up for myself." And Daddy
said Pinky let loose of his sleeve and got halfway across the
street before he turned around and said, "See you in the courthouse, Mayor."

iv

IT WASN'T that Pinky came from bad people, Daddy said, because
a Throckmorton was no worse than most and better than some.
According to Daddy, we'd known three generations of them in
Neely, where they had seen fit to move from Kannapolis which
had become home to a family of Tullahoma Tennessee Throckmortons whose ancestors had gravitated southward out of
Clarksburg West Virginia after originating in Philadelphia where
Daddy said the first Throckmorton stepped off the boat and
threw down his luggage. Daddy said Pinky's granddaddy got
on at the cotton mill as a foreman and proceeded to work his
way up into the executive offices where he earned a respectable
salary with which he bought up a considerable amount of company stock, stock that he willed to his widow who willed it in
her turn to her only child, Braxton Porter Throckmorton jr.,
who arrived at the full blush of manhood with no avocation
and so lived off the benefits for awhile. Daddy said Braxton
Throckmorton jr., who was Pinky's daddy and went by Poppa
in dealings that didn't call for a signature, was the family

throwback and so was not like his daddy or his daddy's daddy or his granddaddy's daddy but liked to think he was most related to and derived from a particular duke or prince or some such potentate in England, Daddy called him, who was a Throckmorton by the most obscure attachment possible and who Poppa said had been the first gentleman in the whole United Kingdom and Europe too possessed of enough social daring to decorate the lid of his snuffbox with a jewel. Daddy said Poppa liked to think the same species of unbridled recklessness and bravado coursed through his veins and set him off from regular humans, which was the explanation he gave whenever folks accused him of being lazy and foolhardy.

Daddy said Poppa married a Fuller girl but not until after his thirty-fifth birthday, when folks had already concluded he would not marry and not until after her thirty-seventh birthday when folks had already concluded she could not marry.

So everybody assumed Poppa Throckmorton would have to go to work at last, what with a new wife and, soon enough, a little one on the way, but Daddy said he merely persisted in the Throckmorton recklessness and bravado which he most regularly displayed from a rope hammock strung between two pillars of the Throckmorton front porch and suspended from a half-dozen sixteen-penny nails that Poppa had hired a negro to drive in and bend over. Then with the arrival of Braxton Porter Throckmorton III, who would be Pinky, folks became more truly convinced and satisfied that Poppa would have to take employment and earn a respectable salary, but Daddy said even after the new baby the only labor Poppa could ever be accused of was holding open the front door for the men who came to pay for and fetch away the furniture as he sold it off item by item. And according to Daddy it wasn't a year and a half later that Mrs. Throckmorton was expecting again and so fired up new speculation around town as to what Poppa would now be pressed to do for money which in this case, Daddy said, could not include selling off furniture since he had already unloaded two sideboards, a hutch, three sets of bedsteads with the accompanying mattresses and springs, four stuffed chairs, a dining room table, a pair of matching velvet ottomans, a maple dry-sink, countless dressers and marble-topped endtables, two sets of stemware, and a box of silver, so Daddy said nobody bothered to suppose that even one more stick of furniture could be brought out through Poppa's front doorway without a Throckmorton riding on top of it or somehow attached to it anyway. But when the former Miss Fuller had her second Throckmorton, who she named Evelyn Maynard after her daddy and her daddy's daddy, Poppa still did not seem inclined to do anything by way of getting a living but continued to display the usual recklessness and bravado from the porch hammock, only now, Daddy said, folks sometimes saw him scribbling ciphers in the air with his finger, which was taken as a considerable advancement on his part.

Daddy said little Evelyn Maynard was coming up on two months when the package arrived from New Jersey and sat unclaimed in the post office for the better part of a week before Poppa managed to get himself upright long enough to go down and claim it. Of course, Daddy said, once it had lingered with the mailmen for a day or two there wasn't anybody in town who didn't know where it was from and who it was to and who would not have attempted anything short of opening to find out just exactly what it was. So the traffic was extraordinarily heavy in front of the Throckmorton house on the afternoon Poppa picked up his package, and Daddy said he took it on into the hammock with him and opened it there. According to Daddy, most folks were a little disappointed and the rest were surely puzzled by what Poppa drew out of the box, which Daddy said was nothing but a stereoscope and a parcel of picture cards both of which entirely delighted Poppa who did not unwrap the cards right away but put the stereoscope eyepiece up to his face and looked out into the front yard. Daddy said he did not suppose Poppa's package contained more than a dozen picture cards altogether, and he said when Poppa finally unwrapped them he stuck the first one into the clip and studied it for a full quarter-hour, all the while sliding it up and down the focusing arm and talking to himself underneath the eyepiece. Daddy said he could only speculate as to what Poppa might have been seeing since he had not been exposed to any great variety of stereoscopes himself but had only looked through Great-grandmomma Benfield's on several occasions and had once made use of our neighbor Mr. Phillip J. King's model at the fullblown insistence of Mr. King himself, Daddy said, who had received in the mail from his cousin in Baltimore a stereoscopic picture of the frontside of a naked woman which

Daddy said went a ways towards pointing out the virtues of
the contraption. But Daddy didn't imagine Poppa Throckmorton had come into the possession of even a single picture of
the frontside or backside of anything naked since he would
look at each one himself for a few minutes before calling out,
"Momma," and thereby bringing the former Miss Fuller out
the side door and onto the porch where she would grab up the
stereoscope herself, adjust it as she saw fit, and look through
it for maybe ten seconds before pulling it away from her face
and saying, "It does look real, Braxton," to which Poppa would
reply, "Don't it though," and take the thing back from her.
Daddy said it was probably a few landscapes and most likely
a dead-on look into the breech of a rifle or a view of the bottoms
of some old bugger's feet poking out from under the bedclothes,
which were a couple of big sellers for the stereoscope people.
Daddy supposed Poppa might have gotten hold of a few the-
atrical shots as well, maybe one or two like the one Great-
grandmomma Benfield had of a sour-looking woman pointing
a dagger and entitled "Lady Macbeth as portrayed by Mrs.
Veronica Beech-Whitham of the London Stage."

So folks simply thought that Poppa had bought himself a
stereoscope and they didn't discover until the business column
came out in Saturday's *Chronicle* that Poppa had not bought
himself a stereoscope exactly but had instead bought himself
a sizeable portion of a stereoscope manufacturing firm, namely
Riddle and Schneider, Inc. of Woodbridge New Jersey. As it
turned out Poppa had taken what dividends and benefits and
cotton mill stock he had left and manipulated it somehow into
cash money which he immediately turned around and reinvested
by mail in Riddle and Schneider, Inc. who had taken out an
ad in *Harper's Magazine* that Poppa had seen and been struck
with. Of course his daddy's former associates at the cotton mill
advised him against it and Mrs. Throckmorton was herself a
little leery of the undertaking, but Daddy said Poppa stood firm
and unswayable where his investment was concerned and in
answer to his detractors could often be heard to say there was
no future in cotton, but the stereoscope, now that was something
else entirely. Unfortunately for Poppa, however, Daddy said
the market for stereoscopes was not particularly bullish at the
time what with the radio and, in Neely anyway, the promise
of a moving-picture house where the negro grocery store had

been, and Daddy said if he was any judge of trends, the heyday of stereoscopes had probably come and gone a full decade or so before Poppa ever thought to pack his money off to New Jersey. Certainly Mr. Riddle and Mr. Schneider knew what was what in the stereoscope business since, as it came out later, they were already sitting on several hundred crates of the things in a dockside warehouse in Perth Amboy, and according to Mrs. Riddle, who turned out to be the only source of reliable information once Mr. Riddle and Mr. Schneider were gone, the gentlemen had abandoned all hopes of remaining solvent but had concluded that a call for investors in *Harper's* might attract anyway at least a half a handful of people foolhardy enough to fling their money towards New Jersey, which Daddy said was just the sort of recklessness and bravado that was right in Poppa Throckmorton's line.

Of course Mr. Riddle and Mr. Schneider went out of business. Poppa Throckmorton was simply devastated, at least, Daddy said, folks assumed right off he would be since they knew they would have been, and consequently most everybody tried to keep the news from him, especially Mrs. Throckmorton who intercepted the mailman at the front steps and daily rushed the *Chronicle* into the backyard where she set fire to it on the trash heap, which went unnoticed by Poppa since he was still reasonably enthralled with his stereoscope and had not as of yet figured out how to read a newspaper through it. Daddy imagined Poppa could have been kept in the dark for a couple of months anyway if the regular mail carrier, Mr. Foster, had not contracted an oriental stomach virus which caused a substitute mailman from Ruffin to be imported for the route on the day the letter arrived from the attorney's office in Woodbridge New Jersey, a letter which had been mailed in such a thin and insubstantial envelope, according to the substitute mailman, that it could not help but be deciphered once it happened to pass between his eyes and direct lamplight. So the blame could not be laid on anybody from Neely, which was some sort of civic consolation, and it certainly couldn't be laid on Mrs. Throckmorton who sprang out the front door and met the substitute carrier before he reached the steps but who could not have and did not anticipate that he would spy Poppa in his hammock and holler up to him, "Hello Poppa, sorry to hear about your business," which is exactly what he did. Daddy said Poppa yanked the stereoscope away from his face and leapt directly up out of the hammock and onto the porch decking, a marvelous accomplishment in and of itself. Then he said, "What?" and even before he could finish saying it a picture card dropped out of the stereoscope and settled onto the plank floor at the very instant Poppa became devastated, or anyway that's what folks said he became and that's when folks agreed he became it.

Daddy said all of Neely immediately feared for Poppa because devastation was widely known to be such a serious affliction, and the people who were so friendly with the former Miss Fuller as to hand her advice suggested that she stay where she could eyeball Poppa at all hours of the day and night just in case he was not courageous and level-headed enough to be devastated and survive it. So Poppa could not get away from Mrs. Throckmorton until the fourth day after the letter arrived and even then he had to tell her that the pantry was on fire and the baby was choking on a hambone before he distracted her sufficiently to slip off over the porch railing, through the hedge, and on down along the street. Daddy said as it was pieced together later from various ragtail facts and assumptions, Poppa made directly for Mrs. Ware's back door, which was a full block down from his own, and first rapped on the glass of it with his knuckles before pounding on the panels of it with his fist and finally taking up a stick of oak kindling off the stoop and beating the doorframe with it, which eventually attracted the attention of Mrs. Ware who was partially deaf on top of being generally reluctant to open her door to anybody at any hour of the twenty-four. Daddy said she made enough space for her nose and mouth between the edge of the door and the doorframe and said, "What is it, Mr. Throckmorton?" to which Poppa had not yet exactly settled on a reply and so twiddled the stick of kindling between his hands and sucked on his teeth until he collected himself enough to say, "How are you, Mrs. Ware?" Daddy said she pushed the door to a little more so that only the point of her nose remained outside and said back at him, "Well enough, Mr. Throckmorton. What is it you want?" which Poppa still had not exactly decided on and so closed one eye, twisted his mouth up, and looked off towards the eave of the house where he was still looking when Mrs. Ware said, "Mr. Throckmorton?" to which he replied, "Groundhogs, Mrs.

Ware, I've got groundhogs in my crawlspace." Daddy said Mrs.
Ware neither opened nor closed the door to any degree but only
gaped at Poppa and eventually said, "Oh" without ever moving
her lips so that it just seemed to spill out of her mouth on its
own, and Poppa put his hand on one of the window mullions,
Daddy said, and pushed on into the house a little as he told
her, "So I'll be needing Buddy's gun to run them out with."
Buddy, Daddy said, being the dead Mr. Ware and Buddy's gun
being a double-aught-six shotgun which everybody knew Mrs.
Ware kept loaded under her bed so in case of a prowler or any
threat of meanness in general she could fetch it out and probably
destroy the inside of her house with it. As Mrs. Ware told it,
she couldn't stop him, couldn't even slow him down, and before
she got past, "Well, I" Poppa had pushed on by her into the
bedroom where he dove under the duster on the north end of
the bed and came out on the south end with Mr. Ware's shotgun
in his hands and a hairball dangling from each elbow.

According to Daddy, once Mrs. Throckmorton discovered
that the pantry was not afire and there was no hambone in the
house she went instantaneously and thoroughly berserk, he
called it, and bolted headlong down the front steps with little
Evelyn Maynard on her hip and a firm hold on Pinky's wrist
which sort of left Pinky to skid and bounce along behind her
until she pulled up in the middle of the road and screamed,
"Braxton Braxton Braxton Braxton!" in most every possible
direction before finally dropping onto the dirt and wailing like
a madwoman. Of course, Daddy said, most everybody within
earshot showed up in the street to see what in God's name had
come over Mrs. Throckmorton, and some one or two of them
ventured to console her while most of the rest talked among
themselves and speculated as to Poppa's whereabouts, and Daddy
said nobody seemed to get particularly excited or upset, aside
from Mrs. Throckmorton, until Mrs. Ware came forward from
the sidewalk and announced how Poppa had gone off with
Buddy's gun, which inspired a whole new feeling among the
onlookers, who suddenly found themselves attracted and pro-
pelled by the idea that whatever in the world Poppa could
manage with a shotgun would most certainly be worth seeing,
and the whole crowd of them together set off in the direction
of Mrs. Ware's house except, Daddy said, for Mrs. Throckmorton and Mrs. Ware herself who paused long enough to bend

over Mrs. Throckmorton and tell her how sorry she was about the groundhogs.

Poppa got a ride with Mr. Lemont Graham on his vegetable wagon which was harnessed to and being hauled by a pair of ancient mudcolored draft horses and so was not exactly flashing through town when Poppa caught up with it. Poppa came bursting out of a clump of shrubbery beside the road and threw himself on up into the wagon bed among the leafy lettuce and the snap beans and the Irish potatoes. Daddy said Mr. Graham did not become especially excited or distressed at the sight of a man leaping out of the bushes at him in the company of a double-aught-six shotgun but merely looked half over his shoulder and said, "Afternoon Mr. Throckmorton" before clearing off the far end of the wagon seat and inviting Poppa to have it, but Poppa told Mr. Graham he'd prefer to lay in among the Irish potatoes and the snap beans which Daddy said was equally agreeable to Mr. Graham who was simply pleased with the companionship no matter what part of the wagon it chose to occupy. So Poppa burrowed in underneath the potatoes and covered what they wouldn't with several lettuce leaves and a few handfuls of snap beans which left him entirely blanketed in produce except for his face and would have been an absolutely inconspicuous way to travel, Daddy said, if Mr. Graham had not gone the better part of a day without an ear to bend and so passed directly through the heart of Neely carrying on a highly animated conversation with his vegetables which attracted no inconsiderable attention on its own.

But nobody put any of it together right off and the unofficial Throckmorton posse was still fanned out on the wrong end of town when Mr. Graham passed along the boulevard by municipal square and on down the hill to the icehouse where he brought the team to a halt at the edge of the platform and waited for one of the icehouse niggers to load Mrs. Graham's block onto the back of the wagon bed. Now Daddy said there were three or four shiver rats up under the eave next to the icehouse itself, who are nothing but northend boys that hang around the platform waiting for the puny chips and pieces of ice that the niggers figure they can't sell, and he said one of them, a little one maybe seven or eight years old, saw Mr. Graham swing around on the wagon seat and commence to jabber at his heap of Irish potatoes, which was fairly unusual even for the icehouse, and so drew that boy on out to the edge of the platform, where Daddy said he must have supposed he might find out just what there was to say to an Irish potato. As Daddy heard it, Mr. Graham was talking primarily about the sucker problem he'd had the year previous with his tobacco acreage and the boy had already stood there on the lip of the platform looking at him for about a minute or two before Mr. Graham broke off long enough to say, "Hello George," and then set back in with his potatoes. Daddy said that boy spat a flat piece of ice out of his mouth and into his hand and said, "My name ain't George," but Mr. Graham didn't pay him any mind and carried on at some length about his suckers until the nigger lowered the ice onto the wagon bed and went around to settle up with him which left the boy all to himself with the potatoes. Daddy said that boy licked his ice and studied Mr. Graham's Irish potatoes by turns but didn't offer to converse with any of the vegetables until Mr. Graham popped the reins and the wagon jolted away from the platform, and then he brought his face out of his hand, looked directly at the potatoes, and said, "Hello," and Daddy said the potatoes replied, "Goodbye George," and the boy flinched and opened his mouth but never bothered to speak as if he suddenly and singlehandedly concluded it was permissible for a heap of Irish potatoes to call him anything it pleased.

Daddy said by the middle of the afternoon the Poppa Throckmorton rescue team and eyewitness brigade washed through the center of town like a floodtide, catching up and carting off most every bystander and straggler until it got so the width of the street could hardly accommodate the bunch of them. He said one of the shiver rats saw them first as they came abreast of the square and he went after the icehouse niggers who gathered on the platform all bug-eyed and fearful and watched the crowd pour by the courthouse and on down the hill. Daddy said it was probably next to impossible for the niggers to judge the temperament of the crowd at such a considerable distance, so taking a precautionary and, Daddy called it, nearly instinctual measure, they immediately began to accuse each other of violating white women which set off a ferocious brawl between all four of them that started out with just bare fists, Daddy said, but soon after became more complicated and sincere with the introduction of a variety of packing crates, two folding metal chairs, and an assortment of boards and stray planking. Daddy said those niggers beat and bludgeoned each other all up and down the platform leaving a splintery shambles wherever they went and they ended up in a pile by the freezer door once they had all become subdued and more or less equally exhausted. Daddy said the front edge of the crowd had already worked its way to the lip of the platform before the niggers knew anybody had arrived, and he said the deputy sheriff, who was at that time a Doyle of the Walnut Cove Doyles and was extensively known to be about as compassionate as a cattle prod, beat on the platform with a hunk of wood he carried in his belt and shouted, "HEY!" which caused all four of those niggers to pick up their heads at once and look at him. "Any a you seen Braxton Throckmorton come through here?" he said, and Daddy said those niggers eyed each other momentarily before completely deflating onto the decking where they stayed until the deputy said, "HEY!" again, which still didn't get much more than a ripple out of them but did bring a little towheaded boy away from the icehouse wall and on out to the edge of the platform where he spat a sizeable chunk of ice into his hand and said, "I seen part a somebody come through here." Some one or two of the crowd recognized him as Punk Kirby's boy, S.D., who had no documented name other than the letters which Punk himself said stood for Sundrop, as in the cola. So Daddy said the deputy adjusted and regulated himself for a child and tried again. "Tell me, S.D.," he said, "just what is it you seen?" And S.D. slurped up what part of his ice had melted, then pointed to the lip of the platform and said, "I seen somebody right there." "What was he doing there, S.D.?" the deputy wanted to know. And according to Daddy, S.D. got a little disgusted with Deputy Doyle and said, "He wasn't there. I was there. That's where I seen him." "Well where was he?" the deputy asked him. And S.D. pointed along about where the deputy himself was standing and said, "He was yonder in a wagon under a pile of arsh potatoes," which Daddy said sort of stupefied Deputy Doyle for a couple of seconds, long enough anyway for the widow Mrs. Ware to ask herself out loud, "What in the world was he doing there?" And Daddy said S.D. pondered his chunk of ice and scratched himself and then looked at Mrs. Ware with his face all twisted up in puzzlement and confusion. "I can't imagine," he said.

So they all lit out along the Danville road on foot and by horseback and cartload and ultimately, Daddy said, in the company of the banker Dunford Hicks's specially appointed T model Ford with the revolutionary planetary transmission, personalized brass headlamps, and silver-plated winged horse radiator cap, and driven of course, Daddy said, by Mr. Dunford Hicks himself who carried along with him Pinky and little Evelyn Maynard in the front seat and, in the back seat, the former Miss Fuller who had collapsed in a swoon and so reclined with a damp rag on her forehead. Needless to say Mr. Lemont Graham and his talking produce had already put an appreciable stretch of road between themselves and the Throckmorton posse, but Daddy said with Mr. Graham showing himself for the regular chatterbox he was inclined to be and what with the team of draft horses before him and the heap of Irish potatoes behind him, he saw considerably more of where he had been than where he was going which pretty much left the horses to forge ahead when they chose to and dawdle when they chose to and leave the road entirely whenever they felt the urge to wander. So Mr. Graham and Mr. Throckmorton and Mrs. Graham's block of ice, which Daddy said was steadily becoming mostly puddle, were not making a very direct route of it to Mr. Graham's Oregon Hill farm, and presently as Mr. Graham eyed the horizon at his backside by way of readying himself to strike in on the advantages of Rhode Island hens, he caught sight of a tremendous, billowy cloud of dust churning and swelling above the treeline behind him just where the road angled off to the east and bent out of view, and he automatically opened his mouth and said, "Well what in the hell is that?"

According to Daddy, Poppa didn't stir right off but rolled his eyes towards Mr. Graham and asked him, "What?"

"That there," Mr. Graham told him.

"Where?" Poppa said and lifted his head out from the hole he'd made for it.

"Yonder behind us," and Mr. Graham pointed.

And Daddy said Poppa shed himself of a half bushel of potatoes as he raised up at the waist and sat on his elbows from where he could see the dust on his own but not the cause of it since it had yet to clear the treeline.

"Maybe it's a hurrican," Mr. Graham said, "one a those little hurricans."

And Daddy said Poppa brought his legs free and fetched out Mrs. Ware's shotgun just as the first wave of the posse outstripped the trees and rounded the bend in the road.

"No," Mr. Graham said, "can't be no hurrican cause it's got legs."

And Daddy said Poppa leapt down off the wagon bed and lingered momentarily in the road while he decided between the blueberry brambles off to his left and the combination mimosa forest and honeysuckle thicket off to his right.

"Maybe it's a cattle stampede," Mr. Graham said. "Maybe Hockaday's cows got loose and come through town wrecking and rampaging everything."

And Daddy said Poppa beat it down the bank, through the mimosas, and bored straight into a tiny gap in the honeysuckles.

"But don't appear to be cows," Mr. Graham said. "Looks more like people. Maybe it's the Independence parade."

And Daddy said Mr. Graham now hollered a little and divided his attention between the road and the honeysuckle thicket where he could hear Poppa swearing and thrashing around in an attempt to make a way for himself.

"No, no," and Daddy said Mr. Graham had begun to shout, "it's August, ain't it, and anyway no parade gets it like these folks. They in the goddammed awfulest hurry I ever seen." And Daddy said pretty soon Poppa had thrashed himself on out of earshot which called for Mr. Graham to stand full up on the wagon seat, fill himself with air, and more or less bellow, "Wild looking bunch a people, I tell you that, and nary a rope between them like maybe they gonna gnaw somebody to death, just chew him right in half. Now wouldn't that be a thing to see, huh? Huh? I suppose so. Yes sir, I guess it would be."

Daddy said Mr. Graham was still hollering into the thicket when the front edge of the Throckmorton rescue battalion arrived at his wagon where they all grabbed hold of their knees for the best part of a minute before any of them could manage a breath to speak with, but finally Deputy Doyle was able to bring himself erect long enough to say, "Where is he?"

"Who?" Mr. Graham asked him.

"Throckmorton," the deputy said.

"What's he done?" Mr. Graham wanted to know.

"Just where is he?" the deputy asked him again.

"Throckmorton?" Mr. Graham said.

"Yes, Throckmorton," the deputy told him. "Where'd he go?"

"What's he done?" Mr. Graham wanted to know.

"Nothing," the deputy said. "Where'd he go?"

"What're you after him for?" Mr. Graham asked him.

"He's a sick man," the deputy said. "Now where'd he get off to."

"He looked alright to me," Mr. Graham said.

"He ain't regular sick," the deputy told him. "He's been devastated."

"Oh," Mr. Graham said. "Well he went off into that thicket yonder," and Daddy said before Mr. Graham could bring his arm back down the deputy had taken the forefront and commenced to lead the entire crowd through the mimosas and on into the seam in the honeysuckle hedgerow that had swallowed up Mr. Throckmorton, and Daddy said it was such a tiny opening and such a ponderous crowd that by the time everybody got beyond the honeysuckles most of the thicket was still thicket except for the part where the seam had been which was brushpile. And Daddy said after Mr. Graham had watched the tailend of the posse disappear behind the mimosas and into the hedgerow he sat down on the wagon seat and propped his head up on his knuckles. "Devastated," he said, "Hmm." And Daddy said Mr. Graham held silent council with himself for some considerable minutes before he eventually climbed over the seatback onto the wagonbed, kicked the block of ice off into the road, and raked all the produce out behind it.

Daddy said once the posse had cleared the hedgerow they spread themselves thin across Mr. Harland Lynch's pasture and swept on through his upper tobacco field calling out for Poppa at regular intervals, while Mr. Dunford Hicks in his finely appointed automobile led a squad of carts and wagons an additional half mile along the highway to Mr. Harland Lynch's access road which the deputy's plan called for them to search and secure before rendezvousing with the foottroops at, what the deputy called, Mr. Lynch's westernmost watering pond, which Daddy said was not then and has never been anything but a mudhole. But Daddy said the mobile unit had hardly gained the access road and only half the foottroops had left the tobacco field when the gun went off, and Daddy said fortunately for Mrs. Throckmorton she was still somewhat delirious, partially berserk, and riding in a Ford, the combination of which caused her to take the gunshot for a backfire. But he said three other women who were not married to Poppa and who did not know him except to call his name fainted outright and had to be hauled up onto the road, where they revived in time to run along behind everybody else and help search for the corpse.

Deputy Doyle, being expert in this sort of thing, figured the shot to have come from behind a cluster of tenant houses due southeast, he guessed, and maybe a touch west too from the watering pond, or what amounted to straight down the road, Daddy said, where two sets of Jeffersons, three sets of Broadnaxes, and one set of Carothers shared four shacks, one shallow well, and a common outhouse. Daddy said all but for Lester Broadnax the negroes were off taking first pullings in the bottom acreage and Lester himself had seen the posse early enough to clear out for the woods undetected, which left the foottroops free to crawl over and through and under the tenant houses and just generally infest them for as long as it took to become plain to everybody that there were no negroes there and no Throckmorton either. So Daddy said most of the posse milled around outside on the packed dirt except for some few of the more adventuresome members, who struck out through the woods beating the undergrowth with sticks, which Daddy said the majority considered a frivolous and unnecessary undertaking up to the very second one of the men in the woods yipped and gave tongue like a hound and so set the entire posse stomping and crashing through the trees and the groundcover all the way down to a shale ledge by a creek where one of the brushbeaters had discovered Lester Broadnax who crouched on a rock, Daddy said, and appeared visibly shaken and agitated by the sight of a whole herd of whitefolks bearing down on him at a full gallop.

The same man who found Lester had found along with him Mr. Buddy Ware's double-aught-six shotgun, which Daddy said he had broken open at the breech and sort of wore over his arm like a velvet overcoat, and once the posse had become a little less thundrous he opened his mouth and intoned, Daddy called it, "Look here, deputy, what I found," and then he held the gun over his head so everybody could see it. And Daddy said Deputy Doyle stepped up onto the rock with Lester Broadnax and that brushbeater and he edged on out towards the creek until he stood right overtop of Lester and then he put one hand on his hunk of wood and the other on the butt of his pistol and he set his feet apart and fixed himself to talk but before he could even separate his lips Lester said, "I ain't done nothing. I ain't!" in a wild, high voice and then temporarily lost his senses which caused him to tumble off the ledge into the creek bed. Daddy said once Lester had been fished out of the creek and had calmed himself down enough to get his throat to make noise again he spun out the whole horrible tale, which was very disturbing and dismaying for most everybody right off, but Daddy said after a few minutes it all began to sink in and the entire posse, almost without exception, agreed that Poppa had taken Mr. Buddy Ware's gun and done the only thing he could do with it: he sold it. Lester Broadnax had fired it into the air, had buffed the barrel with his sleeve, and then had owned himself a shotgun for two dollars and twenty-five cents. And Daddy said while most everybody stood around and looked at each other, Mrs. Ware edged and squeezed and pushed her way up to that brushbeater and snapped, "Gimme that," as she snatched Mr. Ware's weapon out of his hands. Then Deputy Doyle exhaled most profoundly, said, "Well hell," and led the troops up out of the forest.

Daddy said Mr. Dunford Hicks and his mobile battalion had only just reached the stretch of road before the tenant houses when thick clumps of posse commenced to issue from the woods. And he said Mr. Hicks found out the deputy and took him by the elbow so as to lead him to some private place away from the road and the Ford in particular. But Daddy said Deputy Doyle wasn't looking to be steered around by the elbow and so right away shucked himself of Mr. Hicks who decided to take what information he could get where he could get it and asked the deputy, "Is it over?" And Daddy said the deputy shot back at him. "Shit yes, it's over." And Mr. Hicks said, "He's gone then?" in a most sorrowful voice. And Daddy said the deputy told him, "He's gone alright." And Mr. Hicks looked at the ground and said, "Delivered from his torments, delivered and redeemed. We shall miss him." And again the deputy said, "Well hell," and left Mr. Hicks by himself on the apron of the road where he launched into a soaring eulogy and had already carried on at some length before anybody bothered to tell him that Poppa was still as miserable and tormented as everybody else, which Mrs. Throckmorton herself learned about the same time and so managed to clear her head enough to climb out of the back of Mr. Hicks' Ford and haul little Evelyn Maynard and Pinky along with her down to the edge of the woods. Daddy said the tail end of the posse was still coming up from the creek bank and out from the trees but nobody could tell Mrs. Throckmorton anything she didn't already know, and he said after everybody had come out of the woods, except for Lester Broadnax, who did not intend to come out right yet, Mrs. Throckmorton peered in among the trees and called out, "Braxton Braxton Braxton Braxton!" then leaned in with her ear and waited for a reply. And Daddy said what part of the posse couldn't fit in the carts and wagons struck back out across Harland Lynch's tobacco field towards the honeysuckle thicket and the Danville road while Mrs. Throckmorton continued to pace up and down the treeline with little Evelyn Maynard on her hip and Pinky flailing and moaning behind her, and Daddy said she called out Poppa's name at ever increasing intervals until she stopped calling it out altogether and finally came away from the trees and out from the tenant shacks when Mr. Hicks got her attention with his brass carhorn and hollered to her from the driver's seat, "You coming or what?"

Daddy said Poppa showed up around noon of the following day, or got as far as the porch anyway after having slept at the front gatepost until the mailman came along to deliver him with the mail, and Daddy said Mrs. Throckmorton let it out all over town that Poppa had suffered a serious illness but was on the mend now and would be his regular self soon enough. But before the week was out Poppa had sold off four pieces of stemware and skipped out again with nobody to chase him this time except for Mrs. Throckmorton who could not tote Evelyn Maynard and drag Pinky so far as the end of the street before she gave out. And Daddy said he didn't get back to the porch this time or even to the gatepost but collapsed along about the icehouse, where the deputy found him and brought him on home, and again Mrs. Throckmorton tended to him and nursed him and gave it out all over town that Poppa was ill and would recover, and Daddy said he spent several days convalescing in his hammock before he disappeared again and with nobody at all to chase him. But Daddy said this time Poppa brought himself back home carrying with him his illness in one jug and two jarfuls, and Daddy said Poppa lowered the jug and one of the jars down into his well on a rope and took the other jar with him to his hammock, where in the course of the afternoon he drank the entire undiluted contents of it from a galvanized coffee cup and then banged the cup on the porch floor most savagely until Mrs. Throckmorton herself drew in the rope and fetched him the other jarful. And Daddy said now it was the former Miss Fuller who asked for and received a fair price for her grandma's cedar chest, and who sold the last Throckmorton silver service to a dealer in Greensboro, and who let it be known around Neely that she was available to take in laundry and piecework. And Daddy said about once a week while Poppa lay near senseless in his hammock, Mrs. Throckmorton would leave little Evelyn Maynard and Pinky with her momma and would walk north along the boulevard past the square and the icehouse and on out of town to the break in the honeysuckle thicket where she would cut up through Mr. Harland Lynch's tobacco field and skirt on by his tenant shacks and into the trees down to the creekbed which she would follow to the deepest part of the woods. Daddy said Mrs. Throckmorton always came back through town carrying the jars in a flour sack where they rattled and clanged together as she walked.

So soon enough there was nothing left to them but the house, and Mrs. Throckmorton herself struck up a deal for it. With a portion of the money she hired out a wagon which all of the remaining Throckmorton furniture and possessions could hardly fill up, and Daddy said she gave over a little change to Poppa, who hired and paid for the same negro he had hired and paid for before, directing him to pull and unbend the nails and haul the rolled up hammock on his shoulder behind the wagon. Daddy said they moved on a Saturday in the rain with little Evelyn Maynard and Pinky on the seat alongside Mrs. Throckmorton who drove the team while Poppa lay sprawled across the loose items to keep them from blowing. And everybody watched, Daddy said, from doorways and windows as Mrs. Throckmorton guided the horses onto the boulevard away from the square and the courthouse and out to southend where she had bought a little white clapboard house in among a dozen other little white clapboard houses, and Daddy said since there was no porch anywhere but only a stoop on the front and three wooden steps at the back, Poppa picked out a pair of trees in the sideyard and had the negro drive and rebend the nails and so suspend the hammock between them while little Evelyn Maynard and Pinky and Mrs. Throckmorton emptied the wagonbed.

Daddy said the people of southend never bothered to gape at the Throckmortons since they had enough misery and hardship of their own to keep them occupied, but most everybody else found time to parade by the house just to see Poppa swinging in his hammock in the sideyard, and he said the general feeling was that Poppa had disgraced his family and shamed his blood, but Daddy said that was not the case exactly; he said Poppa had simply miscalculated his ties. According to Daddy, who researched it and studied it all, Poppa was not so attached to the snuffbox Throckmorton as he thought but owed considerably more to the West Virginia clan of his kinfolk who had pooled their willingness and knowhow to construct an extraordinary and utterly unforgettable collection of vats and troughs and copper tubing that was less a still than a refinery and which operated on such a scale that it was said to have produced liquor more than brewed it. And Daddy said then or now all anybody had to do was walk into a town or even a widespot most anywhere in the Allegheny Mountains and say the name out loud and every available voice would answer back, "Jesus, them Throckmortons." So Daddy said Poppa's main failing was nothing but pure miscalculation which left him in a very sad and unfortunate predicament, not that he had disgraced the family name, which he hadn't, and not that he hadn't turned out to be a throwback of sorts, which he had, but just that he wasn't thrown back near far enough, which he never would be.

So Poppa lasted it out in his hammock, Daddy said, until his liver took him under which left Mrs. Throckmorton to raise the boys, and Daddy said in spite of everything that had happened and in spite of everybody who remembered it, Mrs. Throckmorton lived to be an old woman which Daddy didn't figure to be any great blessing in this instance considering how things turned out. Daddy said once little Evelyn Maynard left babyhood he gave Mrs. Throckmorton all grades of trouble right on up into manhood and direct to middle age. Along about his fifteenth year he decided he didn't much care for Evelyn or Maynard either and went by Bubba instead, and Daddy said

as Bubba Throckmorton he began to run with the wrong crowd
of people and had already been in and out of jail four times
for various disturbances before his twenty-first birthday on the
occasion of which, Daddy said, the former Miss Fuller presented him with an all expenses paid excursion to the Dix Hill
facility in Raleigh where he went to take the cure. But even
at twenty-one Bubba was too saturated to dry out, not just
saturated with liquor, Daddy said, but with heritage too, so the
cure failed the first time and the time after that and the time
after that, and Daddy said once Bubba hit thirty he was already
pure post-stereoscopic Poppa, so there was nothing for him to
do but live at the homeplace with his Momma, and there was
nothing for her to do but buy him a rope hammock of his own
since Poppa had stipulated and specified that he wear his into
the casket like a shroud. And Daddy said on account of Bubba
the Throckmortons achieved a sort of immortality, or two generations worth anyway, since Bubba took to swinging between
the trees Poppa had swung between and since some of the folks
who had gaped at Poppa and the sons and daughters of the rest
of the folks who had gaped at Poppa could now pacify themselves gaping at Bubba, who Daddy said carried the Throckmorton torch, or in this case the alcohol lamp.

Pinky, however, got on with his life a little more successfully
than Bubba did. He married one of the Jeeter girls whose family
had inherited a chicken ranch in Draper and so had relocated
there from Rock Hill South Carolina. There were five Jeeters
altogether, Momma and Daddy Jeeter, Grandma Jeeter, and the
two Jeeter daughters, who had legitimate Christian names that
got no sort of wide circulation and who were known instead
as the fat Jeeter and the bald Jeeter. Daddy said the fat Jeeter
was what Momma might call hefty, which according to Daddy
was a lady's way of saying she had the girth of a tractor tire,
and Daddy himself said the fat Jeeter was a girl of tremendous
quantity who cut an imposing if not disgusting figure. But
Daddy said she was the one Pinky lost his head over at first
and he wooed her and courted her and kept her in chocolates
for the best part of three months before the wind changed,
Daddy said, and blew what flame there was from the fat one
over to the bald one and Pinky began to call on her and bring
her candied fruit since chocolates made her scalp break out.
Daddy said the bald Jeeter had not been born bald but lost her

hair in childhood during a bout with scarlet fever and had been as slick as an egg ever since. And Daddy said once she got old enough to care that she was hairless her Grandma Jeeter made her a pair of wigs out of a combination of human and horse hair, one of which was satiny black while the other, taken mostly from a chestnut mare, was a lovely natural brown and heightened the otherwise drab features of the bald Miss Jeeter's face. And Daddy said once Pinky married the bald one and left the fat one to go her own way, most everybody agreed he had done a wise thing since the bald one was not always bald or always brunette or always chestnut-headed, but the fat one was always fat. Daddy said Pinky had simply opted for variety, which nobody much was willing to blame him for.

Pinky worked as a day laborer right after his marriage but soon enough took a job with the post office downtown where he sorted mail and sold stamps at the window. According to Daddy, Pinky was as tight as twelve cent shoes with his money and for the first two years of their married life him and the bald Jeeter lived in half a shack down by the cotton mill which they did not leave until Pinky had saved and scraped and otherwise strangled enough dollars to put a downpayment on his granddaddy's house which his momma had sold on account of Poppa's infirmity, Daddy called it.

Daddy said Pinky and the bald Jeeter girl moved into the Throckmorton house in the winter of 1938 which gave rise to considerable optimism throughout Neely that come spring folks would have a Throckmorton to gape at on each end of town, and everybody concluded that would go a ways towards making the whole business more convenient and agreeable. But Daddy said spring arrived and Pinky proved out to be less accommodating than folks had hoped. He kept on at the post office like a regular Trojan, Daddy said, and nights and weekends him and the bald Mrs. Throckmorton worked over the old homeplace from top to bottom in an effort to make it respectable and maybe a little bit awesome once more. And Daddy said people were generally disappointed and fairly much appalled when summer came and went and Pinky never even strung up a hammock, but then Daddy said Pinky was not Bubba and Pinky was not Poppa either but was some of both of them and a little of something else. Of the two remaining Throckmorton heirs, Daddy said Pinky became known as "the other one" while Bubba was unanimously considered "the one who drinks," as in "which one was it, the one who drinks or the other one?" Not that Pinky didn't drink, Daddy said, and not that he drank less than Bubba who even in 1938 was saturated enough to steep in nothing but his own juices for a few days without risking full consciousness, but just that Pinky kept his liquor in the crook of the porch support and drank it in seclusion, which was pretty much discounted as any sort of Throckmorton-induced alcoholic dependence but was instead broadly and publicly taken as a form of polite imbibing, Daddy said.

But Daddy said Pinky was as much his father's son as Bubba was, only in the other direction. He said, like Poppa, Pinky had a little of the potentate in him while Bubba could only own up to a perforated stomach and the ruins of a liver, but unlike Poppa, Pinky was also blessed with a dash of Fuller which Daddy supposed might have supplied him with the determination and wherewithal, he called it, that Poppa could never quite muster in his day. So according to Daddy, Pinky wasn't much like Bubba and wasn't exactly like Poppa who had only talked about his regal attachments while Pinky tried to act like one, which meant he blustered, Daddy said, since that's what Pinky assumed potentates did best. The bald Jeeter was not given to drawing attention to herself and so was not much help to Pinky where blustering was concerned, but Daddy said once Pinky had settled into the homeplace and had gotten himself promoted out of mailsorting and up to clerking only, he developed a full swagger for outdoor use, a kind of bloated lordliness, Daddy called, for the Throckmorton parlor, and his own particular way of blowing around in the post office like maybe he'd invented the envelope. Now Daddy said people generally don't sit still for this sort of thing but they let Pinky play the big fish for awhile since most everybody figured he had a generation or two of Throckmortons to live down and so would have to truly apply himself to this potentate business if he wanted to buff up the family name even the least little bit, and anyway, Daddy said, nobody could get his fill of Pinky as long as there was a Bubba swinging between two trees in his Momma's sideyard and clapping the empty galvanized coffee cup against the near trunk after Poppa's example, so the sight of one Throckmorton and the recollection of another tended to dilute and generally offset any full-scale blustering undertaken by the third one. And Daddy said it got so that the worst thing anybody could say to Pinky was, "I remember your Daddy." He said it got so that wherever Pinky was Poppa was too and whatever Pinky did Poppa had already done it, he said it got so that the faster Pinky ran and the harder he worked his arms the quicker Poppa pulled even with him. Daddy said Poppa was Pinky's lead necktie.

So all of the blustering and blowing around Pinky could manage simply would not get it, and Daddy imagined Pinky might have never found his niche in Throckmortondom if a peculiar set of circumstances hadn't come along to open up whole new vistas for him. Daddy said along about six months after the bald Jeeter had delivered Pinky a daughter into the world, the Throckmortons began to have some trouble with their upstairs toilet. Nothing much would go down it, Daddy said, or anyway nothing much that went down it stayed down it and no amount of plunging on Pinky's part could persuade the toilet to swallow any of the sorts of items it usually made off with very casually and without complaint. So Pinky called in for consultation and advice one of the few local plumbers, Mr. Casper Epps, who Daddy said did respectable work if you could find a sharp enough stick to poke him with. Now Daddy said Mr. Epps had a brother, Justin, who was a servant of Jehovah in Decatur Georgia and recent to Pinky's toilet problems Justin had written Casper to tell how he had constructed an entire sermon around samples of Casper's sinfulness and personal vice, which had been received very enthusiastically by the congregation, and Daddy said since Casper had yet to amount to much otherwise he was proud to have been displayed so prominently and to have earned such a reception and consequently he took it upon himself to cultivate and catalog his shortcomings and dispatch a biweekly report to his brother so that between the two of them they might better show the congregation what transgression is all about. Casper's plan was to work his way systematically through the seven deadly sins taking in a number of the less lethal ones along the way, and he had most recently begun to air out his slothfulness, which he was already partial to, when Pinky called him about the toilet. So they agreed to meet the following morning and Casper, of course, didn't show up, so Pinky called him the next day and made another appointment and again Casper didn't come, so he called him a third time, all fed up and indignant, and threatened and browbeat Casper until he had squeezed a commitment out of him for noon of the day after, and when Pinky left the post office to go home and keep the appointment he found Casper asleep in the square on one of the benches underneath the statue of Colonel Blalock. Pinky took hold of Casper's collar and dragged him on home with him.

The little Throckmorton girl was responsible for the trouble though nobody knew it yet nor would know it until Mr. Epps had unbolted the toilet and turned it upside down. The bald Jeeter had insisted they name the baby Ivy after the fat Jeeter in hopes of smoothing out relations between them which had become a little strained on account of Pinky, and Daddy said the bald Jeeter left little Ivy on the bathroom counter while she cleaned out the tub and somehow the baby got hold of a small tin of toothpowder which she accidentally dropped into the toilet bowl where it sank on out of sight and became wedged in the crook just this side of the drainoff. Daddy said Casper leaned over the bowl and peered into it and Pinky leaned over behind him and peered into it for himself, and then Casper poked the handle of the plunger as far down into the neck as it would go and Pinky took the plunger from him and poked around for himself, and then Casper lifted the lid off the tank and fiddled with some of the paraphernalia and Pinky stuck his hand in the tank too and fiddled a little for himself, and then Casper told Pinky he didn't know just what was wrong with the toilet and Pinky told Casper he didn't know himself. So Casper set out after his tools and Pinky made the mistake of letting him which left the Throckmortons without an upstairs toilet until the following Tuesday, when the time came for Casper to take up another vice.

He had considered Adultery, but Daddy said Casper was not one of your more alluring plumbers and so had settled instead on what he called Shortness, which according to Daddy was mostly sharp-tongued ill-mannered rudeness with wings and had its appeal for Casper since he could be short all day without ever having to hunt up a consenting adult to be short with him. And Daddy said by Tuesday morning Casper already had two full days of discourteous behaviour under his belt and had managed to work himself up for the third day by kicking Mrs. Greenly's schnauser on his way to the Throckmortons, so Daddy said Casper was truly ripe and surly when he arrived at Pinky's front door and began to beat on it with the handle of his mallet. It being midmorning, Pinky of course had long since gone off to his seat at the stamp window and the bald Jeeter was well underway with her housework which she usually performed skin-headed leaving a wig on Pinky's hatrack by the door so she might have it handy in case of a caller, but Daddy said Casper gave the front door such a thrashing with his mallet handle that Mrs. Throckmorton thought maybe the house was on fire, or all her relatives had fallen over dead, so she tore through the parlor and into the front hallway and Daddy said she had already swung the front door partway open when she recollected her hairlessness and plucked the chestnut wig off the hatrack and slapped it onto her head as best she could. And according to Daddy, Casper had crossed the threshold and gotten himself into the house before Mrs. Throckmorton had the chance to be thoroughly disappointed, and he had started on up the staircase, Daddy said, when he turned his head ever so slightly and told her, "I come to fix your toilet." Then he stomped on up three more steps before he stopped cold, Daddy said, and brought himself full around to face Mrs. Throckmorton who he treated to nearly an entire minute of genuine chicken-necked gawking, Daddy called it, before he reeled in his jaw enough to say, "Your hair's crooked." And Daddy said Mrs. Throckmorton got this kind of sour stomach grin on her face and her right hand sort of drifted up into the vicinity of her hairpiece and felt all around it until she got hold of the bun over her left ear and gave the whole business a quarter turn towards the backside, which pretty much set things to rights, Daddy said, or at least satisfied Mr. Epps who stomped on up the rest of the staircase and into the bathroom.

Pinky came on home once the bald Jeeter had wailed at him over the telephone and told him how the plumber had blown into the house like Atilla himself, but before Pinky could get so far as the stairwell Casper had already drawn the water off the toilet, unbolted the thing from the floor, and extracted the toothpowder tin from the neck of it; however, along about when he was resetting it over the drainhole he saw the opportunity for some active sinning and began pouring all of his resources into coveting Pinky's brass lavatory taps which proved to be such a taxing endeavor that he lost his hold on the commode and it fell over directly atop the wooden toilet seat snapping it cleanly in two. So by the time Pinky arrived in the upstairs Casper was already holding the piece of broken toilet seat under his nose and eyeing it like maybe it had come off some antique upright creature and he couldn't figure from just exactly what part. And Daddy said even before Pinky could haul himself into the bathroom proper and park his bulk up against the vanity or the towel rack, which Daddy said Pinky was inclined to do since he did not possess the usual lean and wiry Throckmorton frame but had constructed for himself a modified and overblown variation of it that called for buttresses and cross braces whenever they were available, and Daddy said even before Pinky could take some relief against the edge of the door on his way to the vanity or the towel rack, Casper shook the detached piece of toilet seat at him and made a noise in his throat that started out very much like articulate English but went axle deep and became snared in something Casper had to dredge up and evacuate into the toilet bowl, which was very handy though still waterless, before he could tell Pinky just what it was he wanted to tell him, which he did not get around to until he'd wiped his mouth three or four times with the back of his hand and which, even then, didn't turn out to be anything but, "You know what?" followed by a most impressive tattoo, Daddy called it, that Casper played on the commode porcelain with the broken piece of toilet seat.

And Daddy said Pinky situated himself against the overhang of the vanity counter and crossed his arms in front of him. "What?" he said.

"Your wife's bald," Casper told him, "and I broke your toilet seat." And Daddy said Casper handed the piece of wooden ring to Pinky so maybe he could see for himself it was far enough away from the hinged section on the commode not to be a part of it any longer.

And Pinky examined what piece of the seat Casper had handed to him before setting it on the counter beside him and crossing his arms again. "I know," he said. "How'd it happen?"

And Daddy said Casper didn't answer directly but repositioned the toilet over the drainhole and tightened it down with a wrench. Then he hooked the waterline back into the underside of the tank and began to collect his tools together but still didn't offer Pinky any sort of response until Pinky asked him again,

"How'd it happen?" and Casper brought himself to his feet, snatched up his toolbox, and said, "I ain't got no call to know how it happened. Maybe she was born that way." And Daddy said Pinky sort of lifted his face and blew a breath towards the overhead light.

They reached an agreement about the toilet seat, Daddy said, so Pinky didn't commence proceedings against Casper right off, probably did not know he was going to commence proceedings against him since he had never commenced proceedings against anyone before and so as of yet had no way of knowing jurisprudence would lay claim to him and be his calling just as recklessness and bravado had laid claim to his daddy. Casper agreed to order the toilet seat from an outfit in Atlanta and replace it for nothing if Pinky would sand it and stain and varnish it on his own, but Daddy said Pinky found this sort of arrangement entirely unacceptable at first since he'd had no hand in the destruction of the toilet seat and saw no reason for him to have a hand in the replacement of it, so by way of compromise Casper told Pinky he could take his toilet seat and go straight to the devil with it, which set Pinky to reconsidering the initial offer since as of yet he did not possess the proper spine for hard bargaining but was only capable of all variety of indignant noises with which he entertained Casper for a day or two before deciding that the first arrangement was not so entirely unacceptable after all. So they reached an agreement about the toilet seat, Daddy said, and Casper told Pinky he'd go ahead and order it, but Daddy said riotous and sinful living was certainly no sidelight and consequently didn't leave Casper much time to conduct himself like a regular businessman, so the outfit in Atlanta did not hear from Casper Epps right off and understandably, Daddy said, did not up and dispatch any sort of toilet covering towards Neely on its own, which meant that Pinky, even after he waited what he considered to be a reasonable amount of time, could never discover a commode ring addressed to Casper Epps from Atlanta in the back of any mailtruck or in the bottom of any mailsack or in any dark and neglected corner of the post office itself.

So the toilet seat never got so far as Neely, never got so far as out of Atlanta, and probably would have never arrived at all if Pinky hadn't happened to run up on Casper at Mr. Bill Castleberry's Leaf Market Dinette and Cafeteria adjacent to the warehouse and just around the corner from the square. Casper was attempting to hone up his gluttony on the fillet of sole which was always the chef's choice on Tuesdays unless the truck got waylaid in Greensboro which would leave the chef to choose between the chopped hamburger steak and grilled weiner with navy beans, but the fillet of sole had turned out to be a little fishier than Casper generally preferred and so caused him to attempt to gorge himself on a helping of boiled potatoes, a sprig of parsley, two lemon slices, and a dribble of cole slaw, which Daddy said was the sort of meal a good Roman might sneer at and inhale but which Casper was forced to consider a gluttonous repast, Daddy called it, since he couldn't get the fillet of sole beyond his nose and Mr. Castleberry had run out of lemon pie. So Casper was gnawing on the parsley stem and trying to look bloated when Pinky sat down beside him at the counter and began to tell him how shameful it was that a big toilet seat conglomerate like that outfit in Atlanta couldn't get their orders out in any reasonable amount of time. He said people like him and Casper shouldn't have to hold up their dealings just because some fiddleheaded shipping clerk in Georgia was as slow as Christmas and he asked Casper if he knew what it was like to have to bolt into the downstairs everytime nature beckoned in the night, and when Casper didn't even venture an honest guess, Pinky said to him, "It's no treat, I'll tell you, it's no treat at all," and then he went on as to how he might just write a letter to Atlanta, as to how he might just make enough trouble to get that toilet seat for nothing. And Daddy said Casper put both elbows on the lunch counter and extracted the remains of parsley stem from his mouth. Then he turned around just enough to see Pinky with his near eye and said, "What toilet seat?"

Of course Pinky blew up, Daddy said, but he blew up in stages and the first one was the quietest of the bunch. Daddy said Pinky just leaned himself towards Casper and put his face up next to Casper's face and sort of whispered in the general direction of Casper's ear, "What toilet seat? What toilet *seat*?" Then he moved on to stage two, Daddy said, which was very much like stage one only louder and led directly into stage three, which was also like stages one and two except for the pounding on the countertop that Pinky used to punctuate himself everytime he said "toilet" and every time he said "seat." Daddy said the explosion, such as it was, built towards and culminated in stage four, which saw Pinky rise up from his stool and stalk all the way out onto the sidewalk and then back inside again to the lunch counter, which he beat on four times hard with both fists and screamed at Casper, "WHAT TOILET SEAT!" and Daddy said everybody in Mr. Castleberry's dinette who had not left off eating previously left off eating now and the cook himself looked out from the kitchen through the slot in the wall and overtop two orders of tuna salad.

Daddy said Mr. Castleberry's Dinette and Cafeteria was in what folks call the grip of dead silence, except, that is, for the sound of Pinky's fingertips against the formica countertop, which he was playing like a snare drum and continued to play entirely throughout what Daddy said folks call the anxious moments, and Daddy said the quieter and stiller things got, the louder Pinky drummed his fingers so as to provide a way for any excess of passion and sheer hot-headedness to seep off from him and thereby prevent the risk of instantaneous human combustion which Daddy said Pinky had heard of and wished to avoid.

Daddy said the whole scene could have been played out in a very grand and dramatic fashion if only Casper had taken notice of the grip of dead silence and the anxious moments and had consequently allowed himself to get caught up in the feeling of the thing, but Daddy said Casper was not one of your regular dramatis personae and so just slouched against the countertop on his elbows and gnashed at the parsley stem. And Daddy said even after Casper had gotten his fill of parsley and had flicked the mangled stem onto his plate he didn't seize upon the opportunity before him to launch some sort of poetical barb in Pinky's direction but simply settled for, "Funny thing about that toilet seat—slipped my mind completely." And Daddy said all the patrons along with Mr. Castleberry and the dishwashers and the cook and Mr. Castleberry's girl, June, all of them together took a breath and held it and watched Pinky to see how he would blow up this time, and as for himself Pinky leaned in towards Casper and put his face up next to Casper's face and sort of whispered in the general direction of Casper's ear, "Slipped your mind? Slipped your mind?" and then he repeated himself three or four times, pounding on the counter every time he said "slipped" and every time he said "mind," and of course, Daddy said, folks were already watching the door before Pinky ever made a move to stalk out it onto the sidewalk, and they were already watching the counter before he ever arrived back at it and hammered away on the formica with his fists while screaming at Casper, "SLIPPED YOUR MIND!" So Daddy said Pinky was not much of an innovator in his own right and him and Casper together would probably have made a dreary mess out of the whole production if Casper had not taken a few moments to ponder his predicament and decided he'd be proud he'd been slothful and so kill two birds at once. Consequently, Daddy said, the harder Pinky pounded on the countertop and the louder he hollered at Casper, the taller Casper got on the barstool and the more he drew back at the shoulders until, Daddy said, he began to look more like a rooster than a plumber, and as the patrons reported it later, it seemed that Mr. Epps was on the verge of having the sugar dispenser forcibly introduced into one of his upraised noseholes when he made his exit, and Daddy said everybody who saw it or even heard about it agreed it was a very fine exit, the sort of exit that should not be tampered with and could not be improved upon in this life or any other, and Daddy said it very possibly saved Casper from all grades of violence and certainly pardoned him for having previously squandered the grip of dead silence and a full sixty seconds worth of anxious moments.

He didn't stand up exactly, Daddy said, he just sort of rose from the barstool like a wisp of smoke and then lingered very casually at the counter digging through his trouser pockets with Pinky in his face raining abuse all over him, Daddy said, and generally threatening to do all sorts of damage to Casper's person if he didn't soon enough find himself perched atop his upstairs toilet with a varnished wooden ring between his posterior and the porcelain. Daddy said Pinky beat his fist on the countertop and then shook it under Casper's nose and then beat it on the countertop again while Casper, for his part, continued to poke around in his pockets from which he extracted an ink pen, two folded pieces of paper, one set of keys on a steel ring, a buckeye, a three-bladed knife, and several pennies before he finally dredged up the nickel he'd been after and slipped it under the edge of his plate for Mr. Castleberry's girl, June. And even then he didn't light out for the sidewalk like everybody thought he would but just emptied his hands back into his pockets and left them there and stood quietly by while Pinky delivered himself of his latest dose of outrage and indignation. And Daddy said once Pinky had run down and momentarily fallen silent, Casper freed one of his hands and scratched the top of his head with it before seizing upon the opportunity to speak himself. "Mr. Throckmorton," he said, "don't get the fish." Then he was out the door and gone, and Daddy said it was the grip of dead silence all over again until Pinky had regrouped and recovered enough to clear out himself in what Daddy said folks call a huff.

And still Pinky did not commence proceedings, probably still did not know he was going to commence proceedings since he still had not ever commenced proceedings before and so had yet to feel the tug of jurisprudence at his heartstrings. Instead Pinky did Casper the favor of writing a letter to the toilet seat outfit in Atlanta and also did him the favor of signing his name to it and mailing it off, and Daddy said hardly two weeks had gone by since the high drama at Mr. Castleberry's Dinette and Cafeteria when the boxed-up toilet seat passed through the post office on its way on out towards Casper's digs, Daddy called it, and Pinky took leave from the stamp window long enough to hunt up Casper himself who, all reports indicated, had been lurking around Colonel Blalock's feet for the better part of the morning.

When Pinky found him, Casper had just finished up a lively exchange with Commander Jack Tuttle in the shade of the colonel's left flank. The commander had climbed in on Mrs. Tuttle's side of the bed the night previous and so had inadvertently forgotten to get his watch off her nightstand when he left for work come morning, and what the commander wanted to know from Casper was the time of day. Now Casper had already been wrestling with his angel for near a month and a half and had probably taken it down for the three count on several occasions, so Daddy said he was steadily becoming the closest thing to a regular infidel any Neelyite had ever been exposed to. His mind was increasingly sharp and sinful, and whereas he'd once had to ponder and decide on each separate transgression, he'd since come to rely on his instincts to cart him off into the darkness on their own. Consequently, when Commander Jack Tuttle caught up with him at the colonel's flank and said to him, "Casper, you know what time it is?"

Casper saw right off that here was the opportunity for some Lying, some Taking of the Lord's Name in Vain, and some serious Shortness all at once, and almost before he could look at his watch he said, "Well hell yes goddam it. It's two forty-five," and the commander, being an undertaker and therefore accustomed to all variety of ill treatment, thanked Casper most hardily and went off towards the post office, where, by the clock over the portico, it was very nearly three-thirty.

Commander Jack met up with Pinky in the post office doorway and the commander pulled up short like maybe he was inclined to exchange a word or two or hold a brief rivet seminar on Pinky's behalf, but Pinky just told him, "Make yourself small," and squeezed on by to the outside and hustled himself on down the steps and across the street towards Colonel Blalock. Casper did not exactly see Pinky coming but heard the footsteps and turned around only after Pinky had snatched up a handful of his shirtcollar so he could draw Casper right on up into his face. "Your toilet seat," he said, "my toilet seat," he said, "just passed through the post office and I want you to bring it out to the house this afternoon. Do you understand? This afternoon."

And with his nose hard up against Pinky's nose and his eyes just level with Pinky's eyes, Casper opened his mouth and said, "Well hell yes goddam it. I will."

So Casper went home directly, Daddy said, threw the boxed-up toilet seat into the back of his truck, and then proceeded to ride it all around Neely and into the reaches of the county for the best part of a week without ever once getting near enough to Pinky's driveway to spit at it. But still Pinky didn't commence proceedings, though Daddy assumed he was probably getting the inkling that he might, and through the weekend and on into the next week the toilet seat continued its open-air tour of the county until the following Wednesday when it disappeared altogether along with the truck and along with the plumber Mr. Casper Epps. However, Daddy said, Pinky didn't know right off that the toilet seat was gone or that the truck was gone or that the plumber Mr. Casper Epps was gone either but just supposed that the three of them together might have grown a little travel weary and so parked themselves for a spell. Consequently, Pinky took his lunch hour Friday to ride on out to Casper's digs, Daddy said, and see if he couldn't come away with his toilet seat, but the truck was not in the driveway and, as Pinky found out from Uncle Bill Collier, Casper was not in the state. He had received a letter from his brother Justin in Decatur who, along with his congregation, had become gravely concerned over the increasing volume of Casper's bi-weekly reports and so had planned and organized a redemption festival in Casper's honor which had set in on Thursday evening with a pot luck supper, would pick up again on Friday night with an hour of scripture study followed by coffee and sweetrolls, and was scheduled to climax and conclude on Saturday with a successful redemption sometime between eleven and twelve of the morning and the accompanying picnic and softball game at the Decatur Sertoma part in the afternoon. So Casper was not at home and would very possibly not be home until Monday morning, and Uncle Bill Collier told Pinky he was entirely convinced that the Casper Epps who rolled into Neely on Monday would not be the same Casper Epps who set out for Decatur on Thursday. And Uncle Bill went on to tell Pinky how he thought redemption was a fine thing, and he said he would have liked to have a share of it for himself and probably would have if not for the bladder ailment that prevented him from taking any long trips, and Uncle Bill asked Pinky if he wouldn't like to be redeemed every now and again himself, but Pinky didn't say anything back since he had stopped listening to Uncle Bill a long time before Uncle Bill had stopped talking. Pinky had all he could handle in trying to accept the fact that his toilet seat had actually gone back to Georgia and so could not have been expected to listen and be disgusted at the same time.

And Daddy said now Pinky commenced proceedings, or anyway tried to commence proceedings on his way back to the post office, but since the Neely courthouse is and has always been what Daddy called half land-deep depository and half jail, there was no district judge for Pinky to see and circuit judge and no clerk of court and no courtroom even but only Mr. Earl Jemison's brother Maury, who held hours as the justice of the peace in the afternoons and who told Pinky he'd be more than happy to unite Casper and him in holy wedlock but couldn't do much in the way of settling the toilet seat dilemma. So on Monday Pinky took the entire day off from the stamp window and traveled to the county seat of Eden where he officially filed against Mr. Casper Epps, plumber, for failure to deliver one unsanded, unstained, unlacquered wooden toilet ring and bowl cover unit after having agreed to provide aforementioned toilet implementa by way of a binding verbal contract entered into by Mr. Casper Epps, plumber, with Mr. Braxton Porter Throckmorton III, plaintiff, and duly witnessed by the spouse of the plaintiff, Mrs. Braxton Porter Throckmorton III (née Jeeter, Daddy said).

So Daddy said by the time Casper Epps got back to Neely on Monday he was already party to a legal action and didn't even know it, but then Uncle Bill had predicted things pretty much square on and the ill-mannered, irreverent, altogether human plumber who had set out for Decatur on Thursday never came back to Neely, and instead we got what Daddy called the thirteenth apostle, who looked like Casper Epps, drove Casper Epps's truck, and lived in Casper Epps's digs but was not hardly the same Casper Epps all of Neely had grown to abide and put up with. In other words, Daddy said, the redemption had taken, and what was once essentially Casper Epps must have drifted on up to a loftier plain since, as Daddy saw it, there was certainly not much of him left on the one where his feet were. So it really didn't matter that Pinky had commenced proceedings against Casper since even when Uncle Bill heard about it downtown and, his bladder ailment notwithstanding, went at a jogtrot all the way home and burst into the kitchen, where he found Casper sitting at the table gazing off into the empty spaces with his mouth all fixed and stretched out of shape into the sort of grin that Daddy said was appreciably more idiotic than angelic, and yelled out to him on his way down the back the hallway to the bathroom, "Pinky Throckmorton's done sued you," Casper Epps, who did not respond until Uncle Bill Collier showed up in the kitchen again, said only, "Bless him," and grinned a little more stupidly off towards the cupboards.

So when the deputy delivered the court summons Casper had him on into the front room for coffee and talked to him at some length about the Saviour who Casper called just plain Jesus now without the H. Christ tacked onto the end of it, and when the deputy finally managed to get himself outside again, Casper thanked him for coming, blessed him too, and then deposited the court summons in an endtable drawer without ever so much as unfolding it to see what it looked like. Daddy said consequently when the suit came up in the honorable K.

Benjamin Mortenson's courtroom two weeks following, Pinky was at the plaintiff's table with a notepad full of accusations, and Mrs. Bald Jeeter Throckmorton, in her brunette wig and a comely blue dress, had taken the bench behind him along with her sister the fat Jeeter with who Pinky and his wife had managed to patch up relations and who held little Ivy in her arms and cooed at her. The rest of the gallery was about half full of idle and otherwise unemployed Neelyites.

The stenographer came in and sat down at her table just before ten o'clock and then the bailiff announced Judge Mortenson himself, who clamored up onto the bench blowing and spewing like a stuck whale, Daddy said, and who called for the principals in the Epps/Throckmorton suit to approach him there, which got him only the plaintiff since the defendant still had not arrived, and Daddy said the plaintiff and the judge conversed for a minute or two in very low voices until Pinky became of a sudden what Daddy called wildly bombastic and waved his arms in the air and stomped up and down in front of the bench saying, "It's always like this. I tell you the man's no-count, entirely no-count," and Daddy said Judge Mortenson asked Pinky to be quiet but Pinky kept on, so the judge tried to hammer him back to order with his gavel but Pinky still wouldn't shut up, so the judge commenced rapping his gavel once at the end of each outburst and fining Pinky a dollar for it, and Daddy said before the bald Jeeter could get to the bench and bring Pinky back under control he'd run up a tab of six dollars and fifty cents for six complete outbursts and one partial one.

Judge Mortenson sent a pair of bailiffs after Casper and shuffled the agenda some so he could get the whole Epps/Throckmorton business out of the way by the end of the afternoon. So Pinky took up his notepad full of accusations and surrendered the table to the next plaintiff. All the Jeeters and Jeeter-Throckmortons went to get an early lunch in a diner across the street and everybody ate a sound meal but the bald Jeeter who had taken little Ivy into her lap so as to prevent her from getting caught between the fat Jeeter and her plate, and then they all migrated on back to the courthouse where there was still no Casper Epps, even after the stenographer had sat down at her table once more and the bailiff had announced Judge Mortenson who hauled himself back up onto the bench and settled in there again, but before he could finish laying his papers and official documents out in front of him one of the back doors flew open and the two bailiffs that had been sent off earlier hustled Casper Epps up the aisle between them and deposited him at the defendants table, where he sat quietly with his hands clasped in front of him and treated Judge Mortenson to the same idiotic grin he had used on the cupboards. And Daddy said eventually the judge looked out from under his eyebrows at Casper and asked him, "Where've you been, Mr. Epps," and without ever not grinning even for a portion of a second Casper said back to him, "Your honor, I've been mired in sin," and Daddy said the judge looked at Pinky and Pinky looked at the judge and the two of them shrugged at each other.

Well, Daddy said it did not get much more judicial after that but got a far sight more lively, commencing with Pinky, who wagged his newly acquired silver tongue all around the issue and talked some about the toilet seat and talked some about professional responsibility and talked some about Casper Epps himself and then said a few words about justice and made an observation on the quality of mercy which the bald Jeeter had heard before and understood even less of now and which got Pinky gaveled all the way back to the plaintiff's table and told to play dead there. Then it was Casper's turn and he had plenty to say himself but none of it about the toilet seat, Daddy said, and not much of it directed at anybody but just generally aired out for whatever ears it happened to fall on. He said once he'd been lost but now he was found because he stood on Christ, who was a solid rock, and he said he'd never before guess what a friend he had in Jesus until he'd taken to standing on him, and Daddy said according to Casper all other ground was sinking sand including the modest little lot occupied by his Uncle Bill Collier's house where Casper said he had been mired in sin for lo these many years. Then the judge beat the gavel once, Daddy said, and Casper blessed him, and then he beat it two more times and Casper blessed him again and asked Judge Mortenson if he'd ever been baptized and Daddy said for about a half minute the judge played the bench like a jungle drum and when his arm gave out Casper offered to baptize him right then and there in any sort of basin that might be handy, and the judge by way of a counter offer told Casper he could cork himself up or get mailed to Butner in a Shoebox. So

Casper blessed him again, Daddy said, and the judge rapped on the bench one time hard before leaning down towards Casper and asking him, "Are you the same Casper Epps that plumbed a half bath for Mr. Jimmy Lyle in Ruffin," which Daddy said would be the same Jimmy Lyle that had married Judge Mortenson's baby sister, Muffy, and Casper said no he was not that same Casper Epps ever since he'd been washed in the river of salvation, but yes he'd once been that Casper Epps when he was walking the road to hellfire and eternal suffering. So Daddy said the judge pounded the bench again even harder than the last time and said, "Guilty," and two or three voices in the gallery rose up more or less in unison saying, "Shoot him," and another one came in right behind them with, "Please." But Daddy said the judge only assessed court costs and then directed Casper to drag his little sanctified ass on over to the Throckmortons' and fix their new toilet seat to the bowl, which Daddy thought was unusually fair treatment for Casper considering how salvation and clean living had thoroughly washed all the appeal out of him.

And of course, Daddy said, that was pretty much when the romance commenced, and he supposed it was probably along about when the judge said, "Guilty," that Pinky threw both his arms around jurisprudence and clutched it to his heart. As far as the bald Jeeter was concerned, she was just glad to get out of the courthouse only six dollars and fifty cents to the bad, but it was different for Pinky, Daddy said, because he'd been a Throckmorton a whole lifetime longer than she had and so had never had much occasion to get his hand shook and his back slapped, which kept him behind in the courtroom a full half hour after the bald Jeeter and the fat Jeeter and little Ivy had gone on to the car. Daddy said folks told him he had won something very fine, almost noble, and even Casper Epps himself, who Daddy said was so busy turning the other cheek he could have just as well been on a rotisserie, took Pinky's hand and blessed him, and then left Pinky in the courtroom all by himself except for one of the bailiffs who touched his hat and said, "Afternoon, Mr. Throckmorton," and Daddy said Pinky told him "Afternoon" back and then carried himself all proper and erect down the gallery aisle and to the far doorway where he turned on the courtoom one final time so as to soak in the pure feeling of the afternoon and haul it on away with him since it had not been anything to be a Throckmorton for as long as Pinky could remember and now it was something again at last. And Daddy said Pinky probably had not gotten so far as outside of Eden, maybe had not even started the car when he set in to figuring who he'd sue next.

Even after the verdict, what Daddy said Pinky liked to call the Finding, the Throckmortons didn't get their toilet seat right off just like the clerk of court didn't get the eleven dollars' worth of court costs in any sort of hurry. And even when Pinky finally did get his toilet ring and the clerk of court finally did get his eleven dollars it wasn't from Casper Epps that they got them but from Casper's Uncle Bill Collier, who recognized that salvation had fairly much incapacitated his nephew and took matters into his own hands so as to keep Jesus from getting Casper thrown into the lockup. But Daddy said even Uncle Bill didn't exactly crack like a whip so the court costs did not get paid until a deputy from Eden came to fetch away the defendant, and Uncle Bill delivered the toilet seat to Pinky in the most technical sense only since it was Uncle Bill that climbed into the truckbed and it was Pinky that stood at the tailgate and it was Uncle Bill that wrestled the boxed-up toilet seat out from a pile of wrenches and pipe fittings and it was Pinky that took it from him and drove it home in his car. So all that court business in Eden, what Pinky liked to call the Throckmorton/Epps litigation, did not in any manner amount to, what Daddy liked to call, a happy horseshit. But then Pinky held he was only after the satisfaction which Daddy said was fine since that was all he got anyway aside from the publicity in the *Chronicle* which Daddy said brought with it the opportunity for some renewed blustering, and Pinky, never one to pass up the chance to swagger when it presented itself to him, spent the best part of the month swollen up like a blowfish.

But of course, Daddy said, memory of the Throckmorton/Epps litigation soon enough wore off and faded away for most everybody but Pinky, who Daddy supposed was only then truly discovering that he did in fact harbor in his breast a burning unquenchable desire for jurisprudence. So Daddy said it was probably along about when the speculation concerning and general talk about Pinky's day in court had come as near to ceasing altogether as it ever would that Pinky began to cast around with his eyes open and his ears pricked up wanting to sue somebody but not knowing who to sue or what for. And Daddy said it wasn't until June, near about a year after the Casper/Epps case, that Pinky finally got himself sufficiently offended to make his way to Eden and file with the clerk there. According to Daddy what happened was that Pinky and the bald Jeeter rented a cottage down at Nags Head on the outer banks so as to take little Ivy on her first vacation to the coast where she could see for herself, Daddy said, what sort of boundless joy there was in going numb in the Atlantic ocean, barbecueing her little carcass on the beach, and feeding the flies and mosquitoes for seven days and six nights. Now just prior to their departure the bald Jeeter had scribbled out a note to the milkman directing him not to leave them any milk, whole or butter, until the following Monday which she had dropped into the metal milk keeper by the side door and which she did not think about again until her and Pinky and little Ivy returned from the seashore along towards Sunday evening the three of them together, Daddy said, a little ragged and irritated from all the fun they'd had.

It was, of course, the bald Jeeter that noticed it first, Daddy said, her being the one that normally kept the house clean and sweet smelling, and she sniffed her way through the parlor and the dining room and on into the kitchen where she told Pinky it smelled like something had passed away behind the wains- coating and was going to heaven a little at a time, and she asked him did he smell it himself, but Daddy said the fresh sea air had played such a tune on Pinky's sinuses that he could have taken his supper in a henhouse and not been the worse for it, so he told her the kitchen smelled exactly to him like the dining room which smelled like the parlor, which smelled like the front yard, and consequently the bald Jeeter rooted around on her own in the cabinets and the pantry and all throughout the refrigerator and then just for the sake of variety she swung open the side door and stepped out onto the stoop where the air was thick sure enough, and Daddy said she lifted the lid of the milkbox ever so slightly and near about a week's worth of indescribable ripeness came boiling up from the bot- tom and over the sides and almost knocked the bald Jeeter off the stoop and into the pyracantha bush under the kitchen win- dow. Daddy said the top had blown off each of the quart bottles and most of the milk had managed to get loose in the milkbox where some of it had crusted up and the rest of it was still stewing away.

Pinky told her she should have left a note, told her they didn't have money to be throwing away on spoilt milk, which was probably the sort of talk the bald Jeeter expected since Pinky could still wring water out of a dry dollar bill, and she told him back she had left a note, and Pinky said, "Uh huh," and she told him she remembered dropping it into the milkbox, and Pinky said, "Uh huh," again. But when she had settled her stomach sufficiently to clean the thing out she found the note for herself stuck to the bottom of one of the quart bottles and she took it on into the house and waved it in Pinky's face, and Daddy said once Pinky had stopped it from flapping enough to see just what it was, he went ahead and blew up right there in the master bedroom. Daddy said it was very probably a Castleberresque explosion only a degree or two less violent since there was not actually anyone present to explode at, and he said Pinky was already talking lawsuit before he got well into the hallway, but the bald Jeeter, who did not share Pinky's affection for jurisprudence, grabbed ahold of him and somehow or another managed to make him into a reasonable creature once again. She told him there wouldn't be any trouble to it, that she'd talk to the milkman herself and get the whole business squared away, and then she sent Pinky off to the post office to pick up the week's worth of mail because she figured the walk would do him some good. And Daddy said the walk probably did him good; it was the mail that didn't because he'd gotten— aside from a Sears tool catalog, a *Reader's Digest*, and three identical fliers announcing the Beef Extravaganza at the Big Apple—a bill from the Guilford Creamery for a month's worth of milk and butter with a note typed in at the bottom of the page asking Pinky to please have his payment in the mail by the fifteenth. So he exploded all over again, Daddy said, and by the time he got home he was already too far gone for the bald Jeeter to do a thing with him. She begged and pleaded and tried to wedge herself between Pinky and the sideboard but Pinky just moved her on out of the way and got the pad of paper from the bottom shelf and sat down with it at the diningroom table where he began to draft up his accusations. And Daddy said by midmorning of the following day Pinky was a plaintiff again.

So Daddy said two and a half weeks later there they all were in the courtroom once more, Pinky and the bald Jeeter and the fat Jeeter and little Ivy, and the honorable Judge Mortenson himself saw it clear to call the Throckmorton case ahead of two divorce actions and one custody suit disputed between Mr. and Mrs. Harold Underhill, who had come to despise each other most violently and so could not between them reach any sort of mutually agreeable decision as to who should get the house trailer and who should get the Pontiac. Daddy said the clerk of court called out Pinky's name and he advanced to the plaintiff's table carrying with him his pad full of accusations and the bald Jeeter's note to the milkman, which had long since curdled but still had a little aroma to it. Judge Mortenson, however, did not allow Pinky to sit down at the plaintiff's table but motioned him on up to the bench where the judge had a note of his own, this one from the dairy in Greensboro and which was not an open admission of guilt but did constitute, the judge told Pinky, an offer of two free quarts of milk to replace the ones that got spoiled. Now Judge Mortenson said he considered that a fair and just remuneration, but Pinky told him he'd just as soon go ahead and pursue the litigation as long as he was already there, and Daddy said Judge Mortenson leaned down across the bench and put his face right up snug to Pinky's face and suggested that Pinky take the milk and clear out or get his head bit off. So Pinky reconsidered the initial proposition and decided that yes he would take the milk but wanted to know could he have a letter of apology from the dairy to go along with it, and that's when the judge up and asked him to leave, or actually, Daddy said, told him to get out.

So as far as most everybody knew it was two Findings for Pinky Throckmorton and none against him, and anybody who had previously happened to miss hearing about the Throckmorton/Epps litigation heard about it now in the same breath with the Throckmorton/Guilford Creamery litigation, which Daddy said meant that every time Pinky Throckmorton's name came up in conversation it arrived attached to two lungfuls of proceedings, and it got so that anymore, according to Daddy, nobody hardly felt secure enough to even say "Throckmorton" without some manner of legal background. Daddy said most folks agreed you had to admire a man who stood up for himself in a court of law, so most folks admired Pinky, Daddy said, because they agreed they had to. And as for himself, Pinky blustered and swaggered and carried on and mostly got avoided everywhere he went so that it started to look like he'd never again become sufficiently offended to go to court, and Daddy said in fact it wasn't until eight months later that Pinky managed to get himself offended, or if not truthfully and entirely offended riled up anyway, and even then he couldn't haul his grievance all the way to Eden before it gave out on him. According to Daddy, what happened was that Pinky bought a three-inch paintbrush from Mr. Jackson P. Eaton, owner, proprietor, and namesake of Eaton's Hardware and General Merchandise on the boulevard, and he set in to painting window shutters with it on a Friday evening and took it up again on Saturday and once more on the following Tuesday along about twilight when he noticed that the bristles were pulling off from the brush-handle in huge clumps and sticking all over the shutter louvers. So come Wednesday morning off Pinky went to see Mr. Eaton and get some satisfaction.

Now Daddy said over the years Mr. Eaton had formulated a very particular opinion of his line of merchandise and actually had developed a thoroughgoing philosophy on the significance of hardware in general. As Mr. Eaton saw it, the human race could not possibly go without hardware for even two full days on end before most all activity on the face of the earth would grind to a halt for lack of woodscrews, doorhinges, cowhooks, toilet floats, and the like. Hardware, Mr. Eaton said, holds the world together, and Daddy said he was so fond of that sentiment he had it painted on the front plate glass in a half circle. But according to Daddy when it got down to cases Mr. Eaton was not nearly so farseeing or philosophical, which usually worked out fine since very few of his customers came looking to hold the world together; they had just as soon keep their houses from falling apart. But sometimes despite all the mass and volume of hardware that had been nailed and glued and screwed and wedged and bolted and just generally applied to it, a house fell apart anyway, and whenever such an unspeakable thing occurred Mr. Eaton could not in any degree make himself believe it was the hardware that gave out or broke up since, to Mr. Eaton's way of thinking, hardware simply did not give out or break up without, of course, someone to abuse it. So

Mr. Eaton thought considerably more of his merchandise than of his customers, and Daddy said the most accurate Eaton motto certainly had to be "Never blame the implement, blame the implementor," which Daddy said was not painted on the plate glass but should have been.

Daddy said Mr. Eaton had never let his hair grow out much and usually kept it clipped so short that it stood straight up all over his head, and whenever he was faced with any sort of dilemma that required more than ten seconds' worth of concentrated thought he would reach up with his left hand and rub the palm of it on his topnotch so vigorously, Daddy said, it was a wonder he didn't electrocute himself. And so when Pinky brought his paintbrush in on Wednesday morning, Mr. Eaton took it up in his right hand, set in immediately with his left hand, and proceeded to become so utterly confounded and annoyed with the sorry state of Pinky's brush that he very nearly set his head on fire. He couldn't even talk at first, Daddy said, couldn't begin to think of the words that would adequately express his dismay, and so he just held the paintbrush up between his face and Pinky's face and looked at Pinky through it which was not so difficult to do since the bristles were gone completely all the way through the middle, leaving Mr. Eaton with what looked like two brushes on one handle. And Daddy did not know whether or not Mr. Eaton could have ever stirred himself into speech if Pinky hadn't said to him, "The thing fell apart on me," and then laughed once and slapped the counter as if he did not quite grasp that he was talking about a piece of hardware.

So of course, Daddy said, that sort of touched off Mr. Eaton, who knew for himself that a paintbrush simply could not fall flat apart without some sort of desperado, Daddy called it, attached to the handle, and consequently Mr. Eaton shook the remaining bristles in Pinky's face and said to him, "You been hammering on something with this?"

"Hammering?" Pinky asked him back. "I been painting with it. It's a paintbrush."

And Mr. Eaton ran his finger along about where the brush was most severely defoliated, Daddy said, and then observed mostly to himself, "Looks like somebody's been hammering with it."

Pinky set the heels of his hands firmly on the countertop,

drew his nose in towards Mr. Eaton's nose, and said to Mr. Eaton, "I generally hammer with my hammer and paint with my paintbrush."

"Well," Mr. Eaton said back to him, "just looks to me like somebody's knocked these bristles loose."

"May look that way," Pinky said, "but I hadn't knocked them loose. They come loose on their own and stuck all over my window shutters."

"Window shutters?" Mr. Eaton said. "You been poking this up between them louvers?"

"No other way I know of to get the paint there," Pinky told him.

"And what you been using to clean the brush with?" Mr. Eaton wanted to know.

"Varsol," Pinky said.

"Varsol?" Mr. Eaton asked him.

"That's right," Pinky said.

"And painting louvered window shutters."

"That's right," Pinky said.

"Uh huh," Mr. Eaton said back to him, and laid the brush down directly in between them on the countertop. "Well, there's your problem then. You've got bristle stress compounded by an improper solvent, and I don't know of any brush that'll hold up under such as that."

"Bristle stress?" Pinky said.

"That's right," Mr. Eaton told him. "Let me show you something." And Mr. Eaton led Pinky on back to the paint shelf and took up a quart can of tripolene. "Here's what you been needing. Gentle on the bristles, gentle on the glue that holds the bristles," and he handed the can to Pinky, who read the backside of it while Mr. Eaton went off down the aisle where he plucked another can off the shelf and handed it to Pinky too. "Linseed oil," he said. "A man who cleans his brush in tripolene and soaks it in linseed oil won't ever have a speck of trouble with it." And as Pinky tried to read the linseed oil can, Mr. Eaton fetched a brand new three-inch hoghair brush off the pegboard on the back wall and stuck the handle of it between two of Pinky's fingers. "Now I'm going to sell you the tripolene and the linseed oil outright and regular," he said, "but I'm going to give you this new brush at half."

"Half what?" Pinky asked him.

"Half price," Mr. Eaton said, and set out for the front counter, leaving Pinky to follow him on up there.

But Pinky just stayed where he was, Daddy said, and looked at the can of tripolene and at the can of linseed oil and at the new hoghair brush, which was just like the one he already owned but in far handsomer shape, and when Mr. Eaton turned around and discovered he was all by himself at the front of the store Pinky said to him, "You mean I come in here with a week-old brush that's falling all to pieces and you're going to sell me a new one?"

"At half price," Mr. Eaton said.

"At half price," Pinky said right behind him, and then he set the tripolene can and the linseed oil can on the floor, laid the brush across the top of them, and made for the door. And when he got to the front counter he picked up his own bristle-stressed and improperly solvenated paintbrush, Daddy called it, and said to Mr. Eaton, "I don't believe I'll be needing a new brush this afternoon. Seems I might be traveling to Eden. Seems I might have some business there."

"Eden?" Mr. Eaton said, and commenced to rub his head again.

"Seems so," Pinky told him.

So Daddy said Pinky got the brush for nothing and linseed oil and tripolene for half, which Daddy supposed did not seem like much of a victory on the surface but was in fact a fairly staggering concession from a man who considered hardware to be the glue of the universe and who wore his creed on the front plateglass for folks to gawk at. And so after the paintbrush imbroglio, which Daddy said is what Pinky called it, it was Throckmorton/Epps, Throckmorton/Guilford Creamery, and Throckmorton/Eaton, which amounted to two Findings and one Settlement. Now as far as Pinky himself was concerned the paintbrush imbroglio advanced him most considerably in the public mind, especially once he set back in to painting the shutters with what folks called the fruits of the dispute, or with one of the fruits of the dispute anyway, which would be the paintbrush, while he kept the other two fruits in the crawlspace under the house until evening when it was time to clean up and he got the whole crop together. Daddy said throughout most of a Saturday or towards twilight during the week people would pass by Pinky's granddaddy's and Pinky's daddy's and now Pinky's house and they would find Pinky in the frontyard with one of the shutters he'd taken from its hooks and leaned against an elm tree, and Daddy said people would think to themselves how pleasant it must be to get satisfaction, how proper and fitting it must feel to get a finding or a settlement, and Daddy said some people even began to think that maybe there were worse things to be than a Throckmorton.

So Pinky had advanced himself in Neely and had become fairly well thought of by way of his two proceedings and one imbroglio, and even though he didn't go to court again or even get imbroglioed anymore before the mayor's monkey hosed him down Pinky did manage to surrender an appreciable degree of public good will in an episode that had nothing whatsoever to do with jurisprudence. Daddy said near about midway between Throckmorton/Eaton and Throckmorton/Pettigrew, which were themselves slightly over a year apart, Pinky engineered what Daddy called the great pigeon fiasco, which Daddy said was probably a fairly good idea at the beginning but turned itself into a fiasco almost entirely because Pinky was Pinky. The trouble was the pigeons, Daddy said, and the pigeons were at the post office where they roosted on the windowsills. Now when Pinky worked the stamp window he wasn't bothered much by the pigeons since the stamp window was far enough removed from the front of the building to be nearly out of earshot of all the cooing and scratching around that the pigeons did there. But once Pinky got promoted to route supervisor he took an office on the second floor where he had his own window and his own windowsill and his own assortment of pigeons and pigeon droppings.

Daddy said there has never been any great hue and cry against pigeons in Neely, and he didn't imagine Pinky started out much less inclined towards them than anybody else. He said pigeons simply aren't the sort of thing people tend to get worked up over. They walk through them when they have to and feed them when they want to, and Daddy said as for the pigeons themselves they generally aren't even the slightest bit engaging and don't offer hardly anything to ponder or admire except maybe the near miraculous way they have of turning four ounces of seed and breadcrumbs and hulled peanuts into two pounds of pigeonshit, which mostly gets left on win-dowsills or on Colonel Blalock's sword or the top of his head and so is generally removed enough to be wondered at without having to be smelled too. So Daddy said as far as he could tell, nobody much in Neely has ever been charmed to tears by a pigeon. But then nobody much had ever been set into a rage by one either, at least not until Pinky who moved upstairs assuming he would be alone there and then discovered that he wasn't. What he thought would be a private office turned out to be a sort of duplex with him on the inside of the glass carrying on postal service business and anywhere from one to a dozen pigeons on the outside of the glass carrying on nature's business in addition to the usual preening and squawking and gurgling at each other the way pigeons do.

Daddy said Pinky couldn't stand the commotion right off, didn't even have to wait not to like it, and he spent the best part of his first week upstairs walking back and forth from his desk to the window where he would tap on the glass with his finger and so spook the pigeons off the sill. But soon enough, of course, Pinky saw that this was no way for a thinking man to do things and so took himself down to the post office base-ment where he hunted up an old mophandle and some twine and rigged himself a window-tapping device by suspending the mophandle horizontally from the ceiling and near enough to his desk so that he could draw it back without having to get up and then let it loose to swing against the window glass like a battering ram. And at first, Daddy said, every time the rounded end of the mophandle thunked against the pane the pigeons liked to killed themselves getting away, and after a day or two a thunk from the mophandle would still empty the window sill but the pigeons were a little more casual about it than they had been previously, and after a solid week of near constant thunk-ing all the pigeons who had any claim to Pinky's windowsill got to the point where they knew nothing was coming aside from the thunk itself and so didn't bother to go anywhere but just sort of looked at the mophandle and appeared rather annoyed on account of it. So whereas Pinky started out by swinging the thing back and letting it loose, he began pushing it some to get a louder report, and once the pigeons got accustomed to that he pushed it harder still, and once the pigeons got accus-tomed to that he threw it once and it sailed on through the

window light and dangled against the side of the building but
did drive the pigeons off the sill temporarily.

So Pinky gave up on the mophandle, Daddy said, and instead
consulted on the matter with Mr. Donzo Scales, the post office
janitor and handy man who, at the time of the pigeon fiasco,
had been in the government's employ for just shy of half a
century and appeared to get by very comfortably on his wages
since in the course of the years he had managed to become
nearly all stomach. Daddy said around Neely Mr. Donzo had
come to be known as Lawd Scales because most every time
he opened his mouth it was either lawd yes or lawd no or lawd
something or other, and when Pinky got with him about the
pigeons Mr. Donzo said lawd no he didn't know just what to
do about them, but lawd he guessed he'd think on it, and lawd
yes he'd come up with something, which he did, Daddy said,
and almost immediately. Mr. Donzo cut a piece of three-quarter-
inch plywood into a rectangle the size of Pinky's windowsill
and then hammered a couple of hundred nails through it, Daddy
said, so that it looked like a swami's bed. Then he carried it
up to Pinky's office and put it in the sill and him and Pinky
stood back from the window some and watched the pigeons
try to land on it, which they could not do at first with any sort
of success and so they would beat and flap and hover all around
the thing and attempt to make out just what in the world it
was. Of course, Daddy said, all the beating and flapping and
hovering made more of a racket than any sillful of pigeons had
managed to stir up previously, but Pinky's and Mr. Donzo's
view of it was that as soon as the pigeons realized they could
not sit very restfully atop the pointy ends of two hundred nails
they would give over Pinky's windowsill for some flatter, less
pointy place. So Pinky put up with all the increased flutter and
hubbub, abided it, Daddy said, not exactly optimistically and
serene but with the aid of an assortment of threats and abusive
phrases which he would throw up the sash and deliver to any
departing pigeons and which Daddy said were absolutely unre-
peatable but extremely creative and were usually punctuated
by "Goddamwellbetterleave" and the sound of the panes rattling
as Pinky slammed the sash shut.

And in the middle of the second week most of the commotion did die down, Daddy said, but unfortunately for Pinky
it was just the beating and the flapping and the hovering that

went away and not the pigeons who did not give up Pinky's new spiked windowsill but simply adapted to it. After a full ten days of thorough experimenting the pigeons figured out that they could latch onto the outside row of nails with their little feet and then lower themselves onto the points and sit there on their stomachs without hardly any discomfort. So when the beating and flapping and hovering left off, the preening and squawking and gurgling picked up again, and Pinky could hardly sit down at his desk from shooing off one batch of pigeons when he'd look up to find a half dozen new ones lolling on the tip ends of the nails like Asian mystics. According to Daddy this is the best illustration he has ever come across of why the world is thick with pigeons, and it is and ever has been his theory and hypothesis that if a man could somehow manage to crossbreed a pigeon with a mule he'd have himself an absolutely indestructible creature.

So the piece of nailed plywood wasn't really doing the trick, Daddy said, but Pinky stuck with it for a full week after the pigeons began to occupy the nail points just in case they were not actually comfortable there but had instead all agreed to suffer for the sake of antagonizing him. Daddy said Pinky had simply begun to suspect more of pigeons than they were able to be guilty of, and when he'd enter his office in the morning and switch on the light whatever pigeons might be littered across the spiked windowsill would glance at Pinky with one eye and then coo and rustle enough among themselves to make his ears burn until lunchtime. So the pigeons got next to Pinky, Daddy said, and soon enough he became dissatisfied with merely shooing them off the sill and began to speculate on and devise a plan for the capture of a single specimen to be flushed down the men's room toilet as an example to the others, notwithstanding Mr. Donzo's assurances that no toilet in the building could effectively accommodate anything larger than a sparrow. But even before Pinky had entirely formulated his scheme, actually even before he had halfway finished all the speculating and devising that was called for, he slipped out of his chair and onto the floor one afternoon when the windowsill was particularly bustling with pigeons and crawled around the end of the desk and by the file cabinets along the wall and snuck undetected all the way to the window jamb where of a sudden he got up on his knees, flung open the sash, and made any

number of desperate and lunging attempts to snatch a pigeon
out of the air, all of which were unsuccessful but one of which,
according to Mrs. Greenly, caused the trouble directly while
Pinky held that three of the pigeons in conjunction were completely responsible, to which Mrs. Greenly said it didn't matter
anyway since the effect on Sweetums was exactly the same in
either case, the effect having been caused by, Daddy said, the
nailed piece of plywood, which, pigeons or Throckmorton, got
knocked off the windowsill, fell onto the post office steps and
bounced end over end down to the sidewalk where it hit pointy
side foremost and very nearly aerated Mrs. Greenly's schnauser
who had not been the same ever since Casper Epps kicked him
and who got worse instantly and lit out across the street and
into the square with Mrs. Greenly chasing behind him hollering,
"Come back, Sweetums, come back to Momma," and the effect
itself being, Daddy said, one frantically quivering lump of
schnauser flesh which Mrs. Greenly hauled on into the post
office with her as evidence in her complaint. And after she had
finished with the two employees at the stamp window, and after
she had finished with the bigger wheels upstairs, and after she
had finished with the post office in general, Pinky and Lawd
Scales together carried the nailed board into the basement and
deposited it behind the heat plant.

And Daddy said once Mrs. Greenly and Sweetums had left
for home and once the nailed board had been safely done away
with and once the pigeons had repopulated the windowsill,
Pinky closed himself up in his office again where he allowed
himself a half hour to stew over the circumstances of the afternoon, and after considerable mental turmoil and distress Pinky
decided that the pigeons had caused him enough humiliation
already to warrant anything he might see fit to do to them. So
he gave Mr. Donzo a pocketful of post office money and sent
him over to the FCX after a sack of any sort of poison that
might be potent enough to do away with a pigeon and shortly
thereafter Mr. Donzo returned with an eight pound bag of rat
killer which the clerk had told him was of course designed for
rats but would polish off any sort of vermin, of which he
considered a pigeon to be one. And Daddy said along with the
rat killer the clerk had provided Mr. Donzo with precise instructions on how to portion it out and Mr. Donzo repeated them
word for word to Pinky, or as near to word for word as he

could recall, and Pinky listened very close to him and said, "Alright," once Mr. Donzo had finished, and then proceeded to distribute exactly half as much simply because Pinky was Pinky and didn't figure there was any call to be extravagant, even with rat killer. It was Mr. Donzo that figured pigeons to have enough on the ball not to eat pure and undisguised poison, and so it was Mr. Donzo that got sent after a box of oatmeal, part of which he distributed on top of what windowsills Pinky had already baited and the rest of which him and Pinky mixed in with poison itself before they put it out on what windowsills remained. So by the time Pinky and Mr. Donzo got done with the oatmeal and got done with the rat poison, the post office was nearly one hundred percent vermin proofed, and Pinky left for the evening supposing he'd return the following day, pick up the little feathered corpses off the sills and then go on with his business unplagued for awhile, and Daddy said Mr. Donzo probably supposed much of the same thing.

According to Daddy, the morning of the great pigeon fiasco dawned bright and calm and even before the bald Jeeter had scrambled up Pinky's eggs, half the town was out in the daylight taking the air, so when the commotion kicked up it had an audience that Daddy said was already extremely thronglike long before Mr. Donzo got around to calling the sheriff and the fire chief, probably before he ever thought he would have to.

Daddy said Pinky stopped dead before he ever started out across the square and looked at the crowd and at the pump truck and at the top of the sheriff's hat, which is all he could see of him, and then at Mr. Donzo, who had momentarily set onto the pavement the tin trashcan he'd been carrying with him up and down the street and who had commenced to wave his arms over his head and scream, "Lawd Lawd, Mr. Pinky, Lawd Lawd!" Daddy said the air all around and above Mr. Donzo was thick with pigeons that had bailed off the post office windowsills in twos and threes and were plummeting earthward and expiring, Daddy called it, against the pavement. And Daddy said once Mr. Donzo left off waving and Lawd Lawding, he took up the trashcan by the handles again and attempted to run under and catch as many pigeons as he possibly could which turned out to be no pigeons whatsoever since Mr. Donzo could not very agilely carry both the trashcan and his own stomach and since he could not get well underway after one pigeon without seeing four more in four different directions and setting out after them too, which meant that Mr. Donzo got no pigeons at all and hardly went anywhere. And Daddy said once Pinky made his way through the crowd and stepped into the street, Mr. Donzo stopped from his pigeon collecting long enough to say, "Lawd Lawd, Mr. Pinky, we done it now," and according to Daddy for a moment or two it looked like Mr. Donzo might expire against the pavement along with the pigeons.

In the opinion of the clerk at the FCX, who had been called in by Sheriff Browner to analyze the predicament once all the details and circumstances of it had finally been disclosed, Mr. Throckmorton and Mr. Scales had failed to portion out adequate doses of the substance in question and so had succeeded in making the pigeons as a flock, the clerk said, feel somewhat puny along about midnight and deteriorate until morning when they became outright and convulsively incapacitated, all of which, Daddy said, meant that the pigeons were too sick to fly but heavy enough to fall which they would not have done at all if Pinky had allowed and distributed enough rat killer to knock them over dead where they were. So the pigeons as a flock, Daddy said, crept to the edges of their respective windowsills and threw themselves into the street, flapping a few times on the way down for effect, and Daddy said there was such an abundance of outright and convulsive incapacitation, not to mention pigeons themselves, that Mr. Donzo and Pinky and Sheriff Browner and a firehouse lieutenant and the clerk from the FCX could hardly gather up the most recently expired batch before another one had already launched itself towards expiration, and Daddy said Mr. Donzo's trashcan was all but filled up with deceased birds before it even began to look like there might in fact be an end to all the carnage, Daddy called it, and finally after a half minute with no pigeons whatsoever either landing or falling or departing from the post office, some one of the crowd said out loud to everybody else, "That's it. That's all of them," but before the sound of his voice could die well away another pigeon pitched himself into the air and sailed gloriously down to the pavement. Then a full minute passed, Daddy said, with no sign of a live pigeon anywhere, and this time it was several people that said, "That's it. That's all of them," which they had not even finished saying when three more birds hit the street. And then after a good minute and a half with no expirations, everybody but Sheriff Browner and Pinky and Mr. Donzo said more or less together, "That's it. That's all of them," and it finally seemed like maybe it was until after five or six pigeonless minutes, a pair of birds staggered into view on opposite ends of the post office and entertained the crowd with what was pretty much a synchronized expiration, and then everybody looked and waited and nobody said anything, but nothing else happened, Daddy said, because that was it. That was all of them.

Sheriff Browner didn't charge Pinky or Mr. Donzo either with any sort of misdemeanor, didn't even issue them a citation for littering. According to Daddy, all the sheriff did was to tell Pinky that if he were him he didn't believe he'd do any such thing again, which was not in any way a threat but just a piece of advice the sheriff thought Pinky ought to have. And Daddy said Pinky told the sheriff back that as far as he knew he'd poisoned all the pigeons he was ever going to poison. Now the crowd itself, Daddy said, very obviously appreciated the diversion and probably, as a crowd, did not yet know that it had witnessed an atrocity, though Daddy imagined one or two among them could possibly have suspected that a pigeon massacre might be an atrocity but most likely were not exactly sure if it was or it wasn't, and Daddy said in fact the pigeon fiasco did not officially become an atrocity until the witnesses had circulated various accounts of it which were filtered through, expanded upon, and recirculated by an ever increasing number of non-witnesses until finally two or three or four or maybe even a half dozen versions of the story reached the little pink shell-like ears, Daddy called them, of Mrs. Ira Penn and Miss Joyce Tullock who were respectively the president and vice-president of the Neely chapter of the DAR and together set aside ten minutes of the Wednesday luncheon for a debate and vote on and condemnation of Mr. Pinky Throckmorton's high crime against pigeondom, Daddy called it, which the ladies elected to be an atrocity and very soundly condemned along with Pinky himself while at the same time taking no official action against Mr. Donzo who was an old, fat, uneducated negro which, Daddy said, they figured to be condemnation enough.

So Daddy said what on Tuesday had been your simple fiasco got elevated to an atrocity lunchtime Wednesday and then was distributed as such on the bottom half of the front page of the Thursday *Chronicle*, and consequently all those people who were previously not exactly sure if a pigeon massacre was or was not an atrocity got told for certain that it was and all those people who had not even suspected that it might be also got told that it was and so at least had to consider the possibility whereas otherwise, Daddy said, they probably would have just gone around ignorant and would never even have suspected that Pinky was guilty of atrociousness. But he was, Daddy said, anyway Mrs. Ira Penn said he was right there on the bottom half of the front page of section A of the *Chronicle*, which is actually the only section aside from the advertising inserts which are called section B but are not a section at all and are only stuck inside of section A, according to Daddy, in order to make the *Chronicle* feel like fifteen cents worth of newspaper. At first Mrs. Ira Penn said she was "scandalized" by what Mr. Pinky Throckmorton had "instigated," which would be the pigeon fiasco, and then she said she was "scandalized and distressed," and then she said she was "scandalized, distressed, and deeply saddened," and as far as Mrs. Ira Penn saw it Neely could not yet but would soon "fathom the myriad reverberations of the innumerable death knells sounded Tuesday last for the companions at our feet," all of which the reporter Mr. Upchurch called "pigeons" in parentheses. And Daddy said even though Mrs. Ira Penn could not tick off any specific reverberations right at the moment, just the hint of some on the way stirred up about half of Neely, which would be mostly the female half since not much of the male half paid any attention to Mrs. Ira Penn except for Mr. Ira Penn, who Daddy said was the sort of man who always knew what was good for him.

But Daddy said even after the pigeon fiasco had been officially declared an atrocity and played up as such in the newspaper, nothing much came of it except for an abundance of fiery talk directed mostly at Pinky but partially at Sheriff Browner for allowing him to run free, and throughout all of a Monday and part of a Tuesday the DAR did manage to collect eighty-three names on a petition which requested that Braxton Porter Throckmorton III be made legally bound to purchase for the township of Neely one sizeable and undamaged flock of pigeons to be distributed throughout the municipal square and environs, but when it came Mrs. Nettles's turn to make herself the eighty-fourth signee she left the petition untended on the eating table while she went after her spectacles, and Mr. Nettles, who Daddy said never quite ran on all four cylinders, started up a fire in the cookstove with it and nobody much bothered to draw up another one. So the petition business sort of piddled out and all variety of speculation on and discussion of pigeons died down some and Pinky and the bald Jeeter stayed close to home until the whole atrocity business could blow over, which it eventually did, Daddy said, with the help of a national convention of the DAR in Nashville, Tennessee, what Daddy called a Dowager Jamboree, which so thoroughly distracted the members of the local chapter that they forgot all about the pigeon issue since packing for Nashville did not leave them much time to help sustain the outcry against those innumerable death knells, and so the outcry itself, Daddy said, left off reverberating entirely.

Pinky got off the hook, then, or anyway got pretty much shed of the pigeon fiasco once the whole local unit of the DAR chartered out the First Baptist Church activity bus and headed west for the weekend, and when they returned to Neely all blue-blooded afresh and historically agitated anew, a trashcan full of poisoned pigeons did not seem such an atrocity anymore, and Daddy said not Mrs. Ira Penn nor Miss Joyce Tullock nor any single woman or group of women in or around Neely could appreciably rejuvenate in themselves, or in anybody else for that matter, even the slightest degree of the pigeon hubbub they'd all helped to stir up previously, so all organized opposition to Pinky Throckmorton's pigeon fiasco fell off to nothing, or next to nothing anyway, and Daddy said it began to look like Pinky might recover after all and maybe even bluster once again, but anymore it was not just the bad feeling of the women he had to overcome; the men of Neely had gone a little sour on him too. Now Daddy said if it had just been the women, Pinky would probably have been alright since women are generally opposed to swearing and drinking and pool playing and just about every other thing that makes life worth living, while, according to Daddy, men are generally in favor of them and so most regularly feel obliged to come out on the side of most everything that women come out against. And as far as Daddy knew, no self-respecting native gentleman had ever had a civilized word to say about the local flock of pigeons while they were alive and were not exactly shot through with remorse now that they were dead, so it wasn't the pigeons that did Pinky in, it was just Pinky, and not even Pinky really, Daddy said, but only near ceaseless, interminable, neverending, everpresent talk of Pinky from the women, which meant Pinky Throckmorton to digest over breakfast, during lunch and at the supper table, which meant the evening air all ripe with Pinky Throckmorton, which meant Pinky Throckmorton in the bedroom at night with the house dark after an entire day of Pinky Throckmorton with the sun in the sky and the lights burning. But of course it wasn't just Pinky alone, Daddy said, since talk of Pinky naturally led to talk of Bubba and talk of Bubba led to talk of Poppa and talk of Poppa led to talk of the former Miss Fuller and her Momma and Daddy, the prophetess and the Latter Day Saint—Quaker, and her older sister who was still a Miss Fuller and so gave cause for some comment. And Daddy said once folks had followed the Throckmorton-Fuller line of descent until it narrowed down into a deer run and dead-ended in a thicket, they would light out in the other direction and theorize as to why the bald Jeeter was bald or why the fat Jeeter was fat or just generally wonder at the sorry state of the Jeeter chicken ranch which was going rapidly to pot since the Jeeters had only inherited chickens and so had not been raised to any understanding of them which, according to Daddy, is about as necessary as the henhouse itself. Consequently, what the men of Neely got fed up with did not have much of anything to do with pigeons or rat poison or any sort of atrocity that Pinky might have been the cause of. It was the women that objected to what Pinky did. As for the men, they just got wore out on hearing about it and hearing about Pinky and hearing about all of Pinky's connections, and Daddy said the male portion of Neely had gone such an unreasonably long time with some manner of Throckmorton to digest at every meal that it got where even the sight of a Throckmorton or a Fuller or a Jeeter could set off a severe case of acid stomach in any number of people.

And that was about how things stood, Daddy said, when Pinky got his shirtsleeve in the way of Junious Pettigrew's private functions, which he managed to do nearly a full year after he had successfully made himself what Daddy called atrocious and ubiquitous by means of an eightpound bag of rat poison. Of course, Daddy said, by the time the monkey hosed off Pinky's shirtsleeve by way of Mr. Chester Amos's straw fedora, talk of Pinky had died down considerably, and it had probably been four or five months since the sight of a Throckmorton or any Throckmorton relation had inspired anything more than a little mild heartburn and certainly no fullblown indigestion. But Daddy said nobody much had left off being sour on Pinky, and so when the monkey emptied himself onto Pinky's sleeve by way of the crown of Mr. Amos's straw fedora most everybody was pleased and satisfied at the sight of Pinky hopping all around the sidewalk with his shirtsleeve between his fingers, everybody that is except for Mayor Pettigrew and Miss Myra Angelique, who were just before getting litigated, and maybe not the monkey either, who Daddy said was probably only relieved. And Daddy supposed even Pinky himself was pleased and satisfied since Throckmorton/Guilford Creamery had been his last official dose of jurisprudence and that had gotten itself all settled up before he could even begin to carry on about justice and mercy and the aroma of spoilt milk, so Daddy imagined prior to Pinky there had never been a man anywhere who got pissed on by a monkey and found it pleasing.

As for the mayor, Daddy said he did not much want matters to carry so far as the courthouse, and even after he'd offered to launder Pinky's hosed-off shirt, to which Pinky said No sir, and even after he'd offered to buy Pinky a brand new unsprinkled shirt, to which Pinky said No sir also, the mayor went ahead and took a half a day to drive all the way to Greensboro on Pinky's account where he bought for Pinky two very finely made white shirts with tapered tails and a striped blue and grey necktie that had a 1937 Plymouth worked into the design of it. But along about early evening when the mayor stopped off to see Pinky so as to give him the shirts and the necktie and attempt to settle up things before they got so far as Eden, he never saw anybody but the bald Jeeter and little Ivy Throckmorton since Pinky refused to come down out of the master bedroom and discuss a settlement and would not even consider one where he was. The bald Jeeter, of course, did not share Pinky's passion for jurisprudence and did not hardly feel as comfortable behind the plaintiff's table as Pinky did, and as for little Ivy the only thing she knew about Throckmortons was that she was one, so the two of them together were hardly as hot for a legal action as Pinky was, and little Ivy sat in the mayor's lap while he took coffee and sugar cookies with the bald Jeeter and they all three tried to figure their way out of the litigation, though the mayor and the bald Jeeter did most of the talking since little Ivy knew slightly less about litigations than she did about Throckmortons.

The bald Jeeter told the mayor how all the monkey drippings had come clean out of Pinky's shirtsleeve and the mayor asked her did that satisfy Pinky any, but the bald Jeeter said Pinky told her it wasn't so much his shirt that had been pissed on—if the mayor would see clear to pardon her—but his dignity. And the mayor said that sounded awfully familiar to him. Then Daddy said the mayor asked the bald Jeeter if she thought maybe two new shirts and a silk necktie from Greensboro would settle Pinky down any, and the bald Jeeter certainly could not have thought so but said she did and the two boxes with the shirts in them and the box with the necktie in it went with her up the stairs and into the master bedroom but promptly came back down the steps by themselves and lay piled up in the foyer for a few minutes until the bald Jeeter arrived to pick them up and carry them on back into the parlor, where she told the mayor, "Pinky says thank you anyway." So Daddy said the mayor asked her had Pinky gone to Eden yet and filed, and the bald Jeeter said yes he had. And the mayor asked her was it at all likely that Pinky might unfile, and the bald Jeeter said he'd die first.

Seeing how things stood, then, the mayor set about formulating some manner of defense for him and Sister's monkey, or anyway he intended to formulate a variety of strategies and arguments, but being the accomplished piddler that he was, he let most all of the formulating go until the summons arrived directing him and Miss Myra Angelique and the Pettigrew chimpanzee to show themselves in the Eden courthouse on the morning of April the twenty-second, and consequently it struck home with the mayor that he'd best set about some genuine formulating and devising, Daddy called it, before it was too late. So on the evening of April the fifteenth the mayor sat down at the paymaster's desk his daddy had bought for himself and scratched around in most all the nooks and drawers after a clean piece of paper which he found eventually but not until he'd come across a pile of old snapshots that had to be laboriously piddled through followed by a pair of letters to his momma from his Grandmomma Bennet, neither of which was entirely decipherable and so required what Daddy called perusal, and once he'd done with the snapshots and done with the letters and opened the drawer where the clean paper was he found beside the pile of it a steel cylinder that had previously been a piece of something else and owned up to several movable parts itself, including a spring down the shaft of it which more than anything set the mayor to fiddling with it and wondering at it and speculating over it. And Daddy said he still had not satisfied himself that he knew precisely what it was or even generally what it was when he managed to return it to the drawer and take up several sheets of paper instead. Then he had to find himself a pencil, Daddy said, but the search for it did not lead to much more than several bobby pins and a postage stamp from Portugal since the mayor already knew where the pencils were before he ever started looking. So with the paper before him and the pencil in his hand the mayor set in to formulating and devising and he pondered his alternatives for a number of minutes before he finally licked the pencil point and wrote "April 22" in the top righthand corner of one of the sheets. Well, Daddy said that satisfied the mayor for a while and he passed a quarter hour cleaning out his ears with the eraser before licking the lead tip again and applying it and himself to near about the middle of the page, where he drew an automobile tire and then a fender above it and above that what started out to be a running light but turned into a poplar tree somewhere along the way. Beside the poplar tree he drew a dappled mare in profile and then another tree off its flank, what Daddy said looked most like some sort of hybrid maple— and next to the maple he drew a little pond for it to be on the bank of, and along the rest of the shoreline where the maple tree wasn't he drew a variety of shrubbery and several clumps of cattails underneath a pair of which he sketched a very flattering likeness of Franklin Roosevelt from the necktie knot up. Then he left off drawing for a spell and with his incisors gnawed most every gnawable portion of the pencil shaft before licking the lead point again and setting it back to the paper, and he didn't draw anything this time, Daddy said, but didn't write anything either, at least not until he'd picked the pencil back up, licked the point yet again, and brought it to the paper once more. And Daddy said when the mayor had sufficiently adjusted his grip so that he was satisfied with it, he wrote all at once and in one extended burst of industriousness, "Good morning, your honor." Then he marveled at what he had done, Daddy said, until he became a little drowsy, got up from the desk, and switched the lamp off.

Now as far as Daddy knew, Miss Myra Angelique must have honestly imagined that Wallace Amory jr. was actually formulating and devising a defense during those seven evenings from April the fifteenth to April the twenty-second when he would close himself up after supper in what had been his daddy's personal office and not come out for anything until near about eleven o'clock. But Daddy said the truth of it was that the mayor sat himself down at the paymaster's desk on the night of the fifteenth only and did not get any further than intending to on the other six nights since instead he would throw himself into his daddy's recliner and set in to studying all his legal alternatives with a section of the Greensboro *Daily News* draped over his face, and Daddy said around eleven o'clock the mayor would just naturally wake up and haul himself on to bed. So from the hours her brother kept in the office after supper, Miss Myra Angelique assumed he was formulating and devising somewhat successfully, and since the mayor always washed the newsprint off the end of his nose before she could see it, she did not learn then and did not ever know, as far as Daddy could tell, that when her and the mayor and Mr. Britches, who was still Junious at the time, arrived at the Eden courthouse the mayor's argument in their defense was dominated mostly by a pencil sketch of Franklin Roosevelt. And Daddy supposed Miss Myra Angelique could not have even been made to believe that when the mayor and her and the monkey came up on Judge Mortenson in the hallway and the mayor said to him, "Good morning, your honor," he had used up the extent of his prepared notes.

So for her part, Daddy said, Miss Pettigrew approached the defense table all confident and calm and with Mr. Britches in her arms. Britches was the culprit in the case and made quite a splash in the halls of justice, Daddy called it, with his porkpie hat and plaid blazer and green bathtowel underwear that Miss Pettigrew had outfitted him with purely for the sake of modesty. As for the mayor, Daddy could not recall that he looked much of anything but maybe numb and a little terrified, and he carried in his arms an oversized paper shopping bag that he could not make quiet no matter what he did and which he caught on a newell post just short of the defense table and very nearly ripped all to pieces. And as for the courtroom itself, Daddy said the whole place was absolutely slam full up with people, most of them from Neely, a few of them even designated witnesses for the plaintiff, and everybody else just folks from Eden and Spray and Draper who had heard a monkey was going on trial, had never seen a monkey up close before, and so had dropped in for the morning to remedy that.

Now Daddy said of course Pinky had not yet occupied his chair at the plaintiff's table when Miss Myra Angelique and Mr. Britches and the mayor got situated in theirs, and he did not even enter the courtroom itself until just before the judge did, which Daddy said Pinky must have supposed to be the mark of a seasoned litigator, so he blew on in the back doors and up the aisle and fairly much wrestled with his chair until he got it under just what part of the table pleased him best. Then he slapped his customary list of accusations down on the tabletop before him and let loose most all his breath in one windy blast. Daddy said the mayor certainly heard all the commotion of Pinky's arrival but probably did not see hardly any of the plaintiff's entrance since at the time he was otherwise engaged with the clerk of court who wanted to know if the monkey had a name so that he could make a proper announcement of the case since it was not just Throckmorton vs. Pettigrew but was instead Braxton Porter Throckmorton III vs. the Pettigrew Chimpanzee, and as the clerk figured it any monkey who went around in a plaid sportcoat and a porkpie hat was bound to have some sort of personalized designation aside from just plain chimpanzee so the clerk asked the mayor what his chimpanzee went by, and Daddy said that's when Wallace Amory decided not to call his monkey Junious anymore simply because he did not wish to bind up his cousin's name with what the mayor supposed would very likely be a court conviction, so he looked at the monkey for inspiration and landed on Mr. Britches instead since they were what he was most noticeably without.

Consequently, it was Braxton Porter Throckmorton III vs. Mr. Britches Pettigrew that the clerk announced to the court

just before bringing out Judge Mortenson, and Daddy said it
wasn't until everybody had sat back down that the mayor finally
got a look at Pinky who was busy adding a few last touches
to his list of accusations and who had behind him for support
a whole benchful of Jeeters including of course the bald Jeeter
and the fat Jeeter and along with them their momma and daddy,
who were neither passably bald nor fat between them, and
along with their momma and daddy Grandmother Jeeter herself,
who was by now so old and wispy that she probably should
have been dead ten years previously but had found something
or another to clutch at and cling to and so wasn't. As for
Throckmortons, aside from little Ivy and her daddy there was
only one in attendance, that being the former Miss Fuller who
had never watched Pinky litigate before and probably would
not have this time if he had not insisted she take the opportunity
to see a Throckmorton succeed at something if for no other
reason than the pure novelty of it. So the mayor looked at Pinky
scratching up a few new accusations with his pencil and looked
at all of the Jeeters and Jeeter-Throckmortons and Throckmortons behind him, and then fished out from the shopping
bag all thirty pages of his defense, which he figured could stand
a bit of elaboration since twenty-nine of them were still blank
and since he did not have for his own inspiration and support
an entire benchful of in-laws and relations but only one sister
to his far left and one monkey to his near left, though of course,
Daddy said, the gallery was just as warm for the mayor as they
were sour on Pinky which might have helped Mr. Wallace
Amory some if he had only known it.

According to Daddy, most everybody was anticipating a
partial midmorning and entire afternoon full of accusations and
arguments and objections and sworn testimony and all variety
of evidence, circumstantial and otherwise, along with enough
gavel beating to drive ten pounds of twenty-penny nails. But
as it turned out, Judge Mortenson was not disposed to any of
it except maybe for the gavel beating, which he opened up
with before asking the mayor and Pinky to get to their feet,
and with the defendant and the plaintiff standing before them
the gallery expected to hear a few stanzas of the national anthem
from the one followed by a smattering of wild bombast from
the other as a sort of prologue to the regular proceedings, but
the judge was simply not disposed to hearing from either one

of them and so set in to talking himself. "Mr. Pettigrew," he said, "Mr. Throckmorton, I've been studying over the facts of this case and have talked to several people who were there to see what happened and have heard from several more who weren't anywhere around but figure they know what's what anyway, and now I'd like to check with the two of you just to make sure I've got everything straight. Is that agreeable to you both?"

And Daddy said the mayor let go with a plain "Yes sir" but Pinky tried to attach an additional dozen or so words to the end of his which got him hammered into silence and directed to stay that way.

"Now Mr. Pettigrew," Judge Mortenson said, "this chimpanzee belongs to you, does it not?"

"Yes sir, I paid for it," the mayor said.

"And you're in the habit of letting him run loose in the frontyard, is that right?"

"Well not loose exactly, your honor," the mayor said. "We generally hook him onto a rope so he won't run off."

"I see," the judge told him. "And you've put up a flagpole for the monkey to climb while he's hooked onto this rope, is that right?"

"Yes sir," the mayor said.

"And this monkey has somehow or another gotten into the habit of relieving himself off the top of this flagpole. Am I correct?"

"Yes sir," the mayor said, "you are."

"And am I right in saying he most usually relieves himself into the same camellia bush?"

"Yes sir," the mayor said, "he does."

"And is this camellia bush on your property?" Judge Mortenson wanted to know.

And Daddy said the mayor told him, "It does grow out through the fence a little, your honor, but the most of it is on our property."

"I see," the judge said. "And when the monkey doesn't hit this camellia bush that grows mostly on your property what does he usually hit?"

"Sometimes just short of it or to the right or the left," the mayor said, "but sometimes I'm afraid he hits the sidewalk and every now and again when the wind is just right his business carries on out into the gutter."

And after the judge had clasped his hands together and set his chin on top of them he opened his mouth and said, "Tell me, Mr. Pettigrew, do most all monkeys relieve themselves the way your monkey does?"

"No sir," the mayor replied, "most monkeys don't. Our monkey was trained to use a toilet himself and still does when he's made to, but the veterinarian Doctor Stockton in Greensboro says the height of the flagpole agitates his bladder sufficiently to make urination almost entirely unavoidable."

"Well, Mr. Pettigrew, did you ever consider taking the flagpole down?"

"We did, your honor," the mayor said, "but according to Dr. Stockton it's better for the monkey to climb and urinate than not to climb at all."

"I see," the judge said and thanked the mayor and told him he could sit down.

Now Daddy said all throughout Mayor Pettigrew and Judge Mortenson's discussion of Mr. Britches's affliction Pinky had managed to refrain from lodging any outright objections but had squirmed and grunted and spewed so that he had succeeded in making an annoyance of himself anyway which put him on sharp terms with the judge right from the start, and before Pinky could even inflate himself properly for his side of the discussion Judge Mortenson glared down from the bench at him and said, "So he hit you then, did he?"

"He most certainly did, your honor," Pinky replied and Daddy said he wanted to vent a little outrage on top of it but the judge beat the gavel once and dared him to.

"And why is it you were where you were, Mr. Throckmorton?" the judge wanted to know.

"I'd just come to watch him, your honor, same as everybody else," Pinky said.

"But then I don't suppose you had a wager on the goings-on like everybody else."

"Well I might have had a little one," Pinky admitted. "I don't exactly recall."

And Judge Mortenson said, "Then I don't guess you'd remember whether or not it was five dollars on the lower right-hand side of the camellia bush now would you?"

And Daddy said Pinky ruffled up a few pages of his accusations before telling Judge Mortenson that yes, maybe that did ring a bell with him.

"And does the fact that gambling is illegal in this state ring a bell with you, Mr. Throckmorton?"

"But your honor," Pinky said, "it was only a friendly wager."

"It was still a violation, Mr. Throckmorton," the judge told him.

"Yes sir," Pinky said, "and I'm sorry for it."

And the judge said back to him, "I see," and Daddy said the judge shuffled his papers some and Pinky messed around in his accusations a little before the judge started in on him again and asked him, "Was it a direct hit, Mr. Throckmorton?"

"Do you mean the monkey water, your honor?" Pinky wanted to know.

"I do," Judge Mortenson said.

"Well yes sir, it was a direct hit," Pinky told him, "but I myself was not the recipient of the fullest directness of the monkey's relief and can only lay claim to having been tributized by a portion of it on my right shirtsleeve."

And Daddy said it appeared for a second or two that Pinky was about half set to step out from behind the plaintiff's table and roam awhile, so the judge took up the gavel as a precaution and asked him, "Do you mean to say it did not hit you directly?"

"Yes sir," Pinky replied, "it did not hit me directly."

And Daddy said the judge looked at Pinky like he wanted to chew him up and spit him back out again. "Well then, what did it hit directly?" the judge asked him.

"Your honor," Pinky said, "the full brunt of the monkey water descended almost precisely upon the very center of the crown of Mr. Curtis Amos's straw fedora, which is itself made from some variety of lacquered wheatstraw and which Mr. Amos recollects to have been purchased at Eaton's Hardware in the township of Neely in the spring of 1943 somewhere along about April perhaps prior to Easter but perhaps not."

Daddy said Judge Mortenson banged the gavel sharply twice, but before he could work himself up to a reprimand with barb enough for the occasion a straw fedora made itself obvious above the heads in the gallery and commenced to swing back and forth like a train signal. "I suppose that's Mr. Curtis Amos's straw fedora," the judge said, and directed Pinky to it with the gavelhandle.

"Yes sir," Pinky replied once he'd turned back around, "that is the hat in question your honor."

"And I suppose those are Mr. Curtis Amos's fingers attached to the brim of it," the judge said, "which leads me to suppose that the remainder of Mr. Curtis Amos is somehow connected to it also, do you not agree, Mr. Throckmorton?"

"I concur with you completely, your honor, on this matter."

So the judge raised his voice slightly and addressed himself to the gallery. "Mr. Amos," he said, "are you in fact attached to your hat?"

And without showing himself yet Mr. Amos replied, "I am, your honor."

"Would you mind standing up, Mr. Amos?" the judge asked him.

"No sir," Mr. Amos said, "I wouldn't mind it." And Daddy said the hat disappeared into the gallery and the judge and Pinky and everybody else waited for Mr. Amos to show himself for the longest while but there was no hat and no Mr. Amos either, so finally the judge said to him, "Mr. Amos, would you stand up please?"

"Why yes sir," Mr. Amos replied, "I will," and stood up.

"Tell me, Mr. Amos," the judge said, "did Mr. Pettigrew's monkey relieve himself directly onto your hat?"

"Your honor, as far as I know he poured most all his business right here," and Mr. Amos held up the fedora in one hand while he indicated the crown of it with one finger of the other.

And Daddy said it looked like Mr. Amos was just before embarking on an elaboration when Pinky pointed to the fedora for himself and broke in with, "Exhibit A, your honor," which to the utter astonishment of most everybody did not even get him gaveled once but only mustered a quick "Shut up" out from the side of Judge Mortenson's mouth, and once he'd gotten the go-ahead from the bench Mr. Amos went on to say how he was probably not the one to tell just what part of the crown the monkey emptied himself onto since he was underneath it at the time and so couldn't see.

And Daddy said the judge told Mr. Amos he appreciated his candor and then came straight out and asked him, "Mr.

Amos, why aren't you here sueing this gorilla since by all accounts he gave you the nearest thing to a bath anybody got?"

"Well it's like this, your honor," Mr. Amos told him back, "all the evidence up and evaporated on me," and Mr. Amos laughed and the judge laughed and everybody else but Pinky laughed and the proceedings got sort of loose there for a few minutes until Judge Mortenson beat them back into the proper mood and addressed himself to Pinky again. "Tell me, Mr. Throckmorton, did your evidence evaporate on you?"

"Yes sir," Pinky said, "it did eventually, but it left spots all up and down the sleeve."

"Well, Mr. Throckmorton, did you try laundering the shirt to get the spots out?" the judge asked.

"Yes sir," Pinky said.

"Well, did they come out?" the judge asked.

"Yes sir, they did," Pinky told him.

"I see," the judge said. "Tell me, Mr. Throckmorton, who was it that laundered your shirt for you."

"My wife did, your honor."

"Did Mr. Pettigrew ever offer to clean it?"

"Yes sir," Pinky said, "I believe he did."

"But you didn't want him to."

"No sir," Pinky replied, "I didn't."

"I see," the judge said, and took hold of his chin momentarily. "Tell me, Mr. Throckmorton, did Mr. Pettigrew ever attempt to give you anything else by way of settlement?"

"Yes sir," Pinky told him, "he did."

"And what was that?" the judge asked.

"A shirt," Pinky told him.

"A shirt," the judge said.

"Well, actually, two shirts," Pinky told him.

"Two shirts," the judge said.

"Well really it was two shirts and a necktie," Pinky told him.

"Two shirts and a necktie," the judge said. "I see." And Daddy said the judge grabbed onto his chin again and studied Pinky or anyway studied the air overtop of Pinky's head. Then he let loose of himself and said, "So you didn't want the shirts?"

"No sir," Pinky told him.

"And you didn't want the necktie?"

"No sir," Pinky told him.

"Well, tell me this," the judge said, "if you didn't want a new shirt, not even two new shirts, not even two new shirts and a necktie, what is it you wanted, Mr. Throckmorton?"

And Pinky told him, "I wanted satisfaction, your honor."

"Satisfaction?" the judge said. "And just what part of you is it that needs satisfying, Mr. Throckmorton?"

"My dignity, your honor," Pinky said.

"Your dignity," the judge said right behind him.

And that was near about the end of Pinky's honeymoon with jurisprudence though nobody knew it yet, certainly not Pinky or the mayor or Miss Myra Angelique or the bald Jeeter or any other part of the gallery, maybe not even Judge Mortenson himself, who would be the one to lay Pinky low and who, Daddy said, had most likely never considered or even imagined that anybody at all could get attached by his heartstrings to such a thing as a courthouse. So even after Pinky had said "dignity" and even after Judge Mortenson had said "dignity" right behind him, nobody knew it was over and everybody watched the judge lay the entire side of his face into his open hand and set about what looked to be thinking but what turned out to be steaming and churning and boiling, and consequently, Daddy said, most everybody expected the judge to say something wise and judicial when he again said anything, so nobody was any less surprised than Pinky when the judge started in like a wildman and fairly much blew up all over the bench. "Let me tell you something, Mr. Braxton Porter Throckmorton the third, you're not gonna find your dignity in a court of law; if you don't have it when you come in here you're not gonna have it once you leave. I can give you justice and I can give you compensation but that won't make you dignified if you aren't already, and I'll tell you this Mr. Braxton Porter Throckmorton the third, you aren't already. First it's a toilet seat and then it's spoilt milk and now it's monkey urine, and here the man's tried his best to make things right with you but you won't take his necktie and you won't take his shirts and you won't let him clean yours. Well I have had it with you, sir, I have had it. Your dignity. Your dignity!" And Daddy said Judge Mortenson took up the gavel and near about brutalized the entire length of the benchtop with it. "This case is dismissed," he said.

For Pinky's part he'd only started to go numb and so could

still make his tongue work sufficiently to get out "But your honor . . ."

And Daddy said the judge pointed the gavelhandle at Pinky and told him it was a good thing there was no law against being a horse's ass. Then he beat on the bench again and said, "Dismissed!"

And Pinky came in right behind him with "But your honor . . ."

And again the judge beat the bench and said, "Dismissed!"

Then once more it was Pinky with "But your honor . . ."

And Daddy said this time Judge Mortenson didn't beat the gavel but stood up with it in his hand and whipped it at Pinky as hard as he could and Pinky tried to cover himself with his arms and all the Jeeters and Throckmortons behind tried to cover themselves with their arms and all the people on the bench behind them tried to cover themselves too, and Daddy said the gavel struck the front edge of the plaintiff's table and kicked up into the air spinning like a pinwheel, and even before it had a chance to rattle across the hardwood floor Judge Mortenson hollered, "DISMISSED!" and lit out to his chambers with the tails of his robe flying behind him.

Of course, Daddy said, the gallery became all unglued with stomping and hooting and whatnot, and some people stood around and told each other how they'd never seen anything like it before while most everybody else tried to reach across the front bannister and slap the mayor's back or scratch the monkey or shake Miss Pettigrew's fingers. Understandably, however, that was not how it was for the plaintiff's relations, who did not get up right away since they had nothing to hoot or stomp about, and that was not how it was for the plaintiff himself, who Daddy said had circled out from the backside of the plaintiff's table and stood alone in front of the bench. The bald Jeeter came up behind him for a half minute and tried to tell him a kind thing and console him but Pinky bucked her away with his shoulders and so got left to himself once more, and Daddy said Pinky stuck his hands in his pockets and studied the floor planking like it was the most sorrowful conglomeration of grooved boards and ten-penny spikes he'd ever had the misfortune to stand on and look at. Daddy said plain and simple it was Poppa all over again.

As Daddy recollected it, the mayor broke loose from the

crowd first hauling his shopping bag behind him and then Miss Myra Angelique and Mr. Britches made their way clear of the gallery and approached Pinky from his blind side so that he never got wind of anybody coming before they had already arrived. And Daddy said Pinky looked at the mayor and looked at Miss Pettigrew and looked at Mr. Britches and then looked at the floor again, and Daddy said the mayor told him, "Pinky, I'm sorry for all this," said it right in front of everybody though the gallery was still buzzing somewhat and so probably did not catch all of it. But Pinky still looked at the floor, Daddy said, even after Miss Myra Angelique had told him she was sorry too, which most of the gallery did hear since they had seen what was going on by then and had all quieted down to listen. Then the mayor set the bag beside him and pulled out from it the two boxes with the shirts in them and the box with the necktie in it and he tried to give them to Pinky as he told him, "We want you to have these, Pinky. We owe this to you at least," and Miss Myra Angelique said, "Take them, Mr. Throckmorton, please take them," and Daddy said still Pinky left his hands in his pockets and looked at the floor. So the mayor gathered all the packages up in the bend of one arm, and Daddy said right there in front of everybody he put his free hand on the back of Pinky's neck and told him, "I'd be pleased if you'd have these, Pinky, I'd be very pleased," and not of a sudden but soon enough Pinky said, "Thank you, mayor," and reached out his hands for the boxes.

So the gallery got a double bonus that afternoon in Eden since they had already witnessed a trial nobody had ever seen the likes of before and now they got the chance to hear Pinky Throckmorton say Thank you, which not a one of them could have predicted. And as for himself, Daddy said, Pinky very nearly got alright or anyway became undevastated in a hurry and most everybody decided it was on account of the two shirts and the necktie which the Pettigrews did not have to give to Pinky and did not need to give to Pinky but which they gave to Pinky anyhow because they were decent people. But in Daddy's view the two shirts and the necktie part of it did not amount to much of anything and it was only the decent part of it that counted, because Daddy believes and has always believed that the big and obvious things don't hardly ever make any difference and it is only the countless little things all taken together that ever do or undo what gets done or undone. Daddy said most all the satisfaction the gallery got came from the two shirts and the necktie, but the satisfaction that was Pinky's came mostly from the four fingers and the thumb on the back of his neck which never would have ended up where they ended up if the mayor had not been decent and which never could have undone everything that was undone if Pinky had not recollected that he was a little decent himself. So he very nearly got alright, very nearly recovered from what Daddy called the jilting, and before he left the courtroom Pinky hooked his arm around the bald Jeeter's, and managed to pat Mr. Britches on top of his porkpie and say, "Hey monkey."

v

MR. PIPKIN wrestled his hat off his head so as to allow his ears to breathe for a few minutes and one of the firefighters stood up from the runningboard long enough to climb out of his rubber overhauls right there in front of all of us, and once he had them balled up in his arms he said to Mr. Pipkin, "I's just before suffocating," and then he redirected himself towards what Daddy called the cutting edge of the throng which me and him and Mr. Newberry had become a part of ever since we'd moved up next to the sawbucks, and he said to all of us, "I was, I's just before suffocating." Then he draped his overhauls over a section of firehose and sat back down on the runningboard.

Mr. Pipkin pushed his hat down onto his head and prized his ears back up under the band of it once he figured they were properly oxygenated, Daddy called it. And then, of course, he set in to clawing and picking at himself which Mr. Newberry said was a kind of hobby with the firechief, so it wasn't until after Mr. Pipkin had studied over most all of his wounds and temporary deformities that he said to Sheriff Burton, "Well let's suppose he is, then."

"Ain't no supposing to it, Pipkin," the sheriff shot back at him. "Where you think this sneaker come from?"

And Mr. Pipkin watched the sheriff shake the sneaker at him again, and then he looked up at the top portion of the water tower which was still illuminated by the spotlight on the cab of the firetruck, and then he watched the sheriff shake the sneaker at him a little more before he finally said, "I still don't see no monkey."

And the sheriff told him, "He's up there alright."

"Fine," Mr. Pipkin said. "Then let's suppose he is."

And the sheriff asked Mr. Pipkin if he was a jackass or what.

So Mr. Pipkin just picked at himself and ruffled the hair on his legs until the sheriff agreed to suppose along with him, and then Mr. Pipkin said, "Fine," and left off his hobby for a bit. "Now Myrick here tells me," he started in, jerking his head towards the fireman directly beside him, "that he read somewhere or another how what that monkey puts out'll eat through your clothes and burn your skin up. He says it's like acid and you could probably clean a patio with it."

"Myrick, did you tell him that?" the sheriff wanted to know.

And Myrick shook his head yes he did.

"Well, where'd you read such a thing?" the sheriff asked him.

And Myrick engaged in what looked like thinking for an appreciable few moments before telling Sheriff Burton, "Somewhere."

"I never heard anything like that," the sheriff said, talking to Mr. Pipkin now. "What comes out of a monkey probably ain't much different from what comes out of us. Probably ain't any different from what comes out of Myrick."

"Well maybe not," Mr. Pipkin said, "but let's just suppose that monkey's up on top the tower, and let's just suppose I send one of my men up after him, and let's just suppose that monkey cuts loose all over whoever it is I send, now can you guarantee me my man won't get his clothes eat right off him and his skin all burned up?"

"Listen, Pipkin," the sheriff said back to him, "even if that monkey was putting out straight acid, you and me both know he hasn't had any pressure in years and doesn't do anything but dribble anymore."

And before Mr. Pipkin could respond, Myrick leaned over to him and said something into his ear, so that when Mr. Pipkin did open his mouth again he told the sheriff, "Myrick here tells me it don't matter if it is a dribble."

And the sheriff asked Myrick if he was a jackass or what.

By that time didn't none of us think that monkey had a hope of setting foot on solid ground again if he didn't bring himself down, since to a man the firemen came out for Myrick and his data, Daddy called it, which meant after all the supposing about the monkey Mr. Pipkin finally supposed not him nor any of his men would go up and get it, and as for the deputies they told Sheriff Burton they'd rather not risk being doused with anything that could clean a patio and all three of them appeared set to pluck their badges off their pocket flaps and attempt to retire again if the sheriff pressed them on the matter. So Sheriff Burton set in to casting around for an alternative and after five minutes or so of not much of anything to see or hear except Mr. Pipkin pursuing his hobby, the sheriff told the throng of us there how he had been considering and now had definitely decided upon the formation of a crack monkey retrieval squad composed entirely of civilians, and maybe Mr. Small had stared into the sheriff's ear for about ten minutes too long, I don't know, because he got to be squad leader. Of course nobody much even tried to volunteer except for boys whose Momma and Daddy would not let them climb up the water tower, so it looked like the monkey retrieval unit would be all leader and no squad until Mickey, Carlton, and Jerome Roach stepped forth out of the throngs without any older, more responsible Roach to hinder them since Mr. Roach had gone home to eat supper and Mrs. Roach had gone home to cook it. Now the Roaches had owned a monkey previously, which was at present, of course, reposing in a legal envelope, so on behalf of Carlton and Jerome, Mickey explained to the sheriff how the three of them were highly experienced in handling the creatures which was more than qualification enough for the job since the sheriff was not looking for any qualifications at all, so after five or ten seconds of ponderous examination and review, Sheriff Burton took the Roaches on as squad for his squad leader.

Naturally when the sheriff and his deputies and his newly appointed monkey retrieval squad leader and newly formed monkey retrieval squad collected there in front of us to talk tactics, we paid the most of our attention to them and so nobody whatsoever saw Aunt Willa limp out of the darkness from across the street and slip on up behind us to the base of the water tower, and I suppose she had already said it two or three times before anybody ever heard her say it since she always talked in that same flat, lifeless voice that you couldn't really hear unless you were listening for it and nobody had been listening for it. Then she said it again and we all heard part of it. Then she said it again and we all heard all of it and turned around to find Aunt Willa calling out to Miss Pettigrew's monkey in a voice that could not possibly carry up past the breadsack.

"Come on down h'yer," she said. "Come on h'yer, you ape."

So the throng did an immediate about-face and me and Daddy and Mr. Newberry were suddenly so far off the cutting edge that all we could see was the backs of people's heads, which meant of course that the sheriff and the deputies and the crack monkey retrieval squad and the firemen and the firechief Mr. Pipkin were just as suddenly farther off from the business at hand than we were and, being authorities, none of them could hardly stand it, not even Mr. Small and the Roach boys who figured they were fullblown authorities now too. Consequently, the sheriff and the deputies and the monkey retrieval squad and the firemen and the firechief Mr. Pipkin pushed their way on through the throngs of us there and collected around Aunt Willa who didn't pay them anymore notice than she'd paid anybody else and who was entirely occupied with watching the top rim of the water tower and saying, "Come on down h'yer, you ape" everytime she could get the breath to say it.

Now as it was me and Daddy and Mr. Newberry could hardly hear Aunt Willa from where we were but we watched the top of the tower anyway since none of the three of us had anywhere near the knowledge of monkeys Myrick possessed and thought maybe an ape had the ears to pick up what a human couldn't. But apparently some one of the authorities imagined the monkey could use all the help he could get and so dispatched Carlton Roach after the official sheriff's department bullhorn which was in the trunk of the patrol car Mr. Small had delivered his soliloquy off of. However, even after the bullhorn along with Carlton Roach disappeared back into the throng, me and Daddy and Mr. Newberry did not hear anything in the way of amplification for what seemed an improperly lengthy amount of time, and they didn't find out until the next evening at the viewing that Aunt Willa had refused to talk into the bullhorn at first since she had never talked into one before and would not talk into this one until the sheriff himself put it up to her face and held the trigger down so that Aunt Willa did not have to do anything more than she had been doing already.

So now it was "Come on down h'yer, you ape" in that same flat, lifeless tone but loud enough to sail a ways past the top of the water tower and with some nearly unbearable squeaking before and after it on account of the bullhorn, and maybe it was the squeaking and maybe it was the words themselves but anyhow some one or the other of them drew Mr. Britches out to the top edge of the tower and first we saw the crown of his porkpie followed by his hairy face underneath it and then he looked at us and we looked at him until he drew back out of sight for a few moments and then reappeared a little closer to the ladder from where he looked at us once more and we looked at him again. Of course Aunt Willa continued to call out for him with every breath and probably that monkey had been around her enough to know she'd keep doing it until the last trumpet drowned her out or until he hauled his little self on down the ladder whichever came first. So the next time we saw him he already had one foot on the top rung and was clutching at the railings, and then he brought the other foot into view, the one with the sneaker still on it, and proceeded directly on down the ladder without hardly stopping for anything, not even to relieve himself.

Mr. Britches had just barely touched the ground with his five unsneakered toes when the crack monkey retrieval squad converted itself to a breadsack retrieval unit and the Roach boys set in to fighting for the right to go up the ladder with Mr. Small as their moderator only since he preferred to stay where he was. Somehow or another Jerome got first crack at it and Mickey got slated as his backup just in case he fell off. Carlton was put down for third since he'd been sent after the bullhorn and so had performed a duty already, and Mr. Small was charged with talking a fireman into going up if the Roaches got all broken to pieces in the process and could not continue. But as it turned out fetching the breadsack only called for one Roach, that being Jerome of course, and when he brought it down he was relieved of it immediately by a deputy who was in turn relieved of it by Sheriff Burton who stretched it out full length in front of him and studied it for awhile in silence until he finally opened his mouth and said, "Merita." Then the sheriff unknotted the neck of the sack and drew out Miss Pettigrew's clutch purse which he studied just like the sack itself before he ever began to fumble at the latch of it. Sheriff Burton gave over the breadsack to the deputy on his right once he got the purse open so as to free his hand to reach inside it and remove first one scrawny white rose and then one scrawny red rose, both of which he gave over to the deputy on his left so as to keep his hand free to reach back inside Miss Pettigrew's purse and extract from it not even a half sheet but a quarter sheet of paper folded once in the middle. Then the deputy who had the breadsack, who also happened to have the sneaker, got the purse along with the two of them, and the sheriff unfolded the piece of paper with both hands and looked carefully at the side that had been folded shut before flipping it over and looking just as carefully at the side that had been folded open. And once he'd satisfied himself that he'd seen all there was to see of it, he allowed the piece of paper to circulate among the authorities and the throng crowded in around them, and it was the people in the front who told the people in the middle who told us people in the back that Miss Pettigrew's piece of paper said "heart's ease" in blue ink. So then most everybody was saying, "heart's ease" to himself or to somebody else or just into the air except for the sheriff who had set in to calling for Aunt Willa and so most everybody else set in to calling for Aunt Willa with him but nobody could raise her anywhere. And then the sheriff yelled for Aunt Willa and most everybody yelled for Aunt Willa with him except for the deputy to his left who said, "Sheriff?" And then the sheriff yelled for Aunt Willa again and most everybody yelled again with him except for the deputy to his left, who said, "Sheriff?" And then the sheriff wondered out loud where she went and a whole load of people wondered right along with him except for the deputy to his left, who said, "Sheriff?" Then nobody said anything until the deputy said, "Sheriff?" again, and Sheriff Burton spun around and screamed at him, "What in the hell is it?"

"What you want me to do with these roses?" the deputy wanted to know.

And Sheriff Burton asked him why didn't he stick one in each ear and whistle Dixie.

Mayor

So now they all said it was a romance because she had died on account of it, or anyway most everybody who had ruminated over Miss Pettigrew's half sheet of folded paper seemed to think it was a romance except for Daddy, who had ruminated over the half sheet along with everybody else and seemed to think it was not a romance at all. Even after the roses and the folded note Daddy still called it madness, but now that Miss Pettigrew had thrown herself off the water tower Momma came right out and insisted it was a matter of the heart which Daddy said was only proper coming from Momma since she had a natural leaning towards that sort of thing anyway. So Daddy let Momma tell him Romance outright, which she never would have done except for the roses and the folded note, and somehow or another he kept himself from telling her Madness back. Daddy said he figured he was obliged every once and again to let Momma exercise her leanings.

On the morning of the viewing, which was a Saturday and also the morning after the expiration, Momma called it, Mrs. Phillip J. King dropped by for a cup of coffee in the breakfast room and over a Sara Lee pecan twirl her and Momma together constructed what Daddy called the Miss Myra Angelique Pettigrew shrine and memorial. Daddy himself had started out in the breakfast room, but soon after the arrival of Mrs. Phillip J. King him and his newspaper had traveled by way of the sitting room to the front porch which was the only part of the house where Daddy could get far enough away from Mrs.

Phillip J. King not to hear her and only then if he shut the aluminum storm door and paneled front door both, which he did immediately. Daddy did not have much stomach for Mrs. Phillip J. King. So by the time I got up, Daddy had already put both front doors between himself and the rest of the house and Momma and Mrs. Phillip J. King had already done away with near half the pecan twirl between them. Of course Mrs. Phillip J. King, being what she was, would not let me sit down at the table until I had kissed her on the cheek and had kissed Momma on the cheek and then she asked me if all my dreams had been sweet ones and I tried to tell her "yes ma'm" but she was already talking to Momma again before I could get it out. So I cut myself some pecan twirl and Momma brought me a glass of milk and I tried to dispatch with both of them as I watched Momma and Mrs. Phillip J. King talk about Miss Pettigrew, but I don't guess I have much stomach for Mrs. Phillip J. King either since I couldn't hardly get anything down. According to Momma, the trouble with Mrs. Phillip J. King is she doesn't have to come but from next door and so most always looks as frightful in our house as she does at home, and Daddy says it is a rare day when any neighbor to the Phillip J. King house and grounds gets to see Mrs. Phillip J. King with her hair combed out and her clothes on since she most regularly shows herself in the world looking like something that's just crawled out from the bedlinens.

Momma says Mrs. Phillip J. King is a handsome woman when she puts her face on, but I don't believe Daddy would walk across the street to look at her and I can't ever make myself say "handsome" and "Mrs. Phillip J. King" in the same breath, not that she's a homely woman, or even a plain woman, but just that no amount of handsome on top could ever make me forget what the underneath was like. It just seems to me that Mrs. Phillip J. King is forever preparing to be handsome but never is. Most always when I see her she is punishing herself with some new and experimental variety of beauty treatment that she has read about in the back of a magazine or seen on t.v. and which usually calls for some manner of vegetable or tropical fruit, and every once and again the occasional crushed toadstool, to be mixed together with a specified moisturizer and a quantity of cold cream and then smeared from ear to ear just before bedtime.

So I set aside my milk and my portion of pecan twirl since they both smelled like Mrs. Phillip J. King's present beauty treatment, which seemed to me to have some banana in it along with maybe a touch of sweet onion, and I listened to Mrs. Phillip J. King and Momma tell each other how what Daddy called Madness was actually Romance. Mrs. Phillip J. King said he had been dashing, but Momma would not go along with dashing and said to her mind he had been not unattractive, but Mrs. Phillip J. King couldn't see fit to drop all the way from dashing to not unattractive, so her and Momma negotiated a description and arrived at reasonably good-looking, which was mutually agreeable though it seemed for a minute or two that Mrs. Phillip J. King might hold out to have the reasonably struck from the official version. But Momma went on to tell her how she thought his nose had a fanciful bend to it which distracted Mrs. Phillip J. King away from the reasonably because, as she told Momma back, she had always thought his nose had a fanciful bend to it herself. Mrs. Phillip J. King called it a Roman nose and she said there wasn't anything uppity or snotty about it but it was purely a sign of nobility. And Momma said he certainly carried himself like a Roman, which sparked Mrs. Phillip J. King to wonder if maybe he hadn't come from Romans, if maybe that wasn't why he was a Republican. But Momma said she recalled he was a notable Democrat. And Mrs. Phillip J. King said, "Maybe he was." And Momma said she believed so. And Mrs. Phillip J. King said, "Maybe he was" again.

Mrs. Phillip J. King is what Daddy calls a legwagger so it is near impossible to watch her talk without getting yourself hypnotized or half agitated or maybe a little dizzy and nauseous, and of course I got hit with the dizzy and nauseous part of it once the legwagging and eau de garden salad aroma took up together and came at me. What few bites of pecan twirl I had managed to get down were organizing to come back out for an airing, so I excused myself to Mrs. Phillip J. King and Momma and went off to the bathroom to hang my head over the toilet.

Consequently I was not present when Mrs. Phillip J. King decided she could not let reasonably good looking rest peacefully and resurrected the whole business with the argument that a moustache under that fancifully bent nose would have most certainly made for dashing. But Momma could not see clear to allow for a moustache since there had not been one actually; however, Mrs. Phillip J. King insisted that if Momma could just imagine a finely manicured and dignified Douglas Fairbanks-style moustache under that Roman nose then all of the rest of the features would surely come together and pretty much scream Dashing at her. But even with a moustache thrown in Momma could not sit still for any degree of dashing though Mrs. Phillip J. King campaigned rather fiercely for Considerably Dashing and then Somewhat Dashing and then A Touch Dashing, so Momma for her part felt obliged to retreat some from reasonably good looking and her and Mrs. Phillip J. King settled on passably handsome with Mrs. Phillip J. King supplying the handsome and Momma of course supplying the passably. As a result what had been reasonably good-looking when I left for the bathroom, where I splashed my face with water and managed to recover without giving up any pecan twirl, had already become passably handsome before I could get down the back hallway and into the breakfast room again, so I did not have much of any idea who Mrs. Phillip J. King was talking about when she leaned in towards Momma on her elbow and said, "Pepsi-Cola."

And I looked at Mrs. Phillip J. King and then looked at Momma, who was herself looking at Mrs. Phillip J. King, before I took the chair opposite to the one I'd been in previously so as to put the tabletop between me and any legwagging I might otherwise be tempted to watch, and before I got settled in good Momma laid both her hands flat out in front of her and said, "Pepsi-Cola?" for herself.

I could tell by the way Mrs. Phillip J. King's shoulders jumped back and forth that she was wagging one or the other of her legs to bring the cows home so I set in to counting the rubber grapes in Momma's centerpiece as a kind of digestive diversion and after I'd gone through all seventeen of them I started over again and counted the teethmarks on each separate grape, all of them mine of course since Momma and Daddy do not chew on rubber grapes and do not care for me to, but as for myself I've never found anything more entertaining to chew on than a rubber grape since you can squeeze all the air out of it with your teeth and then attach it by the stemhole straight out from the end of your tongue. Understandably, then, there was at least a half dozen clear and utterly distinguishable teethmarks for every grape, so I hadn't hardly gotten well into the bunch with my calculations before Mrs. Phillip J. King was going on about Pepsi-Cola again. "Pepsi-Cola," she said. "Yes I believe it was Pepsi-Cola because I'm near certain it was Mr. Womble that ran the Nehi outfit."

And Momma set straight up and said, "Helen?" which was what Momma called Mrs. Phillip J. King to her face while I called her Mrs. King and Daddy called her Mrs. Phillip J. King until she got out the door and partway down the sidewalk when he called her the bride of the beast.

But Mrs. Phillip J. King just went straight on ahead and said, "Yes it had to be Pepsi-Cola. He owned the bottling plant you know in Burlington. I mean his daddy, now I don't think he ever owned it himself, but his daddy did and made a killing putting out Pepsi-Cola until he sold the whole business and made another killing doing that. Momma said it was just a ton of money that changed hands. She was brought up in Burlington you know."

"But Helen," Momma said.

"Lord they were filthy with it, just absolutely gloriously rich." And Mrs. Phillip J. King pointed her finger at Momma. "Now you talk about dashing," she said, "his daddy was the picture of it. Momma used to say he had cheekbones up to the hairline and teeth like pickets. And wear a suit, Lord I guess he could. Now of course I never saw him in life and it was many a time I thought Momma was just going on when she had no need to be, but my Aunt Mary, Momma's sister, had kept a picture of him she'd clipped from the Burlington *Courier* and even though Uncle Roy had set a glass on it and left a ring right direct through the center of his face I knew him for a dashing gentleman just from the way he held himself. Momma always said he had the shoulders of a sailor."

"But Helen I thought that . . ." Momma said.

"And they tell me his wife was just a gorgeous woman but not from around here of course. Between you and me, Inez, I'd as soon scour this countryside for hen's teeth as gorgeous women, so Momma said he went out and got one all the way from Delaware or Ohio, she couldn't ever remember exactly which, but I imagine it was Delaware since P.J. tells me," P.J. being Mr. Phillip J. King, "that Delaware is one of your urban states, lying like it does snug up against New York City, and P.J. says it takes an urban state to bring out the gorgeous in women since urban states are where all the money is, and P.J. says there is plenty of money in Delaware mostly on account of the Duponts, and she might have even been a Dupont herself, anyway I don't know that she wasn't and she was probably from Delaware I imagine, which is where they all come from. And lets you and me face it, Inez, money and a proper upbringing can make almost any woman gorgeous. I mean, after all you don't hardly ever see a Loretta Young come popping out from the cotton mill."

I guess Momma had begun to think it would never happen, but finally Mrs. Phillip J. King was forced to take a breath. However, even after what seemed near five minutes of pure exhalation all she did to replenish herself was sip at the air, so Momma must have prepared ahead because the very second Mrs. Phillip J. King switched over from outflow to inflow Momma managed to say, "Cookies," one time fast.

"Now you take a gorgeous woman and you marry her up to a dashing man," Mrs. Phillip J. King went on to say, "and you throw in near about a million dollars just to make things stylish and proper and you can pretty much count on any number of children along about as gorgeous and dashing as they are. They didn't have but two as far as I know, and the first to come along was the girl who Momma said was named Ashley Marian or Marian Ashley or some such and I do believe she got into the last five of the Miss Alamance County pageant that year it was won by the godchild of a friend of one of the judges and so was not ever considered a square contest. And of course me and you know her brother Alton was a handsome man, passably handsome anyway, and I recall Momma telling how he'd been outright dashing in his youth. Cheekbones, Momma said, he was all cheekbones and she said he had this dimple right in the middle of his chin that worked on the women like a bullet, I mean killed them dead."

"But Helen," Momma said, "I thought it was cookies, and I don't recall any dimple."

"Momma told me he grew out of it when his bone structure settled," Mrs. Phillip J. King said. "And he'd already lost all the fine lines to his face don't you know by the time him and Miss Pettigrew struck it up together, so I guess the dimple had just filled in before he ever hit Neely. Momma said it was a fine dimple, a deep and noble dimple. She said you could probably lose your thumb in it."

"And wasn't it cookies, Helen?" Momma asked.

"Wasn't what cookies?" Mrs. Phillip J. King asked her back.

"Wasn't it cookies instead of Pepsi-Cola?" Momma wanted to know. "Didn't Mr. Alton's Daddy make those savannahs with the white cream filling and those little oval shortbread cakes that came in the blue sack?"

And Mrs. Phillip J. King got a little hot on account of the cream-filled savannahs and the shortbread cakes and she said to Momma, "Now Inez, he might have dabbled in cookies later but I can tell you for a fact it was Pepsi-Cola at the first because Momma said it was Mr. Womble at the Nehi and Mr. Foster at the Coca-Cola and Mr. Tod W. Smith at the Sundrop and Mr. Nance at the Pepsi-Cola, and Momma herself told me it was Pepsi-Cola that made him his money but I don't ever recall a whisper of cookies passing her lips. And even if he went into cookies later, the cola business had already gotten him rich enough not to need to. No, I don't recall any savannahs or shortbread cakes in a little blue sack and I certainly would remember that seeing as how I simply adore shortbread cakes."

"So it wasn't cookies then?" Momma said.

"No ma'm, it was Pepsi-Cola that got them filthy with it, and I mean absolutely and gloriously filthy with it. Don't you know Mr. Alton's daddy built his wife a mansion on thirty-seven acres just the Durham side of Burlington, and Momma said it was made out of some kind of brick that had to be sent for from across the ocean. And of course all the fixings were brass you know except for the doorknobs that were made from pure cut crystal and had to be sent for along with the brick. Now the momma and daddy of Mrs. Dupont Nance had thrown in with their daughter a sizeable portion of furniture for dowery, and Momma said it so very nearly filled up the entire house that all Mrs. Dupont Nance had to buy was several wool rugs, which she got directly from the mill there in Burlington, and all Mr. Alton's daddy had to do was get hold of any number of pictures for the walls which Momma said he got from God knows where and which turned out mostly to be pictures of ducks, some of them flying off to the frame on the left-hand side and some of them flying off to the frame on the righthand side and some of them taking off from reedy marshes and some of them landing in them and some of them just bobbing on top of them." Then Mrs. Phillip J. King left off talking and left off legwagging and stared at Momma's centerpiece in a very earnest way until she could get enough breath to tell me and Momma how it seemed to her that Mr. Nance had possessed a great fondness for ducks. And Momma said that was very possible.

According to Mrs. Phillip J. King the reason Mr. Alton ended up as rich as he ended up and got to be as notable as he got to be was because his sister did not inherit anything of what she was supposed to inherit. Miss Ashley Marian or Marian Ashley Nance married a Wainick before she turned twenty and knowing full well that her momma and daddy did not approve of Wainicks since none of them came from much of anything but other Wainicks who did not come from much of anything themselves. Mrs. Phillip J. King said Miss Ashley Marian Marian Ashley Nance tried to tell her Momma and Daddy that her Wainick, who was Frank Wainick, was a different strain of Wainick, a sort of Wainick with gumption, Mrs. Phillip J. King called it, and Miss Ashley Marian Marian Ashley invited her parents out to Mr. Frank Wainick's dairy farm so they might see for themselves what a very clean and proper operation it was. But Mrs. Phillip J. King said that Mr. Alton's daddy and Mrs. Dupont Nance did not take up the invitation and went ahead and disapproved of Frank Wainick along with all the rest of the Wainicks. So when Miss Ashley Marian Marian Ashley got married she did not receive any money and did not receive any furniture, not even a single picture of a duck as far as Mrs. Phillip J. King could tell, and on the day the honeymoon commenced Mr. Alton's daddy revised his will so as to make his daughter a Wainick entirely. Consequently, Mrs. Phillip J. King said, Mr. Alton Nance ended up gloriously rich instead of just plain rich and ended up notable instead of only heard of.

"Now of course," Mrs. Phillip J. King said, "he didn't see much of any money until he turned twenty-one and got a whole load of it, and Momma said he set to racing through that like he might wear out his daddy's fortune before any one of them could manage to die rich. It mostly went towards girls, you know, I mean dozens and dozens of them which is what Momma said and Momma was hardly ever given to stretching the truth. And you have to remember, Inez, that this was probably ten or twelve or maybe even fifteen years before his cheekbones gave way, so he was just purely dashing and gloriously rich and Momma said he could simply wink at a girl and very nearly make her fall over. And of course with all those girlfriends he absolutely had to have some sort of suitable way to get from one to the other, so Momma said he sent off to London, England, for a touring car which came over to New York City in the bottom of a boat and arrived in Burlington on a train. Momma said Mr. Alton himself drove his new vehicle out from the boxcar and onto the platform and folks collected all around the fenders and tried to figure out how in the world he would guide the thing with the steering wheel being where it was." Then Mrs. Phillip J. King told me and Momma confidentially that most people in Burlington were about as worldly and refined as houseflies. "But they became accustomed to his foreign made automobile," Mrs. Phillip J. King said, "and they all got used to seeing some one of his girlfriends or another riding where he should be and him driving where she should be, but Momma said of a sudden it stopped being a whole pack of women that got rode all around town and through the countryside to Graham and Pittsboro. She said of a sudden it was one woman who was really not even a woman yet but was the honorable congressman Mr. Robert L. Dundee's baby girl, Sissy Dundee, who Momma said might have been seventeen at the time but probably wasn't. And Momma said Sissy Dundee claimed the seat beside Mr. Alton all for herself and her and him went around Burlington together and sometimes got so far as Raleigh of a Sunday, and Momma said she heard they slipped off to Richmond once for the entire weekend, but Momma imagined that was just a tale since the congressman and Mrs. Dundee were not the sort of people to bring up a hussy. So Miss Sissy decided that he was for her and Mr. Alton decided that she was for him and Momma said it got so you couldn't have kept the two of them apart with a wall of fire, so of course whenever Congressman Dundee got all his political friends together for a party Miss Sissy and Mr. Alton usually made an appearance which is most likely when he started meeting all those Republicans."

"Democrats," Momma said.

"Democrats too," Mrs. Phillip J. King said back.

Then Mrs. Phillip J. King told me and Momma how Miss Elizabeth Mercer Dundee and Mr. Alton Daniel Nance were joined together in holy wedlock at four p.m. on the fifth of June in between two ligustrum hedges out back of the congressman and Mrs. Dundee's house, and she said her momma told her everybody who was anybody went to watch it except for Mrs. Ashley Marian Marian Ashley Nance Wainick who Mrs. Phillip J. King said was a little miffed with her people and so stayed clear of the whole business.

"They went to Paris, don't you know," Mrs. Phillip J. King said, "for a full month, and Momma told me they stayed at the Ritz Hotel right there in downtown which put Miss Sissy directly in the middle of a whole block of dress shops and which put Mr. Alton near enough to the big museum to stroll to it. Momma said nobody appreciated a good picture like Mr. Alton, who probably took after his daddy to a degree but was able to stand for something other than ducks. And Momma said whenever Mr. Alton got weary from looking at pictures or studying statuary, he would hunt himself up a bench somewhere along about the Eiffel Tower and spend several hours on it reading a portion of what book he happened to be carrying in his jacket pocket at the time. Momma said nobody appreciated good writing like Mr. Alton. And she said whenever Mr. Alton could talk Miss Sissy into it, her and him would go to the opera house after dinner and hear a performance. Momma said Miss Sissy did not have much feeling for music and so would usually spend the best part of the evening trying to see who was looking at her, but as for Mr. Alton, Momma said nobody appreciated a fine melody like he did. She said he was highly cultivated in most every area."

Mrs. Phillip J. King told me and Momma they steamed to England when the month was out, and she said Miss Sissy and Mr. Alton visited around the countryside for several weeks and then settled in temporarily in the manorhouse of a viscount and viscountess who Mr. Alton's daddy's money had gotten him introduced to previously. According to Mrs. Phillip J. King, Miss Sissy and Mr. Alton slept in the actual bed that Queen Victoria had once sat upon to have her shoes removed and her feet rubbed by a serving woman. Mrs. Phillip J. King said Queen Victoria had not been particularly dainty as queens go and so was ever exhausting her arches, she called it. And Mrs. Phillip J. King told me and Momma how as a momento the viscountess gave to Miss Sissy half of a teacup that the Prince of Wales's valet had knocked off a serving tray with his elbow and broke on the floor, and for his part the viscount presented Mr. Alton with a silver-tipped walking stick that somebody or another had left in the front coat closet, he could not remember who exactly but was certain it hadn't been Queen Victoria or the Prince of Wales's valet. Mrs. Phillip J. King said Mr. Alton and Miss Sissy and their piece of teacup and their walking stick departed for New York in mid-August when the viscount told them the weather would be most favorable, and Mrs. Phillip J. King said it would have been except for the hurricane which was supposed to have drifted off in the other direction but did not and so kept the water stirred up all the way across the ocean. Consequently, there wasn't much of anything to do but sleep since hardly anybody could hold a fork still enough in front of his mouth to snatch from it whatever might be on it or to even want to, except of course for Mr. Alton who Mrs. Phillip J. King said had the constitution of a walrus, which she intended as a compliment. So Mr. Alton took his meals alone in the dining room and afterwards had brandy and played canasta with two waiters and a bartender which left Miss Sissy to herself below decks where she could go ahead and curl up beside the toilet on a blanket and not be underfoot.

Mrs. Phillip J. King said Mr. Alton and Miss Sissy had not planned to stop over in New York City for more than an evening, but once the boat docked Miss Sissy was so worn out and dried up that Mr. Alton got them a room at the Waldorf Astoria for a week, and Mrs. Phillip J. King said Miss Sissy attempted to regain her regularity with a near steady stream of chocolate parfaits minus the nuts while Mr. Alton lived almost entirely off of medium rare beefsteaks that he would have brought directly to the room along with Miss Sissy's ice cream. Mrs. Phillip J. King said nobody enjoyed a good beefsteak like Mr. Alton. By the end of the week Miss Sissy was well enough to wander out of the sight of a toilet, and according to Mrs. Phillip J. King Mr. Alton took her out to the parks and the museums and the Bronx zoo and after that to Coney Island where he somehow or another finagled her onto the parachute drop and got her sick all over again. So Miss Sissy went back to her parfaits and Mr. Alton went back to his medium rare beefsteaks only now she took hers upstairs and he took his downstairs since Miss Sissy held it against Mr. Alton that he did not tell her the parachute drop would do what it did. And Mrs. Phillip J. King imagined they would have made it up before they left New York if Mr. Alton had not accidentally knocked Miss Sissy's overnight bag off the dresser and then stomped on it attempting to catch it, all of which pretty much finished what the Prince of Wales's valet had started. So Mrs. Phillip J. King said by the time their train Pulled into the Burlington station, Mr. Alton and Miss Sissy had already begun to dislike each other a little.

According to Mrs. Phillip J. King they set up house in a bungalow just behind Mr. Alton's daddy's mansion and the four of them shared domestics, Mrs. Phillip J. King called them, which simply meant that the maid and the chef and the gardener were ever beating it back and forth from the mansion to the bungalow or from the bungalow to the mansion so as to keep all the Nances from doing much of anything whatsoever themselves. Mrs. Phillip J. King said Miss Sissy gave each of her friends a sliver of the Prince of Wales's valet's teacup and told them all that the Prince himself had hurled the cup and the saucer too into the Viscount's fireplace in a fit of passion. Mrs. Phillip J. King said her own Momma had told her that the Prince of Wales was in fact a highly passionate man, so Miss got by with the teacup story and she kept the biggest piece of the handle for herself and had it strung on a chain and made into a necklace, and Mrs. Phillip J. King said of course whenever Miss Sissy wore her teacup handle necklace everybody who hadn't heard it firsthand already wanted to know just how the piece of handle came to be separated from the rest of the teacup and Miss Sissy would oblige them with her version, which did not remain one version exactly, Mrs. Phillip J. King said, since she guessed Miss Sissy had the Prince of Wales hurling that teacup against most everything in the Viscount's house but the Viscount himself and most times it was on account of the Viscountess who Sissy said the Prince of Wales had eyes for. Mrs. Phillip J. King said her momma told her nobody could tramp all around the truth like Miss Sissy Mercer Dundee Nance.

Now according to Mrs. Phillip J. King Mr. Alton Nance

went around Burlington with his silver-tipped walking stick near about as regularly as Miss Sissy did with her teacup handle necklace, and Mrs. Phillip J. King said whenever people wanted to know where such a fabulous walking stick could have come from Mr. Alton would tell them that the Viscount fetched it out from a coat closet and gave it to him and he didn't know anything about it aside from that. Mrs. Phillip J. King called this Mr. Alton's usual straightforward bearing and she said it was just a part of what people adored in him aside from his natural good looks and sweet disposition.

And once Mrs. Phillip J. King broke off long enough to change directions I managed to ask her, "What's a viscount anyway?"

And Mrs. Phillip J. King told me it was near about the same as a count.

"Like Dracula?" I said, who was the only count I knew of right off.

But Mrs. Phillip J. King said it wasn't like Dracula at all. She said Dracula was an Italian kind of count and Mr. Alton's viscount was an English kind of count, so while Dracula didn't have anything in the world to do but chase folks all over the countryside, Mr. Alton's was all the time being called upon to represent the royal family at parades and such.

"Sort of like a Duke?" I asked her.

And she said yes, a viscount is like a duke who is like a prince only there are more viscounts than dukes and more dukes than princes. Then she asked me did I see what she meant.

And I said, "Yes ma'm" so as to let her get on with it.

Mrs. Phillip J. King told me and Momma that Mr. Alton's father-in-law, Congressman Dundee, threw a welcome home party for Mr. Alton and Miss Sissy right there between the ligustrum hedges where their wedding had been, and Mrs. Phillip J. King said all of Congressman Dundee's Republican friends were there and some Democrats too, she added, and she said her Momma told her Mr. Alton hobnobbed with the politicians and Miss Sissy hobnobbed with the politicians' wives and the men talked about campaigns and fund raising while the women talked about the Prince of Wales who was still a fairly fresh topic in Burlington. And Mrs. Phillip J. King said before the week was out Mr. Alton's Daddy and Mr. Alton's Momma threw a welcome home sitdown dinner at the Nance mansion, and she said all of the men raved over the roast duckling and the women raved over the sauce on top of it and then left the men by themselves at the table where they talked about finances and profits while the women took coffee on the patio and quizzed Miss Sissy on the Prince of Wales. And Mrs. Phillip J. King said it was the next weekend that Mr. Alton and Miss Sissy threw a party of their own on the lawn outside the bungalow, and she said her momma told her half the guests were friends of Congressman Dundee and half the guests were Mr. Alton's daddy's former business associates, and she said the men mostly stood around with their hands in their pockets and talked about baseball while the women continued to dissect the Prince of Wales who they had already very nearly worn out but not entirely.

So Mrs. Phillip J. King said it shaped up that Mr. Alton's daddy's friends and Mr. Alton's daddy-in-law's friends were Mr. Alton's friends too which was fine with Mr. Alton but which also meant that Mr. Alton's momma's friends and Mr. Alton's momma-in-law's friends were Miss Sissy's friends too, which Mrs. Phillip J. King said was not particularly fine with Miss Sissy since that made all her friends old enough to be her mother while one of them was. According to Mrs. Phillip J. King Miss Sissy desired a little more pizzazz in her life than Mr. Alton seemed inclined to allow for. Mrs. Phillip J. King said Miss Sissy needed pizzazz like she needed food, which Mrs. Phillip J. King said her momma told her was on account of Miss Sissy's tropical disposition. "Hot, don't you know," Mrs. Phillip J. King said.

"Hot?" Momma asked her.

"Yes ma'm. Hot." And Mrs. Phillip J. King said it turned out that Miss Sissy had a touch of hussy in her after all.

"A Dundee of the Congressman Dundee's?" Momma said.

And Mrs. Phillip J. King told her, "Yes ma'm. Flat out loose."

And Momma shot her eyes at me and said to Mrs. Phillip J. King, "Unprincipled."

And Mrs. Phillip J. King said, "Yes ma'm. Unprincipled too."

Of course nobody knew right off that Miss Sissy was loose and unprincipled, probably not even Miss Sissy herself. According to Mrs. Phillip J. King all anybody knew was that

Mr. Alton kept on with his Daddy-in-law's politicians and with his daddy's former business associates while Miss Sissy did not keep on with their wives. Instead Miss Sissy took up consorting, Mrs. Phillip J. King called it, with several girls she'd known in school all of whom Mrs. Phillip J. King's momma had told her traveled with a fast crowd which Mrs. Phillip J. King said was the same as loose which Momma said was the same as unprincipled. According to Mrs. Phillip J. King Mr. Alton didn't object to or interfere with Miss Sissy's renewed connections because he had a pure and trusting heart and so most likely did not even suppose that Mrs. Sissy could manage anything sinful, and aside from his pure and trusting heart Mr. Alton, along with his daddy, was at the time pretty thoroughly preoccupied with what Mrs. Phillip J. King called a scorching dispute which sounded to me more in the way of a Throckmorton imbroglio than anything else. What had happened was Mr. Alton's daddy had decided there was really no reason for him to settle for a painted duck dropping into a painted pond when he could have the real feathered kind setting down in legitimate water if he only applied himself to the pursuit of it, so Mrs. Phillip J. King said he did apply himself to the pursuit of it and applied Mr. Alton to the pursuit of it also which gave the both of them something to do since Mr. Alton's daddy had already retired from his occupation and Mr. Alton himself had yet to embark on one. Of course they started with the pond since the Nance property had not come supplied with one already, and Mrs. Phillip J. King said Mr. Alton and Mr. Alton's daddy staked it out over a creekbed that ran near the backside of the Nance acreage so as to put a sizeable pine grove between the ducks and the Nance mansion and bungalow. Mrs. Phillip J. King said a duck was a very private sort of creature.

Mr. Alton oversaw the clearing of the land and Mr. Alton's daddy oversaw the actual digging of the pond and the eventual stocking of it with the sorts of fish Mrs. Phillip J. King said a duck would go tail up over. Then Mr. Alton and Mr. Alton's daddy together built a number of duck boxes for the animals to breed in and set them out around the pond along with a load of bread crusts and several dozen decoys. And Mrs. Phillip J. King said of course they got all the ducks they wanted almost right off, and Mr. Alton's daddy made a bench out of a hewn log and put it back a ways in the pine grove so he could sit on it and watch the ducks approach from over the far treetops and drop into the pond with all of the grace and agility of bowling balls which Mrs. Phillip J. King said is natural for a duck. So Mr. Alton's daddy and Mr. Alton when he chose to would sit on Mr. Alton's daddy's hewn log bench in the seclusion of the pine grove and study any number of the creatures as they fell out of the sky or climbed back up into it, and Mrs. Phillip J. King said Mr. Alton's daddy and Mr. Alton too could not have been more satisfied with the way the ducks took to the pond and took to the duck boxes, so she said the trouble when it started was not ducks exactly; the trouble was almost purely Gottliebs.

Mrs. Phillip J. King said a whole assortment of Gottliebs lived just beyond the back reaches of the Nance property on about an acre and a half of packed dirt. They had started out in two houses with Grandmomma and Granddaddy Gottlieb in the one and their boy Buster Gottlieb and his wife Cynthia June Cuthbert Gottlieb in the other, but Mrs. Phillip J. King said right from the first Buster had a way of keeping Miss Cynthia loaded up with a Gottlieb year round and it didn't seem that she would hardly drop a new one before another one was already in the breech, so once Buster and Miss Cynthia's house got packed full with Gottliebs they sent the next few on over to Buster's momma and daddy's house, which wasn't but fifteen or so yards away, and then a few after that and a few after that until both Gottlieb houses were slam full up with Gottliebs. Mrs. Phillip J. King said consequently Buster and his daddy had to do some expanding and they slapped together a room on the end of Buster's house so as to catch the Gottlieb overflow, but Mrs. Phillip J. King said that was just a temporary solution since what Gottliebs there were already got steadily bigger and what Gottliebs there hadn't been continued to arrive, so Buster and his daddy set at it again and this time they stuck a room on the end of the other house and several Gottliebs spilled over into it relieving the pressure for a spell. And Mrs. Phillip J. King said just when it looked like Miss Cynthia was all done with Gottliebs she had a set of twin girls followed by a single male Gottlieb all three of which forced Buster and his daddy into the construction business again, and this time they went ahead and put a room between the new one on Buster's house and the new one on Buster's daddy's house and thereby connected the two houses together so that all the Gottliebs could mix and circulate freely. Mrs. Phillip J. King said Buster and his daddy let it out that what they had built was a breezeway, but she said her momma told her it most resembled a mine shaft without the earth on top of it.

Mrs. Phillip J. King said back in those days if you weren't a Nance or a Dundee you didn't have much of anything and if you were a Gottlieb you didn't have anything at all. She said Buster and his daddy didn't own but the two houses and the breezeway and the acre and a half of baked ground the whole mess sat on top of, and they helped tend another man's tobacco when the season called for it but otherwise just trapped and fished and tried to wish a few vegetables up out of the hardpan. And Mrs. Phillip J. King said her momma told her that in November of the year preceding Mr. Alton's daddy's duck pond the Gottlieb fortunes took a turn for the worse when Granddaddy Gottlieb very nearly killed himself on account of a carp; Mrs. Phillip J. King called it a serious mishap. She said Granddaddy Gottlieb had set several bank hooks along the Haw River on the afternoon of a Tuesday and had left them overnight until midmorning Wednesday when he walked the four miles to the river bottom to see what he had caught. And Mrs. Phillip J. King imagined he hadn't hauled in but a few bream and the rest bare hooks when he arrived at the last line and commenced rolling it up on the pole, but she said the hook seemed to have set itself into a log or at least a sizeable treelimb and it was all Granddaddy Gottlieb could do to bring in a half foot of line at the time for fear of breaking it off otherwise, so it was a tedious process, Mrs. Phillip J. King said, but finally Granddaddy Gottlieb drew the first lead sinker out from the water and then the second one and then the third one and then he brought in another handful of line and looked to see what sort of trash the hook might have snagged itself up on, and Mrs. Phillip J. King said Granddaddy Gottlieb found himself nearly eye to eye with a carp about the size of a full grown collie. Now it seems that the carp and Granddaddy Gottlieb saw each other at almost the same instant, and though Granddaddy Gottlieb knew right off he was looking at enough dinner for all the Gottliebs in both houses and the breezeway too, he did not know right off how to get the meal so far as the riverbank, not to mention the dinner table, while the carp for his part took action almost immediately and streaked for the deep water. So just as Granddaddy Gottlieb was deciding whether he would go into the river or not, he got yanked off the bank and went into it. And they set in to thrashing and wrestling and beating around in the water, Granddaddy Gottlieb and the carp, and Mrs. Phillip J. King told me and Momma it must have been a truly glorious and inspiring sight what with all that determination and all that valor and all that sheer brute strength and animal instinct coming together in the wilds of the Haw River bottom in November. Mrs. Phillip J. King said just the thought of it made her shake and tremble all over. She said mortal combat had a way with her.

It seems Granddaddy Gottlieb would get the upper hand on the fish and then the fish would get the upper hand on Granddaddy Gottlieb and then the two of them would go at it even for awhile until one or the other of them would take the advantage again temporarily. And Mrs. Phillip J. King said it didn't appear that the carp could best Granddaddy Gottlieb or that Granddaddy Gottlieb could best the carp, but then once they both became fairly much worn out Granddaddy Gottlieb managed to lock one arm around the carp's midsection, and with his free hand he groped in the back of his britches after the pistol he always carried there but what he found was only his underpants because the thrashing and the wrestling and the beating around in combination with all that glorious and inspiring determination and valor and brute strength and animal instinct had caused Granddaddy Gottlieb's pistol to fall down his britches' leg and into his right boot. So with his one arm still tight around the carp's midsection, him and the fish together went down to the river bed after the pistol and three or four breaths later Granddaddy Gottlieb fetched up into the air what Mrs. Phillip J. King called the instrument of death which Granddaddy Gottlieb had made himself out of a filed-down rifle barrel and a shotgun trigger and a revolver hammer and a hunk of whittled oak for a grip. So Grandaddy Gottlieb leaned back as far as he could and brought the front end of the carp out of the water long enough to introduce it to the instrument of death, and Mrs. Phillip J. King said the shot played among the treetops and echoed and resounded throughout the valley while apparently killing the fish also since the carp became what Mrs. Phillip J. King called vanquished.

At first it was all Granddaddy Gottlieb could do to get his carp and himself out of the water and onto the river bank, and Mrs. Phillip J. King said he crawled on up into the underbrush and stretched out there for near three quarters of an hour in an attempt to recover his wind. Of course he was sopping wet all over, which is hardly any way to go around in November, so by the time he did get his breath back he was already genuinely ill and had to endure a number of shuddering fits before he could gather the strength to heft the carp up onto his shoulder. And as Mrs. Phillip J. King figured it Granddaddy Gottlieb was the rest of the morning making it from the river bottom to the Gottlieb acre and a half, what with the shuddering and the carp working together to slow him down, and she said it wasn't until he got in sight of the bi-winged and breezewayed Gottlieb manor that he was set upon by a slew of little Gottliebs who relieved him of the carp and carried it on into the kitchen in triumph. And Mrs. Phillip J. King said the Gottliebs feasted off their granddaddy's carp; she said they all got carp steaks and carp fritters and carp meal patties except for Granddaddy Gottlieb himself who got pneumonia.

Mrs. Phillip J. King said he was laid up throughout the winter and the spring and on into the summer which was a sorry time for Granddaddy Gottlieb and the rest of the Gottliebs also since circumstances put Buster at the head of the Gottlieb households and breezeway too, and Mrs. Phillip J. King said though Buster was highly accomplished at making heirs he could not be depended on for much of anything else. So Mrs. Granddaddy Gottlieb and Mrs. Buster Gottlieb boiled a plenty of bones that winter and that spring and the Gottliebs lived off broth mostly along with a few bream or bass every once and again and the occasional unfortunate grey squirrel all of which the little Gottliebs provided without the aid of their daddy who Mrs. Phillip J. King said spent the winter in a soft chair by the hearth where he lamented the Gottlieb predicament, and she said in the spring he moved out onto the back porch so as to do some beweeping in the open air. As Mrs. Phillip J. King figured it, the first of the Nance ducks did not begin to drop over the treetops into the new Nance pond until the sap had started to rise in April of the year of Granddaddy Gottlieb's pneumonia, and since Granddaddy Gottlieb was sick under a comforter and the Mrs. Gottliebs were busy boiling bones and the little Gottliebs were off fishing and trapping and such it was left up to Buster to notice the ducks, which of course he failed to do at first burdened as he was with all the lamenting and beweeping, but Mrs. Phillip J. King said one morning on towards May Buster happened to come down off the porch into the backyard to stretch himself and just as he was working his neck a duck shot over the roof and disappeared beyond the pine trees at the back of the Gottlieb property. And Buster said to himself, "A duck," and studied the sky over the roof of the house until two more sailed out of sight beyond the trees. And Buster said out loud but still to himself, "Two ducks," and shaded his eyes with his hands and watched until five or six came over together. And Buster hollered, "Lord at the ducks!" which brought Mrs. Granddaddy Gottlieb and Mrs. Buster Gottlieb both out the kitchen window from the shoulders up and the two of them shouted more or less together, "What ducks?" which woke up Granddaddy Gottlieb who demanded, "Where's a duck?" but who had failed to bring his head sufficiently out from under the comforter and so was not heard by anybody but himself.

And Mrs. Phillip J. King said before Mrs. Granddaddy Gottlieb and Mrs. Buster Gottlieb could draw themselves back into the kitchen and exit properly through the door a pair of drakes shot past the peak of the house and dipped below the pine trees and the two women together screamed, "Ducks!" and Buster hollered behind them, "Get the gun!" and Granddaddy Gottlieb rolled the comforter down below his chin and shouted, "What ducks?" And Mrs. Phillip J. King said Mrs. Buster Gottlieb fetched her husband's shotgun out from behind the bedroom door and stormed into the backyard with it while Mrs. Granddaddy Gottlieb grabbed up her husband's single shot rifle from the closet in the hallway and hit the porch at a gallop. Unfortunately Mrs. Granddaddy Gottlieb was not nearly so spry and sure-footed as she had once been and she stumbled somewhere between the porch planking and the first stairtread but happily managed to catch herself on the bannister and a little less happily managed to keep her hold on the rifle by the only piece of it her fingers could find to latch onto which turned out to be the trigger, and Mrs. Phillip J. King said the gun didn't discharge into the sky exactly but more into the backyard so that Mrs. Granddaddy Gottlieb very nearly bagged her boy

Buster who in leaping wildly sideways touched off one barrel of the shotgun which did not discharge into the sky exactly either but emptied itself against the back part of the house with a tremendous racket, and Mrs. Phillip J. King said somewhere amidst the uproar and confusion Granddaddy Gottlieb, wrapped up to the neck in his comforter, stuck himself partway out the bedroom window and with his pistol blew the topnotch out of one of the pine trees. "I got him," Granddaddy Gottlieb hollered. "I got the son-of-a-bitch," and he threw his arms up over his head by way of celebration, Mrs. Phillip J. King said, which caused him to fall over frontwards partway out the window but not entirely to the ground and he hung upsidedown against the siding with his thighs caught on the windowsill and Mrs. Phillip J. King said what with the lingering pneumonia Granddaddy Gottlieb was too weak-limbed to pull himself back up into the house and too weak-headed to shut up for five seconds about the duck that he'd been too weak-eyed to see was not a duck at all but just a piece of a pine tree. And Granddaddy Gottlieb beat the clapboard with his pistol butt and yelled to his wife to go off through the pine grove after his bird until finally he wore himself out and dozed off just as he was.

An assortment of little Gottliebs who had been playing together across the road in a bramble thicket came beating it around the side of the house and into the backyard to see who'd been shot and why and there with Granddaddy Gottlieb hanging upsidedown out the bedroom window it seemed he'd gotten the worst of it and all the little Gottliebs set in to screaming and wailing and demanding to know how come, and Buster and Mrs. Buster and Mrs. Granddaddy had only just begun to quiet them down when the littlest Gottlieb, who was Tanya Alice, took her finger out of her mouth long enough to point it at the sky and say, "Ducks." And Mrs. Phillip J. King said Buster brought the shotgun to his shoulder and fired off the remaining barrel before he ever bothered to take a bead so the near about half dozen mallards disappeared over the treetops untouched and before the little Gottliebs could even begin to draw their fingers out of their ears their granddaddy roused up and commenced to slamming his pistol butt against the clapboard again. "I got one. I got the son-of-a-bitch," he hollered.

But the truth of it was, according to Mrs. Phillip J. King, that a flying duck proved considerably more difficult to hit than a pine tree or a section of clapboard siding, especially with a pistol or a rifle and even with a shotgun. So after two full days of some very heavy gunfire interspersed with duckless periods of silence, the Gottliebs were still living off boiled bone soup and fish, and to make things worse all that sitting around and squatting in the backyard had given Buster and Buster's oldest boy, little Buster, and little Buster's brothers Dale and J.G. painful and severe sunburns on their forearms and the tops of their feet, and as for Granddaddy Gottlieb, who refused to remain in the bedroom or even to dangle out the bedroom window but instead took up a position in the backyard in a kitchen chair with his comforter around his shoulders and his pistol in his lap, he did not contract any noticeable sunburn himself but instead came down with a rare and unusual case of double hemorrhoids, which Mrs. Phillip J. King told me and Momma right there in the breakfast room must have felt like a couple of ears of corn and the shucks too.

And Momma said, "Helen!" and jerked her head in my direction.

And Mrs. Phillip J. King said to Momma, "Well, Inez."

And I said to Mrs. Phillip J. King, "The shucks too?"

And Momma said, "Louis!" very quick and sharp.

And Mrs. Phillip J. King told me, "The shucks too."

So they hauled Granddaddy Gottlieb's bed on out into the backyard and when Granddaddy Gottlieb wasn't inside the house soaking in the galvanized tub he was outside under his comforter with his pistol in his right hand and his eye fixed on the sky, and Buster and little Buster and Dale and J.G. buried their feet in the dirt and wore their winter shirts, which meant that most everything that could be remedied was remedied except for the bone soup and the fish. And Mrs. Phillip J. King said towards the end of the third day after the Gottliebs had opened up on a number of ducks flying single and nearly as many flying in bunches without telling a one, Buster and little Buster and Dale were setting themselves to carry Granddaddy Gottlieb and his bed back into the house when a sizeable flock of some variety of duck or another came flapping and honking over the rooftop, and seeing as how Buster and little Buster and Dale had their hands full of bedposts and Granddaddy Gottlieb had already stuck his pistol into the back of his pajama bottoms in preparation for the trip, that left only J.G. to see to the ducks, and Mrs. Phillip J. King said he was sitting on top of an upsidedown no. 10 can, which itself was sitting on top of a stump and without bothering to get up he raised the shotgun, leaving the butt of it against his stomach, and squeezed off both barrels at once the force of which, of course, blew him backwards off the can and off the stump too and near about drove him into the ground, so Mrs. Phillip J. King said J.G. found himself in no position to see that he'd hit a duck or to even care that he had since it very possibly seemed to him at the time that he would never draw breath again. But Buster and little Buster and Dale and Granddaddy Gottlieb too saw that duck turn over once in the air and then dip out of sight behind the pine trees, and Buster and little Buster and Dale let loose of the bedposts to go after it and so dropped Granddaddy Gottlieb in the middle of the backyard, which proved to be unfortunate for him since he fell directly on top of his home-made filed-down rifle barrel pistol and consequently undid most all the healthful effects of a whole day's worth of soaking on his condition.

Mrs. Phillip J. King said her momma told her it so happened that Mr. Alton's daddy was taking in the twilight from his hewn log bench in the woods when the momentum of J.G.'s duck carried it on beyond the trees and into the water with the rest of the flock, but Mrs. Phillip J. King did not suppose Mr. Alton's daddy noticed one of his ducks was dead when it hit the water since the live ones dropped into the pond with about as much abandon and since Mr. Alton's daddy was most attracted to the splashing down and the lifting off and not the swimming around in between which of course the whole flock immediately engaged in except for the dead one, which sort of bobbed on the backwash and then drifted off to itself. So Mr. Alton's daddy rolled from one shank to the other and made himself comfortable on the log bench while he waited for a new selection of ducks to swoop over the treetops and set down in the pond for the night, but instead of ducks what he spied was a species of Gottlieb that wandered out from the scrubby undergrowth on the far bank and took to poking around the reedy shallows with a stick. This particular Gottlieb happened to be little Buster though Mr. Alton's daddy did not know it was little Buster, did not even know it was a Gottlieb since the Gottliebs were not the sort of people that a Nance would have anything to do with. Mr. Alton's daddy simply knew it was not a duck and could see for himself it was poking around in a place where only ducks should be poking around, so Mrs. Phillip J. King said he became very understandably annoyed and rose up from his hewn log bench so as to charge little Buster, Mrs. Phillip J. King called it, to identify himself. "You there, young man," Mr. Alton's daddy shouted across the lake, and for no more than a second or two the top of little Buster's head became little Buster's face before it went back to being the top of his head again. And Mrs. Phillip J. King said Mr. Alton's daddy demanded to know just who Buster was and what he was doing and why he thought he had any right to do it on the bank of the Nance duck pond. But the top of Buster's head remained the top of his head this time until two more Gottliebs, a big one and a little one, came out from the scrubby undergrowth and caused the top of Buster's head to become the back of his head momentarily. And Mrs. Phillip J. King said the sight of three Gottliebs where there had been only one previously stirred up sufficient indignation in Mr. Nance's daddy to cause him to jump on top of the hewn log bench from where he set in to charging all three Gottliebs to tell him just why they were where they were and just who they were anyway, and all the commotion and indignant screeching did not have much of any noticeable effect on little Buster but the uproar from Mr. Alton's daddy did cause the tops of big Buster and Dale's heads to become their faces momentarily before going back to being the tops of their heads again.

Mrs. Phillip J. King said of course the trouble was that none of the three Gottliebs could find the duck. They had been all through the pine grove without any success and now had ended up in the undergrowth around Mr. Nance's pond, which was as far as they figured a dead duck could fly to. But even after considerable poking and prodding around in the reeds and high grass none of them could find much of anything except for Dale who ran up on a banded water snake and tormented it for awhile until his daddy made him stop. And Mrs. Phillip J. King said it wasn't until little Buster couldn't turn up the duck anywhere else that he decided to look out into the pond for it and found it floating upsidedown in the middle of a pack of rightsideup ducks, and he pointed at it with his stick and called out to his daddy who pointed at it with his arm and called out to Dale who pointed at it himself. Mrs. Phillip J. King said from where he was Mr. Alton's daddy could see all the pointing and could see all the rightsideup ducks but couldn't make out the dead one and so still did not understand exactly what the Gottlieb invasion was all about, still did not even know it was a Gottlieb invasion, and he clapped his hands sharply twice as an attention getter and hollered, "You there, you there," several times in an attempt to turn the sides of the Gottliebs' heads, which was all he could see now, into faces once again. But Mrs. Phillip J. King said the Gottliebs didn't pay any mind to Mr. Alton's daddy no matter how many "you theres" he cut loose across the pond since the Gottliebs were busily engaged in what Mrs. Phillip J. King called a discussion. And once Mr. Alton's daddy left off his hand clapping and left off his shouting he could hear some of the noise the discussion was generating, especially after it became what Mrs. Phillip J. King called heated with most of the heat supplied by Dale who apparently had some strong objections to whatever it was little Buster and big Buster were agreeing to, and Mrs. Phillip J. King said things became outright fiery before big Buster grabbed Dale by the one arm and little Buster took hold of the other and the two of them together flung him on out into the pond, which seemed to bring the discussion to an abrupt close.

He just flapped around a little at first, according to Mrs. Phillip J. King, but once he got his bearings he sort of dog-paddled out towards the flock of rightsideup ducks that was still keeping company with the solitary upsidedown one. Of course the sight of a Gottlieb coming at them across the pond, or anyway the sight of the head of a Gottlieb which is all that was out from the water, drove the ducks on towards the far bank and the flock discharged the carcass behind it which Mr. Alton's daddy still could not make out very clearly even after Dale had taken hold of the duck's feet and had commenced to churn his way back towards big Buster and little Buster which the duck was preventing him from doing with any sort of ease or much success. As Mrs. Phillip J. King explained it, the dogpaddle is strictly one of your four-limbed strokes and here Dale was trying to pull it off with three free limbs and a duckladen one which in combination kept him off the pond bottom but did not exactly carry him skimming across the water. So in the interest of keeping the carcass count down to one,

Dale decided he'd best not try to swim and haul the duck too and instead he tossed the duck out ahead of him and paddled up to it so as to toss it out ahead of him again. And Mrs. Phillip J. King said it was while the duck had taken to flying once more that Mr. Alton's daddy got his first good look at it and knew it for one of his teals and of course the sight sort of rejuvenated his agitation and touched off a whole new assortment of "you theres" and "young mans" and "I says" along with enough hand clapping for a legitimate ovation. But the Gottliebs did not pay any attention whatsoever to Mr. Alton's daddy, and Mrs. Phillip J. King said once little Buster saw that Dale was very possibly not going to drown he lit out through the pine grove for home to tell his momma and his grand-momma to take the bones off the fire. That left big Buster to haul Dale up out of the pond by the britches' bottoms and he offered to carry the duck for him but Dale said he'd fetched it and he wanted to carry it so him and his daddy left the pond bank for the scrubby groundcover and left the scrubby ground-cover for the pine grove and by the time they arrived at the treeline Mr. Alton's daddy had left off his hand clapping and had given over his "you theres" and "young mans" and "I says" for an extended series of "Heys" which he delivered like pistol shots. And Mrs. Phillip J. King said it wasn't until big Buster had disappeared into the trees that Dale pulled up short of vanishing into them himself and allowed his backside to become his frontside momentarily so that he could raise his duckless arm towards Mr. Alton's daddy and say "Hey" back.

According to Mrs. Phillip J. King that was the beginning of the imbroglio, though she did not call it an imbroglio and did not call it the beginning either. Mrs. Phillip J. King said it was the "overture to discord" which she just up and came out with and which seemed to me near about the same thing as the beginning of the imbroglio once it was translated out of King's English, Daddy calls it. Of course Mr. Alton's daddy was outraged right off, overture or not, and he carried his outrage on home with him so as to give it an airing out over dinner with the former Miss Dupont who did not share her husband's passion for ducks and who was in fact growing increasingly weary of them since most everywhere she looked she saw one, painted or otherwise. So according to Mrs. Phillip J. King, the former Miss Dupont could not work up any sort of appreciable anger, not even when her husband told her he had been "beset by vile poachers," which sounded far nastier and more serious than "invaded by Gottliebs," and consequently Mr. Alton's daddy collected up his outrage from the dinner table and hauled it on down to the bungalow where he suspected he might find somebody to be outraged along with him. Mrs. Phillip J. King said of course Mr. Alton was at home alone, and she cleared her throat at Momma who nodded back at Mrs. Phillip J. King so as to indicate she understood that Miss Sissy was most probably out doing something unprincipled, and according to Mrs. Phillip J. King since Mr. Alton was not presently hobnobbing with his political acquaintances or hobnobbing with his wife either, he found himself free to become worked up and him and his daddy sat outside on the bungalow patio, where they could be outraged together under the stars.

Mr. Alton seemed to favor legal intervention while, in the heat of the moment, his daddy came out strong for what Mrs. Phillip J. King called fisticuffs. But Mr. Alton knew right off and his daddy knew when he'd simmered down some that any one Gottlieb by himself, who they still did not know were Gottliebs and so instead called "that ilk," could most likely take on all the available Nance's at once and fisticuff the whole slew of them into the ground. Accordingly, Mr. Alton and Mr. Alton's daddy worked out a strategy that would commence with negotiations and carry on into the courtroom if the poachers proved to be hardheaded, which Mr. Alton's daddy was sure they would be since they were vile anyway and consequently had nothing to lose by being hard-headed too. So Mr. Alton and his daddy set out from the estate the following morning in Mr. Alton's touring car and hunted up the Gottliebs down an oiled road that bordered the Nance property to the north. Mrs. Phillip J. King said for their part Granddaddy Gottlieb and J.G. and Dale and little Buster and big Buster had moved out from the backyard and around the house to the frontyard, where they had repositioned themselves almost directly between the breezeway and the drainage ditch. The move had come mostly on account of a kind of vile poachers' roundtable that Granddaddy Gottlieb and J.G. and Dale and little Buster and big Buster had taken part in after supper the night previous during which it was decided by unanimous vote that while a duck shot over the Gottlieb backyard might sail on into the Nance pond a duck shot over the Gottlieb frontyard could not possibly get clear of the pine grove, and of course the decision was helped along some by Mrs. Buster and Mrs. Granddaddy who both agreed it was still a little too springlike to be tossing Gottliebs into a lake. So by the time Mr. Alton and Mr. Alton's daddy arrived at the Gottlieb house, Dale and little Buster and big Buster and J.G. had already hauled their granddaddy out into the front yard on top of his fourposter bed which he was confined to more than ever since aside from the lingering pneumonia his case of the double hemorrhoids had become increasingly inflamed and troublesome almost from the very moment little Buster and Dale and big Buster dropped him in the back yard when he took a pistol whipping directly on his affliction.

Mrs. Phillip J. King said Mr. Alton stopped the car in the middle of the road and beeped the horn twice and his daddy leaned his head out the side window and asked all five Gottliebs at once, "What are you gentlemen up to?"

But of course they didn't fall all over themselves trying to answer him. In fact no Gottlieb said anything until little Buster left off burying his feet long enough to turn to big Buster and ask him, "Who is that, Daddy?" And Mrs. Phillip J. King said big Buster laid the rifle across his legs and gave some thoughtful consideration to Mr. Alton's daddy and Mr. Alton and Mr. Alton's touring car before he turned to Granddaddy Gottlieb who was reposing on his frontside under the bedclothes and asked him, "Who is that, Daddy?" And Granddaddy Gottlieb raised himself on his forearms and trained his near eye on Mr. Alton's daddy and then on Mr. Alton and then on Mr. Alton's touring car, and he said, "They's Nances," and then let himself back down onto the mattress where he set in to reposing again.

"I'm Mr. Nance," Mr. Alton's daddy said, "and this is my son who is Mr. Nance also."

"Well, I'm Mr. Gottlieb," Buster told him back, "and this is my daddy, who is Mr. Gottlieb also and this is my boy Buster jr. and Dale and J.G. who are all Mr. Gottliebs too. Now, what is it all us Gottliebs can do for you Nances?"

"You can answer me one question," Mr. Alton's daddy said. "You can tell me what you gentlemen are up to," and he made a very dramatic sweeping gesture with his arm so as to take in all five of the gentlemen Mr. Gottliebs who were sitting before him in kitchen chairs except of course for Granddaddy Gottlieb and except for J.G. who had brought his no. 10 can into the front yard with him.

But before big Buster could decide whether or not him and his daddy and his boys were up to anything and so formulate a reply, J.G. raised his right arm and pointed as high as he could point considering the tender condition of his ribs. "Ducks!" he shrieked, "ducks coming in over the white oak," and little Buster shouldered the shotgun while his daddy brought the rifle out of his lap and while his granddaddy rolled very gingerly onto his backside and raised his pistol with both hands. And Mrs. Phillip J. King said Granddaddy Gottlieb cut loose with his bullet and then big Buster cut loose with his and then little Buster emptied the shotgun squeezing off one barrel at a time so as to keep his shoulder intact, and as for the ducks, Mrs. Phillip J. King said they just kept getting it on over top of the Gottlieb house and beyond the pine grove and into the pond. So consequently Mr. Alton and Mr. Alton's daddy found out first hand what the gentlemen Mr. Gottliebs were up to without big Buster having to bother to tell them.

Of course Mr. Alton's daddy, and Mr. Alton too for that matter, became noticeably agitated and appalled by what Mrs. Phillip J. King called the thundrous barrage, and once the sound of the gunfire had trailed off sufficiently Mr. Alton's daddy clenched his fists and stomped his foot two or three times on the oiled road and told all the gentlemen Mr. Gottliebs outright, "This is an outrage! You cannot, I tell you you simply cannot shoot a duck coming in to roost."

And Mrs. Phillip J. King said big Buster opened up the rifle breech, prized out the empty cartridge with his fingernail, and said to Mr. Alton's daddy, "You're right on it there, Mister. It's all you can do to get the gun up. Now J.G. hit one yesterday, but it took both barrels and some considerable luck and the butt liked to went clear through him." And big Buster stopped talking to Mr. Alton's daddy long enough to say to J.G., "Show him your stomach, son." And J.G. stood up off his can and opened his shirt so the Nances could see the blue places on his belly. "Weren't luck either," he said.

But almost before he could get the words out, Mr. Alton's daddy had commenced to stomping again and Mr. Alton had seen fit to get out of the car and join in. "I won't let you do this," Mr. Alton's daddy said. "I simply will not allow you to shoot my ducks."

"Your ducks?" big Buster said to him.

"Yes sir," Mr. Alton's daddy told him back, "my ducks. They're breeding in my boxes on my property and I demand you stop shooting at them."

And big Buster laid the rifle across his legs and said, "I suppose that is your pond and I suppose those are your boxes and I guess that's your pine grove too, but they's anybody's ducks."

"They're my ducks, sir," Mr. Alton's daddy snapped back at him.

"As long as they're in your pond they might be," big Buster said, "but when they come over top that white oak yonder they're all mine. Ain't that right boys?" And little Buster and Dale and J.G. all put in together with "Yes, Daddy."

"Well, we'll just see about that, Mr. Gottlieb," Mr. Alton's daddy told him.

And big Buster said, "Awright."

And little Buster turned half around in his chair and said, "Daddy, it's ten-thirty."

And big Buster said, "Thank you, son," and turned half around in his chair and told Granddaddy Gottlieb, "It's ten-thirty, Daddy."

And Granddaddy Gottlieb rolled onto his back and hollered, "Nina! Nina!" which brought the top part of Mrs. Granddaddy Gottlieb out one of the breezeway windows. "Nina," he shouted at her, "fill the tub, I'm coming in."

Mrs. Phillip J. King said Mr. Alton and Mr. Alton's daddy did not go home directly but stopped in downtown at the offices of Mr. Wade "Shorty" Glidewell, attorney at law, who Mrs. Phillip J. King said was testing the water in the race for district judge and so had reason to take care of any sort of problem Mr. Alton or Mr. Alton's daddy might be having. Now according to Mrs. Phillip J. King, Mr. Glidewell did not specialize in duck custody cases, and as far as he could recollect there in the presence of Mr. Alton and Mr. Alton's daddy he had never had the privilege of litigating over any variety of duck dilemma whatsoever, but of course he welcomed the opportunity and even before Mr. Alton and Mr. Alton's daddy could get away from his office Mr. Glidewell sent his brother's boy,

Lyle, to find out just where and how often the law of the land and ducks had anything to do with each other. For his part, Mr. Alton drove his daddy on home and the two of them took lunch on the bungalow patio, where Mrs. Phillip J. King told Momma they dined on congealed salad and beef brisket with a delightful fruitfilled pastry cup for desert, and she said the most of their conversation was devoted to running down Gottliebs except for the few minutes in between the brisket and the fruit cup, when Mr. Alton's daddy made a very brave and highly animated speech about a man's right to take wild creatures for his own and so got the blood pumping in Mr. Alton and in himself also. According to Mrs. Phillip J. King the Nances were by nature men of considerable passion, which was of course a fitting complement to their finely chiseled features, which Mrs. Phillip J. King said they both still had at the time of the duck imbroglio since Mr. Alton's cheekbones had not yet given way and his daddy's had retained their structure all along which left him near about as dashing as his son. And Mrs. Phillip J. King said after they had pushed their plates away and after the both of them had clipped their cigars and lit them, Mr. Alton and his daddy took turns carting their hot blood and their finely chiseled features all over the patio. First Mr. Alton's daddy rose from the table and circled it twice with the index finger of one hand crooked around his Havana and the thumb of the other jammed into his fob pocket. He was fairly much off Gottliebs specifically and had gotten himself a little sweltery on the topic of vile individuals in general, instances of which he illustrated with Gottliebs when the application seemed appropraite, and Mrs. Phillip J. King said once he'd played out on the subject he gave over the patio to Mr. Alton, who paced back and forth in front of the cement planter box and worked his arms in the air. It was Mr. Alton's opinion that people weren't worth a piddle anymore, especially Gottliebs. And Mrs. Phillip J. King said the longer Mr. Alton talked the more worked up him and his daddy became until the two of them together were stalking all over the patio and declaiming, Mrs. Phillip J. King called it, in a most passionate fashion.

Mr. Wade Shorty Glidewell's brother's boy, Lyle, was still hunting up duck cases in the legal section of the Burlington library on the morning of what Mrs. Phillip J. King said was day two of the duck imbroglio which was actually day three if you counted the afternoon of the Gottlieb invasion as day one which Mrs. Phillip J. King neglected to do and so arrived at day two instead of day three. And on the morning of day two which was actually day three Mr. Alton and Mr. Alton's daddy, having heard nothing at all from Mr. Wade Shorty Glidewell and having heard nothing at all from Mr. Wade Shorty Glidewell's brother's boy, Lyle, decided between the two of them that they would take what measures they could on their own in the form of a fence between the pond and the Gottliebs. So Mr. Alton's daddy had the gardener make up a load of staubs and him and Mr. Alton carried an armful apiece down through the pine grove and around to the backside of the pond, where they discussed and diagrammed and plotted and wandered around in the trees and where they had even driven a staub or two before the first of what Mrs. Phillip J. King called the distant salvos filled the air and fell, Mrs. Phillip J. King called it, on their ears. Of course the pistol report followed by the rifle report followed by the double volley from the shotgun agitated and distracted Mr. Alton and his daddy all over again and set them to reviling Gottliebs afresh which turned out to be more fitting for the patio than the pine grove since Mr. Alton's daddy, who was driving the staubs, and Mr. Alton, who was holding the staubs, temporarily lost sight of their present undertaking and so had an accident in the form of a direct blow delivered full from the head of Mr. Alton's daddy's twenty ounce hammer squarely onto the first two knuckles of Mr. Alton's right hand. And Mrs. Phillip J. King said Mr. Alton circled the pond twice at a gallop and then tore up through the pine grove towards the bungalow with his daddy behind him in full stride apologizing with what wind he could muster.

According to Mrs. Phillip J. King, by the morning of the third day of the duck imbroglio, which was actually the fourth day, Mr. Alton and his daddy were so completely preoccupied and eaten up with Gottliebs and ducks that neither one of them could breathe a word that didn't carry a hint of imbroglio with it, so nobody but the former Miss Dupont, who did not care a fiddle for ducks except under an orange sauce, was free to pay any notice to Miss Sissy who had pretty much been running amuck, Mrs. Phillip J. King called it, ever since she found out she could get away with it. Of course Mrs. Phillip J. King held by her belief that Miss Sissy was naturally inclined towards

running amuck and so would have anyway with or without a
diversionary imbroglio, but since Mr. Alton had been engaged
for a number of weeks now, first with the digging of the pond
and then with the collecting of the ducks followed by the despising of the Gottliebs, Miss Sissy had managed to run amuck
entirely undetected until the former Miss Dupont drew her first
suspicious breath. Now according to Mrs. Phillip J. King, the
former Miss Dupont was cagey enough to recognize a tropical
disposition when she saw one, but Mrs. Phillip J. King said
since Duponts were raised to allow for the worst in people,
especially a Dundee of the Congressman Dundees, the former
Miss Dupont did not hold Miss Sissy's tropical disposition
against her and figured Miss Sissy could keep the reins on it
well enough herself. Of course that was before the former Miss
Dupont discovered that her daughter-in-law was exhibiting what
Mrs. Phillip J. King called some loosely unprincipled behavior,
which was the same as running amuck, which was the same
as an unladylike showing which Momma landed on once Mrs.
Phillip J. King took plain unprincipled and corrupted it.

As far as Mr. Alton knew Miss Sissy was spending the most
of her afternoons and some of her evenings with an old class-
mate named Marie Ketner, a slightly built brunette who Mrs.
Phillip J. King said her momma told her was a genuine trollop
but who Mr. Alton had only met once and probably then did
not think to wonder if she simmered like she did. According
to Mrs. Phillip J. King, Miss Sissy was ever telling Mr. Alton
how her and Miss Marie Ketner were planning to hop over to
Raleigh and do some shopping or motor to Chapel Hill and
visit the college or take in a matinee in Greensboro, and Mrs.
Phillip J. King said sometimes they did get as far as Raleigh
and occasionally to Chapel Hill and every now and again to
the picture show in Greensboro but mostly they never got past
Club 54, which was located on the road to Carboro just outside
the Burlington city limits. Club 54 was a concrete block structure that had been a Texaco station for near about a decade
until the owner, a Mr. Jerome Little of Graham who Mrs. Phillip
J. King said was the sort who could work up a sweat bending
over, decided to get out of the gas business and get into the
roadhouse business. So he boarded up the service bay doors
and filled in the grease pit and bargained with a Baptist preacher
from Pittsboro for a thirdhand piano which Mrs. Little could

beat on almost melodically while her husband sat behind the counter in a cane-bottom chair and sold whatever manner of alcohol he could get his hands on, some of it even bonded.

Now as Mrs. Phillip J. King understood it, Miss Sissy liked a little taste every once and again and Miss Marie liked a little taste every once and again as well, so the two of them took to stopping in at Mr. Little's Club 54 on the way to Raleigh or on the way to Chapel Hill and they would each have a taste to face the road with while taking care to keep themselves away from the riffraff and away from what Mrs. Phillip J. King called the underbelly, both of which tended to congregate at Mr. Little's establishment. And Mrs. Phillip J. King said soon enough Miss Sissy and Miss Marie took to stopping in at the Club 54 on the way to Greensboro even though it was not on the way to Greensboro and they would treat themselves to a bigger taste apiece and so end up in High Point where they didn't even have a picture show. And Mrs. Phillip J. King said it got so that Miss Sissy and Miss Marie would set out from the bungalow for Raleigh or Chapel Hill or Greensboro and would not get anywhere at all beyond Mr. Little's Club 54 where they had even begun to mingle some with the riffraff and the underbelly too. And then it was not just mingling but dancing also, that is it was dancing whenever the patrons could encourage Mrs. Little to bang out something on the keyboard which mostly turned out to be Methodist hymns played in a sort of jumpy, half-syncopated beat that was suitable for dancing if you didn't listen too close. And Mrs. Phillip J. King said since Miss Sissy and Miss Marie were about the only women the Club 54 attracted aside from the Potts sisters, who Mrs. Phillip J. King said had probably come to be female by some sort of divine mistake, Miss Sissy and Miss Marie were ever taking to the dance floor and kicking up their heels to "Whispering Hope" or "Stand Up for Jesus" or "Sweet Hour of Prayer," three of Mrs. Little's favorites. And Mrs. Phillip J. King said it got so that Miss Sissy and Miss Marie could hardly sit down and finish off their little tastes before some gentleman patron or another would buy a whole bottle and insist they have a few snorts out of it, which they generally felt they could not refuse to do without flying in the face of human kindness. So in the course of an afternoon at the club 54 Miss Sissy and Miss Marie most usually became what Mrs. Phillip J. King called

lubricated, and being the genuine article that she was, Miss
Marie would regularly pick out some big strapping fellow across
the room—Mrs. Phillip J. King said Miss Marie's sort was
always partial to the brawny ones—and dance him on through
the door and into the parking lot where the two of them would
mingle in Miss Marie's daddy's car.

Miss Sissy of course did not go in for that sort of mingling
right off, being a married woman and still being possessed of
a few grains of what Mrs. Phillip J. King called Dundee com-
punction. But according to Mrs. Phillip J. King, with that
sandy-colored Dundee hair and those big brown Dundee eyes
Miss Sissy was the sort of woman that made men's hormones
jump to their feet and tapdance, which caused Momma to say,
"Helen!" on the inhale and turn rose-petal pink from the neck
up. But Mrs. Phillip J. King just carried on with what she was
about and told me and Momma, well told Momma mostly, how
all the males at the Club 54 except for Mr. Little, who Mrs.
Little kept an eye on, would pile up all over themselves trying
to get a seat at Miss Sissy's table especially once Miss Marie
had two-stepped on out the door to do some private mingling,
which usually left an additional opening on Miss Sissy's flank.
And Mrs. Phillip J. King said Miss Sissy would stir up a breeze
with her eyelids and roll her head all around on her shoulders
and lick her lips and laugh from way back in her throat and
reach out with her fingers to touch very lightly whoever she
might be talking to at any particular moment, and Mrs. Phillip
J. King said you could near about hear the hoofing of the
hormones above Mrs. Little's piano music.

But Mrs. Phillip J. King said even after it became clear to
Miss Sissy that she had a definite tendency to mingle, which
is certainly the sort of definite tendency she had, she still
refused to do it in the back of Miss Marie's daddy's car notwithstanding Miss Marie's assurances that there was a gracious
plenty room even for a leggy creature like Miss Sissy. After
all, Miss Sissy did have her principles and Dundees of the
Congressman Dundees simply would not compromise on some
things. So Miss Sissy continued to agitate hormones there inside
the Club 54 while Miss Marie continued to entertain what Mrs.
Phillip J. King called clients outside in the open spaces of her
daddy's car. But then Miss Sissy had not laid eyes on much
of anybody at the Club 54 who even made her hormones sit

up straight until one afternoon when her and Miss Marie were on their way to Greensboro and would not even get to High Point, and it was while Miss Marie was fox trotting with the prospects that Miss Sissy first saw the man who caused her hormones to slip into their tap shoes. His name was Jackson Dubois Byrd, and Mrs. Phillip J. King said even before Miss Sissy knew about the Dubois part she gathered from his looks that there was something worldly and exotic about him, and Mrs. Phillip J. King told me and Momma he was from Connecticut as it turned out and so was as good as foreign as far as Burlington was concerned. According to Mrs. Phillip J. King, he'd come south to work in textiles and had rented a house in the mill village on the northeast side of the city where he lived by himself except for a speckled tomcat that he called Dardanelles, which he told Miss Sissy he'd gotten from a book. Mrs. Phillip J. King said Mr. Jack Byrd was brawny in the Miss Marie Ketner sense of the word and owned a wondrously elaborate black waxed moustache that lay across his face like a decorative wrought iron strut. He was not very loud and was not very vulgar, which fairly much distinguished him at the Club 54, and Mrs. Phillip J. King said he first caught Miss Sissy's eye when he showed her how he could make the veins on his forehead stand up and twitch.

It seems Miss Sissy had a soft spot for the hulking shy type, so Mr. Jack Byrd found favor with her right from the beginning and the two of them embarked on what Mrs. Phillip J. King could not bring herself to call a romance but called instead a series of relations which was some form of advanced mingling that Momma would not allow Mrs. Phillip J. King to elaborate on. Of course part of Mr. Jack Byrd's appeal, aside from his brawn and aside from his twitching veins and aside from his flat Connecticut accent that Miss Sissy tended to hear a little French in, was his car and the house that it would drive him and Miss Sissy to. Now the car alone was fit for mingling, but since Dundees were historically non-minglers Mr. Jack Byrd would probably not have ever laid a finger on Miss Sissy if not for the house, because Mrs. Phillip J. King said you needed a house to carry on a series of relations, more specifically you needed a legitimate bedroom, and while Miss Sissy did not have mingling in her blood she seemed well enough suited for a Posturepedic. And of a sudden Momma scratched her head and asked Mrs. Phillip J. King didn't she think it might rain and Mrs. Phillip J. King said, "Lord no, honey," without ever looking out the breakfast room window.

As near as Mrs. Phillip J. King could figure it, Miss Sissy and Mr. Jack Byrd collaborated on the first in their series of relations along about the time when Mr. Alton and his daddy were engaged in plotting and staking out the boundaries of what would be Mr. Alton's daddy's duck pond. By then Miss Sissy and Miss Marie had left off going to Raleigh or Chapel Hill or Greensboro or High Point, had left off even intending to and instead made straight for the Club 54 almost daily where Miss Marie would dance and mingle and where Miss Sissy would wait for Mr. Jack Byrd to get off his shift at the millworks and come pick her up and take her home with him. And then it wasn't even as far as the Club 54 anymore, at least not for Miss Sissy who would borrow Mr. Alton's daddy's Bentley and drive it to the mill village herself and play with Dardanelles in Mr. Jack Byrd's bedroom until Mr. Jack got home from the mill when the two of them would carry on, Mrs. Phillip J. King called it, and the cat would sit on the windowsill and watch. And Mrs. Phillip J. King said Miss Sissy and Mr. Jack Byrd got away clean with their relations for the longest time and probably would have continued to carry on scot free if the former Miss Dupont had had anything else in the world to do but wonder where Miss Sissy and the Bentley got off to most every afternoon. But Mrs. Phillip J. King said since the former Miss Dupont was filthy with it she didn't have anything else in the world to do but wonder and speculate and ponder and suspect, and so she would stand by the parlor window in the afternoons and watch Miss Sissy ease the Bentley out of the garage and on along the driveway to where it bent out of sight behind a hedgerow, and even after Miss Sissy and the Bentley were gone from view the former Miss Dupont would linger at the parlor window, which was where she did her best wondering and speculating and pondering and suspecting.

And it was on what turned out to be the actual day one of the Gottlieb imbroglio that the former Miss Dupont finally decided to do something about Miss Sissy and the Bentley besides just wonder and just speculate and just ponder and just suspect, so almost the very instant Miss Sissy wheeled Mr. Alton's daddy's vehicle around the bend in the driveway and beyond the hedgerow the former Miss Dupont reached across the front seat of her sedan and slapped at the driver's shoulder with the pair of dress gloves she was clutching in her hand, and the driver eased the former Miss Dupont's car out from the far end of the garage and around behind the hedgerow and down towards the street. The former Miss Dupont did not drive herself and had engaged the services of her gardener, Mr. Gallos, who owned a perfectly valid operator's license but who both lived and worked on the Nance estate and so did not have much occasion to drive either. Consequently, Miss Sissy in Mr. Alton's daddy's Bentley opened up a sizeable margin between herself and the former Miss Dupont's sedan, which was understandable since Miss Sissy was traveling at what Mrs. Phillip J. King called the speed of desire while the former Miss Dupont was moving at the speed of a first-generation Greek gardener who did not know exactly what he was doing. So Miss Sissy was already inside Mr. Jack Byrd's bedroom with his cat in her lap long before the former Miss Dupont and her gardener got so far as the mill village which they were not sure was where Miss Sissy went anyway. But between the two of them the former Miss Dupont and Mr. Gallos spied Mr. Alton's daddy's Bentley in front of Mr. Jack Byrd's house, and Mrs. Phillip J. King said the former Miss Dupont instructed her driver to pause a ways down the street so as to avoid suspicion.

As Mrs. Phillip J. King figured it, the former Miss Dupont and Mr. Gallos had already been pausing near about a half hour when Mr. Jack Byrd came sauntering down the street from the mill and let himself in his front door. And Mrs. Phillip J. King said the arrival of Mr. Jack Byrd was followed by two full hours of uneventful pausing on the part of the former Miss Dupont and her gardener, most of which Mr. Gallos spent sleeping and most of which the former Miss Dupont spent wondering and speculating and pondering and suspecting. And Mrs. Phillip J. King said at the end of the two full hours Miss Sissy emerged from the house onto the front stoop all flushed and fresh looking only to be drawn by Mr. Jack Byrd back into the doorway where Mrs. Phillip J. King said the two of them fell into each other's arms and kissed most passionately. And while the former Miss Dupont watched her daughter-in-law kiss whoever it was she was kissing, she figured and concluded that since Miss Sissy had not gone to Raleigh and had not gone to visit the university at Chapel Hill and had not gone to Greensboro or High Point either, she had instead been forced to settle for a short trip into the bedroom and under the sheets with a brawny, moustachioed millworker who was very obviously not Miss Marie Ketner. And the very second Mrs. Phillip J. King said, "sheets" was the precise moment Momma discovered she simply had to have the recipe for Waldorf salad that was located in the back of a magazine on the nightstand in the front bedroom, so I got sent after it while Momma soaked Mrs. Phillip J. King in the meantime. And just as I stepped out of the back hallway and into the breakfast room again with Momma's *National Geographic*, which was the only magazine on the nightstand in the front bedroom, Momma lurched up straight in her chair and asked Mrs. Phillip J. King didn't she believe we were in for a spell of dry air from the east, and Mrs. Phillip J. King tilted her head slightly in Momma's direction and said, "Lord no, honey."

According to Mrs. Phillip J. King the former Miss Dupont intended to tell Mr. Alton's daddy the news of Miss Sissy at the supper table, but the afternoon of the former Miss Dupont's intrigue with her gardener Mr. Gallos turned out to be the afternoon of the actual day one of the duck imbroglio, what Mrs. Phillip J. King called the overture to discord, so Mr. Alton's daddy was already worked up into a sufficient lather by the time he reached the supper table and for the moment the former Miss Dupont decided against stirring him up any further. Consequently, Mr. Alton's daddy ranted about his vile poachers for awhile and then boiled on down to the bungalow still ignorant of Miss Sissy and her millworker, and the former Miss Dupont spent the early evening in what Mrs. Phillip J. King called a revery and made plans to break the news to Mr. Alton's daddy when he had cooled off some, which he had not done by the time he got home from the bungalow and which he did not do throughout the actual day two of the duck imbroglio and which he still had not done on into the morning of day three. So the former Miss Dupont had kept the news of Miss Sissy's waywardness to herself for near about two full days by the time the afternoon of the actual day three of the duck imbroglio rolled around and she lingered at the parlor window almost until dark waiting for Miss Sissy to ease the Bentley out of the garage and on down around the hedgerow, but Miss Sissy and the Bentley did not go anywhere and the longer the former Miss Dupont lingered at the parlor window the more she began to wonder and speculate and ponder and suspect which she had not engaged in ever since she'd figured and concluded but which she took up once more now that there was a good two days between herself and the evidence. And Mrs. Phillip J. King said on the evening of day two of the duck imbroglio, which was actually day three, Mr. Alton's daddy arrived at the supper table relatively collected and un-agitated since it was him that had done the pounding with the twenty-ounce hammer and it was Mr. Alton's knuckles that had received it, but Mrs. Phillip J. King said the former Miss Dupont could not bring herself to tell Mr. Alton's daddy about Miss Sissy even now that he was calm enough to hear since anymore she was not entirely convinced that she had seen what she had seen. So in the early afternoon of the actual day four of the duck imbroglio, the former Miss Dupont and her gardener Mr. Gallos climbed into the sedan in the garage and crouched down low in the seats waiting for Miss Sissy who came along soon enough and took the Bentley on down around the hedge-row and then along the streets at the speed of desire and all the way across town to the mill village where the former Miss Dupont saw all over again what she had seen previously.

And Mrs. Phillip J. King said once the former Miss Dupont saw the passionate embrace in the doorway and all the kissing that went along with it, her and Mr. Gallos lit out for the Nance estate at very nearly the speed of desire themselves so as to allow the former Miss Dupont to tell Mr. Alton's daddy all about Miss Sissy's waywardness while she was still convinced that that was what it was. But the former Miss Dupont could not find Mr. Alton's daddy in the big house and could not find him or Mr. Alton either in the bungalow, and Mrs. Phillip J. King said that was because it was day three of the duck imbro-glio which was actually day four, the ultimate day of the duck imbroglio, and which meant that Mr. Alton's daddy and Mr. Alton along with Mr. Wade Shorty Glidewell and Mr. Wade Shorty Glidewell's brother's boy, Lyle, were all around at the Gottlieb acre and a half engaged in some earnest negotiating. What had happened was Mr. Wade Shorty Glidewell's brother's boy, Lyle, had finished up his research the day previous and on the morning following him and his uncle had gotten together in his uncle's office so as to consult, Mrs. Phillip J. King called it. And she said around midday Mr. Wade Shorty Glidewell and Mr. Wade Shorty Glidewell's brother's boy, Lyle, arrived with their findings at the Nance estate where they were invited by Mr. Alton's daddy to take lunch with him and Mr. Alton on the bungalow patio prior to any sort of duck related discussion. So Mrs. Phillip J. King said the four of them had cutlets with brown gravy and waxed bean salad which was followed by sponge cake under sherbert which was followed by Mr. Alton's daddy's Cuban cigars for everybody except Mr. Wade Shorty Glidewell's brother's boy, Lyle, who said he did not have the constitution for them.

And Mrs. Phillip J. King said once all the dishes were cleared away but for the coffee cups, Mr. Wade Shorty Glidewell opened up his satchel and Mr. Wade Shorty Glidewell's brother's boy, Lyle, opened up his satchel and the two of them together covered over the tabletop with heaps and piles and bundles of precedents and alternatives and interpretations along with a separate folder full up with notes and illustrations devoted entirely to who had done what to a duck and how he'd answered for it. And right off Mr. Wade Shorty Glidewell told Mr. Alton and told Mr. Alton's daddy that as far as the records showed duck litigation was a delicate business. He said the litigants, who were most usually on the duck's side of the matter, were not uniformly successful in winning judgements against the offending parties, who did most of their offending, according to Mr. Wade Shorty Glidewell, with shotguns and whose sentiments most usually ran contrary to ducks. And Mr. Wade Shorty Glidewell went on to say that his brother's boy, Lyle, had found out that a litigant could hardly hope for a judgement without the aid of what Mr. Wade Shorty Glidewell called a palpable trespass on the part of the offending party. And Mr. Alton's daddy said he had a palpable trespass, said he'd seen with his own eyes three Gottliebs in the midst of one. But Mr. Wade Shorty Glidewell said that him and his brother's boy, Lyle, had pondered over it together and had both agreed that as far as Mr. Alton's daddy's trespass was concerned, the three Gottliebs to say they didn't more than cancelled out the one Nance to say they did. So it was the studied opinion of Mr. Wade Shorty Glidewell and it was the studied opinion of Mr. Wade Shorty Glidewell's brother's boy, Lyle, that Mr. Alton and Mr. Alton's daddy should not commence any sort of legal proceedings against the Gottliebs since they were not in possession of a clearly indisputable palpable trespass and since, as far as Mr. Wade Shorty Glidewell understood the law of it, only those ducks harbored within the bounds of the litigant's legal holdings, territorially speaking, could be said to belong to the litigant while any creature flying to or flying from the lawfully described boundaries of the litigant's property was legally subject to the threat of violence and destruction from whosoever might be willing to raise a gun at it, which Mr. Wade Shorty Glidewell said could be anybody, even a Gottlieb.

Consequently, it was Mr. Wade Shorty Glidewell's conclusion, to which Mr. Wade Shorty Glidewell's brother's boy, Lyle, concurred, Mrs. Phillip J. King called it, that Mr. Alton and Mr. Alton's daddy should not pursue any sort of legal action against the Gottliebs but should instead seek to negotiate with them for an immediate settlement and so put an end to what Mr. Wade Shorty Glidewell called the senseless massacre, which already counted among its casualties the single duck from day one along with the untold myriads, Mr. Wade Shorty Glidewell called them, from days two and three and now day four. And Mrs. Phillip J. King said the idea of myriads, especially untold ones, won Mr. Alton and won Mr. Alton's daddy over to Mr. Wade Shorty Glidewell's view of the matter since Mr. Alton and his daddy could not have known and did not know that the Gottliebs hadn't felled anything after the initial day of the imbroglio and so were still working on a one-duck massacre.

The arbitration party, Mrs. Phillip J. King called it, rode round to the Gottlieb acre and a half in Mr. Wade Shorty Glidewell's European sedan and they were greeted, Mrs. Phillip J. King said though she did not mean greeted exactly, by a whole front yard crawling with Gottliebs in various stages of development and evolution and including the five duck brigade Gottliebs who were positioned on day four of the imbroglio pretty much as they had been on day two except for Granddaddy Gottlieb who on account of the vast improvement in his posterior condition had left his bed in the house and so was sitting on a feather pillow in a straight-backed chair with his comforter wrapped loosely around his shoulders. Of course Granddaddy Gottlieb was in possession of his homemade filed-down rifle barrel pistol, the muzzle of which protruded between the folds of the comforter, and big Buster himself was in possession of the rifle which lay across the tops of his thighs with the bolt open, while it was Dale's turn to have at the shotgun, which left little Buster free to pick at his toes and gave J.G. the leisure to squat atop his no. 10 can and spit at ants with his head down between his legs. So what Mrs. Phillip J. King called the Gottlieb vanguard appeared on day four almost exactly as it appeared on day two but in actuality things were considerably different since the Gottliebs were almost entirely out of ammunition and about as far gone in patience. Granddaddy Gottlieb had only five rounds left for his pistol while big Buster's shirt-pocket held the three remaining rifle shells and the shotgun was loaded with the last two cartridges, one of which was filled with buckshot while the other was filled with salt and so left Dale the opportunity to obliterate a duck with the one barrel or season him with the other. Consequently, the Gottliebs were not altogether displeased at the sight of Mr. Wade Shorty Glidewell's European sedan complete with two Nances since they had been sufficiently humiliated by ducks already and invited the chance to tangle with people for awhile.

Mr. Alton's daddy was the first one out of the car and across the oiled road to the Gottlieb acre and a half where he said his hellos to big Buster and Granddaddy Gottlieb and the Gottlieb boys, and he was followed by Mr. Alton, who was followed by Mr. Wade Shorty Glidewell and Mr. Wade Shorty Glidewell's brother's boy, Lyle. "You remember my son, Mr. Nance," Mr. Alton's daddy said, mostly to big Buster, "and this is my attorney, Mr. Glidewell, and my attorney's aid, Mr. Glidewell."

"Mr. Nance. Mr. Glidewell. Mr. Glidewell," big Buster said, twitching his head at each one of them in turn. And then he pretty much pointed his topnotch at Granddaddy Gottlieb and said, "This here is my daddy, Mr. Gottlieb, and them over there are three of my wife's children, Mr. Gottliebs too."

"Pleasure," Mr. Glidewell said.

"Pleasure," Mr. Glidewell's brother's boy, Lyle, said.

"Uh huh," big Buster said back at them.

"Of course we've come about the ducks, Mr. Gottlieb," Mr. Alton's daddy began. "We'd like to work out some sort of settlement and so put an end to the . . . to the . . ."

"Bloodshed," Mr. Wade Shorty Glidewell provided and which

was followed almost immediately by a sharp "Ha!" from J.G. who never raised his head from between his legs to say it. "I have discussed the matter thoroughly with Mr. Nance sr. and his son, Mr. Nance jr.," Mr. Glidewell continued, "and after exhaustive considerations we have concluded upon a mutually beneficial compromise."

"That so," big Buster said.

"Yes sir," Mr. Glidewell told him, and Mrs. Phillip J. King said Mr. Alton and Mr. Alton's daddy drew in a little tighter around Mr. Glidewell since they did not recall any exhaustive considerations themselves and so wanted to hear firsthand just what variety of compromise they'd become a party to. "Of course," Mr. Glidewell set in, "it is not Mr. Nance's desire to take this issue into the courts."

"I don't guess it is," big Buster said back to him, "since as far as I know they ain't yet made the law that keeps a man from sitting in his own front yard and shooting his own gun at anybody's ducks."

"Yes, well, be that as it may, Mr. Nance has kindly agreed to defer all legal proceedings in the hope that an equitable compromise outside of the courtroom might render any future confrontations unnecessary."

And big Buster looked at Granddaddy Gottlieb and then looked at Dale and then looked at little Buster and then looked at J.G., who was still spitting on ants with his head between his legs. "Whut is it we get?" he said when he finally decided to look at Mr. Glidewell again.

Now according to Mrs. Phillip J. King, Mr. Wade Shorty Glidewell figured that he would take it upon himself to strike up a bargain with the Gottliebs when he pulled up in front of the Gottlieb acre and a half and saw with his own eyes that not a single Gottlieb out of the entire five duck brigade Gottliebs seemed very much carried away with the sport of the hunt, so Mr. Glidewell's keen legal mind set in to gyrating, Mrs. Phillip J. King called it, and Mr. Glidewell deduced and calculated and arrived at the conclusion that since the sport of the thing did not seem to have much appeal for the Gottliebs, they must be in it for the ducks alone. And Mrs. Phillip J. King said with an additional gyration or two Mr. Glidewell reasoned that there were more ways to bag a duck than with a rifle and so commenced the negotiations straightaway. "A duck," he said, "or a drake if you prefer, fully dressed from the market and delivered to you on a monthly basis."

"A duck?" big Buster said back to him.

"Or a drake, if you prefer."

"A duck a month?" big Buster said.

"Precisely."

"For how long?"

"For as long," Mr. Glidewell told him, "as Mr. Nance wishes to keep you from shooting at his ducks." And Mrs. Phillip J. King said Mr. Glidewell looked sideways at Mr. Alton and at Mr. Alton's daddy and both the Nances together nodded their approval.

"A duck a month," big Buster said and gaped to his left at his daddy and then to his right at his three boys. "Why mister," big Buster said, "I can get a whole year's worth of ducks in an afternoon" which was followed almost immediately by a sharp "Ha!" from J.G. who this time raised his head up from between his legs to say it.

"That is our offer, Mr. Gottlieb. We do hope you'll consider it," Mr. Glidewell said.

But big Buster hardly waited for him to close his mouth. "You and him over there," he said pointing to Mr. Wade Shorty Glidewell's brother's boy, Lyle, "and them two Nances yonder had best collect up together and take another vote. I got no use for your one duck a month."

"What sort of offer did you have in mind, Mr. Gottlieb?" Mr. Glidewell wanted to know.

"I was thinking more along the lines of two ducks a day, fully dressed, acourse."

"We'll confer," Mr. Glidewell said.

"You do that," big Buster told him.

And according to Mrs. Phillip J. King, Mr. Wade Shorty Glidewell and Mr. Wade Shorty Glidewell's brother's boy, Lyle, and Mr. Alton and Mr. Alton's daddy all gathered around the front left fender of Mr. Glidewell's European sedan and recommenced the exhaustive considerations that they had not ever commenced in the first place. And Mrs. Phillip J. King said Mr. Alton's daddy was all for knuckling under to the two ducks a day and so be done with it, but Mr. Alton convinced him that even a Gottlieb could be made to bend some and Mr. Wade Shorty Glidewell took up with Mr. Alton while Mr. Wade

Shorty Glidewell's brother's boy, Lyle, leaned against the front headlamp with his hands in his pockets and chewed on a weed in what Mrs. Phillip J. King called silent contemplation. She said Lyle was not much given to snap judgements.

And when the conference finally disbanded, Mrs. Phillip J. King said Mr. Wade Shorty Glidewell approached big Buster with a freshly considered counter offer. "One duck," he said, "dressed and delivered fortnightly," which sounded considerably better to big Buster than one duck a month and sounded considerably better than two ducks a month until he found out that that was what it was and so stamped his foot twice and went back to insisting on his two ducks a day. And Mrs. Phillip J. King said the Nances and their attorney and their attorney's aid collected again at the front left fender of Mr. Glidewell's car and again Mr. Alton's daddy was prepared to give way but once more Mr. Alton and Mr. Glidewell teamed up to talk him out of it while Mr. Glidewell's brother's boy, Lyle, sucked on his weed stem in silence. And this time Mr. Glidewell came away from the conference with a counter offer that sparked big Buster to only one stamp of the foot, so Mr. Glidewell immediately counter offered again and again big Buster stamped his foot but a little less vigorously than before so Mr. Glidewell counter offered again and this time big Buster did not stamp at all but instead conferred with his daddy ever so briefly before coming out with a counter offer of his own. And Mrs. Phillip J. King said it went back and forth for a goodly time with each party chiseling away at the other until finally the great flurry of counter offers on top of counter offers slowed up almost to a standstill and after a period of somber and weighty consultation with his clients, Mr. Wade Shorty Glidewell made what he called the ultimate and irrevocably final concession at one duck fully dressed and delivered every fourth day, to which big Buster said, "Done," even before he looked at his daddy, who, in the heat of the negotiations, had sunk down nearly out of sight in the folds of his comforter.

"Then we're agreed," Mr. Glidewell said.

"Well, we're nearly agreed," big Buster told him. "To tell you the truth," he went on, "around here we don't much care for duck. It's tough and stringy, don't you know. So if you're going to bring us something every fourth day why not make it a chicken instead."

"A chicken?" Mr. Glidewell said and looked at Mr. Alton's daddy, who said, "A chicken?" and looked at Mr. Alton.

"Uh huh," big Buster told them, "and it'd be alright with us if you went ahead and roasted it, wouldn't it, daddy?" But the comforter chose not to respond outright so big Buster took the silence as an affirmative.

"One roasted chicken every fourth day," Mr. Wade Shorty Glidewell said, and looked sideways at Mr. Alton who looked sideways at his daddy who nodded at Mr. Glidewell who looked full on big Buster once again and said, "Done."

And Mrs. Phillip J. King said big Buster shook hands with both the Nances and shook hands with both the Glidewells and she said all the involved parties seemed pleased and satisfied especially Mr. Alton's daddy, who was a fiend about ducks but had no love for chickens whatsoever. And even before Mr. Wade Shorty Glidewell could wheel his car around in the road and head back for the Nance estate, big Buster and little Buster and Dale and J.G. all had hold of Granddaddy Gottlieb's chair and were hauling it and the comforter and Granddaddy Gottlieb and his filed-down rifle barrel pistol across the front yard and towards the breezeway.

So Mr. Alton and Mr. Alton's daddy and Mr. Wade Shorty Glidewell and Mr. Wade Shorty Glidewell's brother's boy, Lyle, returned to the Nance estate in triumph, and the former Miss Dupont stood at the parlor window with the tips of her fingers against the panes and watched Mr. Glidewell's European sedan round the hedgerow and accelerate towards the house. She wanted to catch hold of her husband before he made off with his son and with his attorney and with his attorney's nephew so she could begin to tell him all about Miss Sissy and her series of relations with Mr. Jackson Dubois Byrd whose name she did not yet know and who himself did not strike her as being the least bit Frenchified or exotic, even for Burlington. But according to Mrs. Phillip J. King, when the former Miss Dupont finally rapped sharply enough on the parlor window to get the attention of Mr. Alton and his daddy and Mr. Glidewell and his brother's boy, Lyle, they all smiled and waved at her except for Mr. Alton's daddy, who smiled and clasped his hands together and shook them overtop of head and then the four of them rounded the house towards the bungalow as the former Miss Dupont again touched the parlor windowpanes with the tips of her fingers and looked down along the driveway and out past the hedgerow.

Mrs. Phillip J. King said Mr. Alton and his daddy and Mr. Wade Shorty Glidewell and Mr. Wade Shorty Glidewell's brother's boy, Lyle, set themselves up on the bungalow patio from where Mr. Alton's daddy dispatched Mr. Gallos to the kitchen of the big house to fetch back the cook who was instructed to whip up what Mrs. Phillip J. King called a light repast to be served there on the bungalow patio along with a half gallon or so of Mr. Alton's daddy's special imported champagne, what Mrs. Phillip J. King called Brewté Shumpanya, which she said was very rare, considerably ancient, and near about as dry as grate ash. And of course Mr. Alton's daddy and Mr. Alton and Mr. Wade Shorty Glidewell all three rared back and basked in the glory of their negotiated settlement long before the light repast and the champagne got so far as the patio, and Mrs. Phillip J. King said even Mr. Wade Shorty Glidewell's brother's boy, Lyle, managed to bask some himself though he was not much accustomed to basking and so did not pull it off with the grace and ease of his uncle or his uncle's clients. According to Mrs. Phillip J. King, when they finally got around to it they repasted on shellfish and watermelon rind pickles and artichoke hearts and she said they swilled the Brewté Shumpanya out of fluted crystal glasses which her and Momma agreed was the only proper and acceptable way to do it. And Mrs. Phillip J. King said they were still swilling long after they had finished repasting, and on into the early evening Mr. Alton and Mr. Alton's daddy and Mr. Wade Shorty Glidewell took turns analyzing the finer points of the imbroglio while Mr. Wade Shorty Glidewell's brother's boy, Lyle sat silently by until at last he stood up from his chair, raised his fluted crystal glass, and proceeded to toast Mr. Alton's daddy and Mr. Alton and his uncle Mr. Wade Shorty Glidewell, after which he promptly fell over backwards into the cement planterbox.

And as Mrs. Phillip J. King heard it Mr. Alton and his daddy did not desert the bungalow patio even after Mr. Wade Shorty Glidewell excused himself and departed in his European sedan with his nephew heaped up in the backseat, and she said they continued to entertain themselves with a combination of swilling and basking that held them on into the night, so when Mr. Alton's daddy finally did bring himself up from the bungalow to the big house and on into his bedroom to his bed, the former Miss Dupont was already in it. And even before Mr. Alton's daddy could stretch full out and blow once, the former Miss Dupont tugged on his pajama sleeve and called his name in what Mrs. Phillip J. King said was a most woeful and afflicted way. But what with all the swilling and the basking, the swilling mostly, Mr. Alton's daddy didn't make much of any response right away and Mrs. Phillip J. King said the former Miss Dupont very nearly tugged his pajama top clean off him before she got him to talking though he was in no state to talk and so hummed and grunted and did not really exhibit much civilized diction. But the former Miss Dupont figured Mr. Alton's ears were probably fit enough to receive what she had to say even if the rest of him was a little bit overswilled, so she stuck her nose up against the right side of Mr. Alton's daddy's head and said, "Our son's wife is carrying on with a millworker."

"harryathome?" Mr. Alton's daddy replied, and snorted once.

"She is having a romance."

"hohands?"

"She is cheating on your son with a common laborer."

"heating?"

"They meet in the afternoons at his house in the mill village and spend hours doing God knows what."

"honsin!" Mr. Alton's daddy said, which is what he usually said about anything that was not a duck though generally his tongue had a little more snap to it.

"I've seen them" the former Miss Dupont told him. "Mr. Gallos has too. We've followed her to the mill village."

"holloweder?" Mr. Alton's daddy said.

"It's hard to lose a Bentley at that end of town," the former Miss Dupont replied.

And according to Mrs. Phillip J. King, of a sudden Mr. Alton's daddy sat up on the pointy ends of both elbows and glared at his wife. "My Bentley?" he said.

So they both lingered by the parlor window with their fingertips against the panes until Miss Sissy wheeled the Bentley out from the garage and on around the hedgerow, after which Mr. Alton's daddy bolted for the former Miss Dupont's sedan and then waited there for the former Miss Dupont who refused to bolt herself since she knew where they would end up anyway.

And Mrs. Phillip J. King said Mr. Alton's daddy was forced to drive though he did not much like driving but couldn't avoid it since Mr. Gallos was presently otherwise engaged in carrying a delicately roasted chicken with a parsley garnish on a silver platter around to the backside of the duck pond and on through the pine grove. Of course everything but the chicken and the roasting was entirely the idea of the cook, who could not bring himself to put the thing in a paper sack as he had been instructed. So Mr. Alton's daddy drove at something considerably less than the speed of desire and the former Miss Dupont attempted to direct him, but since the former Miss Dupont did not drive herself she generally paid the most of her attention to where she had arrived and not how she came to be there, so she was ever contradicting herself in the middle of a righthand turn or in the middle of a lefthand turn and Mrs. Phillip J. King said it began to look like the former Miss Dupont might direct herself and Mr. Alton's daddy straight into an ambulance ride to the Alamance county hospital. But somehow or another the former Miss Dupont and Mr. Alton's daddy and the former Miss Dupont's sedan ended up in the mill village though they arrived at the backside by the plant, and Mr. Alton's daddy drove systematically up and down the streets until the former Miss Dupont spied his Bentley, which happened to be the only Bentley in the vicinity at the moment and was in fact one of the few Bentleys in the southeastern United States.

Of course Miss Sissy was already inside scratching Dardanelles behind the ears while she waited for Mr. Jack Dubois Byrd to come home and mingle with her, and Mrs. Phillip J. King said the former Miss Dupont and Mr. Alton's daddy had to pause in front of Mr. Jack Dubois Byrd's house for near three quarters of an hour before Mr. Jack Byrd himself came down along the sidewalk from the plant and got indicated to Mr. Alton's daddy by the former Miss Dupont who pointed with her finger and said, "Him." And according to Mrs. Phillip J. King, Mr. Alton's daddy and the former Miss Dupont continued to pause in front of Mr. Jack Dubois Byrd's house throughout the duration of the afternoon's relation, which was of course only one in a series and which by itself lasted close to an hour and a half as Mrs. Phillip J. King figured it. So it was well beyond two hours after Mr. Alton's daddy and the former Miss Dupont arrived at the mill village that they got to look at what they had come to look at in the form of Miss Sissy and Mr. Jack Dubois Byrd caught up together in what Mrs. Phillip J. King called a sweltering embrace right there in the front doorway, and she said the former Miss Dupont raised her arm and commenced to point at them, but Mr. Alton's daddy told her, "Put your finger away. I see it."

So then it was the former Miss Dupont and Mr. Alton's daddy and Mr. Alton lingering by the parlor window with the tips of their fingers against the panes as Miss Sissy wheeled the Bentley out of the garage and on around the hedgerow. And this time it was Mr. Gallos who slipped in on the driver's side since he was in between chickens, and the former Miss Dupont's sedan rounded the hedgerow itself and proceeded to clip along at the speed of a first generation Greek gardener who recollected where to go. Mrs. Phillip J. King said Mr. Alton and Mr. Alton's daddy sat in the back seat on either side of the former Miss Dupont each of them quiet and sullen and most thoroughly engaged in holding onto his kneecaps while the former Miss Dupont fanned her face with an old church bulletin and appeared noticeably flustered and agitated, Mrs. Phillip J. King said, like maybe she'd been chatting with the governor and a burst of wind had blown her dress up over her head. And Mrs. Phillip J. King said Mr. Gallos and the former Miss Dupont and Mr. Alton's daddy and Mr. Alton paused in sight of Mr. Jack Dubois Byrd's house and in sight of Mr. Alton's daddy's Bentley for a full half hour before the shift changed at the mill and Mr. Jack Byrd came home along the sidewalk and got indicated to Mr. Alton by Mr. Alton's daddy, who pointed with his finger and said, "Him." And according to Mrs. Phillip J. King it was another two hours before Mr. Alton was made to look at what the former Miss Dupont and Mr. Alton's daddy had brought him to look at, and Mrs. Phillip J. King said when the time came Mr. Alton's daddy raised his arm towards the doorway and said, "There."

As Mrs. Phillip J. King figured it, that was probably when Mr. Alton's cheekbones began to give way, though she did not call them cheekbones anymore and so would not allow them to merely give way. Instead Mrs. Phillip J. King told me and Momma that was probably when his features commenced their emotional erosion, though she insisted Mr. Alton remained unerodedly dashing to the naked eye for any number of months after he witnessed his wife, Miss Sissy Dundee, and Mr. Jack Dubois Byrd wrestling in Mr. Byrd's doorway under the close scrutiny of a speckled tomcat. But anyway that was when Mr. Alton's finely chiseled bone structure began to break down on a microscopic level, according to Mrs. Phillip J. King, who said the deterioration was further advanced by Miss Sissy herself who could not be made ashamed of what she had done no matter how much sinfulness and damnation anybody held over her head. Mrs. Phillip J. King said Miss Sissy had simply become far too tropical for redemption. Of course Mr. Alton blamed it all on himself at first, said if he'd never gotten her on the parachute drop at Coney Island none of this might have happened, but Mrs. Phillip J. King said presently Mr. Alton recollected that he wasn't much more fond of Miss Sissy than she was of him, and so he became a little less tormented than he had been previously and left most of the agonizing up to his momma and daddy and up to the congressman and Mrs. Dundee, who had to share all the Dundee agony and shame between them since Miss Sissy would not be saddled with any of it.

Now according to Mrs. Phillip J. King rich, cultivated people generally go about their agony and their torment in a most civilized and proper fashion and so what had started in a roadhouse on the 54 highway and then carried on into the north Burlington mill village got fairly much finished off over four courses of supper at the Dundee estate. Mrs. Phillip J. King said the appetizer and the entree belonged to the congressman and Mrs. Dundee along with Mr. Alton's momma and daddy all of whom insisted that their daughter and son-in-law respectively, who became the parties in question for the sake of discussion, work together towards a speedy and blissful reunion. But during the fruit plate and the dessert, the congressman and Mrs. Dundee along with Mr. Alton's daddy and the former Miss Dupont all found out together that the parties in question near about despised each other. The fruit plate belonged to Miss Sissy who could not find a decent or sorrowful word to say to Mr. Alton even after her momma and Daddy and Mr. Alton's daddy and the former Miss Dupont tried between the four of them to hoist up all of Miss Sissy's mingling and hold it over her head which apparently had no effect whatsoever on Miss Sissy who went after her apple slices and her melon balls with what Mrs. Phillip J. King called shameless gusto. The dessert of course fell to Mr. Alton who picked at his merangue with his fork as he told his wife and his in-laws and his momma and daddy how he had been wounded most mortally in his pride and so did not think he could ever again bathe Miss Sissy in the glow of his affections. Mrs. Phillip J. King said that aside from his microscopically eroding features Mr. Alton was afflicted as well with a heart turned barren and cold where once had thrived the flowers of devotion nurtured by the warmth of desire, which Momma told Mrs. Phillip J. King was a very fine turn of phrase on her part, for which Mrs. Phillip J. King was highly gratified.

Mrs. Phillip J. King said what came of the four course supper at the Dundee estate was that the congressman and Mrs. Dundee and Mr. Alton's daddy and the former Miss Dupont and Miss Sissy and Mr. Alton all decided and agreed that the parties in question should undergo a trial separation until what the congressman called the riff could be mended, and Mrs. Phillip J. King said everybody at the table was pleased and satisfied with the decision since when the congressman and Mrs. Dundee and Mr. Alton's daddy and the former Miss Dupont said trial separation they meant trial separation and when Miss Sissy and Mr. Alton said trial separation they meant divorce. So when Mr. Alton moved back up to the big house and left Miss Sissy by herself in the bungalow all the Nances and Dundees together agreed it was surely for the best, and Mrs. Phillip J. King said almost immediately things went on pretty much as they had gone on before except for Miss Sissy who was relieved of the keys to the Bentley by Mr. Alton's daddy until she had herself delivered to Mr. Jack Byrd's house by one of Burlington's two taxi cabs and retrieved from it by the other all of which put her in the Bentley once again and allowed things to go exactly as they had gone on before. Of course Mr. Alton and his daddy had polished off their imbroglio and so Mr. Alton's daddy returned to his hewn log bench in the pine grove from where he watched anybody's ducks drop over the treetops and into his lake without what Mrs. Phillip J. King called the accompanying fuselade to distract him. As for Mr. Alton, he took up politicking again and engaged himself in advising public figures, which Daddy had told me he did mostly with his wallet, while the former Miss Dupont continued to linger at the parlor window in the afternoons with her fingertips against the panes and watch Miss Sissy wheel the Bentley around the hedgerow and out of sight.

According to Mrs. Phillip J King, Mr. Alton and Miss Sissy tried the separation for a full year and then tried the divorce after on account of a longstanding state law that decreed it was the natural order of things for conflicting spouses to despise each other from separate and individual dwellings for twelve months time before legally dissolving their vows and so becoming friends again. But Mrs. Phillip J. King said she did not believe Mr. Alton and Miss Sissy ever became friends because twelve months worth of steady mingling on the part of Miss Sissy and on the part of Mr. Jack Dubois Byrd finally succeeded in swelling Miss Sissy up with a minglette, news of which unloosed an emotional gulleywash on Mr. Alton's features. So Miss Sissy and Mr. Alton went ahead and became divorced with about the same feeling they had for each other when they became separated and Miss Sissy moved on out of the bungalow and back to the Dundee estate while Mr. Alton moved out of the big house and into the bungalow once again. And according to Mrs. Phillip J. King, Mr. Alton was just holding his own at reasonably dashing when Miss Sissy's daddy the Congressman Dundee, discovered that Mr. Jack Byrd was invaluable to him for his political advice and so hired him on as an aid which opened the way for Miss Sissy to take him on as a husband, and Mrs. Phillip J. King said the ceremony transpired on the twenty-third of July between the Dundee ligustrum hedges, so almost exactly where Miss Sissy Mercer Dundee had become Miss Sissy Mercer Dundee Nance she became Miss Sissy Mercer Dundee Nance Dubois-Byrd which Miss Sissy's daddy got legally hyphenated as a wedding gift for the happy couple, mostly for the happy bride. As for Mr. Alton, he steadily continued to become less finely chiseled and by the time the baby little Jackson Mercer Dubois-Byrd got brought into the world, which was a ways short of nine months after the ceremony, Mr. Alton had long since left off being purely dashing, had even left off being purely reasonably dashing, while for her part Miss Sissy discovered that the last thing on earth she wanted was a baby now that she had one, and for his part Mr. Jack Dubois-Byrd entertained the congressman's constituents by making the veins stand up on his forehead and got sent out for sandwiches whenever he was handy.

Mrs. Phillip J. King said Mr. Alton was a sizeable while putting Miss Sissy behind him and she said he could well have eroded clean down to homely if not for the luck and happenstance that sent him to what Mrs. Phillip J. King called a political feeta in the company of Judge Wade Shorty Glidewell where Mr. Alton got himself introduced to a gentleman who had recently come into considerable prominence on account of a chimpanzee and where he got himself introduced to that gentleman's sister also. According to Mrs. Phillip J. King, it was not love at first sight exactly since Mr. Alton, eroded and gulleywashed as he was, did not set women all aflutter anymore, and since Miss Myra Angelique, reserved and dignified by nature, was not much given to wild flights of impetuosity, Mrs. Phillip J. King called them. But she said it was love eventually even if it was not love at first sight exactly, and according to Mrs. Phillip J. King it got so that no Republican or Democrat either could hardly throw a feeta of any scale or variety without attracting Miss Myra Angelique and her brother the mayor, and without attracting Mr. Alton and his ever-settling features. And as Mrs. Phillip J. King recollected it, feeta number one saw Miss Pettigrew and Mr. Alton share an hors d'oeuvre plate and pass between them many polite remarks while feeta number two brought Miss Myra Angelique and Mr. Alton together on the dance floor where they negotiated themselves through several waltzes with exceptional success until Mr. Alton led Miss Myra Angelique directly into the corner of the punch table and so put her out of commission for the remainder of the feeta. And Mrs. Phillip J. King said it was not until feeta number five at the legion hall in Greensboro when Miss Pettigrew passed her arm through Mr. Alton's and allowed him to escort her out onto the slab patio where the two of them took the evening air together, and Mrs. Phillip J. King said there is something about standing on a cool cement slab under the stars that breeds romance like mosquitoes.

She told me and Momma she would never forget it. She told us it would never pass from her memory. "Of course I's only a baby, don't you know," Mrs. Phillip J. King said, "I mean I wasn't hardly out of my ringlets and my smock when P.J. and me said our I do's and he brought me here to this place to settle, but it will never leave me, not ever, Inez, I mean the sight of him driving along the boulevard in his touring car with the sunlight playing against the fenders and sparkling off the tire spokes, and me hardly out of my ringlets and my smock and not ever having been much of anywhere and not ever having seen much of anything and then there's his foreign automobile on the boulevard taking the sunlight like a diamond and him behind the wheel of it erect and dapper and very nearly finely chiseled. I mean to tell you Inez it was just, it was simply, it was absolutely . . ."

"Dazzling?" Momma said.

And Mrs. Phillip J. King told us, "Lord yes."

She said his cheekbones had made a partial recovery after the commencement of the romance with Miss Pettigrew and Mrs. Phillip J. King tried to get by with plain handsome but Momma insisted on tacking the passably to the front of it, so Mrs. Phillip J. King went round about the other way and told me and Momma how Mr. Alton had taken to sunning himself on the bungalow patio and so had become what Mrs. Phillip J. King called swarthy.

"Swarthy?" Momma said.

"Yes ma'm," Mrs. Phillip J. King told her, and then she asked us did we know that Dupont was a French word for bronze, which we didn't not either one of us. So Mrs. Phillip J. King went on to tell us how even a plain to reasonably good-looking gentleman could be improved upon considerably if not outright dramatically by a touch of swarthiness in his complexion, and of course, she said, if you start out with a man who is passably handsome already, who in fact tends much more towards the handsome than the passably, then a bit of the bronze, la Dupont she called it, could make him into a regular Dick Powell in the course of a cloudless afternoon.

But Momma would not allow for a regular Dick Powell and would not allow for purely handsome either because, as Momma saw it, swarthiness was at best a seasonal improvement that offered up the illusion of handsome by covering over the passably on a temporary basis. So Momma and Mrs. Phillip J. King negotiated once again with Mr. Alton's attractions and together they agreed to let Mr. Alton hover up around the handsome end of passably handsome in the summertime and drop back down to the passably end of it for the rest of the year. So Mrs.

Phillip J. King said Mr. Alton was hard up against the underside of handsome the first time he took his touring car down along the boulevard and towards municipal square. She said it was early September and Mr. Alton had built up an entire August's worth of swarthiness, and as Mrs. Phillip J. King recalled it, not Mr. Alton nor his touring car either had ever looked so majestical on the streets of Burlington as they did once they hit the boulevard in Neely. She said Mr. Alton sat behind the wheel in swarthy splendor and guided his magnificent machine, she called it, along what Mrs. Phillip J. King said were the arbored streets and byways of the fair city. She said the sight was a study in pure dazzlement and again she told me and Momma it would never pass from her memory even if she wasn't hardly out of her ringlets and her smock at the time.

According to Mrs. Phillip J. King, Mr. Wallace Amory could just barely fit into Mr. Alton's back seat, which was made more for suitcases than for anybody, and she said soon after Mr. Alton arrived at the Pettigrew's in all of his dazzlement and in all of his swarthy splendor he lit out again with Miss Myra Angelique to his right side looking very queenly and appropriate, Mrs. Philip J. King called it, and with the most of Mr. Wallace Amory to his backside except for those parts and attachments that could not be squeezed or wedged or otherwise forcibly introduced into the backseat and so hung over the door panels or stuck straight up into the air. So Mrs. Phillip J. King said even though Mr. Alton was just as splendorously swarthy when he left as when he had arrived and even though Miss Myra Angelique was just as splendorously queenly beside him, the general departure lacked the majority of the dazzlement of the general arrival entirely on account of the mayor who was mostly kneecaps and shoetops and appeared to be sprouting out of the back of the car like a weed. But Mrs. Phillip J. King said Mr. Wallace Amory got his fill of Mr. Alton's backseat after two dinners in Winston-Salem, a brunch in Greensboro, and a handful of campaign feetas in Raleigh and consequently left off prizing himself between the trunk and the seatbacks which allowed for a return of what dazzlement had seeped away on account of the flagrant untidiness of the major's appendages, Mrs. Phillip J. King called it. And she said with the dazzlement back along with the splendorous swarthiness and the splendorous queenliness to complement it, the sight of Mr. Alton and Miss Myra Angelique traveling in Mr. Alton's magnificent machine along the arbored streets and byways of the fair city was enough by itself to set your heart to quivering.

Mrs. Phillip J. King said they were a supremely handsome couple and there wasn't anybody in all of Neely who did not believe that the two of them were made for each other, not even Mr. Phillip J. King who Mrs. Phillip J. King said was about as romantic as steel wool. Of course the mayor thought it was a marvelous match, at least he did at first, and Mrs. Phillip J. King said whenever Mr. Alton and Miss Myra Angelique would go off together in Mr. Alton's touring car the mayor would set out from the Pettigrew mansion and stroll uptown before all the quivering could die away where he would accept the congratulations of most everybody since most everybody was pleased for Mr. Alton and pleased for Miss Myra Angelique and pleased for the mayor who was equally pleased himself, at least at first. And according to Mrs. Phillip J. King every once and again Mr. Alton would wheel into town all splendorous and sparkling and would not make off with Miss Pettigrew but would remain in the Pettigrew mansion with the mayor and with Sister where they would all take dinner together and then retire to the ballroom for the remainder of the evening. And Mrs. Phillip J. King said Mr. Wallace Amory would throw open the window sashes and the draft would draw the ends of the milky sheers outside across the sill and Mr. Alton would pop the cork on a bottle of champagne and Miss Myra Angelique would start up the phonograph and set the needle down on Miss Ethel Merman's rendition of "The Lullaby of Broadway" which she was particularly fond of and so always commenced with. And as Mrs. Phillip J. King figured it, the music and the golden light from the ballroom and the mild October night air all conspired together to attract most anybody with feet and a will to move them, and consequently Miss Merman could hardly get through the refrain twice before the first few arms would pass between the palings of the imported wrought iron fence out front. And Mrs. Phillip J. King said eventually whoever was pressed up against the fence would find people at their backsides pressed up against them who in turn would get pressed up against themselves, so by the time Miss Myra Angelique could set the needle down on Mr. Bing Crosby's

"Swinging on a Star" folks would already be backed up into the street to watch her and Mr. Alton glide past the open windows and on around the ballroom. But Mrs. Phillip J. King said Mr. Alton by nature was more of a swiller than a dancer which put him mostly in the company of the champagne bottle and left Miss Myra Angelique to tour the dance floor with the mayor who did not much care for Mr. Bing Crosby but showed a marked preference for his brother Bob's lively version of "The Big Noise from Winnetka." So sometimes it was Mr. Alton and Miss Pettigrew and sometimes it was Miss Pettigrew and the mayor and sometimes, after they had popped enough champagne corks between them, it was the mayor and Mr. Alton who whirled past the ballroom windows with their cheeks pressed hard together and their arms around each other while Miss Myra Angelique cackled and clapped her hands and left the record to spin on the phonograph platter until the needle bump bump bumped against the final groove.

Mrs. Phillip J. King did not know how Mr. Wallace Amory found out when he at last did find out, she did not know who he knew in Burlington or who he knew in Neely who had relations in Burlington and thereby got secondary access to what it was Mr. Wallace Amory discovered. All Mrs. Phillip J. King could tell me and Momma was that the mayor did find out, found out before October was up and intercepted Mr. Alton at the Pettigrew front door one Tuesday evening, which left off being just Tuesday evening once Mr. Alton got intercepted and became instead the mournful night of reckoning, Mrs. Phillip J. King called it. She said Mr. Wallace Amory hauled Mr. Alton on into the study and slid the towering twin mahogany doors tight shut behind them. Then he spun on his heels, Mrs. Phillip J. King said, and confronted Mr. Alton directly, asked him outright was he or was he not freshly divorced.

"Freshly divorced?" Momma said.

"Yes ma'm," Mrs. Phillip J. King told her. "It was a pure and absolute revelation to him, Inez. Mr. Alton had never let on, had never whispered a breath of it, and of course Mr. Wallace Amory was scandalized to find it out for himself. After all, Inez, we are talking about the man's very sister."

"Freshly divorced," Momma said.

"Yes ma'm," Mrs. Phillip J. King told her.

And according to Mrs. Phillip J. King, Mr. Alton could not

manage an answer at first so Mr. Wallace Amory reconfronted him all over again and demanded that he make reply, Mrs. Phillip J. King called it, and Mr. Alton traveled all roundabout the question for any number of minutes before he finally did admit he was divorced but not all that freshly. And Mrs. Phillip J. King said just the admission of the divorce alone even without the freshly threw Mr. Wallace Amory into what she called a fit of passion which apparently gets thrown mostly with the feet and the hands since Mr. Wallace Amory stomped throughout the study and beat on most anything that looked like it would not beat back. Mr. Alton of course tried to justify himself, tried to explain Miss Sissy and tried to explain Miss Sissy's mingling, but Mrs. Phillip J. King said it was most always near impossible to talk sense to a man in a fit of passion, so once Mr. Alton finished up his defense Mr. Wallace Amory said he believed he'd throttle him anyway and the two of them set in to scuffling across the floor and into the furniture with Mr. Wallace Amory having the upper hand right off since Nances were about as much given to scuffling as they were to fisticuffs.

Now when the scuffle itself broke out Miss Myra Angelique was upstairs in the middle of her twalet, Mrs. Phillip J. King called it, and ordinarily she would have heard all the grunting and the banging around since the study was fairly much directly underneath her, but Mrs. Phillip J. King said as it turned out the night of the mournful reckoning was particularly tumultuous weatherwise on account of an inky cloud that had settled in over Neely along about dusk. And Mrs. Phillip J. King said by the time the mayor grabbed hold of Mr. Alton's lapels and threw him into the settee, which was the first place he threw him, the rain was coming down in sheets and torrents and bucketfuls and the profound inkiness of the evening was getting some relief from the lightning bolts which rent the night sky in fiery jagged slashing streaks, Mrs. Phillip J. King said, and which of course drew along with them a whole chorus of great rolling thunderclaps that shook not only the Pettigrew window panes but the sashes too.

"A thunderstorm?" Momma said.

"Yes ma'm," Mrs. Phillip J. King told her.

"In October?"

"Yes ma'm." Mrs. Phillip J. King said it was a lower level atmospheric disturbance of the most violent and unusual kind.

Consequently Miss Myra Angelique did not hear any of the beating and banging around that was going on directly underneath her, and since she had a whole half a twalet ahead of her when the scuffling commenced the mayor got to toss Mr. Alton most all throughout the study before Miss Pettigrew ever touched her dainty foot to the top stairtread and set about gliding on down to the main floor.

According to Mrs. Phillip J. King, the majority of the scuffle had run fairly much like the outbreak of it with Mr. Wallace Amory doing most of the beating and Mr. Alton doing the best part of the banging. But she said near about the time Miss Pettigrew got halfway down the stairway Mr. Alton forgot himself momentarily and delivered what Mrs. Phillip J. King called a telling blow to the boney part of the mayor's nose which somewhat compounded and inflated the mayor's fit of passion and turned it into an outright rage, especially once Mr. Wallace Amory put his fingers to his nostrils and drew back a tiny smear of blood. So Mrs. Phillip J. King said by the time Miss Myra Angelique hit the foyer, Mr. Wallace Amory had already backed up to the mantelpiece and fetched down from over top of it his great-uncle's naked sabre which was all bestudded about the handle with jewels and gems and which had been carried to several operas and toted in any number of parades but had not ever before sliced up a Nance which was what the mayor seemed to have in mind when he took hold of the hilt with both hands and raised the blade up over his shoulder. And as Mrs. Phillip J. King understood it, the mayor was all set to advance on Mr. Alton and filet him when Miss Myra Angelique slid open the towering twin mahogany doors and let herself into the study. And according to Mrs. Phillip J. King, once Miss Pettigrew drew up short and saw what there was to see she let out a wild anguished cry that rent the night pretty much like the lightning did, and then Mrs. Phillip J. King cut loose with a wild anguished cry of her own to show us what one sounded like.

Daddy must have heard it, even through both front doors, and must have decided right off to come into the house and on back to the breakfast room to watch Mrs. Phillip J. King suffer whatever variety of calamity it might take to draw that sort of shriek out of her. So he was already parked against the doorway between the kitchen and the breakfast room when

Mrs. Phillip J. King collected up enough breath to tell me and Momma and now Daddy too how Miss Myra Angelique flung herself at the mayor so as to keep him from swinging the naked sabre against even the most insignificant little swarthy piece of Mr. Alton. But the mayor cast Miss Pettigrew aside with one mighty hand, Mrs. Phillip J. King called it, and with the other waved the pointy end of the sabre at the tip of Mr. Alton's nose. "This man is divorced," he said. However, as Mrs. Phillip J. King recollected it, Miss Myra Angelique did not waver for even a second before she flung herself at the mayor all over again and wrapped both her arms around his legs. "Run!" she screamed. "Save yourself!" and apparently that was about all Mr. Alton needed to hear since he was already straddling a windowsill before the sound of the words could die off altogether. And Mrs. Phillip J. King said Miss Pettigrew managed to keep ahold of the mayor until Mr. Alton got clear of the window and partway around the house, and even when Mr. Wallace Amory did free his legs, Miss Myra Angelique grabbed him around the waist and got dragged on out through the front door and onto the porch where she was finally deposited in a heap when Mr. Wallace Amory had had enough of the extra baggage. So Miss Myra Angelique lay on the porch decking and sobbed while the mayor proceeded on out into the front yard and stood under the lightning rent sky in the sheets and torrents and bucketfuls of rain and waved his great-uncle's naked sabre over his head as he hollered after Mr. Alton who brought his touring car away from the curb and disappeared down the boulevard.

And Mrs. Phillip J. King drew a luxuriously long breath. "First Miss Sissy," she said, "and then this. What a tragic figure."

"Such a tragic figure," Momma said and let out about as much air as Mrs. Phillip J. King had taken in.

And Daddy, who had not bothered to say anything just yet, finally opened his mouth and told the both of them, "He was a slimy individual," which stood Momma straight up out of her chair and spun Mrs. Phillip J. King full around in hers and together they pretty much wailed at him, "Louis Benfield!"

ii

MR. RUSSELL NEWBERRY told me and Daddy he believed it was a Louisiana tag, but he'd hardly closed his mouth good when Mr. L.T. Chamblee and Mr. Raford Britt's eldest boy, Coley, said it was not any such thing. Mr. Chamblee recollected the outline of a palmetto tree behind the numbers and so insisted it was a South Carolina plate, while Coley Britt, who could not recall any specific vegetation, said he'd been reading ever since he was nine and guessed he ought to know the words West Virginia when he saw them. Along about then Mr. Covington came out through one of the service bay doors wiping his hands on a rag, and before he could even tell me and Daddy how do you do, Mr. Newberry and Mr. Chamblee and Coley Britt were all over him wanting to know was it Louisiana or was it South Carolina and especially was it West Virginia since Coley Britt had fairly much put his education on the line. But Mr. Covington just looked at the three of them as he finished wiping his hands and then stuck the rag partway into his back pocket and said, "Whut?"

"Where was it they come from?" Mr. Chamblee asked him.

"Who?" Mr. Covington said.

"That man and his wife," Coley Britt told him. "Just where was it they come from?"

"Up that way," Mr. Covington said and flung his arm in a direction the road didn't go exactly.

"What sort of plates did they have, Bill?" Mr. Newberry wanted to know.

"Jump got his gas for him," Mr. Covington said. "I didn't ever see the plates."

So while Mr. L.T. Chamblee set in to bellowing for Jump to come out from wherever it was he'd gotten off to, Coley Britt told Mr. Newberry, "West Virginia's up that way."

And Mr. Newberry told him back, "So's Alaska."

"Well they couldn't have driven down from Alaska in a Pontiac," Coley Britt said.

And Mr. Chamblee broke off his bellowing right in the middle of it and told Coley Britt, "Hadn't no Pontiac been in here all day. It was a Chevrolet as big as life."

"For God sakes, L.T.," Coley shot back at him, "that thing was a Bonneville pure and plain."

"Tell him Russell," Mr. Chamblee said, "tell him what it was."

But Mr. Newberry said he didn't know one car from another and all he could recollect for certain, aside from the license plate, was the color, which he remembered as a dull green all over.

And Mr. Chamblee conceded that it did look a little green to him at first also. "But it turned out to be blue," he said, "turned out to be a blue Caprice Classic."

Then Daddy asked Coley Britt if, in his estimation, a man could drive a blue Chevrolet Caprice Classic down from Alaska, and Coley looked at Daddy out from the side of his face like maybe he was sizing him up for a tire-iron necktie. "How about from Michigan?" Daddy said, and Coley spat twice on the asphalt and appeared to be formulating some sort of genuine threat when Jump Garrison, who was actually Coolidge Garrison but got called Jump, came out from around the far side of the station where he'd been hosing down Mr. Covington's rest rooms so as to keep them as clean as all the signboards said they were. Jump was what Daddy called a blue-gummed negro which meant he was about the color of the bottom of a full hole. He had been with Mr. Covington for going on seven years and so had become somewhat attached to the gas pumping business and especially to the gas pumper's uniform which he kept all pleated and creased like a tuxedo and which was no end of pride to him except maybe for the shirt since it did not say "Jump" in the little white oval over the pocket and did not say "Coolidge" either but said "Bill" instead, even after seven years.

He came round the corner mopping himself with a brick-colored rag, which he carefully folded and slipped into his back pocket once he was done with it, and even before he could manage a full stop and clasp his hands behind his back so as to stand fairly much at ease Mr. Covington asked him, "Jump, you remember a blue Chevrolet coming through here today?"

"A Caprice Classic," Mr. Chamblee added.

And Jump licked the inside of his bottom lip. "No sir," he said.

"You remember a green Pontiac," Mr. Covington asked him.

"No sir."

"How about a blue Pontiac or a green Chevrolet?"

"No sir," Jump said.

"They was a man and a woman," Mr. Chamblee told him. "They won't from around here."

"Yes sir," Jump said, "I remember. Them two come through in a green Buick with a black vinyl top."

"For Chrissakes, a Buick?" Coley Britt said and laughed and then he said it again and laughed again and then he made a most mean and vicious remark against negrodom in general which Jump Garrison accepted with the blandest of expressions like maybe Coley had merely speculated on the weather.

"I give him fourteen dollars and fifty cents worth a Good Gulf," Jump said, mostly to Mr. Covington, "and then I checked his oil, which was awright, then he come out around the front a the car and asked me to put some water in his battery. He told me he paid nearly ninety-seven dollars for that battery and he wanted to keep it slam full up with water. He said a man had to be willing to pay for quality, he said he was lucky he could afford to. But the battery didn't need any water so I put some in the radiator instead and checked the belts and wiped the duster off before I closed the hood up. Then his wife decided she had to go right away and couldn't wait for me to get the key so she took it off the wall herself and he give me a twenty and followed me into the station, but before I could take out for the gas he got himself some nabs and got his wife some peanuts and come away from the drink box with two Brownies but he opened the first one up before he shook it so I let him put it back and get another one and I only took out for the two Brownies along with the nabs and the peanuts and the fourteen dollars and fifty cents worth a Good Gulf. Then me and him went on back outside and presently his wife come round the corner and give me the key. Then him and her both want to know where they can find Miss Pettigrew. And I say to him, 'What Pettigrew?' And he says back to me, 'Miss Myra Angelique Pettigrew.' A course I didn't know what to tell him, so I figured I'd fetch Mr. Covington and let him do it for me, but I looked up here into the service bay and seen him in the grease pit under a Torino so I guessed I'd have to do it for myself and as I figured it there wasn't any way to go about it but head on so I said to him, 'I'm awful sorry, Mister, but Miss Pettigrew's dead. Died yesterday.' And along about midway through the sorrowful news him and his wife both turned up their Brownies, then she ate one a his nabs and he ate some a her peanuts. 'I know that,' he says to me. 'Where is she?' Well, then I tell him I suppose she's at Mr. Commander Tuttle's and he wants to know where that is so I get him out alongside the road and show him how to hit the boulevard and tell him where to cut back past the square and he thanked me and seemed considerably gracious so I went ahead and asked him flat out if he was some sort of Pettigrew relation. And he finished off his Brownie, handed me the bottle and said, 'You're looking at the heir, buddy.' Then his wife handed me her bottle too and him and her got back in the Buick and damned if he didn't light out in exactly the wrong direction."

"Well Jump, where was it they were from?" Mr. Chamblee asked him.

"Didn't neither one of them say," Jump told him back.

"The tags, Jump," Mr. Newberry said. "Where were the tags from?"

And Jump said he never noticed the tags, said the gas tank was on the right rear fender so he never had call to circle round behind the car.

Then Coley Britt said, "They sounded like they were from West Virginia, didn't they, Jump?"

"I guess so," Jump told him. "What's that sound like?"

And Coley Britt made another observation about negroes that was a little meaner and a little more vicious than the first one.

Mr. Russell Newberry came away from Mr. Bill Covington's Gulf Station when me and Daddy came away from it ourselves and Jump Garrison went back to hosing down the bathrooms while Mr. Covington excused himself into the service bay, which left Mr. L.T. Chamblee and Coley Britt on the bench out front against the stucco wall where Mr. Chamblee got back on his palmetto tree almost immediately and Coley Britt leaned forward with his forearms across his thighs and appeared set to strike in on the history of his reading habits whenever the moment presented itself. And though Mr. Chamblee and Coley Britt still could not agree as to whether or not it was South Carolina or West Virginia they both appeared considerably relieved at the withdrawal of Louisiana from the proceedings.

As for Mr. Newberry, he told me and Daddy he was not so thoroughly convinced it was Louisiana after all but was dead certain it had not been South Carolina or West Virginia and so had automatically volunteered Louisiana which was ever prominent in his mind on account of his sister's husband who hailed from Natchitoches which Mr. Newberry could never say the same way twice. Then Mr. Newberry stopped in the middle of the sidewalk, braced himself, and told me and Daddy Natchitoches two times fast which Daddy said sounded like both sides of a heated argument in Portuguese.

Between the two of them, Daddy and Mr. Newberry decided we had best head on over to Commander Tuttle's Heavenly Rest and put an end to this license tag business forever which worked out exceptionally well since that seemed to be where we were going anyway. But we hadn't hardly set foot on the far side of the boulevard when a green Buick with a black vinyl top turned out from a sidestreet and passed us almost before we knew it was coming. I don't believe I ever saw the front end of it and I don't imagine I'd have ever seen the back end of it either if not for Mrs. Pettigrew heir who turned out to be Mrs. T. Fay Rackley, the "T." being the survivor of something her daddy had burdened her with that she could not in good conscience dispose of entirely but had very nearly cancelled out anyway. Mrs. T. Fay Rackley was riding with her window rolled all the way down into the door and her head partway out the opening when Mr. Pettigrew heir drove her up the boulevard past me and Daddy and Mr. Russell Newberry. And along about when the front view of the Buick was becoming the side view of the Buick, Mrs. T. Fay Rackley laid the back of her head down next to the vent window and said, "Well, Sugar!" in one of those high unbearable voices that usually bypasses the mouth and exits through the noseholes. Naturally the sheer unpleasantness of it caused me and Daddy and Mr. Newberry together to seek out the guilty party who Daddy and me saw was riding in a green Buick and who Mr. Newberry saw was riding in the green Buick, so Mr. Newberry was the only one of us to turn around quick enough to see the license plate but of course he was the only one of us who couldn't hardly see anyhow which meant we could still be sure it wasn't South Carolina or West Virginia and could remain reasonably certain it wasn't Louisiana either but could not say precisely what it was.

So between the two of them, Daddy and Mr. Newberry decided we had best not head over to Commander Tuttle's after all since there was no longer much call to pay the commander a visit, and instead me and Daddy and Mr. Newberry swung around in the opposite direction and made for wherever it was the Buick had made for which we figured had to be the Pettigrew house since there wasn't much else in Neely worth coming all the way from Louisiana or West Virginia or even South Carolina to see. And although we swung around in pursuit of that Buick a time before it got wherever it was it was going we weren't hardly the first people to catch up with it once Mr. Pettigrew heir pulled up alongside the curb by the imported wrought iron fence and him and Mrs. T. Fay Rackley let themselves in through the gate and poked around in Miss Pettigrew's flower beds for a spell before they climbed the front steps up onto the porch and beat on the door. By the time we arrived, Aunt Willa had already let them into the foyer, and out on the street that car was thick all around with admirers who circled it from frontside to backside and from backside to frontside and puzzled over every little attachment and embellishment like they had never seen such a contraption as a Buick before. Even Coley Britt and Mr. L.T. Chamblee beat us to the license tag and we came up on the two of them stooped over it in the midsts of a fiery exchange. "That's what I thought it was all along," Coley Britt said. "I told you that's what I thought it was."

"I'll be goddammed if you did any such thing," Mr. Chamblee told him.

"L.T. I said clear plain if it weren't West Virginia that's what it would be."

"The hell you did," Mr. Chamblee said.

"They're near about the same place, L.T. You can stand in one and spit into the other."

"But they ain't the same place."

"Well at least neither one of 'em has a thing in the world to do with a palmetto tree."

"I tell you I seen a palmetto tree on this exact car," Mr. Chamblee said.

And Coley Britt asked him, "Well where is it then, you jackass?"

And when it looked like Coley and Mr. Chamblee were just about set to flail each other to death, Daddy stuck his head square between the two of them so as to get to the license tag himself. "Yep," he said. "Just like I told you, Russell. Kentucky." And then he drew his head out again and grinned at Mr. Coley Britt and grinned at Mr. L.T. Chamblee, and I do believe if the both of them had not been all frozen up and transfixed with rage they would have made a very sincere attempt to take Daddy apart entirely.

But then Aunt Willa turned the monkey out so everybody forgot about the Buick and forgot about where the Buick was from and took to the fence. Me and Daddy and Mr. Newberry got us a place right up next to the gate, and I guess there was a dozen people flanking us on either side when Aunt Willa hooked Mr. Britches into his tether and turned him loose. Of course he shot directly up the flagpole and stood on the knob at the top looking thoroughly self-possessed and satisfied and wearing the exact same outfit as the day previous except for the sneakers, one of which was under a chair in the front hallway and the other of which Sheriff Burton had confiscated in the name of conscientious law enforcement. And as we all stood there at the fence watching the monkey perched there on top of the flagpole watching us, Aunt Willa went back up onto the porch and into the house but left the front door standing open and consequently we all heard Mr. Pettigrew heir say, "What's this here?" which drew us off from Mr. Britches who had himself commenced to surveying the horizon. You really couldn't see on into the foyer, you really couldn't see clear up to the back of the porch on account of Miss Pettigrew's awning and the shade it threw everywhere, but it seemed you could hear well enough, so we all sucked in our breath and waited to find out what Mr. Pettigrew heir's this here was exactly, but no matter how still we held ourselves and no matter how hard we listened all we could hear was a kind of flat, bothered silence that turned out to be Aunt Willa's response. "But what's it for?" Mr. Pettigrew heir said, and Aunt Willa droned at him for another spell until Mrs. T. Fay Rackley opened up both her noseholes and shrieked, "Why Bugs, look at that yonder." "Where?" Mr. Pettigrew heir asked her. "Right yonder," she wailed at him, and apparently right yonder was somewhere other than the foyer and took the three of them on into the back of the house because that was all the talking and all the droning and even all the screeching we heard for awhile.

So in the meantime for amusement most of us watched Mr. Britches, who had fairly much doused the flagpole and who was squatting on the knob engaged in picking at the fur on his belly which was just the sort of undertaking to undo most everything a blazer and a porkpie hat might appear to accomplish. Then a portion of the crowd grew weary of watching Mr. Britches be a monkey and went back to circling the green Buick that was very nearly from West Virginia, and just when it seemed like the Pettigrew house had gone ahead and swallowed up Aunt Willa and Mrs. T. Fay Rackley and Mr. Pettigrew heir, a window sash on the far end of the first level sailed up with a thunderous rattle and Mr. Pettigrew heir himself stuck his head outside and sucked at the afternoon like he'd been under water for a quarter hour. Of course the whole time the window was open we could all hear Mrs. T. Fay Rackley exercising her noseholes over a floorlamp that had been made from a butter churn and the only thing in the world she wanted was for Mr. Pettigrew heir to look at it which he did not seem the least inclined to do right up to the moment Mrs. T. Fay Rackley fetched him away from the window with one hand and slammed the sash down with the other. So we all went back to watching the monkey and pondering the Buick and Daddy and Mr. Newberry leaned backwards against the fence and smoked Daddy's Tareytons off Mr. Newberry's matches until finally a second floor window went flying up with about as much fuss and rattle as the other and Mr. Pettigrew heir popped out clear down to his midsection and siphoned off considerably more of the afternoon than he'd been able to manage previously. As far as we could tell, Mrs. T. Fay Rackley was working her noseholes over a bedstead this time and she could not seem to decide whether it was an oak bedstead or a fur bedstead or a walnut bedstead or a loblolly pine bedstead, so she asked Aunt Willa who apparently did not know or would not say because after the spell of silence that was Aunt Willa's response, Mrs. T. Fay Rackley set in to screeching at Mr. Pettigrew heir about it and allowed him to protrude into the afternoon for only a short while longer before she caused him to disappear a little prematurely again.

We didn't see Mr. Pettigrew heir for a considerable while after the bedstead episode, which is what folks were beginning to call it, and we didn't see Aunt Willa or hear from Mrs. T. Fay Rackley either, so understandably interest in the monkey and the Buick proceeded to erode some and I do believe even Daddy and Mr. Russell Newberry were growing somewhat weary of the Tareytons by the time Mr. Pettigrew heir showed himself high up in the gable of the house behind a little round attic window. Of course we all watched him try to get it open, first by tugging at it, then by pushing on it, then by beating it with the heel of his hand, then by tugging at it again, but no matter what he did short of putting his foot through it the little round attic window wouldn't budge, probably because it was never meant to. And then Mr. Pettigrew heir was gone from sight again for what turned out to be a while just as considerable as the one previous, but we all bore it a little more bravely this time since Mr. Paul Needham and his daddy little Buford had been away to the drugstore after a Coca-Cola during the entire of the attic window episode, which was what it was getting called all around, so everybody got to take a turn telling the both of them just what it was they hadn't seen and the process kept us all thoroughly occupied until near about when Mr. Pettigrew heir himself scampered on out the front door and down off the porch into the yard which turned out to be a reasonably rare thing to witness since Mr. Pettigrew heir did not appear to have the architecture for scampering.

He brought with him into the afternoon a long-handled shoe-horn that he'd grabbed up somewhere and right off he shook it at Mr. Britches who was still squatting on top of the knob on top of the flagpole but was too busy picking at himself to notice. Then Mr. Pettigrew heir and his long-handled shoehorn continued on up the sidewalk to the gate where me and Daddy and Mr. Newberry were still holding the fence up, and once Mr. Pettigrew heir stopped to fumble at the gatelatch Mr. Newberry took the opportunity to tell him, "Lovely day," which seemed to be just enough to set Mr. Pettigrew heir off and he let loose of the latch, wagged his shoehorn in the general direction of the Pettigrew house, and said, "Whole goddam place smells like monkey clean up to the rafters."

"You don't mean it," Daddy said.

"Yes sir, I do. Some people just ain't worth a happy shit, can live any old how and stand the stink just fine, not to mention the hairballs up there the size a melons, and it ain't like you could air the place out. Hell, half the windows are painted shut. Just between you and me," Mr. Pettigrew heir said, and indicated Daddy with his shoehorn, "you'd think a woman with her kind a money would have the great good sense to hire herself a nigger with some gumption stead a that thing she's got. I'd as soon take that monkey for my wife as take that nigger for my housekeeper."

And Daddy and Mr. Newberry glanced at each other quick and sideways before Daddy smiled at Mr. Pettigrew heir ever so slightly and asked him, "Are you a full-blooded Pettigrew?"

"No sir," Mr. Pettigrew heir told him, "I'm a Rackley, Conrad Rackley. Her daddy's sister was my momma."

"But you get the whole load, do you," Mr. Newberry said.

"I guess so," Mr. Rackley told him, "but ain't much of it worth having." Then he laid his backside against the fence, crossed his arms over his chest, and studied the front of the house up and down until he arrived at a piece of dental molding that had pulled away from the eave and was sagging somewhat pathetically overtop a second-story window. "Look at that there, ain't that the sorriest mess. Who built this heap anyway?"

"Your uncle, I believe," Daddy told him.

"Ain't surprising," Mr. Rackley said. "He never was worth a big goddam."

And Daddy and Mr. Newberry looked at each other again but before either one of them could conjure up any sort of polite remark Mrs. T. Fay Rackley herself came scampering out the front door and down the steps and along the sidewalk with both her noseholes at full flare. "Bugs! Bugs!" she screeched, "look what I got," and she arrived at the fence cradling in her hands a small porcelain figure of a hobo sitting on a stump.

"Get in the car, Momma," Mr. Rackley told her.

"Ain't this the most divine thing," she said. "Ain't this just about the most divine thing you've ever seen."

"Surely," Mr. Rackley told her. "Now get in the car."

And Mrs. T. Fay Rackley along with her noseholes and along with her porcelain hobo and his porcelain stump underneath him slid into the front seat of the green Buick while Mr.

Conrad Rackley circled round to the far side where he managed to get hold of the doorhandle before Coley Britt came up behind him and said, "Excuse me, but wherebouts you from in Kentucky, the West Virginia end?"

And as Mr. Conrad Rackley turned to answer, Daddy put his hand on my shoulder and said, "Louis."

"Yes sir," I said back.

"I want you to take a good hard look at that man there," he told me. "That's what we call an asshole."

So I paid some considerable attention to Mr. Conrad Rackley, who had laid his backside against the car door, and to Mr. Coley Britt, who was once again talking about spitting into West Virginia, and then I looked back at Daddy and asked him, "Which one?"

"Pick," he said.

iii

MOMMA WORE her navy dress with the little white speckles all over it and her blue scullcap, the one with the veils and the plumage, and on account of the seriousness and sheer gravity of the occasion she fished out from her jewelbox the diamond broach Grandmomma Benfield had presented her with on her wedding day and pinned it to the left side of her collar. This was by no means a frivolous bauble studded all over as it was with precious and semi-precious stones in no readily describable design, though Daddy was given to insist it put him in mind of Rhode Island, a likeness which Momma did not particularly hold with. She said it was one of your free-form abstract broaches with some considerable substance to it which made it an appropriate item for particularly weighty occasions like viewings and funerals and Mrs. Estelle Singletary's autumn harvest brunch. So Momma pinned the broach to the left side of the collar of her speckled navy dress and it hung there about as light and dainty as a railroad spike. As for Daddy he started out in his brown slacks and his green and brown striped necktie and his gold poplin sportcoat that was not pure gold exactly but was nearer to the color of butterscotch candy, and he wore the entire ensemble out of the bedroom, up the back hallway, and into the living room, where Momma met him and sent him to the bedroom again on account of the combination of brown and green and butterscotch which she found wholly inappropriate for the occasion. Momma said this sort of thing called for a dark suit, so Daddy changed into his grey one and came out of the bedroom, up the back hallway, and once more into the living room, where Momma complimented him on the improvement before she took him by the arm and escorted him down the back hallway and on into the bedroom again so as to personally relieve him of his brown and green striped necktie, his gold socks, and his oxblood wingtips.

They finally got off at near about 7:30 after Momma had kissed me on the cheek and told me not to turn on the oven or strike any matches and after Daddy had shook my hand and told me not to run off and join the circus or enlist in the navy until they got back. Of course Momma would not leave the porch until I had latched the screen door behind her, but almost before I could get the hook through the eyelet she grabbed ahold of Daddy's elbow and lit out for the commander's with Daddy trailing in her wake like a grey flannel pennant. Time was I could have gone along with them and seen for myself whether or not Miss Pettigrew was as dead as everybody claimed her to be, but two years previous Commander Tuttle, who would be Commander Avery Tuttle in this case, had drawn up and instigated a very pointed and specific policy against children under the age of sixteen attending any sort of open casket proceedings prior to the funeral itself. Of course the commander's policy excluded what he called siblings of the immediately bereaved since, as Commander Avery figured it, they would be sufficiently saddled and bound up with lugubriousness as to be incapable of much mischief. But children of most anybody else had to get left at home since, as Commander Avery saw it, the siblings of friends and acquaintances of the deceased were too far removed from any sort of direct line of bereavement to be weighted down or sobered or saddled or even the least bit bound up by much of any degree of lugubriousness themselves, and if there was one thing Commander Avery simply could not bring himself to tolerate it was a light-hearted sibling in a funeral parlor. So the commander had drawn up and instigated his very pointed and specific policy and had drawn up and broadcast a very pointed and specific motto to go along with it. "More sharper than a serpent's tooth," the commander would say "is it to have an unlugubrious child near the deceased." And armed with his policy and armed with his motto the commander seemed satisfied that he could avoid the sort of trouble that had beset him once in the past, trouble which nobody much held against the commander except for the commander himself, and trouble which had involved the earthly remains of the saintly Mr. Zeno Stiers, the carcass of one heathen guinea pig named Artemus Gordon, and, of course, one relatively unlugubrious child.

Most everybody called it the Bridger Mishap though there was not much mishap to it and what mishap there was sent Mr. Zeno Stiers all the way to his eternal reward while dispatching Mr. Derwood Bridger only so far as Mrs. Stiers's forsythia bush which was not nearly so glorious a place to wind up. But it was the Bridger Mishap anyway, probably because Mr. Stiers, having sailed off to the everlasting, was not available for subsequent comment which left Mr. Bridger with a monopoly on the facts and circumstances of the matter, a monopoly he made some considerable use of from the very moment he crawled out of the forsythia bush since it was his pelvis that had been fractured while his tongue had come through the ordeal fairly much unimpaired.

Mr. Bridger was a fireman by occupation. He drove the rear section of the hook and ladder unit which meant he did not do much of anything but hold a hose for the majority of the year except at Christmas-time, when Mr. Pipkin himself would take the front wheel and Mr. Bridger would take the back wheel and the hook and ladder would come screaming out of the Omega firehouse making a great variety of clamorous, riotous, and outrageously offensive noises and carting along with it, aside from Mr. Pipkin and aside from Mr. Bridger, a full complement of slickered but hatless firefighters who clung all around the perimeters of the truck like so many cockleburs. Up the boulevard they would fly with the siren wailing and the bell clanging and the airhorn on top of the cab bellowing periodically in a flat, utterly unmusical baritone that you could feel in your molars, and together Mr. Pipkin and Mr. Bridger would manuever the rig into the square and bring it to a lurching halt in front of the courthouse, where a crowd would have already collected on the far side of the street, and the whole assortment of slickered, hatless firefighters would simultaneously disengage themselves from the truck and bolt up the courthouse steps and in through the open doorway while Mr. Bridger commenced to raise the ladder. Then in a flash they were all back outside again and down the steps and onto the truck once more, each of them hauling a cardboard packing crate on his shoulder, and the point man was usually halfway up the ladder before Mr. Bridger could get it set full well against the cornice and then the rest of the squad was hard up behind him and all of them running in as much as anybody can run up a ladder hauling a packing crate, and by the time the last man could step over the cornice and onto the portico roof Mr. Bridger would have already manned his position just inside the courthouse doors and Mr. Pipkin would have already joined Sheriff Burton and Coach Littlehohn at the forefront of the crowd, which would by now be fairly much breathless with anxiety and anticipation.

Usually the candles went up first, one on each end of the portico. They were about three feet high apiece from the base all the way up to the tip of the yellow plastic flame, and each candle required a pair of firefighters to secure it: one to hold it upright and another to bolt it to the coping. During the candle installation the remainder of squad usually engaged itself in unpacking reindeer from the cardboard boxes. They came two to a box already harnessed abreast and entirely put together otherwise except for their heads which had to be snapped into place. If things were proceeding on schedule, the reindeer unit would be fishing out Donner and Blitzen, who were numbers five and six, by the time the candle detachments converged on the center of the portico roof and commenced to unpack Santa's sleigh from its crate. The sleigh came separate from the runners and separate from the bag of toys and goodies that went in the backseat and separate of course from Santa Claus himself who was made out of a single piece of molded plastic and who always got wedged and stuck back in the most unimaginable places from year to year and so generally had to be hunted up. Consequently, the candle detachments, which had united to become the sleigh detachment, rarely had Santa situated by the time the reindeer were all regimented by pairs and set to be hooked into the singletree so everybody, no matter what squad, unit, or detachment joined the hunt for Santa Claus except for Lieutenant Holland who moonlighted as an electrician and so was traditionally appointed to plug in all the plugs and splice in all the wires. And Santa Claus usually turned up along about when Mr. Holland was getting done with everything he had to do, and when he did in fact get finished with the plugging and the splicing and taping he would signal to whoever might be closest to the cornice who would lean out over the street and holler, "Now!" to Mr. Pipkin who would in turn holler, "Now!" to Mr. Bridger who would throw a switch inside the courthouse door and thereby cause the lightbulbs in the candles and the lightbulbs in the stomachs of the reindeer and the lightbulbs in the sleigh and in the bag of toys and goodies and the lightbulb inside of Santa's head to all come on at once. Then Mr. Pipkin would shout, "Time!" and Sheriff Burton would shout, "Time!" and Coach Littlehohn would shake his stopwatch in front of his face and announce the results. Anything under fifteen minutes was respectable, anything under fourteen minutes was exceptional, and anything approaching twelve minutes and thirty-seven seconds was historical since that was the record established in 1965 with the aid of a terrific tailwind down the boulevard and with the invaluable assistance of the late Mr. Robert W. Harwood who by all accounts had an extraordinary way with a ratchet wrench. Mostly it was fourteen to fifteen to fifteen and a half minutes from then on except in 1974 when a member of the sleigh detachment mishandled Santa Claus and dropped him into the street.

Otherwise Neely did not have much call for a hook and ladder and so did not have much call for a driver of the backside or the frontside either. As a result, Mr. Derwood Bridger mostly held a hose, or anyway held a hose whenever he was battling a blaze, which was something the Neely fire department did not do much of, so in actuality Mr. Derwood Bridger only annually drove the backend of the hook and ladder, rarely held a hose, and mostly played canasta in the firehouse game room. That was when he was working, but on his off days when he wasn't working he painted houses which was near about the only thing Mr. Bridger did that seemed the least bit like labor. And most everybody said he was as capable a house painter as there was roundabout, and some people even judged him to be without peer when it came to cutting in conflicting colors or trimming out window mullions. They figured him for a regular DaVinci with a two-inch sash brush. Consequently, Mr. Bridger was ever up on a ladder in between canasta tournaments and he kept fairly much booked up solid from one year on into the next.

Now when Mr. Zeno Stiers's wife, Mrs. Anne Elizabeth Bailey Stiers of the northeast strain of the Swannanoa Baileys, decided that her and Mr. Stiers's house could stand to be freshened up some, naturally she called Mr. Bridger and he came out directly to estimate the charges. That was in early September of 1975 and together Mr. Bridger and Mrs. Stiers walked around the house and Mrs. Stiers studied over a paint chart while Mr. Bridger measured and counted and ciphered and periodically pointed out patches of mildew and rotting window sills and split siding so as to impress upon Mrs. Stiers what a sorry heap she lived in. Then him and her got back around to where they'd started from and Mr. Bridger squatted on his heels and figured up the plump sum which was his standard price for rejuvenating sorry heaps and Mrs. Stiers agreed to it almost immediately, primarily out of sheer embarrassment since she did not think of herself or wish to be thought of as the sort of woman who would live in just any old ramshackle place. So they set in to arriving at a color scheme straightaway and Mrs. Stiers showed a preference for Peyton Randolph Grey with a touch of Palace Arms red here and there and some Bracken House Biscuit as a highlighter, and Mr. Bridger suggested Bafferton Blue for a base with Peyton Randolph Grey for trim and Nicholson Shop Red shutters, which Mr. Bridger said was an altogether richer and more luxurious red than the Palace Arms, and though Mrs. Stiers was all for luxuriousness in her shutters she did not much care for the blue and the grey together, so Mr. Bridger told her she might try Moir Shop Fawn on the siding and Bracken House Biscuit on the trim along with the Nicholson Shop Red shutters which proved to be a combination Mrs. Stiers was very fond of for a few minutes until she realized how her and Mr. Bridger had ignored the greens completely and so she selected Holt Storehouse Grey which happened to be a grey that was actually green and Mr. Bridger suggested Blair House Green which happened to be a green that was actually extremely green and the two of them together arrived at Bracken House Biscuit for the window sashes which of course was not the least bit green but would, according to Mr. Bridger, bring out the subtleties of the other two colors, and Mrs. Anne Elizabeth Bailey Stiers of the northeast strain

of the Swannanoa Baileys was not much accustomed to subtleties in her house paint and so was temporarily taken with
the novelty of it which left her incapable of objectively gauging
the variation in her enthusiasm between the fawn and the biscuit
and the red and the grey-green and the green-green and the
biscuit, and to complicate matters further the Bafferton Blue
and Peyton Randolph Grey were beginning to kick up some
affection with her since they were not wholly without subtleties
themselves. Consequently, Mrs. Stiers could not bring herself
to decide on a paint scheme right away, so her and Mr. Bridger
set in through the paint chart again and argued the virtues and
detractions of most every color until finally after some considerable debate and thoroughgoing circumspection Mrs. Stiers
and Mr. Bridger agreed to paint the house white, everything
that is except for the shutters, which would be Bridger's Cellar
Green which was not a chart color exactly but was where the
gallon of paint was that Mr. Bridger had a mind to get rid of.
So him and Mrs. Stiers shook hands on the color and shook
hands on the price and then Mr. Bridger told Mrs. Stiers he'd
see her at the tail end of April and maybe later but certainly
not before.

    Naturally the months between the estimate and paint job
served to dull Mrs. Stiers's enthusiasm and somewhere between
September 1975 and April of 1976 she managed to fairly thoroughly forget about Mr. Bridger, which did not matter much
in her case, but Mr. Zeno Stiers forgot about him too and that
proved to be of considerably more consequence on account of
Mr. Stiers's infirm and delicate condition. Mr. Zeno Stiers had
loaded a shredder at the American Tobacco Company most all
his working life but was forced to take an early medical retire-
ment because of acute emphysema complicated by an artery
ailment. All along Mr. Stiers's doctor had strongly insisted on
surgery for the artery trouble, but Mr. Stiers had just as strongly
insisted against it and instead they settled on a potent little blue
pill to be washed down every day before lunch with a glass of
orange juice. The doctor said it was meant to aid the heart,
but Mr. Stiers always believed it assisted the emphysema by
mistake since it took his breath and sent him to bed all weak
and muddleheaded until near about suppertime. So what with
his medical predicament, which was none too rosy, it was
understandable that Mr. Stiers did not fret away the days between

September and April waiting for the painter to come whitewash his house, and though Mrs. Stiers did not forget about Mr. Bridger completely she did forget about him sufficiently to convince herself he had said July or maybe even August but certainly not before.

But he had not said July and had not said maybe even August either, and Mr. Bridger, who was by all accounts incredibly slow but exceedingly reliable, arrived as promised at the tail end of April which turned out to be fifteen minutes past 1:00 p.m. on the afternoon of Wednesday of the thirtieth of the month. Now of course Mrs. Stiers was not looking for Mr. Bridger until the tail end of July or maybe the tail end of August— she could not decide which—and consequently she had gone on about her regular tail-end-of-the-month business, which at 1:15 p.m. on the thirtieth of April 1976 put her crosslegged in the middle chair at Miss Patricia Rascoe's "Hair by Trish: An Old World Salon" with her head almost completely covered up in slivers of foam rubber. As for Mr. Zeno Stiers, by 1:15 his emphysema and his little blue pill had already ganged up on him and sent him into a kind of snoring coma, so Mr. Bridger could not announce himself at the front door or the back door either and proceeded to remove his extension ladder from the station wagon roof and set it up against the front of the house. It was Mr. Bridger's general policy to commence work on any sorry heap by reglazing what windows called for it, and once he had surveyed a few of the bottom ones and determined the panes were held in mostly by sheer good fortune, he armed himself with an assortment of putty knives and scrapers and a lump of glazing compound the size of a softball and climbed up the ladder towards the guest bedroom window on the far end of the front of the house.

Mr. Bridger has never been the sort of man to revel in working up a sweat and for the most part of his adult life he has managed to resist the temptation to tire himself unduly. Consequently, Mr. Bridger works at what he calls a leisurely pace which does not in fact have much pace to it but consists mostly of lingering spells of recovery interrupted by occasional spurts of earnest labor. So in his usual fashion Mr. Bridger pecked and scraped and poked at the glazing on the guest bedroom window for a furious several minutes and then gave himself near about a quarter hour off which he spent in sight-seeing from the top of the ladder and which was followed by another burst of industriousness that Mr. Bridger managed to maintain just to the verge of perspiration. And after two and a half hours of working what Mr. Bridger likes to call steadily, he had partially reglazed two windows, had cracked a pane in a third one and decided to skip over it, and had set about pecking away at the fourth one which opened onto the master bedroom, where Mr. Stiers was sleeping on top of the bedspread in a sleeveless undershirt and a pair of oversized cotton briefs. According to Mrs. Stiers, her husband, Zeno, was not one of your light sleepers even in his natural and unmedicated state, so all of the scraping and the poking and the rattling around that Mr. Bridger was subjecting the window to did not cause Mr. Stiers to stir much right off and even after Mr. Bridger set in to whistling "It's a Grand Old Flag" through his teeth Mr. Stiers only made a solitary noise in the back of his nose and then proceeded with his coma. And as Mr. Bridger figured it, when Mr. Stiers finally did wake up it was not on account of any single sharp and particular noise but was on account of the accumulation of all the scraping and the poking and the rattling around and the whistling. And as Mrs. Stiers heard it from her husband himself who was coherent throughout most of the following afternoon, he sat directly up on top of the bed and listened at the pecking and the tapping and the whistling coming from the vicinity of the windowsill and decided to himself it must be a pigeon or a redheaded woodpecker notwithstanding the fact that whatever it was was whistling "The Wichita Lineman" which would have been unusual for a woodpecker and unheard of in a pigeon, but then Mr. Stiers was not one of your more melodic souls and never watched Glenn Campbell on television.

So Mr. Stiers got up out of the bed with the intention of shooing a bird off his windowsill, but when he crept across the floor and jerked the draperies apart he did not find a pigeon or a woodpecker or even an assortment of sparrows but instead found himself face to face with Mr. Derwood Bridger, and all of Mr. Stiers's doctors conferred together and agree the shock of a Mr. Derwood Bridger where a pigeon or a woodpecker should have been had induced in Mr. Stiers what they all called an authentic paroxysm which dropped him to the carpet straightaway. As for Mr. Bridger, he had not expected to see Mr.

Stiers, especially in his undershirt and his cotton briefs and unannounced on top of it, but then Mr. Bridger is by his own account not a very excitable person and so handled the situation as best he could which Daddy has always said probably explains why he did not howl on his way into the forsythia bush where he was joined by his softball-sized lump of glazing compound and by his putty knife and his scraper and very nearly by his aluminum extension ladder which Mr. Stiers succeeded in shooing away from the window along with Mr. Bridger.

Daddy holds it was a fifteen-foot drop at the outside and Mr. Russell Newberry generally contends it was less but will allow for fifteen while Mr. Phillip J. King usually puts it at eighteen but has been known to venture into the lower twenties. On the official record duly certified by Sheriff Burton and signed by the chief eyewitness, little Buford Needham, the distance of the fall is given as "considerable" which was all little Buford would agree to since he did not come on the scene until after Mr. Bridger had already crawled out of the forsythia bush and so could not witness to any exact footage. Mr. Bridger himself holds it was at least a thirty foot fall, maybe thirty-five, and Daddy says that surely would have been a spectacular thing to see since Mr. Bridger would have had to leap twenty feet straight up into the air before he ever began to drop. And Daddy cannot bring himself to understand how a fully inflated canasta-playing fireman could fall from thirty-five feet and come away with just a fractured pelvis, but Mr. Bridger simply attributes his good fortune to the density of the forsythia bush in conjunction with his occasional attendance at the eleven o'clock Presbyterian service.

Of course Mr. Bridger had already dragged himself into the front yard by the time Mrs. Stiers got home from Miss Rascoe's "Hair by Trish" but his faculties were sufficiently jumbled on account of his fifteen to thirty-five foot fall to prevent him from providing Mrs. Stiers with a sound explanation as to why he'd had to crawl out of the forsythia bush in the first place. Instead he told her all about a mongrel hound his daddy had given him when he was eleven and told her about his Uncle Rutherford Bridger who had retired from the railroad to raise goobers in Pitt County and explained to her how a fish filters his air out of lakewater. Then he rolled his head from side to side in the grass and said, "Mr. Zeno is sure enough a sight in his under-clothes."

"Mr. Zeno?" Mrs. Stiers asked him.

"Yes ma'm," Mr. Bridger told her. "I ain't never seen such legs."

And that was the last Mr. Bridger saw of Mrs. Stiers until two full days afterwards at the hospital where she had come to sit with her husband, and as Mr. Bridger tells it he laid alone in the grass for a solid hour and was fixing to crawl to his station wagon and drive himself to the doctor when little Buford found him and offered to call an ambulance. And according to little Buford's sworn and duly certified testimony, Mr. Bridger struck in right off with a few unseemly comments on the topic of Mr. Stiers's underclothes and then passed several minutes reviling a man named Peyton Randolph, who little Buford could not recollect though he did testify to an acquaintance with a Mr. Jimmy Randolph of Madison-Mayodan and theorized that the two of them were from the same bunch. Finally Mr. Bridger came to himself enough to suggest to little Buford that he go on in the house and use the telephone and maybe hunt up Mrs. Stiers while he's about it, and little Buford said he found the front door standing half open and so stuck his head inside and hollered up the stairs but nobody answered. Then he let the rest of himself inside as well and called out for Mrs. Stiers and called out for Mr. Stiers but still nobody said anything back, so little Buford helped himself to the telephone in the back hallway and then set out all over the house in search of any Stiers he could come up on which turned out to be Mr. Zeno who was sprawled across the heat duct by the bedroom window in his sleeveless undershirt and his cotton briefs and who looked to little Buford to be very convincingly dead, but then little Buford did not have much experience in authentic paroxysms.

The ambulance came directly, or anyway Mr. Bridger and little Buford heard the ambulance coming almost as soon as little Buford had returned to the front yard. And as the siren grew steadily louder and more irritating, Mr. Bridger and little Buford followed the sound of it off the Richardson Road, along Lawsonville Avenue, and onto Lamont Street where Mr. and Mrs. Stiers lived. Then the two of them together watched the ambulance itself sail on past the house with all of its exterior apparatus flashing and moaning and screeching most unbearably, and before either one of them could wonder out loud where it was going it turned around a ways up the road and came sailing back by the house from the other direction and went into Lawsonville Avenue what sounded to little Buford like sideways. Then it flashed and moaned and screeched off to the north for a block or so before ducking off the avenue again and Mr. Bridger and little Buford listened somewhat forlornly as it wailed and howled its way almost entirely out of earshot, but presently it turned around in somebody's driveway and slid back out onto the avenue heading towards Lamont Street once more and little Buford Needham, at risk of some considerable peril to his bodily person, met the ambulance at the intersection and directed it into the Stiers's front yard.

The driver hopped out first and then stuck his head back inside the vehicle and said, "I told you it was back here and look for yourself, it ain't no Spanish adobe, ain't nothing foreign about it. Great Creeping Jesus Christ, I believe I'd just fall over dead if you ever wrote down an address." The sheer force of all this displeasure seemed to push the other fellow out the passenger door and he stood beside the ambulance with his arms crossed and studied the right front hubcap in humiliated silence while the driver persisted in reminding him how unfit he was to draw breath. He said it was siding, just plain pine siding, with pickets around the front porch and double-hung windows and aluminum gutters and downspouts, and then he turned around to little Buford and demanded of him, "Does this look like an adobe to you? Does any damn thing around here look the least bit Spanish?" And little Buford, who Daddy says is probably the most obliging individual he's ever had the pleasure to know, made a conscientious survey of the house and grounds before he ventured to say, "No sir, not a thing." And the driver laid both his arms on the roof of the ambulance and looked across it to where the other fellow stood in his revery over the hubcap. "Holy creeping son a God," he said. "You ain't worth two farts in a bucket."

Now Mr. Bridger, who was still stretched out in the front yard next to the forsythia bush, was taking all of this in with some attention since, by his own admission, he enjoys a fiery exchange as much as the next man, but nonetheless he was becoming a little anxious for some treatment and so when it appeared that the driver had creeping Jesused himself out, Mr.

Bridger gave vent to a moderate selection of anguished moans and thereby jarred little Buford who in turn reminded the driver who told the other fellow to see if he couldn't find the medical bag. "It's black grain leather," he said, "and looks a little Italian." But the driver hadn't hardly gotten to Mr. Bridger and the other fellow hadn't hardly cleared the front end of the ambulance with the black Italian medical bag when little Buford recollected to tell the both of them that there was a gentleman upstairs in far graver condition, perhaps so grave as to be dead. And immediately the driver leapt away from Mr. Bridger like he was a snake and followed the other fellow, who had already made a midcourse correction, through the front door and into the house and they had not been under the roof for a half a second when the driver hollered, "Upstairs, UPstairs, you pigheaded bastard," and then everything was quiet once more and little Buford and Mr. Bridger were again alone in the front yard beside the forsythia bush and little Buford put his hands in his pockets and set in to whistling "Rocky Top" but before he could get well underway Mr. Bridger grabbed ahold of his ankle, shook it as best he could, and said, "Well shit, Buford."

The two ambulance attendants stayed upstairs with Mr. Stiers long enough to convince little Buford he had not been a corpse after all, and when one of them finally did come back downstairs and out into the front yard it was the pigheaded bastard who was not worth two farts in a bucket and he sailed through the front doorway at a gallop and across the lawn over to the ambulance out from the back of which he fetched a canvas stretcher that he wrapped his arms around and fairly much sprinted off with, but before he could get full across the lawn again and back up to the house Mr. Bridger moaned at him from beside the forsythia bush and though it was not one of your more anguished moans it was sufficient to turn the pigheaded bastard's head which proved to be a sad and untimely thing since it left the pigheaded bastard in no position to see the ends of the stretcher catch on opposite sides of the doorframe and so in attempting to dash on through the doorway he very nearly broke himself in half.

As little Buford calculated it in his official testimony, Mr. Zeno Stiers came out into the frontyard atop the stretcher not more than five minutes after the pigheaded bastard had recovered his wind enough to get up the stairs, and little Buford swore and certified it appeared to him that Mr. Stiers was about as near to corpsehood as he could get without actually having crossed over. Little Buford said he was an ungodly bloodless shade of white, but when Sheriff Burton asked for something a little more vivid to set down in the official statement little Buford decided that Mr. Zeno's pallor was closest to the color of lowfat milk, which the sheriff found considerably more appealing. And according to little Buford, once the attendants had situated the stretcher in the back of the ambulance the driver jumped in behind it and the pigheaded bastard slid under the wheel and the ambulance itself struck out for the hospital with the flashing and the screeching and the general uproar preceding it and following it and just hovering all around it like a swarm of bees. And little Buford said he shot his eyes sideways at Mr. Bridger who was looking so extraordinarily displeased that it would have been difficult to judge what sort of savagery might have ensued if Mr. Bridger had been able to draw himself upright.

The hospital sent another ambulance eventually but not before Sheriff Burton had arrived and commenced his statement taking which by tradition started out with the victim, and though Mr. Bridger told the sheriff a great variety of things in a very hot and unrestrained fashion, Sheriff Burton chose not to pencil any of them into the record and instead wrote "Delerious" next to Mr. Bridger's name. Of course little Buford turned out to be far more cooperative since his pelvis was not in the leastways fractured and together him and Sheriff Burton sat side by side on the Stiers's front steps and constructed little Buford's official testimony with great efficiency and dispatch and very few hindrances except for one exceedingly sharp and tormented shriek from Mr. Bridger when he attempted to crawl across the yard and strangle the both of them. But a new pair of ambulance attendants hauled Mr. Bridger off straightaway and Sheriff Burton's statement taking proceeded fairly smoothly thereafter. Needless to say, the chief sticking point was Mrs. Stiers who could not be found in the house and was very obviously nowhere in the yard either, so Sheriff Burton and little Buford and the better part of the crowd that had congregated on the front lawn walked all over the property shouting for her but soon enough the sheriff was satisfied that Mrs. Stiers was out of earshot and so licked the end of his pencil and wrote "Vanished" next to her name. And that was pretty much the end of the statement taking so the sheriff wagged his nightstick at the crowd and dismissed little Buford telling him not to leave town under penalty of law, which little Buford himself had insisted he get told to satisfy the desperado in him.

Nobody could locate Mrs. Stiers right away, not even after her neighbors and two deputies and Sheriff Burton himself had begun to search for her in earnest, and when she finally was found she was not found by anybody who knew she was missing but was discovered instead by Mr. Charles Henley Gruber who had gone out to his lespodeza patch to fetch in his cow and got Mrs. Stiers in the bargain. She was sitting a few yards off the cow's right flank with her legs curled up beneath her and when Mr. Gruber arrived she was telling the cow a great many things about herself and Mr. Stiers and about their life together, and Mr. Gruber, who had seen hysterical women before, knew right off he was seeing another one while for her part Mrs. Stiers had never had occasion to lose her wits previously and so did not realize she had lost them now. But she had lost them; three doctors and two nurses all agreed she had lost them and they gave her a shot and shined a flashlight in her eyes and looked in her mouth and then left her to sleep directly across from the nurse's station in a room shared by Mrs. Mae Ruth French of the Oregon Hill Frenches who, on account of her stroke, thought she was riding the ferry between Swan Quarter and Ocracoke and so buzzed the duty nurse every minute or so to find out why.

At first the doctors did not tell Mrs. Stiers that Mr. Zeno would not live, though four of them had gotten together with two interns and decided privately he would not. Instead they shined a flashlight in Mrs. Stiers's eyes and looked down into her throat and made her swallow a bullet-sized pill out of a little white paper cup, and even by mid afternoon of the day following the Bridger Mishap when it was perfectly clear to everyone that Mrs. Stiers had fully regained her senses, the doctors still did not tell her Mr. Zeno would not live though they had not changed their minds about it. And in the early evening when three of them together stopped in to observe Mrs. Stiers's faculties, they would only tell her that Mr. Zeno's was a "serious case, a most serious case," and then the youngest among them walked round to Mrs. French's bed, put his face up close to Mrs. French's ear, and said, "How's the water today?"

"Rough," Mrs. French replied. "Oooh, so very rough."

The hospital discharged Mrs. Stiers two days after the Bridger Mishap and she went home long enough to change clothes and come back, and for the rest of the morning and all of the afternoon and on into the evening she sat in a chair beside Mr. Zeno's bed in the ward for serious cases and watched Mr. Zeno's eyelids flutter. Mr. Zeno himself would come to his senses from time to time and talk to Mrs. Stiers in a very strained and nearly indecipherable whisper but mostly he slept on his back with his mouth open and Mrs. Stiers watched his eyelids flutter and kept a folded Kleenex in her hand to wipe away the saliva before it could run across his cheek and onto the pillow. On her way out of the hospital Mrs. Stiers dropped in briefly to see Mr. Bridger who was in traction down the hall, but no matter what brand of pleasantry she attempted on him he would invariably respond with "Where in the hell did you get off to?" which Mrs. Stiers could not answer with any accuracy and did not wish to discuss anyway. So her and Mr. Bridger didn't have much to do with each other after that and instead Mrs. Stiers spent all of her time at Mr. Zeno's bedside, where she was interrupted on the afternoon of the third day after the Bridger Mishap by three doctors, an intern, and two nurses who had stopped off at the ward for serious cases in order to examine Mr. Zeno. One of the doctors shined a flashlight in his eyes and other one looked into his mouth while the intern adjusted all Mr. Zeno's tubes under the scrutiny of the two nurses, and then the five of them together cornered Mrs. Stiers on the far side of the ward and the first doctor, with his elbow in one hand and his chin in the other, told her Mr. Zeno's was indeed a serious case. "A very serious case," the second doctor added at the invitation of the first, and then the intern and the two nurses shook their heads most dolefully.

"Very serious?" Mrs. Stiers wanted to know.

And the two doctors consulted for a half minute before the first one told her, "Extremely serious."

"Yes, extremely," the second one said. And though they chose not to tell Mrs. Stiers, the two doctors present and the intern and the pair of nurses along with three additional doctors, another five interns, six more nurses and a radiologist had all concluded and agreed that Mr. Zeno would most probably not last out the night.

But he did anyway, notwithstanding the twenty professional opinions to the contrary, and when it became clear that Mr. Zeno was going to survive into the afternoon of the fourth day following the Bridger Mishap, an impressive assortment of medical personnel collected around his bed and ran several hours worth of tests on him to find out how in the world he could do it. But the results were all inconclusive, the doctors called it, and so did not convince them to change their minds about Mr. Zeno, who they figured could not possibly hold on until the morning. But he did anyway and nobody could understand why, so Mr. Zeno's personal physician, Dr. Danbury of Ruffin, was called in along with a specialist from Winston-Salem who was at the time entertaining a doctor friend of his from Pennsylvania and brought him along as a bonus. And Dr. Danbury and the specialist from Winston-Salem and his doctor friend from Pennsylvania all examined Mr. Zeno together and then conferred for a full half hour before throwing in with the five doctors, six interns, eight nurses, and solitary radiologist which made for a total of twenty-three professional opinions running contrary to Mr. Zeno. And though Mr. Zeno carried the load bravely for several hours, at 2:53 p.m. on the afternoon of the fifth day following the Bridger Mishap he finally yielded to the accumulated weight of informed medical opinion and expired. There was really nothing else he could do.

It was a sorrowful few days in Neely after Mr. Zeno passed away. Stierses converged on Lamont Street from all over the southeast and most everybody from one end of town to the other went around with Mr. Zeno's virtues on their lips. Of course it was an exceedingly black time for chickens as well. Legions of them got fried and roasted while a considerable few showed up in pot pies and casseroles boiled off the bone. There was beef too and pork barbeque and potato salad and bean salad and macaroni salad along with at least a metric ton of sweetened iced tea and enough molded gelatin to fill a bathtub. According to Daddy by the time he got to the Stiers's house, which was the evening following Mr. Zeno's expiration, the buffet had overflowed off the kitchen and diningroom tables onto a bureau and two nightstands that had been especially imported for the occasion. And Daddy said once he had shaken hands with near about twenty Stierses he dished himself up an assortment of prepared poultry and was coming up fast on the cobblers and the pound cakes when he first noticed, with measurable awe and trepidation Daddy called it, that he was sharing the dining room with perhaps the largest collection of deviled egg plates ever assembled under one roof. Daddy says it was a somewhat sobering revelation to him. Here he was enjoying a bounteous meal at Mr. Zeno's house while Mr. Zeno himself was off at the mortuary being siphoned. But Daddy says he simply decided that is the way things are on God's earth—the dead get embalmed and the living get seconds.

Now almost precisely two hours previous to Mr. Zeno's passing there was another death in Neely. At approximately 12:48 p.m. on Sunday the fifth of May, 1976, Jack Vestal lost his Guinea pig, Artemus Gordon, following a brief illness. Jack and Artemus had been close ever since Jack's ninth birthday in 1973 when his momma and daddy presented Artemus to him in a shoebox with holes in the top. Artemus Gordon had been one of your rarer breeds of Guinea pigs. He was white with brown spots and had little clumps of hair standing up all over his body like maybe he'd been reared in a wind tunnel. Jack always said he was smart as most people, but the only thing I ever saw him do was take in leafy lettuce and process it, mostly all over the bottom of his cage but every now and then underneath Mrs. Vestal's naugahide sofa, which was where he generally got off to whenever Jack turned him loose. It was on the morning of May the third, 1976, that Jack first noticed a decline in Artemus Gordon's condition. His cowlicks had wilted in the night and he looked to Jack a little puny around the mouth, but when Jack called in his mother for a second opinion she said it was the humidity or maybe a combination of the humidity and the sour stomach so her and Jack pulverized one of Jack's daddy's Maalox tablets and fed it to Artemus Gordon in the furrow of a stalk of celery. But when Jack got home from school Artemus Gordon was so thoroughly unimproved that Jack called together his associates for a consultation, and Marcus Bowles and Bill Ed Myrick jr., who lived on either side of Jack, along with Laurence Ridley, who lived with his mother's sister around the corner, all collected in Jack Vestal's bedroom and observed the patient with some considerable gravity and attention. Almost straightaway Marcus Bowles decided it was the pink eye or anyway a peculiar strain of the pink eye with a little mange thrown in which Marcus said would account for the wilted cowlicks, but Jack resisted Marcus's diagnosis and Bill Ed Myrick called him a dumb fuck and Laurence Ridley said it was certainly not the pink eye and was not the mange either but was instead a clearcut case of gonorrhea. But since Laurence Ridley had only heard of gonorrhea the day before from his cousin Denise, who was studying social diseases in health class, he could not come up with a convincing set of symptoms right away and so could not persuade Jack in the least and could not persuade Marcus, who was still campaigning for the pink eye although with noticeably diminished vigor, and could not even begin to persuade Bill Ed Myrick, who called him a dumb fuck and then reminded Marcus that he was a dumb fuck also. Bill Ed said it was not pink eye; he said pink eye was what cows get. And he said it was not gonorrhea; he said gonorrhea was what Miss Tamara Gayle Grantham gave to his uncle. He said it was not a disease at all but was instead a very obvious case of advanced old age. Bill Ed had read somewhere, he could not remember where exactly, that a Guinea pig ages thirty-seven years for every one year of its life on earth and so by simple calculations Bill Ed figured Artemus Gordon to be upwards of one hundred and eleven years old and he said he hoped he looked so good when he was one hundred and eleven. And though Jack hesitated for several minutes he presently called Bill Ed a dumb fuck, which inspired Marcus Bowles and Laurence Ridley to call him a dumb fuck also, and in the absence of any logical and medically sound alternative Jack ground up another Maalox tablet and gave it to Artemus Gordon in the furrow of a celery stalk.

By midmorning of Saturday, May the fourth, Artemus Gordon appeared to be partially recovered in that a half dozen of his cowlicks had righted themselves in the night, and the prognosis remained hopeful and promising throughout most of the afternoon, during the course of which Artemus Gordon did away with two pieces of un-Maaloxed celery and went after a hunk of cabbage with uncharacteristic zest. But by suppertime he had unexpectedly declined into a crisis. He refused all manner of vegetables and began to look a little down in the cowlicks again like maybe he'd been dipped in Brylcream. 9:30 p.m. found him leaning against the bars of his cage with his little pink tongue dangling out of the side of his mouth and by 10:15 when Jack Vestal went to bed it did not appear that Artemus Gordon would be around to greet the morning. But somehow he managed to survive the night and though he was not particularly robust at breakfast time he was sufficiently enthusiastic to notch out the lettuce leaf Jack dropped in through the top of the cage.

As was their custom, at 10:20 a.m. all four Vestals—Jack and his sister, Kimberly Ann, and his momma and daddy—walked downtown to the Baptist church for the eleven o'clock service. Along the way Jack contracted from his momma and daddy sacred and sworn promises to pray for his afflicted guinea pig while his sister, Kimberly Ann, who got all squeally in the presence of most any rodent and was very openly pulling for the affliction, remained noncommittal. But as Jack figured it, his momma and his sister would cancel each other out and leave him and his daddy to carry the day, which Jack would only have to assist in since his daddy was a church deacon and so had influence in this sort of thing. The Reverend Lynwood Wilkerson was suffering from a spring cold and he held up the service several times as he rolled the congestion up out of his throat and bent down behind the pulpit to spit it into a can. Consequently, the general prayer, which ever preceded the weekly tithing, did not get underway until twenty minutes to twelve and even then Reverend Wilkerson blessed one thing and praised another for an uncharacteristically long spell before he finally turned the floor over to the congregation, and as R.B. Jemison from his pew up front set in to wailing for the arthritis to give him some relief, Jack commenced to talk with God in a very low and humble whisper. He prayed that Artemus Gordon did not have the pink eye and he prayed that Artemus Gordon did not have gonorrhea and he prayed that Artemus Gordon was not one hundred and eleven years old. Then he looked sideways at his sister, Kimberly Ann, and saw that her mouth was still moving, so he prayed for Artemus Gordon all over again and finished up just as Mrs. Harold Cosgrove Benedict of the Draper Benedicts was demanding some special attention for her nephew's wife's child who had been born with three big toes.

Unfortunately, however, all the low and humble whispering that Jack and his daddy could muster together was not enough to save Artemus Gordon, and the Vestals returned home from the service to find him curled up dead atop his notched out lettuce leaf. Of course Jack went mad with grief right off and threatened all grades of violence to Kimberly Ann, but his daddy prevailed upon him with a few threats of his own and thereby reduced Jack to a state of excessive lugubriousness which lingered through lunch and on into the afternoon. For a solid hour he sat by Artemus Gordon's cage and poked at the carcass with the eraser end of a pencil on the outside chance that Artemus Gordon was not so thoroughly dead he couldn't recover, but at length Jack became convinced his guinea pig was in fact irreparably deceased and the realization did not sit well with him. He sobbed most piteously and stomped his feet, which brought his mother and Kimberly Ann in to comfort him, but he sent them away directly and commenced to throw a few of his possessions against the bedroom walls, which brought his daddy in to wallop the fire out of him. However, Mr. Vestal was touched by the grief of the moment and consequently treated Jack to one of his less severe wallopings after which he allowed himself to agree to the purchase of a new guinea pig and thereby took most of the edge off of Jack's lugubriousness.

But as Jack saw it, he hadn't hardly collected his share of consolation and sympathy when Mrs. Pipkin's sister-in-law, Mrs. Irene Price McKinney, called up his momma and told her of Mr. Zeno Stiers's unfortunate demise, which was exceedingly fresh news at the time coming as it had from a hospital orderly through Mrs. McKinney and direct to Mrs. Vestal. But then news of most any demise, unfortunate or otherwise, generally does reach Mrs. Vestal in an exceedingly fresh state on account of her reputation. Mrs. Vestal is what Daddy likes to call a hearse chaser, and she'd think nothing whatsoever of driving an entire day to watch a corpse lie still. Not that she is a reprehensible or ghoulish woman; Daddy says she is no more reprehensible and ghoulish than the sorts of people who will leap up from the supper table and run headlong ten blocks down the street to see a house burn to the ground or watch people bleed after a wreck. It's just that fire and carnage don't hold much favor with Mrs. Vestal and instead she requires an unextraordinary and natural death to get her blood going. Generally speaking Mrs. Vestal attends all gatherings and viewings and funerals and burial services in the honor of an acquaintance, no matter how marginal, and she attends all gatherings and viewings and funerals and burial services in the honor of a relative of an acquaintance, and she attends all gatherings and viewings and funerals and burial services in the honor of a neighbor of an acquaintance, and she attends all gatherings and viewings and funerals and burial services in the honor of an acquaintance of an acquaintance, and when she is hard pressed for exhilaration she attends the gatherings and viewings and funerals and burial services of people whose names indicate to her that they might possibly have been related to and/or did know someone Mrs. Vestal could herself have heard of at one time or another. Understandably Mrs. Vestal is a supremely harried woman, but no matter the great multitude of gatherings and viewings and funerals and burial services she attends from month to month and from year to year, she has never been known to allow a single casket to sink into the dark of the grave without a proper sendoff. Once the preacher wears himself out at the cemetery and gives whoever it is the high sign to switch on the electric chrome-plated casket lowering machine, Mrs. Vestal sets herself and at the first jolt of the belts cuts loose with some wild and genuine sobbing which perseveres until the casket settles onto the vault bottom after which she waves her arm over the open hole, manages to catch up enough breath to blubber, "Farewell, Brave Soul," and then tosses a perfectly good linen handkerchief down onto the coffin lid. Anymore no respectable graveside service considers itself sanctified and suitably concluded without a personalized amen from Mrs. Vestal, and Daddy says for her part she is a most obliging woman, hardly the sort to let a corpse down. He says she is as reliable and regular as indigestion after breakfast. The bounteously sorrowful Mrs. Virginia Ann Crutchfield Vestal, Daddy calls her, friend to the dead.

Now the Zeno Stiers expiration was especially invigorating for Mrs. Vestal on account of her attachments in the affair. She was very nearly acquainted with the immediate family, or anyway very nearly acquainted with the immediate widow, and she had in fact gotten her hair curled two chairs over from Mrs. Stiers on the very day Mr. Zeno was struck down with his authentic paroxysm. This seemed to Mrs. Vestal near about the same as a blood tie, so she jumped into a black dress quicker

than you could say ashes to ashes and her and Mr. Vestal left
the house at a canter. They stopped off briefly and picked up
a bucket of chicken all white meat regular recipe, so as not to
arrive empty handed, but even with the delay I do believe they
had been sitting on the front steps for twenty minutes before
Mrs. Stiers got home from the hospital. Of course Jack Vestal
did not much appreciate his parents bolting off as they had and
leaving him alone with his grief, and he was utterly alone with
it since Kimberly Ann had thought it best to clear out once her
momma and daddy did. So for company Jack called up Laurence Ridley and Marcus Bowles and Bill Ed Myrick, and they
all came over to look at the corpse and each of them in turn
determined it was certifiably and exceedingly lifeless. Then
Bill Ed Myrick, who has a flair for this sort of thing, suggested
they fix up Artemus Gordon with a properly glorious funeral
service and they all agreed to it right off since none of them
imagined a guinea pig could be flushed down a toilet with
much of any success. Marcus and Laurence dug the hole in
the far back corner of the Vestals' lot next to the trash heap
and Jack emptied out his mother's Tupperware lettuce crisper
for a coffin. Bill Ed kicked off the service with a truncated
and semi-corrupted version of the Lord's Prayer that somehow
or another had become polluted and tangled up with various
stray phrases from the Moravian Blessing. There were plans
for a hymn, but the prospect was not greeted with much enthusiasm so instead Bill Ed turned to the text, which in this case
was Mrs. Vestal's copy of *101 of the World's Best Loved Poems*.
He opened the book to a marked page and read at length selec-
tions from Miss Jean Ingelow's "Mopsa the Fairy," none of
which had anything whatsoever to do with guinea pigs but
seemed particularly consoling regardless. The reading was followed by a moment of silence, after which Bill Ed Myrick
shook Jack's hand in a frighteningly earnest sort of way and
Marcus and Laurence raked the dirt back into the hole and
stomped on it. Jack announced that Artemus Gordon had been
a fine pet and Bill Ed and Marcus and Laurence agreed that
he had been, and then all four of them went into the Vestals'
house and ate saltines in front of the t.v.

Jack's momma and daddy did not get home until well past
9:00 in the evening and six hours of uninterrupted grieving had
left the both of them unduly irritable, so Jack did not tell his

momma about the lettuce crisper right away and he did not tell her how Marcus Bowles spilt orange juice on the bathroom floor and for the moment he did not attempt to explain to her why the little glass Chinaman in the living room was missing all of his right elbow. Jack just sat at the kitchen table gnawing on a chicken thigh his momma had brought home to him in her pocketbook and listened to her and his daddy exchange examples of Mr. Zeno Stiers's goodliness. And apparently Mr. Zeno Stiers had been an utterly goodly man because every few minutes Jack expected his mother to temper and besmirch the virtues some with an assortment of vices, as was her practice, but every few minutes he was disappointed with more pure goodliness. "Saintly," his daddy said. "Yes indeed, truly saintly," his momma said, and Jack sucked on his thighbone and ruminated over the destiny of a saintly man.

He did not actually decide to dig up Artemus Gordon until the following afternoon, though he did consider it off and on throughout the night and tended towards it during the course of the school day, but he did not actually decide to dig up Artemus Gordon until after his mother had carried him down to Walgreen's where she bought for him Mr. Singletary's last guinea pig which was an albino of the uncowlicked variety. However, Jack could not bring himself to accept a white, uncowlicked guinea pig straightaway, what with his recent bereavement, and it took upwards of an hour and a half before he could get used to a pet whose hair did not stand up in clumps all over its body. But after he'd fed it several stalks of celery and a chunk of purple cabbage and after it had wet on him once, which Jack took to be a show of affection, he named it Napoleon Solo and finally decided outright he would dig up Artemus Gordon, finally concluded he could bring himself to give up Artemus Gordon's earthly remains in the hope of securing a place of glory for Artemus Gordon's everlasting soul. So Jack exhumed the lettuce crisper and removed Artemus Gordon from it and wrapped him in a handkerchief, and when his parents commenced to dress for the viewing at Commander Avery's Heavenly Rest, Jack commenced to dress also which inspired Miss Kimberly Ann, who got all squealy around dead things, to slip into a frock herself since she did not want to be left at home alone. And at seven o'clock sharp all of the Vestals, except for the newest albino Vestal, left the house and took to the sidewalk two abreast on their way to the commánder's and in the company of one deceased guinea pig Vestal, shrouded in a handkerchief and hidden in a coatpocket, who was on his way to the streets of gold.

Daddy says it was partly the fault of the commander himself though of course the commander has never assumed any degree of the blame for it, but Daddy insists that if the commander had not gone on so about his capacious caskets he would not have found himself with the rodent problem that he eventually found himself with. However, Daddy says the commander is the sort of man who believes it requires more than a rivet to get ahead in the mortuarial game, so he is ever taking to the airwaves of WNEQ—Radio Neely—to advertise his business and aside from the individual reposing rooms and the air-cooled sanctuary and the complete limousine service for the bereaved, the commander invariably includes an assurance of capacious caskets and in a very significant and prominent way as if it is his moral obligation to provide the deceased ample room to sit up on their elbows or play the violin. And Daddy says it was the capacious caskets part of it that stuck with Jack Vestal and worked in combination with Mr. Zeno Stiers's unbesmirched virtue to give him an idea he would not have gotten otherwise. As Jack figured it, Mr. Stiers was unquestionably bound for glory while Artemus Gordon's destination was a little less certain, so as long as Mr. Zeno was going to his reward anyway why not let Artemus Gordon occupy a guinea pig's worth of capaciousness and go to Mr. Zeno's reward along with him. Beatitude by association, Daddy called it.

But even with the great wealth of capaciousness that surrounded Mr. Zeno in his repose, Jack Vestal could not at first find the opportunity to slip Artemus Gordon into his slight share of it, mostly on account of the tremendous assortment of mourners who continuously filed by the casket to pay tribute. Daddy says there is nothing like utter goodliness for drawing a crowd at a viewing. So Jack had to be content with loitering around the coffin for awhile, which Kimberly Ann told him was just the most gruesome thing she'd ever witnessed but which rather gratified Mrs. Vestal who was made proud to see Jack developing an acute interest in an activity so dear to her. And as Daddy tells it, Jack probably gratified his momma to the excess before the night was out since he was not able to transfer

Artemus Gordon out of the limbo of his jacket pocket and into the relative security of Mr. Zeno's saintly capaciousness until near about the tail end of the viewing, and even then the best Jack could manage was a blind backhanded toss that landed Artemus Gordon only slightly beyond Mr. Stiers's elbow.

But nevertheless nobody noticed right away the spotted and partially cowlicked infringement on Mr. Zeno Stiers's duly guaranteed and highly regarded capaciousness, nobody noticed it at all—not the unattached mourners and not the immediately bereaved and not the commander and not the commander's platoon of funeral home attendants who were far too busy maintaining a suitable gravity to notice much of anything. So it probably seemed to Jack Vestal, after a full evening of casket lingering and anxiety, that Artemus Gordon was reasonably assured of at least some portion of saintliness, and on the following morning just prior to the service in the commander's air-cooled chapel when Mrs. Anne Elizabeth Bailey Stiers approached the earthly remains of Mr. Zeno for one final glimpse and did not screech or yelp or roll her eyes or attempt to leap up onto the family pew, Jack figured Artemus Gordon's destiny was certain and secure at last. And it very nearly was except for a Mr. Dunn from Spray who earned his living wearing a three-piece blue suit and driving the commander's hearse. In addition Mr. Dunn was in charge of tucking the loose ends of the satin liner into the casket prior to shutting the lid for all eternity, which he generally managed to pull off with a sort of quiet and somber efficiency that made him seem as good as invisible. But just after he had approached Mr. Zeno and had commenced to vanish a little, he stuck his hand down into the casket and felt something stiff and furry at Mr. Zeno's elbow, so he dropped his head sideways and peered back into the casket which did not do very much at all for Mr. Dunn's invisibility. Of course everybody else became instantly eager to know what it was he was looking at and consequently nobody in the entire air-cooled sanctuary failed to see Mr. Dunn, who took hold of Artemus Gordon by his stubby tail, draw out from Mr. Zeno's casket what looked to be a plump, festive-colored, and poorly groomed rat. Daddy says it was just the sort of thing to run converse to the spirit of the occasion and nobody much knew whether they should be horrified or not, except for the commander, who was most openly horrified and except for Mrs.

Ann Elizabeth Bailey Stiers, who was most openly horrified also and except for Mrs. Virginia Ann Crutchfield Vestal, who appeared to be in some danger of fainting.

Fortunately Mr. Dunn was not particularly frightened of rats, especially dead ones that were guinea pigs anyway, so he stuck Artemus Gordon in his coat pocket and carried through with the business at hand in a reasonably inconspicuous manner. The service itself got underway presently and all throughout the course of it Mrs. Stiers grieved demonstratively, Daddy called it, while Mrs. Vestal fanned herself with a hymnal while the commander began to formulate his unlugubrious child policy even before he knew for certain an unlugubrious child was the responsible party. The rest of the congregation still toyed with the idea of being horrified, and as far as Daddy could tell, the Methodist Reverend Mr. Richard Crockett Shelton who delivered the eulogy did the majority of the listening to it also. In between the funeral and the burial service when most everybody was waiting outside the church doors for the casket to find its way into the hearse, word got out about Artemus Gordon, primarily by way of Mrs. Bowles and Mrs. Ridley, and the news caused the congregation to decide it would not be horrified after all but would most probably be amused instead. Of course the commander was not much amused and persisted in his open horrification, but Mrs. Anne Elizabeth Bailey Stiers seemed to have improved during the course of the service and apparently had reverted to simple bereavement by the time she left the church. Mrs. Vestal, however, had doggedly managed to remain horrified all throughout the eulogy and all throughout Miss Fay Dull's solo performance of "Just a Closer Walk with Thee" and all throughout the Reverend Mr. Shelton's thoroughly exhaustive benediction and when she stepped through the big church doorway onto the portico and saw people looking at her the way they were looking at her, her condition escalated into what Mr. Jackson P. Eaton of the hardware Eatons called a traumatized crisis; he said he had seen one before in the big WW. It was about all Mr. Vestal could do to get his wife and Kimberly Ann into the car and then he had to go back and fetch Jack bodily off the church steps since Jack did not much care to leave his guinea pig in the coatpocket of a man he didn't even know. So when he finally did proceed to the cemetery, Mr. Zeno Stiers in his capacious casket did not bring with him a solitary Vestal in tow which proved to distinguish Mr. Stiers in death by having not been pelted with one of Mrs. Vestal's good linen handkerchiefs and the accompanying salute. As everybody figured it, Jack Vestal absorbed most all of the pelting for him.

Anymore Artemus Gordon is the only thing people talk about when they talk about Mr. Stiers. Nobody ever says a word about virtue. Nobody ever says a word about saintliness. People just wonder out loud if they were as muddle-headed as Jack Vestal when they were his age. But Daddy always says when he dies and is lying stiff in his casket he hopes there are enough muddle-headed children in Neely sufficiently convinced of his destination to pack all of his capaciousness full up with housepets. However, what with the commander's pointed and specific policy, Daddy will probably have to face eternity alone whether he wants to or not since nobody much under four feet tall ever gets into the Heavenly Rest anymore except for Miss Mottsinger who is a midget but has become too old and infirm to see her friends off like she used to. And whenever the children of mourners from out of town, who have no verifiable history of muddle-headedness, get themselves banned from the parlor amid the sometimes vehement and indignant protests of their parents, the commander defends himself with a few words about serpent's teeth, and when the parents say, "What?" the commander replies, "Bridger," who had whistled much too loudly for his own good, and when the parents say, "Who?" the commander simply tells them, "Artemus Gordon," who as it turned out was successfully flushed down a toilet with hardly any ceremony to speak of.

So Momma and Daddy went to view Miss Myra Angelique without me since I was not yet sixteen and consequently posed a threat to Miss Pettigrew's capaciousness. But Daddy said by the time him and Momma got to the Heavenly Rest there wasn't enough room in the parlor to accommodate even the smallest of unlugubrious children and they had to wait on the porch for the crowd to condense some. Momma said as far as she could tell nearly everybody able to come had come. Mr. and Mrs. Phillip J. King were there ahead of them along with little Buford Needham and his son Paul, and his daughter-in-law, Mary Margaret Vance Needham, and the bald Jeeter Throckmorton was there with her daughter, Ivy, who had married an insurance agent from Greensboro and was six months gone with their third child but had been allowed to pass anyway since the commander figured a fetus would be sufficiently bound up not to cause much of any mischief. Sheriff Burton had run the knot in his tie clear up to his neck for the occasion and had come in the company of a ladyfriend from Leaksville who Daddy said Mrs. Phillip J. King insisted was a slut even before she met the woman. She said she could sniff out that sort of thing, said it was a gift. Two of the hardware Eatons were there and one of the body shop Eatons and three pair of unrelated Wattses, two from Ruffin and one from Rosemont Hills out by the golf course. Both sets of Singletarys had come, Mr. Billy Singletary from the five and dime along with his wife, Elise, and Mrs. Estelle Singletary of the autumn harvest brunch and her husband, Patrick, who did not ever talk much except to say, "Yes, dear." Most of the rest of the crowd was made up by a contingent of people from down off the Richardson Road whose names Momma could not call along with a party from Southend which included Mr. and Mrs. Small and Mrs. Small's sister and her husband, Mr. and Mrs. Richard Dabb, who had brought with them a neighbor that worked as a welder at the cigarette plant. And Daddy said Mrs. Phillip J. King told him a funeral home was hardly a fit place for such lowlife as that.

There were, then, plenty of people to see what there was to see but as it turned out there wasn't anything much to see— no Miss Pettigrew, no casket, not even any Rackleys who had turned around and gone home and had probably reached the West Virginia end of Kentucky by the time the viewing got underway. So even when the viewing did get underway nothing got viewed right off except the commander who announced to everybody that there was in fact a body and there was in fact a casket but that there was also some specifications of the deceased, he called them, which prevented any sort of public display of the aforementioned items. Then the commander indicated a pair of shut double doors across the parlor behind which, he said, was an individual reposing room within which, he said, was Miss Pettigrew's personal capacious casket which itself, he said, held the earthly remains of Miss Myra Angelique Pettigrew in satin-upholstered and eternal comfort. So the shut double doors got viewed with some interest until the commander held up over his head a handsome leather-bound album that he announced was the family register and should be signed into, and Daddy said the introduction of the leatherbound album threw the assembly of mourners into noticeable disarray since most people were torn between watching the shut double doors and getting their names onto the first page of the register. Daddy said some of them had even gone back to viewing the commander who they figured to be responsible for their disappointment and confusion. As for the commander himself, Daddy guessed he thought people would just get along home once they had inked their names into the ledger to prove they had gone to the trouble to come in the first place; after all, there was no visible corpse and no visible casket but just two visible doorknobs attached to two visible doors. However, even after everybody had signed in Daddy said it was all he could do to get across the room to the sideboard where the commander kept the complimentary matches. He did not notice that anybody had left except for the sheriff and his ladyfriend, who went outside to rake the air and even before they could get through the door good a station wagon load of Frenches came in to replace them.

So after the family register got filled up there was not any general evacuation from the Heavenly Rest as the commander had expected and folks persisted in viewing what there was to view which aside from the doorknobs and aside from the doors and aside from each other meant the commander. And Daddy said the crowd of mourners commenced to encircle the commander roundabout and closed in on him directly before he could devise any sort of successful evasive maneuver which proved a great disappointment to Daddy considering the Tuttle tradition of courageous resourcefulness under fire. And even as the commander was reaching with two fingers into his fob pocket so as to produce the rivet and wear the crowd down some with tediousness, Mrs. Estelle Singletary latched onto his wrist and demanded of him, "What's she wearing?"

"Who?" the commander said.

"Miss Pettigrew."

"Miss Pettigrew? Well, I do believe she's wearing a dress. Isn't she wearing a dress?" the commander asked Mr. Dunn who Daddy said was standing against the far wall like a piece of blue pinstriped puritanical furniture, and Mr. Dunn shook his head yes it was a dress she was wearing.

"What color dress?" Mrs. Estelle Singletary wanted to know.

"Well I do believe it was a red dress," the commander replied and looked at Mr. Dunn who Daddy said hunched his shoulders and opened his hands and looked back at the commander with a wholly moronic expression on his face. "But then maybe it was Mrs. Mueller we buried in a red dress. Come to think of it I do believe it was Mrs. Mueller. Seems to me Miss Pettigrew's dress was white."

"Are you sure?" Mrs. Estelle Singletary said.

"Well I'm sure now it wasn't a red dress and I do believe it was a white dress, though"—and Daddy said the commander grabbed the end of his nose between his right thumb and forefinger and looked down at the floor in front of him—"it might have been a black dress. I saw a black dress somewhere; now where was it I saw it?" And Daddy said once the commander let go of his nose and looked at Mrs. Estelle Singletary again and looked at the faces of the people all around her, he seemed to realize exactly how inadequate he was proving to be and he jerked his head at Mr. Dunn, who went down into the basement to fetch Mr. Tally, the mortician.

In Neely all of the Tallys are each other's mothers or fathers or husbands or wives or sons or daughters or cousins or in-laws except for the Frank Lewis Tallys who are negroes. And in Neely all of the Tallys, except for the Frank Lewis Tallys, are a very slightly built and sheepish bunch of people, what Daddy calls wispy folk, and perhaps Mr. James Elsworth Tally the mortician is one of the wispiest. Consequently, he did not much desire to seize the opportunity to go upstairs into the parlor and discuss the color of Miss Pettigrew's clothes with Mrs. Estelle Singletary or anybody else, but also consequently he could not prevent Mr. Dunn from taking him upstairs anyway since Dunns were generally not wispy in the least. So Mr. Tally got brought out into the parlor against his will and was deposited next to the commander who Daddy said appeared truly relieved to have the company. "Hello, J.E.," he said, and Mr. Tally, who could not find anywhere to put his hands on account of the black rubber apron he wore that covered up his pockets, nodded at the commander and then crossed his arms over his chest. "Mrs. Singletary here would like to ask you a thing or two about Miss Pettigrew," the commander said, and Mr. Tally glanced sideways at Mrs. Singletary and then looked full on the commander again and replied, "Alright."

"Mr. Tally," Mrs. Singletary said, "what sort of outfit is it that Miss Pettigrew has on?"

And Mr. Tally, who had studied the carpet throughout the course of Mrs. Singletary's question, looked directly at the commander and replied, "Suit."

"A skirt and a blouse and a jacket?" Mrs. Singletary said.

"Yes ma'm," Mr. Tally told the commander.

"Wool?" Mrs. Singletary wanted to know.

"Cotton blend," Mr. Tally replied and very nearly looked at Mrs. Singletary as he said it.

"And what color is it?" Mrs. Singletary asked, and Daddy said the women drew in tight all roundabout her and peered at Mr. Tally as intently as Mrs. Singletary herself.

"It's peach, ma'm," Mr. Tally said, looking full on Mrs. Singletary. "It's a rich shade of peach."

And according to Daddy it did not seem as if Mr. Tally could have said anything more pleasing. "Ah, peach," Mrs. Singletary crooned, and several of the ladies behind her said "peach" themselves in low, excited voices.

"Yes ma'm," Mr. Tally said, "a very rich and beautiful shade of peach," and he smiled at Mrs. Singletary which Daddy said was probably the first time he had ever seen a Tally smile directly at anybody.

"And her condition?" Mrs. Singletary wanted to know.

"Ma'm?" Mr. Tally said.

And the Mrs. Rosemont Hills Watts asked him by way of elaboration, "Was she much damaged, Mr. Tally? Was she much damaged in the accident?"

"Not hardly on the outside," Mr. Tally said, "just a few bruises here and there and a plug out of her left forearm but not hardly anything otherwise. I guess the most of the damage is on the inside; she had to die from something don't you know." And Daddy said Mr. Tally grinned at Mrs. Rosemont Hills Watts and at Mrs. Singletary and at the women gathered all roundabout her and then he grinned at the commander just prior to leering at the carpet for good measure. Daddy said it was probably the first time he had ever seen a Tally attempt a joke.

"Does she look natural, Mr. Tally?" Mrs. Mary Margaret Vance Needham asked him. "Does she have much coloration?"

"I suppose she looks natural," Mr. Tally said. "I really hadn't seen her enough to know what comes in the way of natural for her and that neegra of hers wouldn't give us a photograph, said weren't any photographs to be had. So I guess she looks natural, anyway she came to us all pink in the face and didn't call for much blush or highlighter and I swear to you she looks healthy enough to sit up and say hello."

"And her cheekbones?" Mrs. Phillip J. King said.

"She's got both of them, ma'm," Mr. Tally told her, and winked at Daddy, who was standing behind Mrs. Phillip J. King and who said he had never been winked at by a Tally before.

And Mrs. Phillip J. King snapped back at him, "Are they prominent, Mr. Tally?"

"Oh, yes ma'm," Mr. Tally said, "they're a lovely pair of cheekbones. Not a thing sunk in about them."

And the bald Jeeter Throckmorton, who had been standing quietly beside Mrs. Estelle Singletary with her right arm hooked into the crook of little Ivy's left elbow, cleared her throat and said, "How is her expression, Mr. Tally? Does she appear to be at ease?"

"At ease, ma'm?" Mr. Tally said. "Why yes I believe I'd say her expression is..." and Daddy said Mr. Tally paused and sucked on his top lip and then selected one of his fingers and chewed the end of it and then rubbed his eyes with his knuckle and appeared set to grab ahold of the back of his neck when the commander leaned towards him ever so slightly and directed a brief observation at the side of Mr. Tally's head for which Mr. Tally appeared exceedingly grateful, and Daddy said he thanked the commander straightaway and then turned his attention full on the bald Jeeter Throckmorton and told her, "Serene, ma'm. I'd say her expression is quite serene."

"And overall," Mrs. Estelle Singletary began, "with her peach dress and her natural flush and her serene expression, how would you say she looked, Mr. Tally?"

But according to Daddy even before Mr. Tally could fully consider what part of himself he would suck or chew or rub or grab ahold of Momma said, "Elegant," and Mr. Tally thanked her straightaway and then turned his attention full on Mrs. Estelle Singletary and told her, "Elegant, ma'm. I'd say overall she looks quite elegant."

Nobody seemed to have much use for Mr. Tally after that except for one of the Richardson Road contingent who was burning to know what color Miss Pettigrew's shoes were, so the commander excused him at length and Mr. Tally made his manners in the form of a slight, imperial bow and then went off towards the basement door looking altogether taller, Daddy said, than he'd ever seen a Tally look before. And after Mr. Tally was gone from sight, people went back to viewing the shut double doors but with some renewed interest since they were surer of just what was behind them, and in the spirit of gracious solicitude, Daddy called it, the commander volunteered that all of the fittings on the Pettigrew casket were made from solid brass which caused quite a stir among the mourners and sparked exclamations of "Ah, brass!" from all across the parlor. And Daddy said all of the women who had previously drawn in together around Mrs. Estelle Singletary drew in together around her again before the shut double doors and the crowd of them repeated most everything that had been said by Mr. Tally and most everything that had been said to Mr. Tally. They called Miss Pettigrew serene and easeful and lovely and natural and elegant, called her just about every uncorpselike thing they could think of, but when the commander approached them with his fingers in his fob pocket, the women decided they had exhausted themselves in praise and the crowd dispersed in a kind of agitated flurry.

Daddy said him and Momma departed from the Heavenly Rest in the company of Mr. and Mrs. Phillip J. King and before the four of them could get off the porch Mrs. Phillip J. King had to stop and dab at her eyes with a Kleenex. "A pillar of virtue," she announced. "The purest example of sweetness and light." And Daddy said Momma looked at her but did not offer to elaborate or answer back, and the four of them managed to reach the bottom of the steps before Mrs. Phillip J. King stopped again and this time dabbed at her nose. "An inspiration to us each and every one," she said, but Momma did not even turn her head and Daddy said they had not taken four strides altogether when Mrs. Phillip J. King stopped once more, threw her hands up in the air and passionately exclaimed, "Oh peach is such an exquisite color." Daddy said it was perhaps the passion of the exclamation that startled Sheriff Burton and startled his ladyfriend from Leaksville who both jumped out from behind the commander's elm tree where they had been mourning in private, and as Daddy figured it Sheriff Burton had not yet decided it was just Mrs. Phillip J. King being Mrs. Phillip J. King when Mrs. Phillip J. King herself saw the sheriff and his ladyfriend off in the shadows, dropped her hands to her side, and said, "Hussy!" in a low violent whisper that sounded like a sneeze. Then she was gone, Daddy said, gone off into the darkness leaving no trace of herself but for a used-up Kleenex on the commander's lawn and the sound of her heels pecking at the sidewalk, and Daddy said Mr. Phillip J. King explained to him and Momma that his wife had an exceptionally low tolerance for unprincipled women. "ExCEPtionally low," he told them.

iv

"ROADAPPLES," DADDY said and put his feet up on the porch bannister.

"But a tragic figure," I told him, "such a tragic figure."

And Daddy said, "Roadapples" again and scratched himself.

He had not ever gone into the house but had taken off his grey jacket and his blue speckled necktie and draped them over the back of a chair and me and him together had brought the glider out to the front of the porch so we could prop ourselves against the rail. As far as I could tell Momma had gone direct to the kitchen to turn the taps on and we didn't hear much from her after the sink filled except for every now and again when a couple of plates would bump together. Otherwise there wasn't much noise anywhere but for the crickets and the clicking of Tiny Aaron's wheel bearings as he drove his white Impala up and down in front of our house.

"But Momma says he was tragic," I told him, "and Mrs. Phillip J. King says he was tragic and freshly divorced and very nearly skewered on a naked sabre."

"Roadapples," Daddy said. "More roadapples from the queen patoot." And Daddy prized his hand down in between two glider cushions and brought out a matchpack. "Slimy," he told me, "not tragic." And when he had lit his Tareyton he lay his head back until he was looking at the ceiling.

"Not tragic?"

"No sir," Daddy said.

"And not freshly divorced?"

"No sir," Daddy said.

"And not even very nearly skewered on a naked sabre?"

"No sir," Daddy said.

"Well what then?" I asked him.

"Just slimy," Daddy said.

"But he was only out to take a wife. Momma says so. Mrs. Phillip J. King says so."

"No sir," Daddy said.

"No wife?"

"No sir," Daddy said.

"Well what then?" I asked him.

"Favors," Daddy said.

"Whose?"

"Hers," Daddy said. And when I did not say anything back, and when Daddy had drawn on his cigarette and blown the smoke away and I still did not say anything back, he brought his head off from the glider cushion and asked me, "Do you see what I mean, Louis?"

"No sir," I said.

So Daddy said, "Come on," and got up from the glider and after he'd hollered at Momma through the screen door me and him went down the steps together and along the sidewalk towards town. We stopped at Mr. Gibbons's mailbox long enough for Daddy to extract from it a handful of kitchen matches, all of which he gave over to me except for the one he fired against Mr. Gibbons's retaining wall, and then we made straightaway for the intersection and turned right onto the boulevard. It was not a particularly cool night but was a night full of little breezes that stirred the heat sufficiently to make things comfortable, and after we had walked a block or so Daddy took an exceedingly deep breath and told me he believed it was a night ripe for romance, which was not at all the sort of thing Daddy was given to say. I didn't know what to tell him back so I just poked at the cracks in the sidewalk with a stick I had picked up especially for that purpose, and just when I was beginning to think Daddy had been temporarily moonstruck and would recover he said to me, "Louis, do you know much about romance?"

"No sir," I told him.

And Daddy took another exceedingly deep breath before he stopped dead on the sidewalk and looked at me in a most serious and earnest fashion. "Louis," he said, and then he said it again, "Louis," and then he blew out the best part of his exceedingly deep breath and asked me, "May I have a match please?"

"Yes sir," I told him, and gave him one out of my pocket.

And we walked another block and a half until Daddy had smoked out all the usefulness in his cigarette and just as he was tossing the butt of it aside he said to me, "Louis, a man and a woman have a kind of draw for each other. Do you see what I mean?"

"No sir," I told him, "not exactly."

"Well a man can like a woman," he said, "because she's pretty to him, and a woman can like a man because he's handsome to her. And sometimes a man can like a woman because she's smart or funny or goodhearted and sometimes a woman can like a man because he's all those things too. Do you see what I mean?"

"Yes sir," I told him.

"Now sometimes," he said, "a man starts out liking a woman because she's pretty and she can start out liking him back because he's handsome, and once they've kept company together for awhile they each might find out that the other one is smart or funny or goodhearted and so become more attached on account of it. That's what we call a romance. You follow me?"

"Yes sir," I said.

"But sometimes," Daddy told me, "a man and a woman can start out liking each other on account of looks and then discover they aren't suited otherwise."

"What do you call that?" I asked him.

"We don't call that anything," Daddy said. "But anyway that's not what's important. What's important is that no matter whether a man and a woman get so far along as a romance or not, the thing that draws them together in the first place is always the same."

"Well then what do you call that," I asked him.

But Daddy decided he'd best smoke a cigarette before he answered and then he decided he'd best smoke another one and when he finally did set in on a reply it did not much seem like one. "Louis," he said, "you see a woman has what we call charms and charms are kind of like musk; I mean she airs them out every now and again to draw in a mate. You with me?"

"Yes sir," I said, "I think so."

"Good. Now when she gets ahold of a prospect him and her have to go through this little dance together sort of like quail. First she takes him to meet her people and then he carries her to meet his people and then he gives her a ring to show who she belongs to and eventually they get things finalized at a church by a legitimate preacher who marries the two of them together. And once they're married they can become what we call intimate without people looking sideways at them."

"Intimate?" I said.

But Daddy rolled on ahead of me and recommenced with, "But there are some men, and some women too I suppose, who want to go direct to intimate without ever dancing much. Do you see what I mean?"

And I looked up at Daddy who was looking down at me with his lips turned up in a sickly sort of way and his face partway blue from the mercury light overhead, and I was just about to tell him Lord no, I didn't see what he meant when it hit me like a sledgehammer blow to the forehead. Daddy was talking about plugging, or anyway that's what Everet Little calls it even though his sister, Angela Kirstan, insists the scientific term for it is getting intercoursed which Bill Ed Myrick says his brother tells him is most probably undoubtedly correct since word around town is that Angela Kirstan is taking a degree in it. But we call it plugging even though none of us are real clear on what gets plugged and how. We do, however, figure it will come to us at length and on Friday afternoons, in the pursuit of knowledge, we all collect at the Gulf station and listen to Coley Britt talk about the weekly Poontang Festival in Eden which him and his girlfriend, the former Mrs. Bradford Webb, attend most every weekend. Coley says they generally place in nearly all of the events but tend to specialize in the flying fuck and have been known to take their share of regular unornamented fuck awards as well. But even with his considerable expertise, Coley has yet to clear up for us what gets plugged and how since he is ever contradicting himself and all we've learned from him is that men and women get tangled and locked up together in a vague and inexplicable way and if nobody throws a bucket of water on them they're liable to put fruit on the vine. Of course we all have plans to see this sort of thing for ourselves, since it is fairly much impossible to comprehend otherwise, but when Bill Ed asked his brother to carry us over to Eden to the Poontang Festival his brother fell directly off the bed and could not catch his breath to answer. We have been a little bashful about bothering him with it ever since.

So I looked up at Daddy, who was looking down at me with his mouth all twisted and curled up in the sort of outright pathetic smile you might show the dentist when he comes in to drill your teeth, and I asked him, "Do you mean sex?"

"Well Jesus Christ, Louis," Daddy said, "why'd you let me suffer so?"

And I told him, "Daddy, I couldn't make out what you were up to."

And Daddy grinned at me in an utterly untormented way and asked for a match. "So you know about sex then," he said. "I mean you're pretty clear on it?"

"Yes sir," I told him, "fairly much."

"Good. Good," Daddy said and we continued down the boulevard for a spell listening to the crickets and the jarflies instead of each other, but after Daddy had flung his cigarette away he pulled up short, stuck his hands in his trouser pockets, and said, "Louis, you see women are born with a pureness and they're meant to keep it all to themselves until they get into a romance that turns into a wedding and then they can let loose of it with a free conscience. You see it's the sort of thing you can give away only one time to one man and most women figure the one they get to the altar must be the right one."

"Well Daddy," I said, "aren't men born with a pureness too?"

And Daddy told me, "Now Louis, men are born with a pureness, but they're meant to get shed of it as soon as they can. You see women are intended to keep pure and men are intended to keep from it. You follow me?"

"I believe so," I said.

"Good," Daddy told me. "Good." And we started in to walking again very slowly down the boulevard. "Naturally," Daddy said, "when women are trying to hold onto their pureness and men are trying to get shed of theirs you're going to have some conflict and you're going to have some temptation, but fortunately for men there are some women who don't figure their pureness is worth keeping ahold of and give it up early on so as to provide an assortment of gentlemen a place to deposit theirs. You with me?"

"Like Angela Kirstan Little," I said. "Mrs. Phillip J. King told Momma she's a regular harlot."

"Yes," Daddy replied, "there's one of your depository types." And I felt pleased and somewhat sexually advanced by having recognized Angela Kirstan Little for what she was. "However," Daddy said, "there are some women who manage to retain their pureness even though they are sorely tempted to let loose of it. They get in and out of romances, become engaged and disengaged, and are ever burning for intimacy but somehow or another rein themselves in just before their pureness can get away from them."

"Do most everything but get intercoursed," I said. I was feeling awfully bold by this time.

And Daddy laughed and asked me was that what Mrs. Phillip J. King called it. But I told him I couldn't answer for Mrs. Phillip J. King; I told him it was a scientific term. And Daddy said, "Well then, scientifically speaking they do most everything but get intercoursed," and at the time it looked to me that I would not need the Poontang Festival after all.

"Now aside from the women that get intercoursed," Daddy said, "and aside from the women that stop just shy of it, there is another sort of women that do not ever risk their pureness. They hold it far too close and dear to themselves to put it in the way of temptation and only bring it out once the vows are done with and the honeymoon has commenced. And it's my theory," Daddy said, "that Miss Pettigrew was one of these last ones."

"Pure?" I asked him.

"Yes sir," Daddy said. "Pure and goodly right up to Mr. Alton."

"And she got intercoursed?" I said.

"No sir," Daddy told me. "She got invited to."

Me and Daddy stopped directly across from an oiled road that ran alongside the Pettigrew property and linked up Russel Avenue with the boulevard. "When it was all over with," Daddy said, "when it was all pretty much up with him, the mayor would walk at the end of the day and I'd run up on him fairly regular back in there," and Daddy pointed towards the narrow cross street that was lighted at the boulevard end and lighted at the Russel Avenue end but was all darkness in between, "and sometimes I'd give him a cigarette or two," Daddy said, "and we'd smoke and walk together but he hardly ever said anything much except for once and I don't know what possessed him to talk then but we stopped of a sudden and he grabbed onto my arm and told me, 'Louis, I've ruined her.' 'Who?' I asked him. 'Sister,' he said. 'Sister.' "

And Daddy said he asked him, "How, Wallace?"

"It was him," the mayor said. "It was him and me together."

"Mr. Alton Nance?" Daddy said.

"Yes sir," the mayor told him, "Mr. Alton Nance." And Daddy said the mayor spoke Mr. Alton's name in a very slow and peculiar way like it was a thing of great wonder to him. "He told me he would put me in the congress," the mayor said. "He told me he would make a senator of me. He told me I could be governor one day."

"Did you want to be governor?" Daddy asked him.

"Not until he said I could be. And Louis," the mayor said, "it seemed like such a reasonable bargain at the time. It seemed like such a small price."

"What did?" Daddy asked him.

"Her," the mayor said.

"Sister?" Daddy asked him.

"Yes sir," the mayor said.

"Her hand?" Daddy asked him.

"No sir," the mayor said.

And Daddy said him and the mayor stood together in the middle of the oiled road and did not say anything to each other for a time, and then the mayor scratched in the gravel with the toe of his shoe and said, "I didn't know what I was doing, Louis. I was just shut off from sense for awhile. Don't you see, I'd already gotten enough of everything I'd wanted to believe I couldn't help but get this too. I didn't know what I was doing. And Louis I was right there, I was standing right there beside her and all I had to say was NO or STOP or DON'T, anything at all, and if you could have seen how she looked at me, if you could have just seen it." And the mayor crossed his arms over himself like he was near about freezing and made a face, Daddy said, made a face like people on the t.v. make when they are sad and when they are woeful which is just the face regular people make when they are done in. "Ruined," he said and drew off a breath and said it again.

Daddy could not find anything to tell the mayor back, so the two of them stood there in the middle of the sidestreet without talking and somehow without looking at each other either, and Daddy said he could not think of anything worthwhile to say right off and could not think of anything worthwhile to say at length but was fixing to open his mouth anyway when the mayor wished him good evening and so saved himself.

"But she never got intercoursed," I said.

"No sir," Daddy told me, and we set in down the boulevard once more.

"Never even got tempted," I said.

"No sir," Daddy told me. "But they figured she could be." And we crossed the street to the imported wrought iron fence and put our arms through the palings. A number of people were milling around the length of the block and me and Daddy joined them in watching the Pettigrew house, which was dark everywhere except for the solitary light up in Aunt Willa's window and every now and again Aunt Willa herself would pass into view toting a box or an armload of clothes and the sight of her would stir up a noticeable huzzah in the street.

"But Daddy," I said, "she never got intercoursed and she never even got tempted so why did it matter if the mayor and Mr. Alton thought she could be?"

"Her own brother, Louis," Daddy told me, "her own brother guessed she was ripe for it. It makes a difference."

"So it wore on her?" I asked him.

"That's right," Daddy told me.

"And since the mayor figured she wasn't pure," I said, "and since Mr. Alton figured she wasn't pure, she went ahead and figured she wasn't either."

"That's right," Daddy told me.

" But that isn't fair, Daddy."

"No sir," he said, "it isn't."

"So she didn't jump because Mr. Alton was gone from her."

"No sir," Daddy told me.

"And she didn't jump because the mayor was gone from her."

"No sir," Daddy told me.

"Then she jumped because her pureness was gone from her."

"No sir," Daddy told me.

"No sir?"

"No sir," Daddy said.

"Well how come then?" I asked him.

"Because she was bats," Daddy told me. And just as he had closed his mouth good an exceedingly noticeable huzzah kicked up all around us and we looked towards Aunt Willa's window to find it partway blocked off by the backside of Mr. Britches, who was crouched on the windowsill beating his arms on his head.

Sister

MOMMA WORE the same black dress she had seen Grand-momma Yount off in and the same little round hat with feathers and a half-veil and she carried with her a big shiny black pocketbook with gold clasps that had nothing in it but one of Daddy's handkerchiefs. Daddy wore his lightweight navy suit and his reversible vest blue side out and Momma selected for him a striped burgundy tie that she said highlighted and enhanced the natural flush in Daddy's cheeks and accordingly Daddy selected for himself a pair of burgundy socks as a fitting complement but Momma put them back into the drawer for him and brought out some navy ones instead. I wore my green suit, which was at the time my only suit, and my shortsleeve white shirt with the inkstain in the bottom of the pocket and my green speckled necktie along with my green socks that were not exactly the same color as each other and my black oxford shoes which I did not put on until right when I had to since they tended to lay my toes all together in a kind of bouquet. So I stood on my heels in the living room while Daddy went to the kitchen and passed his hand over all the burners and Momma crouched in front of the vanity mirror and pinned Rhode Island to her dressfront. Then we were out the door and down the steps to the sidewalk and Mr. and Mrs. Phillip J. King, who had been waiting for us on their front porch, put her dog Itty Bit into the house and joined up with us as we went by.

Momma made me go in front and her and Mrs. Phillip J. King walked abreast behind me followed by Daddy and Mr.

Phillip J. King, who were not in the leastways frantic about getting to the chapel and so fell off the pace directly and I would have been pleased to fall off some myself but Momma and Mrs. Phillip J. King drove me on ahead of them and it was all I could do to keep from getting trampled on what with my toes bunched up together and causing me some extraordinary discomfort. I suppose we got to the Heavenly Rest a full two blocks ahead of Daddy and Mr. Phillip J. King, who left off talking about whatever they had been talking about once they came into earshot, and when Mr. Phillip J. King got close enough to see the look on Mrs. Phillip J. King's face he fairly much sprinted to us and left Daddy to lag in on his own which was a source of great irritation to Momma who could not ever seem to convince Daddy that there was any virtue at all in arriving early to anything. And even after Daddy got up with us he insisted on smoking a cigarette which he could not at first find a match for, and once he'd gotten it lit up and had smoked it and stamped it out, Momma directed him towards the chapel doorway where he stopped to pass the time of day with Mr. Tadlock who had come outside to spit. Consequently we did not enter the chapel itself until right on time and we made our way up the center aisle to where Mr. and Mrs. Phillip J. King had saved us a little slip of pew that was just big enough so that the three of us could not all sit down flush at once. Of course I was the one that got semi-levitated and while I was situating myself so as to keep any additional parts from getting pinched into disfigurement, Mrs. Phillip J. King turned her head and looked past me at Daddy with her face all puckered and drawn up like he was a slab of rancid meat and then Mr. Phillip J. King looked at him too but a little more longingly.

By the time we arrived the chapel was already packed tight everywhere with people snug up against each other in the pews and in folding chairs along the aisles and standing two and three deep against the walls in amongst the flowers and the leafy wreaths. There was not much relief on the altar either which was itself full up with clergymen and laypreachers and various other Godly individuals who had all volunteered to take part in the service once word got around that there were no specifications of the deceased to keep them from it. In fact the commander had been caught in the middle of a vigorous and hotly contested debate primarily between the Reverend Mr.

Holroyd of the First Presbyterian Church and the Reverend Mr. Richard Crockett Shelton of the Lawsonville Avenue Methodist Church, both of whom laid claim to the eulogy on account of their prior dealings with Miss Pettigrew, who the Reverend Mr. Holroyd recollected as a devout Presbyterian while the Reverend Mr. Richard Crockett Shelton insisted otherwise, and the matter was complicated somewhat by the introduction of the Reverend Mr. W.B. "Red" Hamilton of the Gospel Light Chapel who was a eulogist of county-wide renown and considered himself the man for the job since sendoffs were his particular specialty. So the commander weighed the candidates each one against the other two and he decided to divvy up the eulogy between the Reverend Mr. Holroyd and the Reverend Mr. Richard Crockett Shelton and as consolation he awarded the Reverend Mr. W.B. Red Hamilton three minutes of fairly much unrestricted praying which the Reverend Hamilton agreed to carry out in one tongue only and with a minimum of stomping and gesticualtion. The Reverend Mr. Lynwood Wilkerson of the First Baptist Church was given the honor of reading the text, and Mr. Ames Gatewood, who ran the newsstand downtown but was notably pious nonetheless, was charged with telling the congregation when to stand up and when to sit down, and in addition the Mayor Mr. Simms and Sheriff Burton and Mr. Jeffrey Elwood Crawford sr. of the town council were distributed across the altar for what seemed to be purposes of adornment only and the three of them filled in any vacancies that might have otherwise been left between clergymen. So the altar itself was loaded with about as much Godliness as it could bear up under and the congregation was spilling out of the pews and into the aisles and roundabout the walls. The only part of the chapel that could have been considered uncrowded, unthronged, and otherwise very nearly vacant was up between the congregation and the altar where Miss Pettigrew's casket had come out from behind its shut double doors and lay on the commander's collapsible chrome trundle with its brass fittings catching the light. All around it on every side were several feet worth of emptiness which was a rare commodity in the chapel just then what with the rest of us packed in on top of each other like lizards, so Miss Pettigrew's scant yard and a half of isolation seemed to leave her utterly and supremely secluded.

The service commenced when Mrs. Rollie Cobb, who was

the pianist at the Seventh Day Adventist Church and who played entirely by ear and mostly in ragtime, stood up from her place on the front pew and approached the commander's upright piano, which was situated just shy of the altar and somewhat to the left of it. Mrs. Cobb was probably nearly four feet tall from the bottoms of her feet to the tops of her shoulders and then was another two feet taller from the base of her neck up to where the heap of hair on her head reached its highest altitude. Understandably, then, she was not a woman of any appreciable velocity since balance was a matter of some consequence with her, so once Mrs. Cobb stood up to approach the piano she was in the process of approaching it for a measurable spell before she finally succeeded in setting herself down on the stool, and when she stabilized her head where it would sit properly upright she launched into a lively prefatory melody that gradually degenerated into "Onward Christian Soldiers" as Mrs. Cobb got her bearings on the tempo.

The choir was under the direction of Miss Fay Dull of the Methodist Church and was composed partly of Methodists and partly of Baptists with a smattering of Episcopalians and Presbyterians along with one Jewish tenor, and the plan was for the choir to enter through the main doorway and then separate with the sopranos proceeding up the middle aisle, the altos proceeding up the left one, and the baritones proceeding up the right one. But the aisles were unexpectedly filled up with chairs which were themselves filled up with mourners, so when the sopranos and the altos filed in through the main doorway they scuttled the original plan and improvised themselves across the back of the chapel which was not nearly spacious enough to allow for the baritones, who remained outside on the landing, where along with the rest of the choir they sang the processional without proceeding anywhere. And what with the piano up in front of us and the sopranos and altos all jumbled up back behind us and the baritones not even under the roof, it was not a very stirring rendition.

After Mrs. Cobb had hammered out an Amen, the Mayor Mr. Simms crossed over to the pulpit and grabbed onto the edges of it like a natural evangelist. He greeted us all, told us what a lovely turnout we were, and then reminded us just who it was that had died which seemed to be his primary function and after he had seen it through successfully he crossed back

over to his chair and sat down in it. Almost immediately the
Reverend Lynwood Wilkerson got up and went to the podium
which he grabbed onto also and after he had announced to us
the text for the day he planted his glasses onto the end of his
nose and set in to reading. Daddy recollected it as Ephesians
or Galatians or Phillipians or Thessolonians, he couldn't decipher which, and I thought the reverend had said Corinthians,
but Momma told us it was Revelations and it was indeed some
highly potent material all about angels with trumpets and angels
with sharp sickles and portents in the heavens and plagues and
fires and bowls full up with the wrath of God along with some
sort of blood-red creature that had near about as many heads
as horns. And the more the reverend read the more he appeared
to enjoy hearing himself do it, and the congregation as a whole
was beginning to seem a little fearful that he might persevere
on through to the end of this book and start in on another one
when Reverend Wilkerson finally closed his Bible, took it up
in his right hand, and shook it at us.

"Yes beloved," he said, "a call, a CAWL for the endurance
of the saints."

And as the reverend was lifting his glasses from his nose
and preparing to surrender the pulpit, Daddy leaned across me
and said to Momma, "A regular ray of sunshine," which Mr.
Phillip J. King heard and snorted at but which did not seem to
give much pleasure to Momma, who cut her eyes sideways
and let it out that she was annoyed.

We were treated to a minute or two of coughing, sneezing,
noseblowing, and general uneasiness among the congregation
once Reverend Wilkerson had returned to his chair, and following some elaborate arm waving between Mrs. Rollie Cobb
at the front of the chapel and Miss Fay Dull at the back of it
Mrs. Cobb got herself properly set and anchored at the piano
and then assaulted the keyboard but with such a limited success
that she had to break off and start in again and the second time
around she got underway in fairly good form. However, Mrs.
Cobb commenced to put a little pace on the melody directly
and it became so frantic with embellishments and excesses that
Miss Fay Dull had a difficult time cueing the sopranos and the
altos, which was all she could cue since the baritones were still
outside on the landing and could not quite see her from there.
So the sopranos and the altos simply jumped aboard at the first

available chink in the tune and the baritones waded in shortly thereafter and they all managed to draw together presently into what sounded very much like singing. This particular selection called for a solo and Miss Fay Dull had nominated herself, so once she choked off the competition to her satisfaction she made a fine entrance into the melody and brawled with it all the way to the refrain where the rest of the choir showed up to help her vanquish it entirely. Then they all sang together for a couple of bars before things got a little uptown in the middle and called for the baritones and sopranos to bark back and forth at each other while Miss Dull trilled away between and underneath them and Mrs. Rollie Cobb bludgeoned the whole business with some rather ponderous fingerwork. We were entertained in this fashion for what seemed an inconsiderately lengthy spell and by the time the melody began to shut down, the whole business had turned into a kind of slugfest for soprano, choir, and Seventh Day Adventist and we were all pretty much relieved to see the animosities brought to a close, especially Daddy whose ears had become as red as firecoals.

Mr. Ames Gatewood rose from his chair once Mrs. Rollie Cobb had left off torturing the commander's piano and he indicated to us that we should rise also, which of course we did, but even before all the coughing and sneezing and nose-blowing had a legitimate opportunity to fade away, the Reverend W.B. Red Hamilton went into consultation with Mr. Gatewood and apparently convinced him that he had indicated somewhat prematurely and consequently had brought to their feet a congregation that had no call to be on them, so Mr. Gatewood overturned his previous indication and about the time we all got used to standing up we all sat down again amid a great flurry of additional coughing and sneezing and nose-blowing. Trouble was Mr. Gatewood had overlooked the Reverend W.B. Red Hamilton's three minutes worth of partially restricted prayer and had skipped directly past it to "The Old Rugged Cross" which we were scheduled to sing about thirty-eight verses of, but Reverend Red caught the slipup and after he had announced his intentions we all hunched up and bent over and prepared to get prayed at. However, once the Reverend Hamilton shut his eyes and raised his hands over his head and addressed himself in holy communication to Almighty Gawd and his son the savior Geezus Christuh, he did not say anything

else for what appeared to be his full three minutes and so caused
to mount up a very real threat of some general uneasiness along
with prospect of more coughing and sneezing and noseblowing.
But at length the Reverend Mr. Hamilton reminded God just
who it was that had died, which seemed to be his primary
function, and then he set in to talking in a very colorful way
about nothing much in particular and in a voice that was considerably more melodic than anything the choir had managed
to come up with so far. The reverend said life is like a beauty
rose that blossoms in the spring, and while some buds perish
in their infancy others will thrive and bloom and linger on into
the summer. But even among these, the reverend said, even
among the thrivers and the bloomers and the lingerers, a great
number will be cut from the vine early on and will perish in
nosegays at the height of their blush and a greater number still
will become tainted and blighted with the rosemold and die
leaving only a handful of blossoms to greet the autumn and be
taken by the frost. And the idea of all this extensive carnage
among the rose population seemed to sink the Reverend W.B.
Red Hamilton into a temporary funk and he did not talk to us
or Gawd or Geezus either until he had recovered himself somewhat and then he said, "However, they are all roses nonetheless.
They are all the fruit of the same vine be they bud or blossom,
be they beautious or blighted, and brethren, after that ultimate
autumn, after that final freeze they will all burst into magnificent bloom in the Ming vase of eternity." And that was when
Daddy chortled, though I did not know it was chortling until
later on at the supper table when Daddy explained to me exactly
what constituted a chortle which sounds very much like a self-
inflicted tonsillectomy and which is hardly the sort of thing
Momma would approve of under any circumstances, especially
under the circumstances that Daddy committed one and especially since Daddy's full-fledged robust chortle inspired in Mr.
Phillip J. King a kind of lame, wheezing variation, and the full
chortle and the half chortle together served to get the attention
of the Reverend W.B. Red Hamilton who did not seem to feel
that the Ming vase of eternity was anything to chortle at. So
Reverend Hamilton left off praying momentarily and appeared
to engage himself in wishing a little hellfire on our pew, and
then he said, "Yes brethern," and repeated most everything

he'd told us before about life being like a beauty rose and death being like a bowl full of water.

I guess the reverend prayed at us for the best part of a quarter hour and never once threatened to talk about Miss Pettigrew who was laying in among her brass fittings directly in front of him. Instead he kept on with his rose bushes and his Ming vase and once he made a rather halfhearted attempt to draw Gawd up as some sort of unduly sentimental gardener—"He who cherishes even the lowliest weed"—but Daddy still had a chortle rattling around inside of himself and I suppose the idea of Gawd in a straw sunhat and white gloves got away with him and the chortle slipped up into his throat and inflated the whole front of Daddy's face swelling his cheeks so that he had to vent some of the pressure off through his mouth and made in the process an inadvertent lip fart that carried on up to the altar and seemed to cause the Reverend Hamilton to squeeze off the metaphor before it could draw any additional fire. After that the reverend skirted a few figurative excesses but by and large avoided venturing into them, and by the time he reached the final salute to Gawd the Father and Geezus Christuh his only begotten son, the Reverend W.B. Red Hamilton sounded almost like a regular Baptist.

Of course it was the thirty-eight verses of "The Old Rugged Cross" after Reverend Hamilton's twenty-minute three-minute prayer, and Momma made me look at the hymnal but Daddy and Mr. Phillip J. King simply stood with their hands clasped in front of them and sang the melody like they were chewing on slabs of tire rubber. Momma sang pleasantly herself and I vainly tried to find a key I could stick with while Mrs. Phillip J. King overrode all of us, even Daddy, with her rhythmic screeching that had all of the pitch and tonality of a lawn rake on a slate blackboard. And I don't imagine we had gotten through even twenty-eight verses when most of the congregation became fagged out and winded and left off singing, and after another verse or two the choir got a little worn out itself and gave up the melody to Mrs. Rollie Cobb who persevered on through the refrain and then tacked on a hasty Amen and dropped her arms to her sides so the blood could circulate through her fingers once more. And by the time Mr. Ames Gatewood stood up to indicate to us that we should sit down, we already had our backsides about as flush against the pew seats as they could get and sneezing and coughing and nose-blowing and general uneasiness was rampant throughout the sanctuary.

Town councilman Mr. Jeffrey Elwood Crawford sr. took the pulpit once he considered that we had settled back into a proper funereal demeanor, and he removed a notecard from his inside jacket pocket and set it down in front of him where he glanced at it two or three times in a skittish sort of way and then studied the frontside, the backside, and the edges also with some acute interest. And when he was satisfied with his grasp of the situation, he returned the card to his inside jacket pocket and announced to us exactly who it was that had died, which was not the sort of news we were any longer receiving with much graciousness. But as it turned out Mr. Crawford's purpose was twofold, and once he came to understand that we already knew exactly who it was that had died, he proceeded on to the introduction of the eulogists, who were sitting on opposite ends of the altar since they were both still suffering from what Daddy called the ranklement of the heated eulogy debate. Mr. Crawford started off with the Reverend Mr. Holroyd who was about twice as old as Reverend Shelton and who Mr. Crawford told us had aged with all the grace and dignity befitting his most esteemed position. A pillar of our community, Mr. Crawford called him, a picture of spiritual well-being, and then he swung around and with an open hand directed our attention to the reverend himself, who was sitting a little slumped over in a folding chair with his hair standing more or less straight up all over his head. The reverend jerked his nose at us and grunted; he was thoroughly creased, wrinkled, liver-spotted, was inestimably wealthy with chins, and appeared to have aged about as gracefully as a winesap apple. Daddy has always contended that if the preaching business ever went bust, the Reverend Holroyd could take up residence under a bridge and earn his living as a troll.

After Mr. Crawford figured we'd soaked in enough of the Reverend Holroyd's spiritual well-being for the moment, he turned his attention full upon the Reverend Mr. Richard Crockett Shelton who was sitting on the far side of the aisle a little sideways in his chair and with his arm thrown over the back of it. Somehow or another the Reverend Shelton had managed to recover from the 1962 Christmas Pageant fiasco, and once he put the shame and humiliation of it behind him he gradually regained his confidence and commenced to improve on his pulpit manner. According to Daddy, the Reverend Shelton had started out as a snoremonger extraordinaire but through several years of hard work and undying dedication had managed to cultivate a kind of flamboyant tediousness which the most of his congregation mistook for ecclesiastical charm, including Momma, who was ever having the reverend over for dinner so as to bring Daddy in contact with some genuine Godliness. But the Godliness never seemed to take with Daddy and he just said the Reverend Shelton had a way of making food taste sleepy. But Mr. Crawford did not touch upon that particular talent and instead told us that the Reverend Shelton was a local bastion of virtue and an unfaltering inspiration to his flock, which Daddy said was notecard talk for pillar of the community and picture of spiritual well-being. And when Mr. Crawford swung around and directed our attention to the reverend himself, Mr. Richard Crockett Shelton bowed towards us without getting up.

The Reverend Mr. Holroyd kicked off the double-barrel eulogy partly on account of his religious seniority and partly, Daddy said, on account of the ever present danger that the reverend might join Miss Pettigrew straightaway. He did not have a notecard or a Bible of his own and not a scrap of paper or a matchbook cover to refer to either, but after he took the pulpit and leered at us for a spell it did not appear that the reverend had anything to say which fairly much excused his empty-handedness. So we looked at him and he looked at us and then some of us looked at him and some of us looked at Miss Pettigrew's casket while he looked at us and then he looked at Miss Pettigrew's casket and so drew some more of us to look at it also and then he cleared his throat and we all looked at him except for Daddy who looked at Momma out of the side of his face. And still the reverend did not say anything but gazed all up in the rafters like he had payed a quarter and was taking the tour, and when he finally did open his mouth and speak to us he did not utter a word we had expected to hear. "I once danced with that woman," he told us. "I do recall it very clearly. It was after Mr. Wallace Amory got elected mayor and him and Miss Myra Angelique put on the ball themselves in their daddy's house. There was a little ensemble playing in one corner of the front room and along the back wall there was a champagne fountain and a buffet with fruits and cheeses and finger sandwiches and a great big meaty smoked salmon that still had the head on it. Miss Pettigrew had decorated the walls and the ceiling with crepe, red crepe and yellow crepe and blue crepe, and banners made out of bedsheets and balloons and ribbons and sprigs off juniper bushes. But you remember," the Reverend Mr. Holroyd told us and looked out over the congregation for the first time since he had begun to speak. "Most of you were there so you must remember. I mean it was all so glorious and splendid, and her, why she was simply beautiful. Beautiful. And in my profession I don't get much occasion to dance with beautiful women, but I danced with her. I said to her, 'Miss Pettigrew, would you consider going round the floor with a man of the cloth?' and she told me, 'How divine.' She touched me right on the forearm and told me, 'How divine,' and then she put me down on her card. I was number eleven and came just after Mr. Emory Hobson. Isn't that right, Emory?"

And directly Mr. Hobson himself, from somewhere up in the front of the chapel that I couldn't see, answered the Reverend Mr. Holroyd in a very high, antique voice that creaked like shoeleather. "Yes sir," he said, "That's right."

"You had hair then, Emory," the reverend told him.

"Yes sir," Mr. Hobson said, "and teeth too."

"And you near about frazzled her out for me Emory," the reverend told him.

"Yes sir," Mr. Hobson said. "As best I could."

"But as I recall, she was a woman of exceptional wind," the reverend said, talking to all of us again, "and I do believe the ensemble had not hardly commenced to sawing away good when me and Miss Pettigrew shot past the buffet table and by the doorway and twirled on down the length of the far wall. Seems to me it was a waltz, a very famous waltz, and time was I could call the name of it but," and the reverend squinted up into the recesses of the commander's semi-vaulted ceiling "it don't seem to come to me just now. I do, however, very clearly recollect the way Miss Pettigrew went round the ballroom. She had the lightest touch with her fingers and on her feet why she was air itself, even made me feel like I could dance a little. And I do remember how we spun on by Mr.

Wallace Amory who was pressed in all around by a great gaggle of women, and I leaned over and said into Miss Pettigrew's ear how I believed Mr. Wallace Amory was surely qualified enough to be the mayor and was probably pretty enough to be the mayor's wife, and she just laid her head back and laughed ever so softly." And the Reverend Mr. Holroyd laughed a little softly himself with the most of the congregation chuckling some behind him, and for a very brief moment thereafter it did appear to me that the reverend was in fact the picture of spiritual well-being, but then he peered out overtop of our heads and into the back reaches of the sanctuary and presently he was thoroughly creased and wrinkled and liver-spotted and chin-ridden all over again. "But that was quite a long time ago," he told us, "and the mayor's gone and now she's gone too. Dead," he said, "dead and gone." And I guess we all supposed the Reverend Mr. Holroyd might be setting us up for a sermonette on suicide and damnation, at least that is what I expected to get and, by the grim look on Daddy's face, that is what he expected to get also. But instead the Reverend Mr. Holroyd did a most extraordinary thing: he left the pulpit, went back to his chair, and sat down in it. Of course we all watched him do it, and of course we all persisted in watching him after he had done it, especially Sheriff Burton who had the seat next to the reverend's and who turned his head sideways and studied Mr. Holroyd like he'd just washed in with the tide. And as for the Reverend Mr. Holroyd himself, he looked at Miss Pettigrew's casket and then looked at the floor beside him and then he looked at Miss Pettigrew's casket again and then at the floor beside him once more and then he crossed his arms over his chest and smiled at the carpet.

Nobody much seemed to know what to do, not anybody in the congregation including the commander, and not the sheriff, and not the councilman Mr. Jeffrey Elwood Crawford Sr., and not Mr. Ames Gatewood of the Reading Rack, and not Mrs. Rollie Cobb or her hair either, and not Miss Fay Dull or any of her sopranos or altos or baritones or her Jewish tenor, and not the Reverend Lynwood Wilkerson of the Baptist church, and not the Reverend W.B. Red Hamilton of the Gospel Light Chapel, which left only the Methodist Preacher Mr. Richard Crockett Shelton who possessed a natural instinct for empty pulpits and so leapt directly up into this one. I don't remember what he said at first and I don't remember much of what he said eventually but I am reasonably certain somewhere or another he took the time to remind us just who it was that had died. I also recall that he had gone to the trouble to set down his half of the eulogy on a heap of folded yellow paper which he produced almost magically from the inside of his robe and then proceeded to read from although he pretended that he wasn't. And I do believe the Reverend Shelton quoted extensively from the works of Mr. Henry Wadsworth Longfellow, who apparently could keep a beat a little more truly than the reverend could. However, I do not recollect much of what Mr. Henry Wadsworth Longfellow had to say either, and only later on at the supper table when Momma was trying to convince me and Daddy that we had been interested in what we had been numbed by did Daddy remind me of one of the reverend's more colorful and enlightening utterances. Life, he had said, is like a butterfly and death is God's insecticide that carries strong and meek alike off into everlasting light. I think even Momma was a little embarrassed and she did not offer much of any objection when Daddy associated Reverend Shelton with the Red Hamilton school of eulogization and prayer.

And although there was in fact an interesting moment in the Reverend Shelton's half of the double-barrel eulogy it cannot be accurately attributed to the Reverend Shelton himself who was simply carrying on through with his tediousness when the Reverend Holroyd uncrossed his arms, jacked himself straight up in his seat, and said, "The Tennessee Four Step, that's what it was," and then recrossed his arms and allowed gravity to draw him back into a slouch. After that I don't believe Reverend Shelton was ever able to recover himself entirely and it seemed he became all lost and confused in his heap of yellow paper and not him or Henry Wadsworth Longfellow or even the two of them all at once and together could straighten things out. So the Reverend Shelton left off his eulogizing a little prematurely and where he had planned to conclude with a smattering of Tennyson, who Daddy said was a lot like Longfellow only taller, instead he blessed and amened Miss Pettigrew and her brass fittings and then abandoned the pulpit.

Unfortunately, Mrs. Rollie Cobb was still waiting for the Tennyson several minutes after Reverend Shelton had already sat down and only when the commander had cleared his throat

raw did she commence to hammering out on the piano what
initially sounded like the "Maple Leaf Rag" but turned into
"How Great Thou Art" once Mrs. Cobb got the reins on it.
The choir sang this one by themselves and it was intended as
their recessional, but since they had not proceeded extensively
they did not have much territory to recede across and so were
already entirely outside with near about three full verses to go,
and as it did not seem that Mrs. Cobb was disposed to leave
off playing, Miss Fay Dull turned around her sopranos and her
altos and her baritones and her Jewish tenor and they polished
off the selection from down along the street. And that was to
have been pretty much the end of it except for the rolling out
of the casket; however, once Mr. Ames Gatewood had indicated
us upright and once Mr. Dunn from Spray and the commander
himself had commenced to roll Miss Pettigrew down the center
aisle towards the chapel doors, the Reverend Mr. W.B. Red
Hamilton found himself so utterly overcome by the immediate
circumstances that he set in to delivering an impromptu benediction which had some English to it but was mostly in Swahili
as far as Daddy could tell, and the Reverend Mr. W.B. Red
Hamilton stomped and waved his arms and generally cut up
like an African until the commander could nod at Mr. Jeffrey
Elwood Crawford sr., who nudged Sheriff Burton, who took
ahold of Reverend Red with both hands and moved him a little
more violently than the spirit had. So at length the commander
and Mr. Dunn managed to get Miss Pettigrew all the way out
the church and down the sidewalk and slid her into the back
of the hearse, and then the commander returned to the chapel
alone and advanced up to the family pew where he stood aside
to excuse the occupants who we had not been able to see
previously and who turned out to be Aunt Willa and Aunt
Willa's sister and Aunt Willa's sister's daughter along with Mr.
Jack Vestal and his wife who had redoubled her efforts at
funerals ever since she gave up viewings and so appeared particularly overwrought and inconsolable, and I do believe it was
all Mrs. Phillip J. King could do to keep from spitting on her
as she walked by.

And that was the end of the funeral part of it but before
Momma could get together with Mrs. Phillip J. King and dis-
cuss how we would get to the burial part of it, Mrs. Phillip J.
King grabbed onto her husband's arm and lit out down the

center aisle and on through the chapel doors, and Momma was not able to find her again until her and me and Daddy got outside and she happened to glance into the family limousine, which was thoroughly loaded up with three negroes and two Vestals in the back seat and Mr. Dunn and Mr. and Mrs. Phillip J. King in the front seat. So Momma turned things entirely over to Daddy and presently Daddy got up with Mr. Russell Newberry and with his wife, Mrs. Coleen Ruth Hoots Newberry, who was known as Little Momma on account of how she only came up to Mr. Newberry's armpit which was not itself at any lofty height. Mr. and Mrs. Newberry had come to the service in their green Pontiac and they were both most pleased at the prospect of passengers to the cemetery. Of course Mr. Newberry's glaucoma kept him from driving and Little Momma had to sit on two sofa cushions and a Sears catalog just to get the point of her nose up overtop the steering wheel. Consequently Mrs. Newberry and Mr. Newberry too were always appreciative of any outside navigational advice since they themselves were somewhat afflicted and since their green Pontiac, with all of its sheer bulk and magnitude, was about the size of a modest cabin cruiser.

So me and Momma and Daddy climbed into the back seat and me and Momma took the windows and Daddy crossed his arms over the front seattop and talked Little Momma away from the curb. We got into the processional four cars back from the hearse which meant three cars back from the limousine which meant two cars back from the hardware store Eatons which meant one car back from an assortment of Oregon Hill Frenches and directly in front of the bald Jeeter Throckmorton and her daughter, little Ivy, with Mrs. and Mr. Estelle Singletary at their rear. And once Daddy had navigated Mrs. Newberry out onto the boulevard and had set her to tailgating the Frenches the tension gave way somewhat and Mr. Newberry leaned his back against the doorpanel and asked Daddy his opinion of the church service which apparently Daddy had anticipated since he answered straightaway that, as far as he was concerned, it was a good thing Miss Pettigrew was already dead. I believe Momma punched Daddy in the ribcage shortly thereafter though I'm not to any degree certain of it; however I do know that Mrs. Newberry reached across the frontseat and slapped at Mr. Newberry when he laughed through his teeth. Then her and

Momma together came to the defense of the Reverend Hamilton and the Reverend Holroyd and the Reverend Shelton and they came to the defense of Mr. Ames Gatewood and Mr. Jeffrey Elwood Crawford sr. and they came to the defense of Miss Fay Dull and Miss Fay Dull's interdenominational choir and they attempted to come to the defense of Mrs. Rollie Cobb also but Mrs. Rollie Cobb and her piano playing turned out to be fairly much indefensible. And on account of the way Little Momma kept wheeling around in her seat when she should have been intent on tailgating Frenches, Daddy and Mr. Newberry decided to leave off antagonizing the women for fear of their personal safety and as a change of pace Mr. Newberry said, "I do wish the casket had been opened up. I don't believe I've seen Miss Pettigrew since she gave that Easter party back in 1972."

"What Easter Party?" Daddy asked him.

"Why the one she gave back in 1972," Mr. Newberry said.

"I don't believe it was 1972, Russell," Daddy told him.

"It was 1972," Mrs. Newberry said, and crimped up half the Sears catalog in twisting herself around to look at Daddy, "but it was a Mayday party; didn't have a thing in the world to do with Easter."

"Mayday?" Mr. Newberry said.

"That's right," Mrs. Newberry told him.

"Well maybe it was," Mr. Newberry said. "I don't know."

"Yes sir," Daddy said, "maybe so."

ii

THEY WERE all three wrong. It was July the fourth of 1970 and we got that from Momma who never forgets a date. She said Miss Pettigrew had not shown herself since the evening of the 1962 Methodist Christmas pageant and so had allowed near about seven years worth of holidays to come and go unobserved when Aunt Willa carried the shoebox full of envelopes across the boulevard and up the post office steps. Local history has it that the Neely postal department had never before and has never since moved any correspondence with the sort of breakneck expediency that Miss Pettigrew's invitations inspired. Nobody even bothered to cancel the stamps, and the entire shoebox which Aunt Willa had given direct to Mr. Gillespie at the counter was in turn given direct to Mr. Eugene Ashburn, who had only recently come in from his appointed round and thereby happened to be handy enough to get made into a special courier. Mr. Ashburn was offered the use of a white jeep with a little special courier billboard on the roof, but six months previous Sheriff Burton had taken away Mr. Ashburn's driving license on account of what Daddy called habitual vehicular stupidity, and Mr. Ashburn figured if he could not be vehicularly stupid in his own car he'd best not risk it in a government jeep. So Mr. Ashburn situated the shoebox full of invitations into the bottom of his leather mailbag and lit out from the post office with regular wingéd feet, Daddy said.

But according to Momma even wingéd feet could not outdistance the index finger, and before the second invitation hit the bottom of Mrs. Royce Venable's mailbox, one of the Mrs. Petrees, Momma could not remember precisely which one, had Mrs. Royce Venable herself on the phone to tell her just what it was she was about to step out her front door and fetch in. And whichever particular Mrs. Petree this was read off her invitation item by item and so stole some of the thrill of it for Mrs. Venable, who fished out her invitation once she got off the line with Mrs. Petree but did not bother to open it until she had made a few calls herself. And Momma said Mrs. Petree and Mrs. Venable together with their furious index fingers thoroughly passed up Mr. Ashburn, notwithstanding his temporary wingédness Daddy called it, and successfully prevented him from putting any more invitations into any more mailboxes. Instead the addressees intercepted him before he could get well off the sidewalk and took the deliveries directly into their hands, everybody that is except Mrs. Phillip J. King, who had miscalculated the progress of Mr. Ashburn since his feet were not usually wingéd at all. Mrs. Phillip J. King figured Mr. Ashburn was still on Lawsonville Avenue when in actuality he had mercuriated himself partway down our street, Daddy said, so Mrs. Phillip J. King was preoccupied in exercising the phone dial when Mr. Ashburn dropped her invitation in through the mail slot and Itty Bit snatched it up off the carpet and very nearly chewed it to pieces. Soon afterwards me and Momma stood at the breakfast room window and watched Mrs. Phillip J. King and her terrier compete in a footrace around the perimeters of the King's back yard. I do believe the dog won in the end, but it was a hotly contested event nonetheless.

Apparently Miss Pettigrew had not taken up a pen for some considerable years when she set about making out invitations to her July the fourth party of 1970, and even Momma was somewhat distressed by Miss Pettigrew's penmanship. She had hoped for something a little more graceful and proper and for a time she seemed inclined to hold with Mrs. Estelle Singletary and Mrs. Treva Jane Boyd McKinney, of the block and mortar McKinneys, who insisted that Aunt Willa had filled out and addressed the invitations and so was responsible for the scrawl. But all of the available evidence, including testimony by several esteemed witnesses, indicated that Aunt Willa had never learned to write and could not read either. So eventually Momma had to bring herself to accept the fact that there were just some things about Miss Pettigrew that were not utterly elegant, and when she had grown accustomed to the idea, Momma decided that penmanship was certainly an expendable item.

On the front of each of Miss Pettigrew's invitations was a big red firecracker just prior to blowing up, and on the inside spelled out in sparklers was LET'S HAVE A PARTY! which seemed to me about as elegant as the penmanship, but Momma did not allow it to strike a nerve with her, probably on account of her previous disappointment and probably on account of how Miss Pettigrew did not persist in calling it a capitalized, exclamation-marked, sparkler-spelled party herself but called it instead a "get together" which seemed to Momma a far more agreeable and civilized sort of thing. Miss Pettigrew's get together was to commence at three o'clock on the afternoon of the fourth of July and proceed on to six in the evening with "refreshments provided." Suggested dress was given as "leisurely" and on the line marked "Location" Miss Pettigrew had taken some obvious care in writing out her address as if she actually needed to. And at the very bottom of the card, behind the firecracker and underneath the sparklers and down below all of the pertinent information, and in thick, clumsy, headlong letters Miss Pettigrew had written "Please do come" which most everybody rubbed their eyes and looked at twice before they even began to speculate as to why it was there.

But of course the speculation did commence eventually, and once folks had done some extensive wondering about the "Please do come" they shifted over and began to wonder about most everything else also. Daddy said he had never before encountered a piece of greeting card literature that was open to such widespread and varied interpretation. At length people generally agreed that the "Please do come" did in fact mean please do come, but the unity broke down entirely when it came to "get together." Nobody much had ever attended a get together before so nobody much was familiar with the genuine characteristics and qualities of a get together as a phenomenon, Daddy called it. Now several people had attended what they considered to be get together-like functions, but even the handful of them could not agree as to exactly what constituted a get together since no one of their get together-like functions had been like any of the others. Mrs. Mary Margaret Vance Needham had attended her get together in a hay barn in Rutherford County where all of the get togetherees had eaten barbecue and square danced, while Mr. Wyatt Benbow, sole surviving Benbow of the Big Apple Benbows, had attended his get together on a tour boat in the Cape Fear River off Wilmington. He recalled that drinks were served and he recollected food also, but to the best of his memory the mosquitoes had done most of the eating. One of the Mrs. Browns, Daddy said it was the one that lived on the ninth fairway but Momma insisted it was not, had gone with her husband to a Christmas get together at a Moose Lodge east of Greensboro and she held forth that a get together was nothing but a party with a holiday to back it up. However Mrs. Phillip J. King disagreed with her most harshly and told everybody how she herself had attended an authentic get together in our nation's capital during the course of which she had been personally introduced to the sister-in-law of President Johnson's daughter. The women, Mrs. Phillip J. King said, wore stunning gowns, the men wore dinner jackets, and everybody ate off crystal plates. And it seemed very apparent to Mrs. Phillip J. King that this was just the sort of thing to which Miss Pettigrew would be accustomed, and in fact Mrs. Phillip J. King was successful in convincing a portion of people that this was exactly the sort of thing to which Miss Pettigrew would be accustomed, but Daddy said fortunately it was only that portion of people who were as foolish as Mrs. Phillip J. King was which did not make for any sizeable number of converts.

As a group, then, folks did not ever exactly puzzle out just what a get together was and instead they turned their attention to the pertinent information so as to haggle about it for awhile. First there was the problem of leisurely dress. Daddy said to him leisurely meant just one thing: green polyester. But that was only one man's view of it, and folks generally felt that their leisurely and Miss Pettigrew's leisurely could not carry anything near the same meaning. So some of the people who had spearheaded the movement to describe a get together set about developing a workable definition of Miss Pettigrew's leisurely, and after several extensive discussions and any number of unofficial and thoroughly unscientific opinion polls, it was concluded that Miss Pettigrew's leisurely was the same thing as everybody else's semi-formal, which was a very agreeable finding as far as the women were concerned but the men did not much relish the prospect of wearing coats and ties on the afternoon of the fourth of July and they all objected to it with as much of an unpleasant uproar as they could muster, most all of them anyway except for Mr. Phillip J. King and Mr. Estelle Singletary who had been broken of their spunk previously and so did not make much fuss.

As a diversion from the coats and ties the women proceeded to focus attention on the "refreshments provided" which was the sort of thing that would naturally lend itself to extensive speculation. Loosely, there were three separate and distinct camps on the refreshment issue and the largest of them was jointly headed up by Mrs. Phillip J. King and Mrs. Estelle Singletary and Mrs. Estelle Singletary's old maid sister, Miss Bernice Fay Frazier. These women along with all of their supporters backed the notion that since Miss Pettigrew's leisurely was the same thing as everybody else's semi-formal then it would follow that Miss Pettigrew's refreshments provided would probably be the same thing as everybody else's sit-down meal. Now there was some dissent and disagreement as to exactly what sort of sit-down meal it might be—Mrs. Phillip J. King held with a late dinner served on crystal while Miss Frazier and Mrs. Estelle Singletary were more inclined towards an early ~ on stoneware but otherwise they were all thoroughly ınd solid. Momma took the moderate position that Miss ⸌ would probably offer up a mixed buffet of meats and s and cheeses and fruits and desserts complemented by some sort of lightly alcoholic punch cooler and she believed the whole affair would be pretty much like a wedding reception without the wedding. And as for Daddy, he lent his support to a very small, undignified, and almost entirely indifferent group of people who figured on peanuts and pretzels and potato chips and possibly a tray of pigs in a blanket with Pepsi-Cola on ice for a chaser.

Of course the refreshments provided part of the invitation ultimately did not get any more clarified than the get together part of it, and after nearly everybody had worn themselves out interpreting and speculating and soliloquizing on the two of them, the general interest temporarily got shifted over to the arrival and departure times which seemed clear and decisive enough to most people but spurred some discussion anyway when the sit-down meal society began to insist that three o'clock until six o'clock meant in actuality four o'clock until seven o'clock. Daddy said it was a kind of daylight savings time for the upper crust, but not Mrs. Phillip J. King or Mrs. Estelle Singletary or her old maid sister Miss Frazier either could convince much of anybody of the virtue in arriving at four o'clock since most people figured the best of the food would be gone by then. So the discussion migrated to about the only thing left it could migrate to which was very obviously Miss Pettigrew's reason for throwing a get together in the first place. People were naturally curious as to why a woman who had not sought public company since Christmas of 1962 would suddenly, come July of 1970, up and invite half the town into her own house and offer to feed them on top of it. This was, on the whole, a matter of exceeding bafflement and most everybody expended some considerable energy in wondering at it. Of course right off a general alarm was raised by the sorts of people that tend to raise general alarms, and it was suggested around town that perhaps Miss Pettigrew no longer possessed the faculties to be entrusted with the preparation of safe and digestible food, that perhaps Aunt Willa had put her up to the party and intended to do some mischief to a whole bunch of white people at once, which some folks said was the way with negroes, who are a very wily breed, especially on the fourth of July. And a few people even insisted that the monkey had a part in it since monkeys are notoriously wily themselves. But the general alarm died off fairly quickly and Daddy says it is simply the sort of thing you have to expect when you share your city with ignoramuses. And once the notion of poisoning was dispensed with, some people took up with the idea that Miss Pettigrew had only lost a little of her senses while other people began to believe she had regained about as much, and then there was Momma, who thought something altogether different. So there were nearly as many opinions of Miss Pettigrew's motives as there were readings of Miss Pettigrew's firecracker-decked, sparkler-laden invitations, and only in their response on the afternoon of July the fourth 1970 did people show themselves to be generally and completely agreed about one thing since everybody who got invited went.

Of course Miss Pettigrew's party being a get together, it was not considered the sort of thing suitable for children so only Mr. and Mrs. Cromer brought their little girl, Sally Anne, since at the time she was about the size of a breadloaf and could not get along on her own. The rest of us collected at the Franklin Street schoolyard, where four Y.M.C.A. volunteers attempted to do us some damage with a series of coordinated activities, and we had already suffered through the wheelbarrow race and the watermelon relay when time came for the greased pig chase. Now the previous July Mr. Tadlock had lent the Y.M.C.A. four of his pigs to be larded up and hounded all over the schoolyard and on up into June of 1970 the folks at the Y figured they would simply borrow Mr. Tadlock's pigs again. But just prior to Independence Day when they finally bothered to get in touch with him, Mr. Tadlock told them he had made his pigs into some considerable sausage and sidemeat and shank hams which he believed had taken most of the pluck out of them. So on short notice the best the Y.M.C.A. volunteers could do was two piglets the size of housecats from Mr. Harland Lynch III and three of Mr. J. L. Graham's Rhode Island hens. Mr. Harland Lynch himself, along with the only one of the volunteers who did not have any natural fear of barnyard animals, saw to the greasing of the pigs, and it was decided by Mr. J. L. Graham and the three remaining volunteers that the chickens were vicious already and so did not require any assistance from the lard bucket to be slippery also.

The animals were turned out for a five minute head start on the crowd of us, but since they did not know what we were about to put them through they did not go hardly anywhere in their five minutes and still were fairly much underfoot when we got the signal to have at them. But it didn't take long for the piglets and the chickens too to come to a thorough understanding of their predicament, and almost before the first two or three of us could manage any sort of proper lunges at them the chickens took off in one direction and the piglets lit out in another. Naturally we broke up into two units and the piglet pursuit squad drove their quarry on down towards the far corner of the schoolyard while the rest of us chased all three of the chickens up into the top of a crabapple tree. Of course crabapple trees are generally dense and brambly and difficult to climb and the one in the Franklin Street schoolyard is near about the same thing as an upright thicket, so we decided to send Trudy Tally up into it after the chickens since at the time she was far and away the slightest and wispiest Tally available. And all of her slight wispiness and wispy slightness together enabled her to slip up through the limbs to where the chickens were, but slightness and wispiness even in concentrated combination are not in the leastways sufficient to dislodge terrorized chickens from the top of a crabapple tree, and every time Trudy Tally took a swat at the birds they would all three peck and claw at her in a most fierce and savage sort of way. Understandably we figured that a slight and wispy male would probably be more effective than a slight and wispy female, so we selected from our unit a couple of scrawny boys, though by no means as scrawny as a Tally, and lifted them up into the crabapple tree. But even when Trudy Tally and the two scrawny boys pooled their energies the chickens still got the best of them, so we sent two regular-sized people up as reinforcements but the chickens brutalized them as well, and shortly afterwards there was a general evacuation from the crabapple tree of everything that was not a chicken, and once we had pondered over the input from Trudy Tally and from the two scrawny boys and from the pair of regular-sized people also, we decided as a unit that we'd just as soon chase Egyptian cobras as Rhode Island hens.

Naturally we abandoned the chickens and struck out after the piglets, which looked to be hemmed up in the corner of the schoolyard. But when we arrived at the scene the only thing left in the corner of the schoolyard was the piglet pursuit unit with no readily perceptible piglets to pursue. Instead some considerable attention was being paid to a square of chickenwire patching at the bottom of the chainlink fence that runs entirely roundabout the school property. Directly in the center of the chickenwire was a very round, cleanly made hole which a sizeable number of witnesses claimed to be a miraculous product of piglet engineering. They said they drove the pigs into the corner and once they had begun to close in on them the pigs themselves grew somewhat wild and desperate looking and seemed a little frothy on account of the lard, and when they could not find an alternate means of escape the larger of the two got a running start at the chickenwire and hurled himself straight through it like a little pork bullet. The second one slipped on through behind him and the last anybody saw of them they were rooting around in the jonquil patch back of Mr. Dupree's house. So we formed ourselves into several distinct squads and fanned out across the neighborhood squealing in what we imagined to be a most appealing way.

Now while we were off chasing pigs and suffering the viciousness of chickens, Momma and Daddy and half of the rest of the town were enjoying the privilege of gaping at Miss Pettigrew for the first time in eight years. Daddy said folks began to congregate across the boulevard from Miss Pettigrew's house along about 2:30 and commenced to gaping at the house itself as a preamble to gaping at the occupant. Daddy said even those people who had intended to arrive fashionably late ended up coming early enough to get in some prefatory gaping themselves. And Momma said somehow or another Mr. Louis Benfield sr. had managed to convince himself that there was in fact a grain of virtue in arriving somewhere early, so him and Momma got in on the tailend of the preamble too and were right in the thick of things when 3:00 hit and the whole crowd went tearing across the street, through the iron gateway, up along the sidewalk, and onto the front porch.

Daddy said Mrs. Estelle Singletary rang the bell which apparently was broken since it didn't bring anybody to the door, and after everybody who could see it had studied the knob sufficiently to convince themselves that it had not wiggled and was not about to Mr. Estelle Singletary made an uncharacteristically gallant attempt at reaching for Miss Pettigrew's brass doorknocker but his wife headed him off and took it upon herself to do the rapping which at length did in fact cause the doorknob to wiggle and the whole door itself to swing open. Momma said the foyer was so dimly lit it was somewhat difficult to focus in on Aunt Willa at first what with the acute shortage of suitable backlight, and even Mrs. Estelle Singletary, who very nearly had her feet on the doorsill, put her face partway into the house and called out "Hello Hello" loud enough to be heard in the basement and she was nearly set to wail away again when Aunt Willa reached out from the shadows and general murkiness and touched her on the shoulder. Daddy said from the way Mrs. Estelle Singletary sucked air it appeared to him there would be some need for an ambulance, but after several minutes of regular breathing she began to look rather lifelike once more and told everybody she was perfectly alright notwithstanding some exceedingly serious palpitations of the heart.

Apparently Aunt Willa had not been much inspired by the holiday or the get together either, because Momma said she did not look any different than she normally looked and had not dressed any different than she normally dressed. She seemed to Momma as sour as ever and she was wearing her usual floweredy smock with most all the color bled out of it and her black button-up sweater and her nylons rolled down around the knee and her blue Keds sneakers. However, she was not wearing Mr. Shep Bristow's fedora, which her head most generally did not ever go around without, and Momma theorized that perhaps Aunt Willa had left the hat off as a means of marking the occasion, but Daddy did not ever think too highly of Momma's opinion on the matter. He said it was not one of your sounder theories; he said it was not the sort of thing Mr. Einstein would be proud of. Momma did not seem to have much faith in it either but she simply did not want to believe that Aunt Willa was entirely indifferent to everything although there was not any substantial evidence to the contrary. So it was Momma who said Aunt Willa invited the whole crowd of get togetherees into Miss Pettigrew's house, and it was Daddy who said she only opened the door and stayed clear of the doorway, which was not his idea of a gracious welcome and did not even begin to constitute an invitation.

Everybody did get into the house, however, which was exactly where everybody had been burning to get ever since the opportunity had presented itself. But Daddy said there was

not much to see right off on account of the general gloom in
the foyer and though the ladies made a great variety of astounding faces and Daddy himself undertook some experimental
sniffing, he said nobody knew for certain that the local aroma
was monkey until considerably later when Mr. Rackley cleared
it up for them. At the time, and primarily out of respect for
Miss Pettigrew, most people suspected it was Mr. Emmet Dabb
who was not locally famous for his hygiene and had a well-
documented history of unsavory fragrances. Daddy said Aunt
Willa did not bother to lead the get togetherees into the ballroom
but instead allowed Mrs. Estelle Singletary to take several
people on into a coat closet by mistake and partway into a half
bath before she finally hit on the short front hallway that led
directly to the get together itself. And Daddy said he could tell
right off it was one of your hybrid get togethers that wasn't
purely a sit-down dinner and wasn't purely a plain buffet and
wasn't exactly a pig-in-a-blanket affair either. There were plates
of course, Daddy said, but they were paper with a picture of
the constitution in the middle where the food went, and there
was a punch bowl full of some sort of champagne concoction,
but there was Pepsi-Cola and cracked ice too. Miss Pettigrew,
or somebody anyway, had prepared some chicken and had
baked a ham and had cooked up a couple of good-sized pork
tenderloins along with several other full-fledged repast entrees,
Daddy called them, but they were accompanied by a gracious
plenty of cucumber finger sandwiches and two cheese balls,
one entirely nutted over and one not, and a considerable bulk
of raddish rosettes and celery stalks and carrot slivers. And
Daddy said there were potato chips also and American cheese
slices and little hunks of liver pudding on Townhouse crackers
and a platter heaped up with apple dumplings dipped in confectioner's sugar. However, there was not any legitimate table
to sit at as Daddy recollected and instead Miss Pettigrew, or
Aunt Willa most probably, had backed up several dozen chairs
to the front wall so as to keep the best part of the floor clear
and unobstructed for dancing, which Daddy said seemed to be
Miss Pettigrew's intention judging from the presence of her
portable record player with the lid up and the plug in the socket.

Of course nobody ate anything right off and nobody danced
anywhere and nobody even attempted to sit down. Daddy said
everybody just stood all bunched up together in anxious expec-

tation of the hostess's arrival and Daddy said it was an extended period of anxious expectation and left him near about dying for a piece of tenderloin by the time Miss Pettigrew finally entered through a swinging door at the remotest end of the ballroom. Naturally everybody gaped at her straightaway since everybody had warmed up their gaping muscles previously, and Daddy said the harnessed energy of all those jaws dropping open at once could have electrocuted an elephant. But Momma said she was well worth gaping at. Momma said she was radiant. She said even from all the way across the ballroom Miss Pettigrew was very obviously radiant and handsome still. Momma said she was wearing a light, stylish cotton knit the color of the driven snow though Daddy could not verify anything but the light and stylish part of it since the driven snow did not ring a bell with him. However they both clearly recollected that Miss Pettigrew carried in front of her a copper tea kettle full of tiny cloth flags on dowel sticks, and Momma said from where she was the flags looked to be a bouquet and Miss Pettigrew herself, in her white dress and with her squirrel-colored hair drawn back into a proper and distinguished bun, appeared somewhat bridely which Daddy could verify since the entire scene had also struck him as highly matrimonial notwithstanding his resistance to the driven snow.

Momma said Miss Pettigrew did not exactly scamper across the ballroom but did not dally on her end of it either and so made forthright progress directly into the midsts of the get togetherees, and Daddy said she caught up the copper teakettle in the crook of her left arm which kept her right one free to shake with and she went roundabout to each of her guests and took them by the fingers and called them by name and asked after their children and their old, ailing relations. She told Miss Frazier she was fretfully sorry her dog had got run over by a creamery truck, and she congratulated Mr. Venable on his promotion at the cigarette plant, and she politely took issue with Mr. Wyatt Benbow's tomatoes, which she claimed were altogether too mealy for the price. Daddy said it was purely mystifying to him how a woman who had stayed shut up inside her house for the last eight years and for the last ten years before that and for the last three years before that could know anything at all about anybody aside from herself. But apparently news siphoned in from off the street and Daddy said Miss

Pettigrew fairly stunned most all her guests with every little ordinary observation she made, which was not what people expected from a Pettigrew, especially from an isolated and peculiar Pettigrew, so the gaping persisted long after it had become noticeable and impolite and just when it seemed folks might get ahold of themselves and make civil expressions, Miss Pettigrew would say something regular and run of the mill and the chins would drop all over again since nobody much had expected Miss Pettigrew to be ordinary and since nobody much had wanted her to be either. So Daddy said the gaping did not die off to any degree as Miss Pettigrew made her way throughout the ballroom shaking fingers and giving out tiny cloth flags as party favors, and when folks found themselves out of position to gape at Miss Pettigrew directly they would gape at each other so as not to squander their astonishment.

Daddy said it did not seem to him that the gaping and finger shaking and the flag giving would ever leave off so the eating could commence, but after Miss Pettigrew had taken up little Sally Anne Cromer in her arms and rubbed their noses together, she made a vague sort of gesture with the back of her hand and said, "Please do help yourselves," which was not one of your point-blank invitations but was certainly enough to put the buffet table in some immediate jeopardy. Momma said the food was exquisite and the champagne punch superb, and even Daddy himself, who forages widely but generally does not pay much attention to what he eats, agreed with Momma that the food was indeed exquisite and the champagne punch in fact superb. And Momma said Mrs. Estelle Singletary took a taste of each dish, working her mouth like a rabbit, and then announced to Miss Pettigrew that all of the refreshments were most adequate, which was excessively high praise coming from Mrs. Singletary and set everybody to gushing over whatever happened to be on their forks at the moment. Of course Miss Pettigrew gee-hawed as modestly as she could, and Daddy said she tried to make out like the food had near about prepared itself, but folks insisted on embarrassing her anyway and Miss Frazier said a few words on behalf of the baked ham followed by Mrs. Petree's tribute to the cheese balls after which Mrs. Phillip J. King delivered a brief but compassionate speech on the texture of the potato salad and everybody else just hummed with their mouths full in a show of culinary delight. But Daddy said even the likes of Mrs. Phillip J. King cannot talk about a buffet forever, so the topic wore itself out directly but did not get replaced straightaway except by the sound of Mr. Emmet Dabb's bronchial asthma and a singularly rich and hearty burp from little Buford Needham who simply could not get his hand up fast enough. Otherwise there was not much noise to speak of and most everyone looked at the floor or studied their fingers and waited for somebody to venture a remark they could all throw in with. And Daddy said he was expecting any moment some sort of idiocy from Mrs. Phillip J. King when Miss Pettigrew herself made several extraordinarily bland observations about the weather, so extraordinarily bland in fact that Daddy, who is not much of a natural gaper, laid his chin flush against his shirtfront and showed Miss Pettigrew his adenoids.

And just along about then came Peahead Boyette's big bang, though nobody knew it was Peahead Boyette right off and folks just generally hovered over their chairseats on account of the concussion, everybody that is except for Miss Pettigrew who grabbed at her throat with the fingers of her left hand and looked altogether pleased, Daddy said, that some sort of engaging calamity had come along to prevent her from pursuing the weather. And it did turn out to be an engaging calamity though Daddy said it did not sound particularly engaging at the time or calamitous either. He said it sounded to him like somebody had tossed an aluminum trash can out of a Leer jet and hit the boulevard dead on, which seemed somewhat peculiar and diverting but did not strike Daddy as in any way disastrous. However, it had not been a trashcan exactly; it had been instead Mr. Peahead Boyette's sky-blue 1961 Ford Falcon in combination with a nickel parking meter and a mature poplar tree. And Daddy said Mr. Wyatt Benbow, who had his back to a window, was the first one to part the sheers and look out and directly he shrieked, "A wreck!" which sent half the get togetherees toward the ballroom windows and the other half toward the ballroom door, and by the time Mrs. Petree could pull her nose off from the glass and holler, "Lord, it's Peahead!" Mrs. Phillip J. King was already halfway down the sidewalk with her ears laid back. Little Buford's boy, Paul, caught up with her at the gate since he was not wearing heels and passed her up across the boulevard, but Mrs. Phillip J. King managed to arrive at the Falcon just a hair's breadth behind him nonetheless and the two of them stuck their heads in through the driver's window and expected to see a goodly amount of gore judging from the impact. But there was no gore to speak of and no Peahead either, not anything really except for a pair of drowned muskrats on the back floorboard.

Of course everybody came pouring out of the house shortly, and Momma said she believed even Miss Pettigrew got so far as the front door before she recollected herself and stayed behind, and soon enough Peahead Boyette's sky-blue 1961 Ford Falcon had fairly much disappeared under a swarm of anxious get togetherees who looked in the trunk, under the tires, and all throughout the engine but could not discover Peahead Boyette anywhere. And it was Daddy himself who found Peahead, mostly on account of his aversion for swarming get togetherees which sent him strolling down the boulevard in the direction of the icehouse and along the way he came across Peahead stretched out flat on his back lengthwise in the gutter.

"Peahead!" Daddy exclaimed and stooped down over what he figured for a corpse.

But Peahead opened his eyes and scratched the end of his nose with his index finger. "Hello Louis," he said.

"Are you alright?" Daddy asked him, and Peahead grunted and sat up on both elbows. "Well what in the world happened?" Daddy wanted to know.

And Daddy said Peahead spat out of the side of his mouth and told him, "Goddam Muskrat."

"Muskrat?" Daddy said.

"Yes sir," Peahead told him.

"You mean a muskrat wrecked your car?" Daddy said.

"Yes sir," Peahead told him.

"Well, you should've never let him drive, Peahead. You know their legs are too short to work the pedals." And Daddy said though Peahead is usually of a highly jocular disposition he just spat sideways once more and laid back down in the gutter.

Daddy said Mrs. Phillip J. King and little Buford Needham saw what he was stooped over near about simultaneously and set out together in a dead heat but after the first ten yards Mrs. Phillip J. King commenced to pull away primarily on account of little Buford's arthritic condition, which did not lend itself to extended sprints. And Daddy said it was quite a frightful thing to have Mrs. Phillip J. King run at you, even in the middle of the afternoon, and Daddy said he got kind of hypnotized looking at her with her shiny black clutch purse in one hand and her tiny cloth flag in the other and with her eyes wild and her hair blown back and her forehead mildly irridescent. In fact, Daddy said he was so overcome by the sight that he did not hear Mrs. Phillip J. King at first when she hollered at him, "Is he dead?" and so she hollered it a second time with a little more conviction and Daddy got ahold of himself sufficiently to tell her No.

"Well, is he injured then?" Mrs. Phillip J. King wailed at him.

"No," Daddy told her, "I don't believe so."

And Daddy said that aside from looking frightful and wild and mildly irridescent, Mrs. Phillip J. King looked somewhat lost for words temporarily and allowed little Buford the opportunity to holler, "Is he alright?"

"Yes," Daddy told him, "I think he is."

And Daddy said Mrs. Phillip J. King arrived shortly thereafter and fairly much threw herself on top of Peahead Boyette and put her face directly in his face and said, "Mr. Boyette? Mr. Boyette?" which caused Peahead's eyes to pop open and instigated some serious squirming and thrashing around on his part.

"Jesus woman," Peahead said and worked himself loose from Mrs. Phillip J. King, "I'm alright, just a little shook up."

And Mrs. Phillip J. King stood upright in the gutter and shouted off in the direction of the sky-blue 1961 Ford Falcon, "He's shook up," which sparked a general stampede, and Daddy said little Buford had not hardly gotten enough breath to say "Hey Peahead" when him and Mrs. Phillip J. King and Daddy and Peahead too found themselves all wrapped up in get togetherees who shot down the curbing and churned all roundabout the four of them like a spurt of frantic ditchwater. Of course everybody wanted to know just where Peahead Boyette was shook up, just exactly where specifically, and Daddy said Peahead picked himself up out of the gutter for fear of being stomped on, sat down on the curbing, and had the audacity to insist he was not shook up after all, not shook up in the least. But a great preponderance of people were nearly violently adamant that he be shook up, so Peahead set in to complaining about a shooting pain in his left wrist which was not one of your more severe and scintillating injuries but was far enough off from perfect health to satisfy most everybody. So once Peahead confessed to a degree of noticeable discomfort, people generally turned their attention to the cause of the accident which was a matter of some confusion to them since the driver was a ways down the street sitting insufficiently injured on the curbing and the vehicle was a ways up the street very thoroughly bent around a poplar tree. So naturally folks began to ask Peahead what in the world happened and Daddy said he looked around to see what the ladies would do when Peahead told them Goddam Muskrat but Peahead did not tell them Goddam Muskrat and instead told them, "Ill luck."

"Ill luck?" Mrs. Estelle Singletary said.

"Yes ma'm," Peahead replied, "a shitpot full of it."

Peahead said the trouble had started on the day previous when he had taken the afternoon off to do some fishing. Now Peahead worked on the dock at the cigarette plant unloading hogsheads and usually when he took time off him and Willis Beeson and either Jimmy Pitts or his brother Sleepy would all ride in Willis's truck down 29 south to the Haw River after catfish. According to Daddy, there are any number of decent and sporting ways to catch catfish. You can angle for them with a legitimate rod and reel or you can run a trot line across the river or set bank hooks or even wade out in the water and wrestle with them, but Daddy said Peahead and Willis Beeson and Jimmy Pitts and his brother Sleepy both were not the sort to be much interested in the ethics of fishing, so whenever they went down to the Haw River they got their catfish the easiest way they knew how which was to telephone for them.

It was Peahead's phonebox, or anyway it was the hand-cranked dynamo out of Peahead's Momma's phonebox, and Peahead had customized it somewhat with fifteen feet of additional insulated wire hooked into each of the two terminals, which Peahead figured was enough to reach to the bottom of any river he could get to. All you did was throw the wires in the water and let them sink down to the river bed where the catfish would be and then you set in to cranking the dynamo and thereby made things a little hot for the marine life. How-

ever, according to Peahead the charge didn't damage much of
anything except for the catfish and it went in through their
whiskers and near about electrocuted them, but Peahead insisted that telephoning was in no way as harmful as fishing with
dynamite which tended to bring everything that was under up,
and Peahead found some considerable sport and challenge in
corraling all the catfish once they floated to the surface. But
nonetheless Daddy said he did not believe it was the sort of
thing you'd ever see Kurt Gowdy do on t.v.

Now on the afternoon of July the third Peahead and Willis
Beeson and Sleepy Pitts took Willis's truck down 29 to the
river and then east to a trestle crossing where the local folks
tended to dump their garbage down the banks and directly
into the water which made for a catfish paradise. Peahead
had a little rubber boat about the size of a bathtub, and he
said when Willis and Sleepy finished blowing it up he got
in it with the phonebox and paddled out around the pilings,
where he commenced to charge up the water. Then he criss-
crossed underneath the trestle cranking and paddling and
cranking and paddling and cranking some more, and Peahead
said soon enough the catfish were coming up like corks all
over the place and most every one of them as big around as
a man's thigh. So Peahead called for Sleepy Pitts to toss out
the hook which was a three-pronged floated gaffer on forty
feet of clothesline and Sleepy Pitts flung it a good dozen
yards ahead of the boat where Peahead could paddle up to
it and hook it into a fish. Then Sleepy Pitts would draw it
in to Willis Beeson, who would take the fish by the tail,
knock it on the head for good measure, and free the hook
so Sleepy Pitts could send it back out into the river again.
Peahead said they had found this a very fine and reliable
system for gathering in their catfish and generally, according
to Peahead, there was nobody better than a Pitts for flinging
the hook. He said Jimmy and Sleepy both could usually lay
the clothesline across whatever fish they were after and fairly
much draw the gaff into him on their own. So Peahead was
not expecting Sleepy Pitts to do what he did but then Sleepy
Pitts was not expecting a train to come when it came. Peahead
said Sleepy Pitts had the gaff going round above his head
and appeared just prior to releasing it when the front end of
the engine broke clear of the treeline and hit the trestle with

the whistle wailing, and Peahead said he liked to have leapt clean out of the boat but he managed to restrain himself somehow and he saw on the riverbank Willis Beeson and Sleepy Pitts both jump straight up in the air, which was fine for Willis since he was not otherwise engaged at the moment but which was not so fine for Sleepy Pitts, who let fly with the three-pronged floated gaffer in the very midst of his agitation. And according to Peahead it was one of Sleepy Pitts's more beautiful flings with a high, gentle arc to it and some considerable distance and though it was a little wide of the catfish it appeared to Peahead to be a direct hit on the boat, so he did in fact leap clean out of it after all and Peahead said the gaffer landed near about amidships and the prongs of it dug into the inflatable port gunwhale which caused the whole business to flip over and sent Peahead's Momma's dynamo to the river bottom.

"So you lost your phonebox," Mr. Emmet Dabb said.

"Yes sir," Peahead told him. "Goddam rubber boat."

"And you lost your rubber boat," Mr. Wyatt Benbow said.

"Yes sir," Peahead told him. "Goddam Sleepy Pitts."

"And I guess you lost the most of your catfish too," little Buford said.

"Yes sir," Peahead told him. "Goddam train whistle."

And Daddy said Mrs. Estelle Singletary's spinster sister, Miss Frazier, laid her hand across the knobby part of Peahead's left shoulder and told him, "You've truly had your share of misfortune of late, Mr. Boyette."

"Shit lady," Peahead said, "that ain't the half of it." And Daddy said Peahead put his fist against his ear and commenced to tell how his entire Fourth of July had gone sour on him. Of course it started out sour in the first place what with his third of July being so thorough a disaster on its own, but Peahead said he had never expected his fourth of July to become such a fullblown and sorry mess. Peahead said him and Mrs. Boyette and little Melanie Marie Boyette were supposed to go over to Mrs. Boyette's brother's house for a barbeque at four o'clock, so Peahead figured he'd have time to run out to French's creekbottom after dinner and check his traps. He went after muskrats and minks mostly and sold the pelts to an outfit in Greensboro, and Peahead said he'd laid five traps in all and was expecting to find a couple of muskrats and maybe a mink or two if his luck had improved any. He parked his falcon alongside the Danville highway like usual and set out down through the woods with his cabbage sack over his shoulder, and Peahead said the first trap he came to had a muskrat in it that was near about dead already and he said he held it under water with the heel of his boot and began to feel somewhat recovered from the events of the day previous. But the second trap he came to was empty and though the third one wasn't, Peahead said he wished it had been. It seems Peahead had caught himself some sort of long-legged waterbird, and though he did not know what species it was exactly he said he was immediately impressed with the vigorous displeasure it showed at having its rubbery foot closed up in the jaws of a steel muskrat trap. Peahead said he tried to get up next to it to let it loose but the bird was feeling considerably antagonized already and managed to scratch and peck and screech and beat around sufficiently to hold Peahead off. So he retreated some and consulted with himself as to what he would do next, and Peahead said that was when he landed on the idea of the cabbage sack and he dumped the muskrat carcass out of it straightaway and commenced to circle the bird with the intention of getting the fiercest parts of it inside the bag somehow or another. And Peahead said it took a very liberal dose of some highly serious circling before the bird let down his defenses sufficiently to allow Peahead a shot at him, but even then nothing much got bagged but the head and part of one wing and Peahead said it seemed to him right off that the bird was a little meaner inside of the sack than out of it. So he did some more serious circling on top of what he'd already done, and when the bird finally did appear suitably confused and give out, Peahead slipped in and snatched the trap off his foot, and Peahead said it was most astounding to see how that bird left there at a dead run.

"With the sack on his head?" Mr. Phillip J. King wanted to know.

"Yes sir," Peahead told him. "Goddam long-legged bird." Peahead guessed it could see out the little holes in the sackcloth, and he said he'd never seen a creature bolt through the woods so, especially a half-maimed bird with a bag on its head, and even though Peahead lit out after it straightaway and chased it

along the creekbottom and up the east bank and back through
the trees to Mr. Donald Holloway's three-acre pond, he did not
figure he'd made up much of any ground at all when that bird
worked its wing loose from the cabbage sack and sailed out
over the water and on up towards the treetops with the bag still
dangling off its head. And Peahead said he watched it light in
among the uppermost branches of one of Mr. Holloway's loblolly pines where it shook and screeched and thrashed around
until it had succeeded in getting shed of the cabbage sack,
which dropped maybe a dozen feet before it hung up on a big
bristling cluster of pine needles.

"So you lost your phonebox," Daddy said, "and you lost
your rubber boat, and you lost a sizeable number of catfish,
and now you lost your cabbage sack."

"That's right," Peahead told him. "Goddam loblolly pine."

"Well is that the end of it, Peahead?" little Buford wanted
to know.

"No sir," Peahead replied. "I guess I lost my concentration
too." And Peahead said his mind was still on that cabbage sack
and that great big rubbery-footed long-legged bird when he
came up on trap number four which had closed itself on a
muskrat, and he said he drowned it with the heel of his boot
and then took it up by the tail and carried it on along with the
previous carcass to trap number five which had ahold of a
muskrat also. Now Peahead said this last one was a little more
freshly caught than the first two so he had to club it on the
head with a treelimb before he could move in to hold it on the
creekbottom, and Peahead figured this was the one that was
not dead after all though when he took it up by the tail and
held it with the other two it looked as thoroughly dispatched
as they did.

Peahead said he carried the two legitimately deceased
muskrats and the one half beaten and half drowned muskrat,
which he figured for legitimately deceased also, up out of
the creekbottom to the roadside where he tossed them onto
the back floorboard of his sky-blue 1961 Ford Falcon. Then
he got into the car himself, turned it around, and headed
home towards Neely, and Peahead said he was still considerably worked up about the cabbage sack long before he ever
got to town and he said he believed it was along about where
the Danville road turns into the boulevard that he began to

actively ponder his tragic vicissitudes of July the third, Daddy called them, to which he added what was so far his solitary vicissitude of July the fourth, and according to Peahead the bunch of vicissitudes in conjunction with the active pondering they had inspired caused the muscles in the base of Peahead's neck to tense up in a knotty lump which gave Peahead some noticeable discomfort. Now the tense knotty lumpiness in the base of Peahead's neck was a fairly new sensation for Peahead since time was most all of Peahead's tension, be it a knotty lump or a lumpy knot, had regularly collected at the bottom of his back just overtop his gluteus maximus. But on the first Sunday in March of 1970 Peahead had decided that since he could not get any relief from his doctor he would attempt to get himself healed otherwise, so him and Mrs. Boyette and little Melanie Marie Boyette all attended the ten o'clock service at the Holy Jesus Chapel which had been Casper Epps's Uncle Bill Collier's living room until Casper Epps's Uncle Bill Collier passed away, when it became Casper Epps's living room and underwent some partial renovation at the hands of Casper Epps himself who turned all the chairs to face in the same direction, brought in a pie tin from the kitchen for a collection plate and renamed the entire front part of his house the Holy Jesus Chapel which was duly documented on a piece of plywood nailed directly into the clapboard to the left of the front door.

Daddy said Casper Epps took up healing shortly after he left off plumbing, which was along about when he blessed Pinky Throckmorton in the Eden courthouse. But Daddy could not think right off of anybody Casper Epps had actually healed, though between 1950 and 1970 he had probably laid his hands on anywhere from three hundred to four hundred people, some of them even consenting to it. Casper himself laid claim to any number of miracles the most prominent of which was the restoration of sight to Mr. Odell Cheek, but Daddy insisted Mr. Cheek had not been blind at the time. Daddy said Casper Epps started out in a brush arbor out back of his Uncle Bill Collier's house between the driveway and the cemetery fence and on fair Sundays he would attract a number of negroes and cotton mill workers and he would lay on hands and chant and preach and sing and made himself somewhat of a reputation easing hangovers. Of course word got around about the hangovers soon enough and people figured a man who could relieve that sort of acute ailment could probably take care of a toothache or an inner ear complaint or any sort of mild gastritis and Casper Epps began to collect a sizeable following on account of his holy talents. Trouble was the brush arbor was a seasonal sort of sanctuary while sickness and pain and suffering is generally a year-round kind of thing, so naturally Casper Epps went to his Uncle Bill Collier with the dilemma and asked for the use of the living room, but his Uncle Bill Collier liked to sit in his favorite chair and read the paper and listen to the Baptist service on the radio every Sunday morning and he did not much like the idea of having a whole bunch of negroes and cotton mill workers do it with him. Consequently, for two years running Casper Epps held service in the brush arbor from April through October and healed by appointment the other six months, but in mid-autumn of 1953 Casper's Uncle Bill Collier finally succumbed to his bladder ailment and Casper Epps was able to transform the living room into the Holy Jesus Chapel and commence to preach in it barely a week before the cold weather set in, which Daddy said was one of those things people tended to point at when they talked about how mysterious the lord was.

Of course in March of 1970 Casper Epps was still a regular bedbug, and Daddy said he was healing hangovers and relieving flatulence and had been thrust afresh into the public eye the summer before when he cured Mr. Alphonse Broadnax of the thirty-seven dollars he carried in his hat liner, which was not what Mr. Broadnax had expected to be cured of. But nonetheless, the healing business was fairly much thriving for Casper Epps and his reputation in the field of alcohol related complaints had remained untarnished through the years, so Peahead said he went ahead and gave Casper Epps a chance after his doctor failed to provide him any relief because, as he figured it, a backache and a hangover were near about the same thing only in different places. According to Peahead, the Holy Jesus Chapel was maybe half full on the first Sunday in March of 1970 and promptly at ten o'clock Casper Epps came out from the kitchen in what looked to be a bathrobe, and he said a few words about God the father and Jesus Christ the holy savior and he blessed everybody generally and then blessed a few folks specifically after which he invited the ailing and infirm among the congregation to come forward for the laying on of hands, and Peahead said everybody but Mrs. Boyette and little Melanie Marie Boyette got up from their chairs and advanced on the podium which presented Casper Epps with a considerable volume of ailments and infirmities to lay his hands on, and Peahead himself lingered at the back of the crowd since he did not feel especially infirm or chronically ailed either and didn't want to get the jump on anybody who was.

Now Peahead said it being the first weekend in March the weather was still right wintery, so Casper Epps had the cook stove in the kitchen fired up and had fed a couple of sticks of wood into it just prior to entering the sanctuary. Of course, Daddy said, before you can feed a stove you have to feed a woodpile, and since Casper Epps was not the sort to chop wood himself or, God forbid, pay money for it, he generally filched it off the pile beside Mr. and Mrs. Bill and Nellie Sapp's carshed and he took such a trifling bit at a time that not Mr. Bill or Mrs. Nellie Sapp either one grew suspicious in the least until they visited Mr. Bill Sapp's nephew in West Virginia for a week and returned to find that in the course of seven days they had used an appreciable amount of wood for two people who had not lit a fire between them. Daddy said Mr. Bill Sapp took action almost immediately. He picked out a couple of choice pieces of dried oak and, with a brace and bit, bored a hole down the center of each one. Then he filled the holes with black powder and stoppered them with a pair of whittled plugs after which he returned the wood to the woodpile and him and Mrs. Nellie Sapp together waited to see whose house would blow up.

However, Casper Epp's house and adjoining Holy Jesus Chapel did not blow up exactly, but as for the cast iron cook stove in the kitchen it very thoroughly exploded. Fortunately nobody was injured by the flying fragments from the first blast or by the firecoals either when the second log went off in the middle of the kitchen floor. But unfortunately there was an injury, not an excessively grave injury but an injury nonetheless inflicted upon Peahead Boyette who was in precisely the wrong place at precisely the wrong time which Daddy said seemed to be a regular sort of thing with Peahead what with train whistles, gaff hooks, rubber boats and such.

As Peahead told it, he lingered at the back of the crowd of infirmities and ailments until there wasn't any crowd left and it was just him and Casper Epps up at the podium. And Casper Epps blessed Peahead so naturally Peahead blessed him back, and then Casper Epps asked Peahead just what sort of suffering he was troubled with and Peahead told him about the sharp pains in his lower back. Understandably, Peahead thought Capser Epps would want to see the problem spot for himself so he pulled his shirt partway up to his shoulders but Casper Epps just laid the palm of his hand on Peahead's forehead and commenced to chanting and moaning and wailing occasionally. Then he drew his hand back and chanted some more. Then he brought it forward and tapped Peahead's skull with his fingertips. Then he drew it back again and moaned some. Then he brought it forward once more and laid his palm on Peahead's forehead. Then he drew it back again and wailed twice very sharply. Then the stove blew up, and as Peahead got it from Mrs. Boyette Casper Epps did not tap Peahead's skull and did not lay his hand on Peahead's forehead but instead delivered a fairly potent straight right that did not entirely cure Peahead but managed to make him unconscious temporarily. And Peahead said by the time he woke up, Mr. Armond Renfrow who had been healed of a sinus affliction and Mr. Tommy Underhill who had received some relief from the itch of a sumac infection on his ankle had managed to stomp out most all the fire on the kitchen floor under the frantic and rather discomposed direction of Mr. Casper Epps who was trying to take the explosion as a goodly omen but could not figure out how. And Peahead said Mrs. Boyette helped him onto his feet and he checked himself all over for injuries which was when he discovered that the pain was altogether gone from his lower back and had miraculously migrated up to the base of his neck where it had collected in a tense lumpy knot and where it stayed ever since.

So on July the fourth 1970 when Peahead's active pondering and his tragic vicissitudes began to mingle and collaborate at the base of his neck, Peahead grabbed ahold of the problem area with his right hand and, as he recollected it, he began to work his head back and forth soon after he'd passed the icehouse and along about when he'd breasted the hill and come into the company of Colonel Blalock. And Peahead said he worked his head to the left side and worked it back to the right side and then worked it to the left side once more and then back to the right side again and that was when he saw the dead muskrat that was not dead after all and did not seem very pleased to be alive either. Peahead said it was sitting on the backseat grinning at him with the kind of grin an animal gets when it's about to tear your throat open, so naturally Peahead made an immediate and instinctual evasive manuever: he unlatched the door and bailed out into the gutter. And Peahead said he sat up on his elbows and watched his sky-blue 1961 Ford Falcon clip off a parking meter, ram headon into a poplar tree, and then finally disgorge itself of one highly antagonized and ferocious muskrat, which slipped out an open window and shot across the square towards the post office. And once he could not see the muskrat any longer, Peahead figured it was safe to relax so he lay down flush in the gutter and tried not to actively ponder any vicissitudes whatsoever.

"Christ, what a wild tale!" Mr. Emmet Dabb exclaimed in what was for him an extraordinary show of enthusiasm.

"Yes sir," Peahead Boyette said. "Goddam muskrat."

According to Daddy Sheriff Burton, who was still Deputy Burton at the time, came up on the group of them right at the tailend of the Peahead Boyette saga and he took a spiral pad and a pencil out of his front shirtpocket and then bulled on into the crowd until he was standing directly overtop of Peahead and he licked the end of his pencil and said, "Now what's all this I hear about a muskrat?" Well of course the question alone was quite enough to drive off that half of the crowd that did not want to hear Peahead's story all over again and it was also quite enough to set off that half of the crowd that wanted to tell it for him, and Daddy said he hung around for a spell but finally gave it up when little Buford, Wyatt Benbow, and Emmet Dabb all at once and together attempted to explain to Sheriff Burton just exactly what a dynamo was.

Most of the ladies headed back towards Miss Pettigrew's when Sheriff Burton got his interrogation underway and Daddy said him and Mr. Phillip J. King walked over to the poplar tree to speak to Sheriff Browner, who at the time was just a little over three years shy of becoming the late Sheriff Browner.

Daddy said the sheriff was sitting on his heels next to the left front tire of Peahead's sky-blue 1961 Ford Falcon and was dragging his fingers across the crumpled fender in a somber and grievous sort of way. As near as Daddy could recollect he'd never known anyone to get so truly worked up and disheartened over somebody else's misfortune the way Sheriff Browner did, and he was certainly a conspicuous figure in the middle of all that excitement and agitation inspired by Peahead's tragic vicissitudes, especially the four-legged one. And Daddy said him and Mr. Phillip J. King and Sheriff Browner had just set in to doing some earnest commiserating together when Momma and Mrs. Estelle Singletary and Mrs. Estelle Singletary's old maid sister Miss Frazier and Mrs. Mary Margaret Vance Needham and Mrs. Royce Venable and Mrs. Treva Jane Boyd McKinney all came out through Miss Pettigrew's gate and recrossed the street looking rather forlorn and dazed. And Daddy said he asked Momma, "What is it?" and she told him the buffet and the party and the dancing were all done with. Momma said when they had gotten to the front porch they found a pile of tiny cloth flags and a few pocketbooks and clutch purses along with Mr. Wyatt Benbow's open weave hat and Momma said Mrs. Estelle Singletary tried the door but it was bolted to so she knocked on it and then she rapped on it and then she veritably beat on it the accumulated sum of which brought Aunt Willa into the foyer at length and she opened the door far enough to stick her head and shoulders outside.

"Yes ma'm?" Aunt Willa said.

"We mean to come in," Mrs. Estelle Singletary told her. "We're Miss Pettigrew's guests."

"Miss Pettigrew says she's weary," Aunt Willa said and commenced to back out of the doorway.

"Weary?" Mrs. Estelle Singletary asked her.

"Yes ma'm," Aunt Willa said.

"You mean you're not going to let us back inside?" Mrs. Estelle Singletary wanted to know.

And Aunt Willa said, "No ma'm" and shut the door.

The ladies all agreed they were stunned and then Mrs. Treva Jane Boyd McKinney suggested flabbergasted and they all agreed they were stunned and flabbergasted except for Mrs. Phillip J. King who was not present and who Momma said had been stunned and flabbergasted and incensed and had gone off around the house in a huff with the intention of getting at Miss Pettigrew through the back door. And Daddy said Momma had not hardly closed her mouth from talking when the stunned, flabbergasted, and incensed Mrs. Phillip J. King cut loose with an unholy shriek from the backyard and soon thereafter showed herself at the corner of the house flapping her arms and stomping her feet like maybe she had a hornet up her skirt. "Oooohh oooohh," she wailed, "get away, get away from me," and she came forward another five yards and flapped and stomped some more, and Daddy said just as Mrs. Phillip J. King was setting herself to air out another high-pitched pitiful lament two creatures passed her up and slipped out of Miss Pettigrew's yard through the front gateway, two odd and maybe even extraordinary creatures, Daddy said, that looked to be somehow related to the pig family but were plastered all over with dried grass and leaves and scraps of paper and dirt. And as soon as they'd made the sidewalk they turned left together and hoofed it along the boulevard past the square and down the hill towards the icehouse. Of course most everybody followed them as far as to where the road dropped off just to see where they went and what they were anyway, and Daddy said once he had decided for himself that they were in fact pigs, he started back to the wreck and came upon Peahead Boyette, who was sitting by himself on the curb tapping the end of his nose with a long sheet of folded white paper.

"What you got there, Peahead?" Daddy asked him.

"Citation," Peahead said.

"What for?" Daddy asked him.

"Fishing with a phonebox," Peahead said. "Goddam Deputy Burton."

"Well," Daddy told him, "don't never seem to rain but it pours."

"Yes sir," Peahead said. "It's all chicken but the bill and that's his pecker."

So Momma and Daddy did not have much of a get together on the fourth of July in 1970 and they had already been home an hour by the time the Y.M.C.A. volunteers and Mr. J. L. Graham and Mr. Harland Lynch allowed us to leave off chasing the pigs which not any of us had laid eyes on since they went through the hole in the fence. There were supposed to be fireworks at the fairgrounds come dark but along about 4:30 a storm set in from the southwest and dumped what Daddy called a scandalous amount of rain all over the county, two feet of which ended up in the courthouse basement where the fireworks were in boxes on the slab floor. So Momma cooked us scrambled eggs for supper and we all three sat on the front porch and listened to the rain blow through the treetops and drip from the gutters, and it was just at dark when we heard Sheriff Browner, though we did not know then it was Sheriff Browner, fire off his revolver six times. "Happy fourth of July," Daddy said and laid his head back on the glider cushion so as to blow a plume of smoke straight up to the beaded ceiling.

iii

ONCE WE'D passed through the stone archway at the cemetery, Mrs. Coleen Ruth Hoots Newberry almost immediately ran square overtop of Mr. Ernest Harold Ratliff with her right front tire. It seems her navigator had been blowing his nose at the time and so had failed to warn Mrs. Newberry of the sharp turn the road took just beyond the cemetery gate which was not the sort of thing Mrs. Newberry could readily see for herself from down below the dashboard. So the Pontiac went up onto the granite curbing and the right front tire passed directly across Mr. Ernest Harold Ratliff's midsection, but I do not believe it did him much of any damage since he had died already in 1958 and so could not be done in again, not even by a Pontiac. The incident, however, did serve to speed Daddy's handkerchief back into his coatpocket and he hung over the front seat most devotedly until we had eased up behind the Frenches and docked there.

The Pettigrew plot was halfway up a hillside just below three cedars of Lebanon that ran across the grade in a straight line. Miss Pettigrew's daddy had provided for his family to lie four abreast under a common headstone with him on one end, his son on the other, and his wife and daughter in between. Off to Mr. Pettigrew's right were about five Mordecais and a sprinkling of Fosters while Mr. Wallace Amory jr. was less than an arm's length removed from three generations of Timberlakes on the other side. The rest of the slope all the way down to where it bottomed out was fairly much covered up in Dardens who apparently had that Gottlieb flair for heirmaking. The commander's men had set up a green canvas awning which stretched over the entire Pettigrew plot and there was room under it for a half dozen chairs on the downslope just below the Pettigrews and just prior to the onslaught of Dardens. Of course by the time me and Momma and Daddy and Mr. and Mrs. Newberry got to the graveside the casket was already sitting atop the commander's shiny chrome casket-lowering device and five of the six seats were already occupied by Aunt Willa and Aunt Willa's sister and Aunt Willa's sister's daughter and beside them Mrs. Jack Vestal and beside her Mrs. Phillip J. King with the sixth chair being held in reserve for Mrs. Ouida Gattis, who had fallen and broken her hip in 1976 and had not been able to do much standing around ever since.

The service did not get started right away because the latter third of the procession had been held up at the Mayview Street light and the commander figured they had as much of a right to a full show as anybody else. So we all lingered there in among the tombstones and Daddy and Mr. Newberry leaned up against Mr. Lester Mordecai's marker and smoked Daddy's cigarettes off Mr. Newberry's matches even though Momma and Mrs. Newberry both told them it was a profane and sacrilegious thing to do, but Daddy said he doubted if the smoke would be much of a bother to Lester. And even after the last third of the procession arrived we got to linger some more while Mrs. Ouida Gattis's son-in-law helped Mrs. Ouida Gattis out of the car and then steered her all roundabout the cemetery in an effort to get her to the graveside without stepping on anybody along the way which was a matter of some significance with Mrs. Ouida Gattis, who did not want to be stepped on herself once circumstances put her in a position to be. So Mrs. Ouida Gattis and her partially mended hip bone and her son-in-law all toured the cemetery together and eventually arrived at the canvas awning and the son-in-law along with the commander lowered Mrs. Ouida Gattis into the vacant folding wooden chair which had been moved partway up the hill for her convenience and appeared to be sitting somewhere in the vicinity of Mr. Wallace Amory jr.'s kneecaps.

The graveside ceremony commenced nearly immediately after Mrs. Ouida Gattis's arrival. It would have commenced precisely immediately afterwards, but when the commander nodded at the Reverend Richard Crockett Shelton who nudged the Reverend Mr. Holroyd with the pointiest part of his elbow, the Reverend Mr. Holroyd just looked all around himself rather vaguely and then went back to pondering the casket which he had been engaged in at the time of the nudge. So the commander nodded once more and the Reverend Mr. Shelton nudged once more and the Reverend Mr. Holroyd looked all around himself to see what the disturbance had been before he returned his attention to the casket. Consequently, the graveside ceremony did not commence immediately but only after a pair of nods, a pair of nudges, and two distinct instances of vague circumspection, and when the graveside ceremony finally did commence it did not commence with a prayer from the Reverend Holroyd as was planned but commenced instead with a few words from the Reverend Mr. Richard Crockett Shelton who cleared his throat, drew off a most prodigious breath, and then reminded us just who it was that had died. Of course the Reverend Shelton had carried with him to the cemetery a burial prayer which he had taken the trouble to set down in longhand on a sheet of yellow legal paper, but seeing as how he was called upon prematurely the reverend was forced to make several observations right off the top of his head as he fished around in his jacket pockets, and Daddy recollected that in the course of the hunt the reverend managed to come out with five completely separate, purely unrelated, and entirely insignificant statements none of which, taken singly, was particularly offensive but all of which, taken as a group, were magnificently inconsequential. And when the reverend discovered the burial prayer tucked away in his right hip pocket behind his wallet he compounded his triumph and soared to new and rarified heights of tediousness with the able assistance of Mr. Longfellow and Mr. Tennyson and especially Mr. William Wordsworth whose natural inclination towards idiocy seemed fairly much indisputable. Daddy said it was the most appropriate burial prayer he'd ever heard since we all died a little in listening to it.

Understandably, after the Reverend Mr. Richard Crockett Shelton's prayer the Reverend Mr. Holroyd could not be roused up into speech no matter how vigorously the Reverend Shelton applied his elbow to the undertaking, so instead the commander nodded at the Reverend Mr. Red Hamilton who had not been scheduled to speak but who was always prepared to. The Reverend Hamilton struck in straightaway with a benediction of his own devising and though it was stirring enough it was certainly not one of the Reverend Red's famous unbridled African benedictions, but then the reverend was being actively discouraged from any sort of fanatical antics by Sheriff Burton who had ahold of a handful of Reverend Red's jacket from the back. So the reverend delivered a fairly brief and altogether unobjectionable sendoff and afterwards turned the proceedings back over to the commander who nodded again at the Reverend Shelton who obliged him by reaching for the switch on the commander's shiny chrome casket-lowering contraption, but before he could get his hand even halfway to it the Reverend Mr. Holroyd came to life of a sudden, stooped over, and threw the switch himself. The entire frame jumped once and creaked and then the webbing commenced to unfurl and Miss Pettigrew sank ever so delicately into the ground. And that was the end of it, or anyway that was the end of the official part of it, but that was not actually the absolute end of it since as soon as the casket touched bottom Mrs. Jack Vestal leapt up out of her folding wooden chair all wild and desperate with grief and she waved her arms and wailed and snorted and eventually shrieked, "Goodbye, brave soul" and tossed her good linen handkerchief on into the grave. And that would have been the end of it usually, but that was not the end of it this time because Mrs. Jack Vestal's handkerchief had hardly lighted on the casket when Mrs. Phillip J. King leapt up out of her folding chair all wild and desperate with grief herself and she waved her arms and wailed and snorted and at length worked herself up into a shriek also. "Adieu, sweet princess," she said and let fly with a clump of Kleenex. And that was in fact the actual and absolute end of it unless you count how Aunt Willa and Aunt Willa's sister and Aunt Willa's sister's daughter all stood up together and momentarily pondered Mrs. Jack

Vestal and Mrs. Phillip J. King in that impeccably bloodless sort of way before exiting out the opposite side of the canopy.

After it was over Daddy and Mr. Newberry smoked some more in the company of Mr. Lester Mordecai while Momma and Mrs. Newberry went off to visit Mrs. Newberry's mother where she was laying in with a smattering of Hootses on the far incline. Two men from the vault outfit who had kept themselves and their truck at a discreet distance off behind some sycamore trees during the course of the service started up the engine once most everybody had departed except for me and Momma and Daddy and the Newberrys and Mrs. Ouida Gattis and her son-in-law, who were very nearly to their car, and the truck lurched out into view with the concrete vault top swinging from a cable over the bed. The driver backed on in among the tombstones and hard up to the commander's canvas awning and him and the other fellow together commenced to clear out the chairs and the flowers and the shiny chrome casket-lowering device and then they dragged the green indoor/outdoor carpet off the dirtpile and rolled it up. Me and Daddy and Mr. Newberry watched them work with Daddy and Mr. Newberry propped comfortably against Mr. Mordecai's headstone and me alongside them trying not to step anywhere Mr. Mordecai could possibly be, and at length after the gravesite was near about vacant Mr. Newberry spat between his shoes and said, "I wonder what in the world is wrong with that old fart Holroyd. Seems to me he's lost his mind."

"You think so?" Daddy asked him.

"Yes sir," Mr. Newberry said, "I truly do. Seems to me it's a pure and simple case of decrepitude, don't you think?"

And Daddy crossed his arms over his chest and looked at his shirtfront for a spell. "No," he said, "no, I don't believe it is."

"Well, what is it then?" Mr. Newberry wanted to know.

And while Daddy was considering his reply, the driver of the vault truck started up a mechanical block and tackle and played out the steel support arm until the vault top was suspended directly over Miss Pettigrew's grave, and as me and Mr. Newberry and Daddy all three watched the concrete slab sway there in midair Mr. Newberry said, "Well?" and Daddy told him, "Not decrepitude, Russell. Futility." And I do not believe that word had left off rattling in my ears when the vault truck driver dropped the vault top into place at a reckless velocity. The concussion shook Mr. Lester Mordecai I am certain and turned Momma and Mrs. Newberry completely around on the far hillside. It was most dramatic.

Me

O_N $_{THE}$ Tuesday after Miss Pettigrew's funeral Mr. Conrad
Rackley returned to Neely in a rented truck the cab of which
he shared with a pair of Masseys who we did not know for
Masseys right off but who we recognized as relations on account
of a common chinlessness, which is apparently the predominant
Massey trait in the West Virginia end of Kentucky. Now the
Neely Masseys, and there are eight altogether, are adequately
chinful people, but each one of them can catch rainwater in
his ears without ever tilting his head. Daddy says there is
probably some jackrabbit in the family somewhere. So nobody
was even guessing Massey when Mr. Conrad Rackley turned
off Scales Street onto the boulevard and proceeded to Miss
Pettigrew's house. There was, however, some speculation that
it was possibly Newsomes, who go almost direct from the
bottom lip to the neck without any distraction, but most folks
figured Newsomes to be strictly a local phenomenon and did
not consider it prudent to make such a serious accusation against
total strangers.

This time Mr. Conrad Rackley pulled up alongside Miss
Pettigrew's wrought iron fence without ever stopping off at the
Gulf station to find out how, and he left both the Masseys in
the truck while he went himself to the front door and beat on
it and kicked it and beat on it again before backing off the
porch and into the yard to holler at the cedar clapboard, and I
do believe Aunt Willa stood in the doorway for a full two

minutes and listened to him yell before she brought herself out
into the sunlight where he could see her.

"I come for some things," Mr. Rackley said, and Aunt Willa
just stared at him. "I's here before," he told her, "and I come
back for some things. Conrad Rackley, you remember me."
But still Aunt Willa just stared at him and did not nod or twitch
or even blink either, and Mr. Conrad Rackley looked to his
left and looked to his right and then glared at the sky straight
up over his head. "Shit woman," he said and made a vigorous
exhalation, "I ain't got time to mess with you. Get on out the
way, I come for some things." And he motioned to the Masseys
who bailed out of the truck cab and followed him up the steps,
across the porch past Aunt Willa, and on in through the doorway, and by all reliable reports the younger Massey had not
hardly disappeared into the foyer when he came out again
creeping backwards across the porch and searching for the top
step with his right foot. It seems he got as far as the apron,
which put him abreast of Aunt Willa, when the older Massey
who turned out to be the younger Massey's daddy came out
through the doorway frontwards and suggested to the younger
Massey that he drag his butt directly back on into the house.
"I ain't," the younger Massey told him, "I ain't about to as
long as that gorilla's running loose," and he continued to probe
for the top step with his foot.

"That monkey won't hurt you," the older Massey told him,
"now get back in here."

"I ain't, Daddy, I ain't about to," the younger Massey said,
and what chin he had was all aquiver.

So the older Massey turned his attention to Aunt Willa and
asked her would she please bind up her monkey somehow or
another and Aunt Willa stepped into the house long enough to
fetch Mr. Britches back out with her and carried him down the
steps to the flagpole while the younger Massey looked on with
some considerable attention. And once he was satisfied that
the monkey could not work free of his tether, he commenced
to back across the porch towards the doorway and eventually
vanished into the foyer.

Mr. Conrad Rackley and the two Masseys rummaged throughout the house for a spell independently of each other, and the
assortment of people who had collected along the wrought iron
fence on account of the truck and on account of the monkey

and on account of the combination of the truck, the monkey, two Masseys, and a Rackley all watched the various window sashes on the front of the house fly open in an agitated and violent sort of way so as to allow the older Massey or the younger Massey or Mr. Conrad Rackley himself a breath of untainted air. And I do not believe the first piece of furniture saw daylight until the entire Pettigrew mansion had been all opened up and cross ventilated like a Swiss cheese and even then it was only an endtable that Mr. Conrad Rackley dragged outside, inspected on the lawn, and promptly carried on back into the house. He did not reappear for the best part of a half hour afterwards and neither did the younger Massey or the older Massey or Aunt Willa either, so the folks along the fence had to amuse themselves with the monkey, who was not hardly a danger to them any longer on account of his pressure problem and consequently was not hardly amusing to them either, even in his plaid sportcoat and his porkpie hat and with his lips turned inside out. Mr. Britches's bladder trouble had gone a ways towards deflating the thrill of monkey watching in Neely. Naturally, then, people were growing noticeably edgy and annoyed in the absence of Mr. Conrad Rackley and the accompanying Masseys, and there was mounting the threat that some one or two of the spectators might go on about their business when at last the air was filled with a kind of syncopated thud-thumping like maybe somebody was dribbling a piano down the inside stairway, and the noise had just barely left off echoing across the front lawn when the Masseys came trotting through the doorway on either end of a bonnet-topped highboy with Mr. Conrad Rackley close behind them cheering them on but not really carrying anything. He directed the Masseys straight to the truckbed, selected a spot for the highboy, and encouraged them to put it there. Then he drove them on back up the front steps and into the house in the most amiable sort of way. They were gone maybe five minutes this time when from out of the foyer came a tremendous splintering crash which seemed to indicate that Mr. Rackley and the Masseys had gotten together and decided to dispense with the dribbling and had simply tossed whatever it was off the second-floor landing. At length the Masseys passed through the doorway carrying between them a kind of a dressing table that was lovely, delicate, and complete except for three legs and Mr. Rackley encouraged them to set it off to one side of the porch.

After that the Masseys did not dribble any furniture and did not launch any either but did carry a great variety of items across the front yard to the truckbed under the cheerful direction of Mr. Conrad Rackley who did not dribble any furniture himself and did not launch any and managed to avoid carrying any also. I suppose all in all Mr. Rackley, with the invaluable assistance of the two chinless Masseys, made off with an even dozen endtables, five or six highboys, a matching pair of cedar wardrobes, countless whatnot shelves and several boxes full of countless whatnots, two pine hutches, one overstuffed leather chair, a ponderous oak bedstead, three pair of andirons, one stackable walnut barrister's bookcase, four Tommy Dorsey albums, two sets of silver service, and one very large gilt-framed portrait of an excessively grim individual who was not then and has never since been verifiably indentified though Mrs. Louise Tullock Pfaff, who got the best look at it, insisted it was Jefferson Davis. And all throughout the hauling and the loading and the stacking Mr. Conrad Rackley persisted in his undying encouragement except for the brief few minutes he spent against the wrought iron fence talking to Mr. Mickey Roach sr. and Mr. Covington from the Gulf station and Mr. Russell Newberry and one of the wispy white Tallys along with two of the standard-sized Frank Lewis negro Tallys. As Mr. Newberry told it, Mr. Rackley wiped some accumulated perspiration off the top of his bald head and said, "Gentlemen, this furniture here is awfully heavy."

"Yes sir," Mr. Mickey Roach sr. replied, "I bet it is."

"Awfully heavy," Mr. Rackley said, and dabbed at himself. "We sure could use some extra hands to help carry it."

"Yes sir," Mr. Mickey Roach told him, "I bet you could." And that was about all of it except for the hard looks followed by some general chortling on the part of most everybody but Mr. Conrad Rackley. So the Masseys continued to carry out the furniture alone and continued to suffer the singlehanded encouragement of Mr. Conrad Rackley until at last the truck was packed full and the door was lowered and latched and the older Massey and the younger Massey each were rewarded with a coffee cup full of tapwater. The departure was exceedingly uneventful to a point. There were no fond farewells, not even a solitary civil goodbye, just two Masseys and a Rackley in the cab of a rented truck which backfired when the engine turned over and then went off from the curb in a cloud of grey smoke. And I suppose the departure would have been entirely uneventful if Mr. Britches had not been startled enough by the backfire to urinate on account of it, and though it was not a thick and masterful stream it was a sort of arc nonetheless and drew a riotous ovation from the onlookers.

Daddy said that was that monkey's last hurrah though we didn't know it at the time and surely that monkey didn't know it either. I suppose only Aunt Willa knew it since she had gone ahead and called the zoo in keeping with the specifications of the deceased, and the people in charge there had immediately agreed to drive the width of the state from Ashboro to Neely if only to pick up a dilapidated, bladder-plagued chimpanzee with a court record. You see, the zoo was a fairly new undertaking at the time and was understandably scant of resources. There weren't any elephants just then or giraffes or zebras or tigers or crocodiles but just a few deer, one reasonably tame black bear, and enough corn snakes to start a Bible society, so I do believe the zoo would have flown a man halfway across the country to fetch back a housecat not to mention hopping over to Neely for a legitimate monkey. Consequently, someone came for Mr. Britches right away, or anyway came for him two days after Aunt Willa had called, which was about as right away as you could hope for from a state-supported institution. Aunt Willa had him dressed to travel in his porkpie hat and his handsome blue blazer and his black Keds sneakers, and Mr. Britches was squatting comfortably atop his flagpole when the green station wagon from Ashboro pulled out off Scales Street onto the boulevard and made direct for the curbing in front of Miss Pettigrew's house. The driver got out and stretched himself. He was dressed in khaki from the feet up, kind of like Jungle Jim, but I do not believe he possessed much of a natural instinct for chimpanzees since he passed through the gateway, along the sidewalk, and climbed the steps to the front porch without ever noticing just what it was that had been run up the flagpole, but when Aunt Willa came out of the house and commenced to reel in the tether that fellow did some extremely serious noticing and in fact could not seem to stop himself from gawking at the porkpie hat and the blazer and the sneakers and the entire monkey in general. He did not appear willing to catch up Mr. Britches in his arms when Aunt Willa offered him the chance to and he did not appear willing to take Mr. Britches by his hairy hand when that opportunity presented itself. Instead he seemed to prefer simple gawking and he persisted in it as Aunt Willa hauled Mr. Britches up the front steps and then turned around and hauled him back down again along with his suitcase, or anyway that's what the man from the zoo called it though it was really not anything but a little canvas valise.

"What's in that suitcase?" he said.

"Clothes," Aunt Willa told him.

"Monkey's clothes?" he said.

And Aunt Willa moved her head just enough to indicate yes.

"Ma'm, our animals don't wear clothes," he said.

And Aunt Willa did not move her head any and did not open her mouth any but just stood where she was about as animated as a treestump.

"They don't wear anything," he said.

And Aunt Willa watched him with one of her most accomplished bloodless expressions.

"Nothing at all," he said.

And Aunt Willa continued to exhibit all the liveliness of a cinderblock.

"Not anything," he said. "Nada. Zilch. You got me?"

And he glared at Aunt Willa who watched him watch her but did not move her head and did not open her mouth.

"Lady," he said, "we're running a zoo, not a supper club. Now get this monkey naked and bring him out to the car."

So Aunt Willa set the valise down on the sidewalk and helped Mr. Britches out of his sneakers and out of his blazer and out from under his porkpie hat and then carried him through the gateway to the back of the station wagon, where she attempted to give him over to the man from the zoo who did not show any more of a natural inclination towards monkeys than he had previously, and consequently Aunt Willa herself deposited Mr. Britches in the steel hound cage and latched the door and shut the tailgate, and I do not believe much of anybody saw him off except for her and except for Jump Garrison who gassed up the station wagon and then stood by the pumps holding the nozzle as he watched Mr. Britches go away down the street with his little hairy fingers around the bars of his cage.

And that was about all of Miss Pettigrew except for the odds and ends and she had lived sufficiently long enough to accumulate a vast assortment of them which Mr. Conrad Rackley and the two chinless Masseys had not even begun to deplete, so Aunt Willa contracted with Mr. Ellis Spainhour of Yanceyville who primarily handled cattle and tobacco but took on estate work when it came his way. The announcement arrived a week and a day after Mr. Britches's departure and it was addressed Occupant so was mine to open since Daddy got all the Mr. Louis W. Benfield sr. mail and Momma got all the Mrs. Inez Yount Benfield mail and since Aunt Sadie did not ever send me five dollars on my birthday anymore which excluded me from any sort of postal involvement except for a monthly *Boy's Life* and that wasn't even in an envelope. So Momma set aside all the Occupant mail for me along with the occasional Resident flier from the grocery store and in the evenings just before supper me and Daddy would sit down in front of the television and open our mail together. He generally got the significant items like bills and bank statements and requests for donations to the Waccamaw Boy's Home while I generally got pizza coupons and sample boxes of catfood, but a week and a day after Mr. Britches's departure I opened up the auction announcement and read it out loud to Daddy, who called Momma in from the kitchen and had me read it out loud to her. It was surely the most vital piece of Occupant correspondence I had ever received.

We do not get too many auctions in Neely. We do not even have a regular flea market, and most usually furniture out on a front lawn means an eviction and not a yard sale. Consequently news of the Pettigrew auction touched off some noticeable local fervor, and even those folks who cannot hardly make the mortgage from month to month began to discuss and debate and speculate over just precisely what portion of the estate they would purchase. Of course there was not a tremendous amount of estate left since a goodly part of it had already been hauled off to the West Virginia end of Kentucky, but there was a sufficient assortment of furniture, kitchen utensils, and personal effects for people to get venomous over. The auction itself was held about noon on the Saturday of the Labor Day weekend

which gave everybody a full ten days to tap their noses and
tug at their ears and scratch their topnotches and just generally
brush up on various bidding techniques, and Mr. Spainhour
and his assistants had arrived early enough to haul the auc-
tionable items outside so by the time a crowd began to collect
in earnest it looked like the house had gotten sick and thrown
up all over the front yard. There were little bits and pieces of
the estate everywhere, loose and in boxfuls and stacked on top
of each other and strewn across tabletops and draped over
shrubbery and canted up against treetrunks and piled all roundabout the wrought iron fence, and people swarmed in through
the gate and covered over the yard and they picked up this and
poked at that and fiddled with one thing and studied another.
I'll be the first to tell you there were certainly some grand items
to be had. I recollect an upright piano in passable condition
and a brass coatrack with all sorts of colorful bends and twists
to it and an oversized pitcher and wash basin—what Momma
called exquisite spongeware—and some kind of mahogany
monstrosity with lion's feet that I could not purely decipher a
purpose for but which was entertaining to look at nonetheless
and a solid silver fruit bowl and a handsome mantel clock with
a clipper ship etched into the glass of it and a table lamp made
from a wagon wheel hub and a velvet upholstered divan, Daddy
called it, which was pretty enough to look at but did not seem
the sort of thing you could watch t.v. from. However, most
everything else was not grand and was not especially appealing
but was just old and mildewed and dusty and termite-eaten,
and all the books and dishes and clothes and framed pictures
and tables and chairs and boxfuls of bric-a-brac lay scattered
across the front lawn like they had been turned up with a
grubbing hoe. There was not anything that did not have some
grime to it, and since there was not anything that did not get
touched or picked up or otherwise handled somehow the grime
circulated freely onto fingers and palms and subsequently onto
shirtfronts and necks and faces and pantlegs. So by the time
Mr. Ellis Spainhour called for the auction to commence and
drove us into a corner of the front yard, we carried a good part
of the available filth with us and looked for all the world like
a band of refugees.

The auction got underway promptly at noon and Mr. Spainhour started things off with the upright piano. Mr. Rollie Cobb

pinched his nose, pulled at both his ears, and snapped his fingers twice in an attempt to bid ten dollars for it, but Mr. Spainhour told him the bidding would start at two hundred and fifty dollars instead and Mr. Rollie Cobb put his hands in his pockets so as to avoid any sort of temporary bankruptcy. For a spell afterwards there was not any pinching or pulling or snapping to be seen from anybody, but once Mr. Spainhour had provided us with an extremely flattering and altogether fictitious description of the instrument followed by a second and then a third request for two hundred and fifty dollars, a man on the sidewalk outside the fence waved his arm at Mr. Spainhour, a man in a floppy tennis hat and sunglasses and green plaid pants, a man from somewhere else who obviously had a far more refined understanding of pianos than any of us did. But just as soon as Mr. Spainhour had his two hundred and fifty dollars, he wanted two hundred and seventy-five and straightaway he got that from a woman midway back in the crowd who looked like some sort of exotic variety of Oregon Hill French but turned out to be a High Point Pembroke. So the man from somewhere else was pressed to three hundred dollars and then to three hundred and twenty dollars and when it looked like he would own a piano at last Mr. Wiley Gant scratched underneath his hat and drove the price up higher which I do not believe he intended or was ever aware of and which seemed an extraordinary thing for him to do seeing as how he had no right arm after the elbow. The High Point Pembroke got back in at three hundred and thirty-five and her and the man from somewhere else were joined by a distinguished grey-haired gentleman in a blue suit who Mrs. Phillip J. King said was a senator. The three of them together were responsible for all of the rest of the bidding except for a brief interruption by Mr. Wyatt Benbow who wrestled most mercilessly with his chin until he got recognized at $372.50, but much to his apparent relief he was immediately passed by the senator who gave way to the High Point Pembroke, who was vanquished at length by the man from somewhere else. The whole business grew a little tedious at the end so we were all pleased to see the piano going, going, and then finally gone though Mr. Wyatt Benbow shook his head and tried to look sick about it.

The lion-footed mahogany monstrosity got dispatched with

next. It went to the High Point Pembroke after some furious bidding, and I think she was fairly pleased to have purchased it although it did not seem to me she had any clearer conception of exactly what it was than the rest of us did, so I suppose by way of consolation she bought the mantel clock also since its purpose was not in any way mysterious or indecipherable. The senator made off with the silver fruit bowl and the wagon hub table lamp while Mr. Estelle Singletary succeeded in buying the exquisite spongeware under what appeared to be a threat of death. Mrs. Mary Margaret Vance Needham got the brass coatrack, and in an exhilarating display of financial abandonment and serious chinyanking, Mr. Wyatt Benbow came away with the velvet upholstered divan. Daddy said it was just the thing for a grocery store magnate to rest his hams upon. And that was the last of the truly grand items though a few marginally grand items did show up here and there in the midst of the innumerable ordinary odds and ends that remained, but after the divan went to Mr. Benbow all the nose pulling and ear tugging and head scratching seemed to lose some of its novelty. So I did not pay much attention to the auction for a time and instead retired to the wrought iron fence with Daddy and Mr. Russell Newberry and Mr. Phillip J. King and Mr. Bobby Ligon of Draper, who all smoked together and spat and then launched directly into a vigorous discussion of the higher sciences. What touched it off was Mr. Phillip J. King's terrier, Itty Bit. Mr. Phillip J. King had her with him on a leash and, being the nervous and thoroughly idiotic creature that she was, Itty Bit passed the time in barking fairly persistently at nothing much in particular. We'd all grown somewhat accustomed to the aggravation of it, so nobody paid any attention to Itty Bit except for Mr. Bobby Ligon, who was sitting on his heels just to her backside, and he spent a full minute and a half in devoted contemplation of Itty Bit's rearend, tilting his head first towards one shoulder and then towards the other.

"You know," he said at last, "I wish you'd just look how that little dog's shithole opens up every time he barks."

And Daddy looked at Mr. Russell Newberry and Mr. Russell Newberry looked back at Daddy and then the two of them together looked at Mr. Phillip J. King who said, "What?"

"I said," Mr. Bobby Ligon told him, "I wish you'd look how that little dog's shithole opens up every time he barks."

"Every time she barks," Mr. Phillip J. King replied.

"Yes sir," Mr. Bobby Ligon said, "every time."

Naturally we all looked at Itty Bit's shithole, and sure enough every time she barked it popped open which was a matter of great wonderment to all of us until Daddy commenced to explain it away. He said the activity at Itty Bit's rear section was simply an illustration of one of Mr. Newton's laws of nature, a law that had not been formulated specifically for terrier's shitholes but would work there as well as anyplace else. According to Daddy it was all a matter of balanced thrust. The barking tended to knock the dog backwards and the shithole kicked her forwards so the both of them served to cancel each other out. "Now if Itty Bit could just work her shithole without working her mouth," Daddy said, "why then she could skim along the ground like a jet."

"No!" Mr. Bobby Ligon exclaimed.

"Yes," Daddy replied, and Mr. Russell Newberry and Mr. Phillip J. King shook their heads yes also.

"Ain't that astounding," Mr. Bobby Ligon said.

"It truly is," Daddy told him.

And I do believe it was sometime during the course of what Daddy called his shithole disquisition that Momma made her purchase since not me or him either saw her make it, blinded as we were by the marvels of nature. She bought an oval hand mirror, not a very fashionable little implement but useful enough. The glass was noticeably aged and discolored around the edges but otherwise highly reflective, and the casing and stem were done up in tiny silver-plated rosettes that ran roundabout the whole business on a vine and were joined opposite the glass by Miss Pettigrew's initials, or most of them anyway since the A had fallen off which left a little M beside a big P beside a brass rivet. So Momma had bought a nice enough item, but she did not seem inclined to show it off and carried it under her arm when she came back to the fence hunting me and Daddy, and when Daddy asked her what she had Momma just said, "A mirror," and did not bring it out for us to see. She had come to tell us she was through with auctions for a spell and would be going home directly, and Mr. Phillip J. King asked her would his wife be going home directly with her, but Momma told him Mrs. Phillip J. King was waiting to bid on the naked sabre and so would possibly be awhile. "Very possibly," Daddy added.

So Momma left us for home and me and Daddy and Mr. Phillip J. King and Mr. Russell Newberry leaned backwards against the wrought iron fence with our elbows through the palings while Mr. Bobby Ligon squatted unsupported on his heels beside us. They all smoked and spat and told stories and made terrier shithole jokes and I spat some myself and partway listened and partway watched the mayor and Miss Pettigrew's belongings get sold off piece by ragged piece. Now that all the grand items had been dispensed with and all the marginally grand items had been taken as well, there was not much of anything left but the shabby, mildewed, termite-eaten stuff, so naturally I was not expecting to see anything of interest when Mr. Spainhour took up by the leg a small upholstered footstool and held it high over his head. Just the sight of it made my ears tingle and straight off I could not figure why my ears should tingle on account of an upholstered footstool; I couldn't exactly figure what tingling ears meant anyway. But shortly I recollected an acquaintance with that footstool which I myself had seen under Miss Pettigrew's very feet in the month of March I am certain of 1977 I do believe. We were selling toothbrushes for the James K. Polk middle school baseball team with the money to go for new uniforms. The old uniforms had developed holes in all the crotches and Coach Mangum did not think it seemly to turn a squad loose in them, so we were attempting to generate funds with Pepsodent toothbrushes in an extraordinary assortment of colors. The coach reasoned they would be easier to move than magazine subscriptions or seventy-five-cent nut clusters, and as it turned out they were fairly easy to move. I sold two to Daddy and three to Momma. Mr. Phillip J. King bought a red one as a gift for Mrs. Phillip J. King. The Reverend Richard Crockett Shelton purchased a pair following one of Momma's sleepy meatloaf dinners. My barber Mr. Lacy went in halves on one with his partner. I inflicted two yellow ones and a blue one on Mr. Russell Newberry, who soaks his teeth at night in a dish. And Miss Pettigrew bought up the remaining half dozen, which is precisely where the footstool comes in.

Of course I had not intended to sell any toothbrushes to Miss Pettigrew; it seemed to me Momma and Daddy and Mr.

and Mrs. Russell Newberry were good for four or five more
between them. But Momma suggested I drop by her house,
and when I resisted the first suggestion she made another one
and when I resisted that one too she gave me two bottles of
damson preserves in a basket and showed me the door. I guess
I circled Miss Pettigrew's lot for forty-five minutes trying to
convince myself that Miss Pettigrew was as regular and ordinary as Momma believed her to be. I'd heard at school she'd
cut off your feet and stew them in a pot, which had seemed
ridiculous at the time but was commencing to weigh somewhat
heavily on my imagination as I passed around the house from
the frontside to the backside to the frontside again. However,
at length I reasoned it was best to risk my feet, the danger
seeming altogether remote and improbable, than to return home
with the damson preserves and surrender up my backside. So
I went in through the gateway, along the sidewalk, up the front
steps, and onto the porch, where I beat on the door with the
fleshy part of my hand and then put my ear to one of the panels
and heard the flooring in the foyer creak and pop. Straightaway
the deadbolt shot back, the doorknob jiggled, and the heavy
front door swung open to reveal Aunt Willa in her usual smock
and scowl ensemble, and she invited me on into the house if
you can call a jerk of the head an invitation. "Hello," I said
once the door shut tight behind me, "my name is Louis Benfield
and I'm selling toothbrushes for the baseball team at James K.
Polk middle school," and then I raised up and sought out some
eye contact. Coach Mangum told us eye contact was an essen-
tial facet of good salesmanship. But my pupils were still fluc-
tuating on account of the sudden and general gloom so I could
not find Aunt Willa's eyes or any other part of her to focus in
on which turned out to be understandable since I was by myself
in the foyer except for an umbrella jug that did not seem in
the leastways interested in toothbrushes. And me and the
umbrella jug had not hardly struck up a meaningful acquaintance when Aunt Willa came back and led me out of the foyer
before I could even begin to tell her I was Louis Benfield from
the James K. Polk middle school.

I followed her down a short, dark hallway, across two broad,
dark sitting rooms, and to the door of what looked to be a
closet which when opened gave onto a tiny den where Miss
Pettigrew sat by the lone window with a book in her lap.

"Hello," I said.

"You are Louis Benfield," Miss Pettigrew told me, "Inez Benfield's boy, and you've come bearing gifts and toothbrushes."

I forgot myself momentarily and put the inside of my mouth on exhibition.

"You see," Miss Pettigrew said and smiled at me in the most delightful sort of way.

And I told her, "Yes ma'm" out of sheer reflex and politeness though actually I did not see much of anything at the time.

"Please sit down, Louis Benfield," Miss Pettigrew said, motioning me to a chair, and I closed my mouth and took it. "You have something for me?" she asked.

"Yes ma'm," I said and leaned forward to give her the basket and the preserves.

"How nice, how very nice." Miss Pettigrew held one of the bottles up to the window and looked through it. "Lovely. Tell your mother they are simply lovely."

"Yes ma'm," I said.

"Beautiful preserves," Miss Pettigrew added.

"Yes ma'm," I said.

And as Miss Pettigrew rearranged the preserves in the basket prior to setting it on the rug beside her chair, a great surge of vigorous activity commenced on the floorboards overhead. It sounded to me like a herd of squirrels in a footrace and had set in so suddenly I near about leapt straight out the window without so much as a goodbye.

Apparently Miss Pettigrew noticed my anxiety because she put her hand to my wrist and told me, "It's just him," and then she rolled her eyes upwards the way apostles used to.

"Yes ma'm," I said, "just him," and I tried to sit back and be comfortable.

Miss Pettigrew soothed me somewhat with a few very bland and harmless remarks of the sort adults are generally prone to, and by the time she got around to exhaling a pair of well-well's, which is what they all get around to eventually, I was feeling sufficiently bold to seek out some eye contact. But I had just barely set in on the crisis at James K. Polk middle school when Miss Pettigrew held up her hand and stopped me. "No need for that," she told me.

"Yes ma'm," I said, "no need for that," and of a sudden

the eye contact seemed to me an incredibly bad idea so I made
some contact with the floor instead and that was when I first
noticed Miss Pettigrew's upholstered footstool. It was sitting
flush in the middle of the only patch of sunlight that fell across
the rug. There wasn't anything extraordinary about it and I
don't imagine I would have even recollected it if not for Miss
Pettigrew's feet atop it though more truly on account of Miss
Pettigrew's ankles, which were connected to Miss Pettigrew's
feet which were resting atop the upholstered footstool. I had
never before seen and never hope to see again such astoundingly
white skin on a living human. It was not your regular old folks
white skin all pale and waxy and eat up with blood vessels,
but was more in the line of your stately princesses white skin,
what people call fair, and best as I could determine it was about
the color of fatback. I don't imagine there was anything whiter
anywhere else in the house and I do not even suppose there
was another patch of skin so pure and unfreckled for three city
blocks roundabout. I tell you they were the most unpuckered,
ungathered, unbesmirched ankles I've ever been witness to and
were a matter of considerable wonderment to me, considerable
wonderment, and I'm generally not the sort to get worked up
over girls and such, especially over old women, especially over
old women's ankles. Occasionally I'll find myself hypnotized
and somewhat nauseous on account of a fuzzy open-toed slip-
per, but usually it is the vitality of it that affects me, and Miss
Pettigrew's ankles did not possess any vitality to speak of.
They were altogether stationary and lifeless. I just suppose in
a place where everything else is scarred and spotted and interrupted all over it's pleasing to find even two ankles' worth of
purity and perfection.

So I watched Miss Pettigrew's ankles in a highly discourteous and unforgivable sort of way, and I do believe Miss
Pettigrew thoroughly wore out her stock of polite observations
before she finally resorted to addressing me directly. "Louis?"
she said.

"Yes ma'm?" And I drew off from the footstool to look
Miss Pettigrew in the face which was hardly so striking a thing
as her ankles and seemed worn and ancient and inhumanly
weary everywhere but the eyes. Miss Pettigrew's eyes were
not in the leastways antiques.

"Louis, tell me," she said, "do you ever look at the stars?"

"Ma'm?"

"Do you ever go out in the summertime and lie on you back in the grass and look up at the sky?" Miss Pettigrew said, and turned her head towards the lone window, which gave onto a very slight portion of the backyard.

"Yes ma'm," I told her, "sometimes. I mean I used to, I used to when I was little but I don't much anymore."

"When you were little?" Miss Pettigrew said, and of a sudden pondered me straight on until I could not look at her any longer.

"Yes ma'm," I said.

"And how old are you now, Louis?" she asked me.

"Thirteen, ma'm. But I'll be fourteen in June."

"Ah," Miss Pettigrew said, "my apologies."

She watched me with those eyes of hers until I wanted to seep off into the cellar through a crack in the floor, and only after a prodigious and excruciating silence did she fetch up a little brass bell off the windowsill and ring it sharply. "Good day, Louis Benfield," Miss Pettigrew told me. "Do give my regards to your people." And I bowed at the waist for some reason I have yet to decipher since it is not and has never been my habit to bow at the waist, after which I followed Aunt Willa into the foyer where she paid me cash money for a half dozen toothbrushes, mostly blue ones.

I left that place in an excessive hurry. I don't know precisely why now, but at the time it seemed the circumstances called for an excessive hurry so I provided one. I did not bother with the front steps but left the porch for the sidewalk and exited through the iron gateway at the height of my stride. As I recollect it now, I ran hard for three blocks, trotted two more, and then walked the rest of the way home, where Momma was waiting for me on the glider in Daddy's grey sweater and with her arms wrapped around herself.

"Did you see her?" she asked me almost before I could get into the front yard.

"Yes ma'm," I said.

"How did she look?" Momma wanted to know, and she got up off the glider and met me on the top step.

"She looked old, Momma. She looked old and tired."

"Well, did you talk to her?" Momma asked me.

"Yes ma'm. I talked to her."

"And what did she say?" Momma wanted to know.

"She asked me did I ever lie on my back in the grass and look up at the stars."

"Did she?" Momma said.

"Yes ma'm," I told her, "she did."

ii

WE WERE expecting Astors or Morgans or maybe even some sort of diluted Rockefeller. I mean it was a grand and prestigious property, a fine old local landmark, and folks roundabout the countryside figured not Astors or Morgans or Rockefellers either would object to owning what a Pettigrew had owned and living where a Pettigrew had lived. So Momma watched for the Astors and Daddy watched for the Morgans and I watched for the Rockefellers though I don't believe I would have known a Rockefeller if he knocked me down in the street, especially an impure and diluted one. But none of it made any difference in the end since no Astors came and no Morgans came and not even the square root of a Rockefeller showed up to take a look see. In fact, nobody at all came for a full month after Mr. Grant and Mr. Owen and Mr. Ellersby, Realtors Inc., planted their sign in Miss Pettigrew's front yard. Then in the second week of October Mr. Grant showed the house to a middleaged gentleman who Mrs. Phillip J. King insisted was a Watlington—she said she had been looking for Watlingtons all along—but who turned out to be a Gill from Madison-Mayodan. By all reports Mr. Gill was enchanted with the lot, was intrigued with the house, and was supported solely by disability benefits. House-hunting was Mr. Gill's passion; house-buying did not much interest him, however. Towards the beginning of November Mr. Ellersby showed the property to a young couple from Greensboro who toured the house and walked all throughout the yard on a Tuesday and then returned on a Thursday with a little black notebook in which they proceeded to record all variety of observations and on the Monday following they came back yet again along with an older woman who bore an acute resemblance to the younger woman but turned out to be her husband's mother. The three of them together along with Mr. Ellersby toured the house and walked all throughout the yard admiring the scenery and consulting the little black notebook. Then they held a series of lengthy and earnest confabs on the front porch and along the walkway and in the sideyard and every now and again behind some shrubbery, after which the older woman who resembled her daughter-in-law but was actually her son's mother got into her son's car along with her son and her son's wife and they all three departed from Neely forever. Of course we were disappointed even though they had not been Astors or Morgans or hybrid Rockefellers but we were not entirely unoptimistic and expected Mr. Owen to succeed where Mr. Grant and Mr. Ellersby had failed. But Mr. Russell Newberry found out from his wife's sister, who moved some property herself, that Mr. Owen had departed from the firm of Grant, Owen and Ellersby, Realtors Inc. on account of heart failure and so no longer handled much real estate but occupied some instead. The news did not crush us altogether but did serve to render us a little more entirely unoptimistic than we had been previously.

Nobody came to look at Miss Pettigrew's house for the rest of November and it sat vacant and untoured and unwandered around throughout December and on into January. Mr. Ellersby showed it one Saturday towards the middle of the month and along about the thirtieth or the thirty-first Mr. Grant waited on the front porch for an hour and a half but nobody ever joined him there. By the first of February there was a sizeable faction of local people who were noticeably annoyed with Mr. Grant and Mr. Ellersby for not having unloaded the property with a little more haste and dispatch. They feared the house might get rundown and the yard might get grown over, and they wanted Mr. Grant and Mr. Ellersby or Mr. Grant and Mr. Ellersby together to contact Mr. Conrad Rackley in the West Virginia end of Kentucky and negotiate the price some. But Mr. Grant and Mr. Ellersby too said the trouble was not with the price. They said the trouble was with the house, or more specifically with the ruinous condition and general dilapidation of the structure and environs. And Mr. Grant pointed out some of the missing shutters and some of the missing louvers in the shutters that were not yet missing, and the aforementioned section of pathetically sagging dental molding, and great stretches of paint that were sitting off from the cedar siding like treebark, and an assortment of shattered window lights and pulverized orange terra cotta tiles, and a crack in one of the chimneys big enough to put your arm through, and three or four yellow pine sills that termites had fairly thoroughly reduced to the consistency of talcum powder. Then Mr. Ellersby set in to ridiculing the living area and called it foul and filthy and excessively odoriferous, after which him and Mr. Grant together slandered the lawn and reviled the shrubbery. At first it was almost more than any of us could bear and there was some vicious talk about realtors for a day or two following the meeting with Mr. Grant and Mr. Ellersby, but once we commenced to look around for ourselves we discovered the conditions were in fact ruinous and the dilapidation was indeed general, all of which proved immeasurably surprising to us.

Of course dilapidation was not the sort of thing Momma needed to hear talk of in February, especially along about the first of the month which would leave her the whole rest of the month to ruminate upon it. So the February Miss Pettigrew's house got sold was an especially bleak one for Momma there at the beginning. She was celebrating near about a decade of false starts and thwarted intentions with Mr. Vanderbank, but I do not believe she managed to get properly underway and instead just sat in Grandma Yount's boudoir chair with the book in her lap and looked out the living room window. On February the eighth Daddy made her a gift of an intensified table lamp from Hudson-Belk, but the additional illumination did not seem to enliven her spirits any, and on the evenings of February ninth through the eleventh Daddy treated Momma and me to three consecutive suppers at the Holiday Inn with about the same effect. Naturally there was some fear we might lose Momma. The living room had reached its peak incandescence and the waitresses at the motel were getting fairly fed up with Daddy's sense of humor which left us with no clear remedy for a regular February much less a February complicated by Pettigrew dilapidation. So we were beginning to expect Momma to succumb straightaway and we were confounded and exasperated and feeling a little undone ourselves when Mrs. Phillip J. King called up with the remedy and brought us around directly.

He was Mr. P. Merriman Bledsoe from Stokesdale, and in Mrs. Phillip J. King's estimation that was a name that showed some promise. However we could not discover the first little thing about him for a week after him and Mr. Ellersby shook hands on Miss Pettigrew's front porch. On account of a steady rain, nobody much had seen him except for Commander Tuttle who had happened by and who recollected Mr. P. Merriman Bledsoe to have been approximately sixty-nine inches tall and twenty-two inches across the shoulders which was about as vivid as a mortician ever had call to be. And we did not find out anything otherwise until Mrs. Phillip J. King cajoled one of the Dudley Circle Petrees to urge her second cousin in Walnut grove to call her brother-in-law in Stokesdale and get the full dope on Mr. P. Merriman Bledsoe and his attachments, but even then we did not find out much of anything otherwise except for an anecdote of Mr. P. Merriman Bledsoe's past that circulated all roundabout Neely like a cyclone. It seems Mr. P. Merriman Bledsoe had started out in business as a screenwire salesman for his uncle. He had worked the eastern part of the state down around Oxford and little Washington and Greenville sometime after Coolidge but a few years prior to Truman which Daddy said would have been the Paleolithic era, things being as they are east of Raleigh. Of course nobody much down that way was excessively passionate about screenwire since you couldn't eat it or drink it or wear it on your feet, so Mr. P. Merriman Bledsoe figured he'd best stir up a little passion of his own if he wanted to make any money. What he did was to carry a fifty pound sack of pure white flour in the back of his truck and whenever he visited a prospective client he'd step up onto the porch first and introduce himself and immediately thereafter would circle around to the outhouse and drop three or four healthy handfuls of flour down the hole. Then he would return to the front porch and sit and talk about most anything under the sun aside from screenwire, and directly a white fly would come zipping around the side of the house and beat himself against a front window or disappear through the door-way and then three or four more would show up to take his place and they'd be joined by another half dozen and presently the air would be fairly thick with albino flies. I do imagine it was a most graphic and effective display of the virtues of a screened-in porch.

Naturally we figured him for a tycoon by now, a screenwire tycoon, and word was he had scoured the state for a garden spot and had decided at last to retire in Neely, winner of the Governor's Award for Excellence in 1966. Of course we all looked forward to making him comfortable and welcome, and the widowwomen roundabout the countryside geared up for the undertaking since there had not been any whisper of a Mrs. P. Merriman Bledsoe. Mrs. Phillip J. King said it would be undeniably refreshing to have a worldly and resourceful gentleman in our midsts, and she expected him to possess a scintillating wit, figured him for a pure stitch she said, and Daddy told her he was a little breathless about it himself since he had never before met a man sixty-nine inches tall and twenty-two inches across the shoulders. But we did not ever get to find out if Mr. P. Merriman Bledsoe was indeed scintillating, did not even get to find out if he was sixty-nine inches tall, because Mr. P. Merriman Bledsoe did not ever come to the garden spot to retire or visit or sell screenwire either. Instead he sent two carpenters in a blue Dodge pickup truck and for the last few days in February and on through the most of March they paraded back and forth across the front threshold hauling new wood in and hauling old wood out and otherwise making a monstrous amount of ruckus with hammers and saws and such. Most people figured it for a general renovation though we could not see what was going on, and Mr. Monk Fanning, a carpenter himself, listened at the fence for a day and a half and said it sounded to him like a general renovation or maybe a partial renovation with complications, he could not detect which. Mr. P. Merriman Bledsoe's carpenters did not seem much inclined to discuss the matter with anybody, and only once, when Mr. Wyatt Benbow found them squatting on Miss Pettigrew's front sidewalk drinking Pepsi-Colas and eating nabs, did we get any information from them at all. Mr. Wyatt Benbow asked them just what it was they were up to and they told him they were drinking Pepsi-Colas and eating nabs.

Towards the end of March the carpenters were joined by three painters who arrived in Neely from the west in a gold Ford Torino with two aluminum extension ladders and one eight-foot wooden step ladder strapped to the top of it. The tallest of them, who was tattooed and leathery and wore his hair hooked back behind his ears, climbed up to the eave of the house and nailed the piece of detached dental molding back into the place. The next tallest of them went all around the structure patching, glazing and replacing windowlights. And the shortest of them, who was apparently the boss, kept Miss

Pettigrew's treestump from running off by sitting on top of it. Together the three of them scraped some paint and pecked at some paint and flecked some paint off with their fingernails, and then the leathery tattooed one mixed together a pint of Clorox, a cupful of laundry detergent, and three or four gallons of water in a five gallon bucket and him and the next shortest fellow used the concoction in combination with a pair of bristle brushes on broomhandles to scrub down the house. For his part the boss squirted the hose, from the treestump when he could manage it and he could manage it a considerable portion of the time on account of Miss Pettigrew's surprising and prodigious water pressure which touched off a lively discussion along the fence since Neely was generally the sort of place where a man had to be patient to get wet in the shower.

The Clorox and the detergent and the brushes on broom-handles took off the first several layers of accumulated grime and as the siding dripped dry the three painters and the two carpenters all gathered on Miss Pettigrew's front sidewalk for a collective squat and they all drank Pepsi-Colas and ate orange nabs except for the tallest painter with the hair hooked behind his ears who washed down a sack of pork rinds with a Truade and thereby struck what Daddy called another blow for rugged individualism. Then they threw their bottles in the yard along with their wrappers and they all smoked and looked at the people against the fence in a most presumptuous sort of way, Mrs. Phillip J. King called it, and they talked among themselves and laughed and swore and spat and one of the carpenters fetched a finishing nail out of his apron and picked his teeth with it. Then him and his associate went directly back to beating on the interior of the house but the painters did not commence to painting straightaway. Instead they caulked for awhile, or anyway the tallest one and the next tallest one caulked while the short one did some impressive coordinating from the tree-stump. And apparently Miss Pettigrew's house was simply rid-dled with cracks because the tallest painter and the next tallest painter used up close to a half case of acrylic caulk and the short treestumped boss painter near about coordinated himself to a frazzle. So the three of them together rested for an hour on the front steps before they endeavored to exert themselves further, and at length when they were resigned to yet another strenuous undertaking the short boss painter sounded the car-

penters and then checked with his leathery tattooed employee
before dispatching the middle-sized painter down the boulevard
towards the Burger Chef.

I do not believe they even removed the gallon paint cans
from the trunk of the Torino until well past two o'clock, and
then, under the supervision of the boss painter, the tallest painter
and the next tallest painter stirred the paint and mixed the paint
and stirred it some more and gawked at it and just generally
mucked around with it until right at three o'clock when it was
time for two more Pepsis and a Truade. Of course the ladders
had to be situated before any serious work could get underway
and since the ground was not precisely level everywhere the
short boss painter and the tall leathery painter went into the
house to hunt up some shems and left the middle-sized painter
in charge of the treestump. I guess there was near about an
hour of daylight left when the first brushstroke finally found
its way onto the frame of one of the upper front windows, and
on account of the weak light there was some anxiety among
the spectators who had waited all afternoon to see the paint
and now that they were seeing it couldn't make out the color
to any degree of certainty. Mrs. Estelle Singletary suggested it
was a kind of autumn beige, but Mrs. Phillip J. King said she
believed it more towards a sweet cream white, while Commander Tuttle insisted on wheatstraw brown, puny wheatstraw
brown he called it. The late Mrs. Doris Lancaster's half sister,
Miss Louise Branch Montegue, was more inclined towards lily
of the valley, which she had in her bathroom but her neighbor
Mrs. Pfaff, who had visited Miss Louise Branch Montegue's
bathroom on several occasions, saw in the trim paint more of
an antique almond than any sort of lily of any sort of valley.
Mr. Ogburn of the FCX made a case for pale camel, but Mr.
Johnny Newsome pulled at his bottom lip and wondered out
loud if pale camel and antique almond weren't near about the
same thing, and Miss Louise Branch Montegue told him that
was probably the truth of it but made no nevermind anyway
since pale camel and antique almond neither one showed much
of any relation to lily of the valley, which Commander Tuttle
insisted did not hardly approach the subtleties of wheatstraw
brown which Mrs. Phillip J. King said could not match sweet
cream white for purity of tone and general lustrosity, which
Mrs. Estelle Singletary tittered at and she could titter in a most

meaningful sort of way. The precise color, then, was still a little up in the air when Mr. Wyatt Benbow, who previously had communicated so ably with the carpenters, laid his arms between two of the wrought iron palings and called out, "Hey buddy, buddy" until he turned the short boss painter around on the treestump.

"Whut is it?" the painter asked him.

"Tell me something, buddy," Mr. Wyatt Benbow said, "just what do you call that color your boys are putting on the windows?"

And the short boss painter briefly looked over his shoulder to where the middle-sized painter was working on a window sash and then turned back around to Mr. Wyatt Benbow and told him, "I call it yalla."

There was an ensuing discussion. For a day and a half there was an ensuing discussion, but after four or five windowsills, a doorframe, and the full eave across the front had been trimmed out most everybody agreed to Sunmist, which Mrs. Jackson P. Eaton jr. had plucked directly off a paint chart. Folks said it was a subtle color, a rich yet pale shade markedly pure of tone and possessed of a matchless general lustrosity, and Mrs. Estelle Singletary said she believed it would strike a handsome contrast with some manner of slate blue. Mrs. Phillip J. King told her possibly but felt it more suited to a full chocolate, while Commander Tuttle played up the virtues of a maroon, and the late Mrs. Doris Lancaster's half sister, Miss Louise Branch Montegue, suggested a soft and wholly capable green. Mrs. Pfaff was convinced an antique mahogany would best set off the brilliance of the Sunmist, and though Mr. Ogburn of the FCX found himself attracted to the idea of a mahogany he could not work up any enthusiasm for the antique part of it and was more truly inclined towards some sort of deep walnut, but Mr. Johnny Newsome pulled at his bottom lip and wondered out loud if deep walnut and antique mahogany and maroon and full chocolate weren't all near about the same thing, and Mrs. Louise Branch Montegue told him that was probably the truth of it.

The leathery tattooed painter and the middle-sized painter took their time finishing up the trim and apparently the short boss painter took his time doing whatever it was he was doing because the three of them were on the job a week and a half

before they ever fetched the siding paint out from the Torino
to stir up and gawk at and muck with. Naturally anxiety along
the fence had reached an extraordinary pitch by the time the
leathery tattooed painter with the hair hooked behind his ears
carried the fresh gallon of paint up a ladder towards the front
eave and commenced to smear it on the siding. A sizeable
crowd had collected to watch him—even Aunt Willa had come
out from colored town where she'd disappeared to once the
monkey was disposed of—but the leathery tattooed painter did
not seem much affected by the audience and he spat and cleared
his nose and swore like usual. The middle-sized painter took
his own full gallon up a ladder on the opposite end of the house
and him and the leathery tattooed painter carried six boards
apiece over to the center where the short boss painter coordinated a masterful and indecipherable seam. Then the leathery
tattooed painter and the middlesized painter lowered their ladders three or four rungs and set in to covering six more boards.
No one along the fence seemed excessively eager to comment
on the color straightaway. Folks generally seemed inclined to
reserve judgement and wait for what they called the full effect,
but as for myself I knew directly this was not one of your
standard pigments, was probably not one of your more exotic
pigments either, but was most likely one of your strictly crim-
inal pigments. I do mean it was offensive in a capital sort of
way. Mr. Wyatt Benbow asked the short boss painter what he
called it and the short boss painter said he called it red, but I
do believe there are those reds with a richness and a paleness
and maybe even a matchless general lustrosity to them and this
was not a red like that. More precisely it was the exact color
of tomato soup when you add the can of milk instead of the
can of water, which is nothing that should be exposed to the
out-of-doors in bulk. By itself the siding color proved to be
nauseating and it was purely debilitating in combination with
the trim, so nobody much waited around for the full effect once
the partial effect had taken ahold of them. Consequently the
leathery tattooed painter and the middle-sized painter baptized
the most of the house without hardly any audience except for
the short boss painter and the two carpenters whenever they
decided to come outside and squat. Nobody had much stomach
for the place once it stopped being white and started being red
and yellow, and what folks could manage it avoided going

downtown altogether which Daddy said was understandable considering how Miss Pettigrew's house had suddenly gone from a showplace to a visual diarrhetic, he called it.

We found ourselves a little less fiery hot to meet up with Mr. P. Merriman Bledsoe after the painters got done and the carpenters left town, so disappointment did not run wild and rampant when word got around that Mr. P. Merriman Bledsoe was not coming to Neely to get met up with. We were, however, somewhat distressed by the black and orange Rooms for Rent sign that was tacked onto one of Miss Pettigrew's porch stanchions by Mr. Ellersby of Grant, Owen, & Ellersby, Realtors Inc. Not that a black and orange Rooms for Rent sign seemed inappropriate on a red and yellow house—the place would have looked naked without it—but just that people could not warm to the idea of rental property right there in the heart of downtown Neely under the very nose of Colonel Blalock. They said it was an exceedingly bad idea; they said you didn't know what sort of ilk such a place would attract. But in truth that was not the problem. The problem was everybody knew exactly what sort of ilk such a place would attract, and it attracted them straight off in great sorry heaps and messes.

Things got underway with a half dozen Otts. There was a momma Ott who used to be a Jones and a daddy Ott who'd gotten laid off from the cotton mill, and four little towheaded Otts who looked to be wearing on their shirtfronts some tiny part of most everything they had eaten or otherwise stuck in their mouths over a year's time. These six particular Otts were a fairly unknown quantity to most of us but they were related by blood to a far more illustrious and remarkable Ott whose acquaintance did not usually make for any sort of lofty recommendation. Spencer Ott, first cousin to the cotton mill Ott and the Mrs. Jones Ott and second cousin to the four filthy little towheaded Otts, had operated the projector at the Palace Theatre downtown from the time he graduated high school on up until his thirtieth year. He lived with his mother at the Ott homeplace on Scales Street and was widely figured for a mild sort of a swish up until his momma's death when he commenced to grieve her by wearing her clothes and the odd thing about it was he looked fairly ravishing in them. He had not been ravishing in trousers as far as I know, so it was a compound shock to most everybody when Spencer Ott showed up in the

A&P in one of his Momma's cotton blend outfits and did considerably more for it than she ever had. He'd gotten from somewhere a walnut hairpiece that fell in lustrous locks and ringlets down his back, and he was a regular artist with a lipstick, so nobody knew it was Spencer Ott until he tried to write a check for his groceries and then nobody wanted to believe it was Spencer Ott, especially the men, who felt a little ill about having looked at him in the way they had looked at him. But of course it was Spencer Ott and it continued to be Spencer Ott for several weeks thereafter all over town in pumps and nylons until some of his momma's relations in Leaksville had Spencer shipped off to the Dix Hill Institute in Raleigh on what Daddy called a fashion scholarship. They turned him out eventually and he returned to Neely long enough to pick up and move to the capital for good where I suppose a pretty face is a little more appreciated, and that left Neely thoroughly Ottless except for the four little towheaded Otts and the Mrs. Jones Ott and the laid off cotton mill Ott who was not especially ravishing in trousers himself.

The cotton mill Ott was fat and homely and near about as crusted over as his children. He weighed maybe two hundred and eighty pounds and I do not believe an ounce of it was gumption. He showed an extraordinary affection for chairs and was ever in one, and as best as we could tell he had a particular fondness for Miss Pettigrew's fan-backed cedar porch furniture since he generally remained in contact with one piece of it or another. The cotton mill Ott tended to take his exercise on the second, third, or sometimes fourth day of the month when the mailman brought the checks, and he would cash them at the Big Apple, purchase about a sack's worth of odds and ends, and then stroll on home with his shoulders laid back and the rest of him laid forward like maybe he was smuggling pumpkins under his shirt. The most of the odds and ends he purchased tended to be of the liquid variety and him and the Mrs. Jones Ott would evaporate them personally while the four towheaded Otts would decorate themselves with Cheez Whiz and peanut butter and run fairly wild throughout their part of the house and all roundabout the yard until their parents regained sufficient consciousness to rein them in some.

By the middle of April the Otts had been joined by five Parhams, three Lyles, a pair of Moffets, four McKinneys who

the block and mortar McKinneys insisted emphatically were
not block and mortar McKinneys, one Gresham, three full-
sized Dardens and one baby Darden, two Madison-Mayodan
Rothrocks, and assorted Smiths who did not seem to bear any
relation to each other. At first we could not help but believe
that Miss Pettigrew's house was incapable of holding such an
unseemly bulk of people and we figured three must be going
out the back door for every two that went in the front. But by
and by we learned from Mr. Whitaker, who delivered a second-
hand stove and a second-hand refrigerator into Miss Pettigrew's
upstairs hallway, that Mr. P. Merriman Bledsoe's carpenters
had not performed a general renovation, and had not performed
a partial renovation, had not renovated to any degree exactly
but had subdivided instead. They had separated the big rooms
into quarters and the regular-sized rooms into thirds and the
little rooms into halves, so the tenants were packed into Miss
Pettigrew's house like bullets in a box. I do not truly know
how many people the place could accommodate, but I don't
believe Mr. Ellersby ever filled it up or ever filled it up for
very long anyway since the rate of turnover was extraordinarily
high and Dardens or Greshams or Rothrocks that had sat on
the porch with their feet on the bannister one day were gone
from the county the next only to be replaced by McGees or
Linleys or some fresh Smiths and once by a puzzling batch of
Hayeses who were all related to each other in some inexplicable
and oblique way that not even Mrs. Phillip J. King could make
any sense of.

So the Pettigrew house and grounds took on what Daddy
called a new complexion; it got so that even those people who
could stomach the red and the yellow could not bring themselves to stop at the fence and lean up against it with their arms
through the palings so as to contemplate Mr. Wallace Amory
sr.'s majestic undertaking on account of the countless Otts and
Parhams and McKinneys and Greshams and McGees and
Hayeses and Smiths that had nothing else whatsoever to do but
litter the majestic undertaking's front porch and contemplate
back. Mrs. Phillip J. King said it was unsettling to be perused
so, and most everybody else agreed to the spirit of the observation if not the phrasing of it. Consequently local traffic along
the boulevard diminished in a dramatic sort of way once folks
became sufficiently unsettled and nobody who was going any-

where downtown got there like they used to get there. That is, almost nobody. Daddy still went like he generally went, went like he'd always gone, and would not confess to even the slightest degree of unsettlement because of it. He said it was his duty to eschew all detours and bypasses. He said it was his obligation to chronicle the demise. Daddy said he had a born gift for chronicling demises and did not intend to squander it on account of a porchful of slackjaws.

So while most everybody else circled all roundabout the city and slipped up on wherever it was they were going from behind, Daddy went direct like always and paid some considerable attention to Mr. P. Merriman Bledsoe's tenants no matter how much considerable attention they paid back to him in return. Understandably, then, it was Daddy that kept us abreast of the advancing general dilapidation and progressive ruination of Miss Pettigrew's house and grounds. He counted the window screens on the portico roof and told us what trash had accumulated in the shrubbery. He kept the Smiths all straight from each other and could tell which were born Smiths and which weren't and what little Smith belonged to what big Smith, and when one of the Hayeses threatened to stomp another one of the Hayeses and then did in fact stomp him, Daddy did Sheriff Burton the favor of identifying the offending Hayes, which proved little or no difficulty for him on account of his intense work with Smiths previously. Of course Daddy was right on top of the story when the Rothrocks decided, for the sake of convenience, to drive their Plymouth around the house to the front yard and park it athwart the sidewalk, and he reported the repercussions among Lyles and Dardens and Otts and Moffets who took a lesson from the Rothrocks's example and filled up the front yard with their own vehicles. And understandably Daddy paid particular attention to Mr. P. Merriman Bledsoe's tenants around the first of each month when the checks would come and things would get exceedingly lively, and usually a few Parhams and a Linley and a Darden and a couple of Hayeses and an Ott and every now and again a Smith or two would all throw in together and try to dismember each other just for the sheer diversion of it.

But nobody else seemed to pay much attention to Mr. P. Merriman Bledsoe's tenants except maybe for Mr. Russell Newberry and Mr. Wyatt Benbow and Mrs. Phillip J. King though she swore several demonstrative oaths to the contrary. Hardly anybody even talked about Miss Pettigrew's house anymore; folks just made ghastly faces over it and tried to recollect what it used to be back when it was something. So Daddy persisted in chronicling the demise very nearly by himself, but after the checks came in October, when the Hayes stomping occurred, there was not much left to chronicle on account of how the tenants, or some one of the tenants anyway, carried the dilapidation and ruination to the very boundaries of utter destruction and beyond which I do not believe he was aiming for but which he hit direct nonetheless. All the Hayeses said it was a Smith and all the Smiths said it was a Hayes and all the McKinneys and the Moffets and the Dardens and the Otts and the Parhams and the Lyles and the Linleys agreed among themselves it was a Smith or a Hayes though they could not be sure of precisely which. There was no doubt, however, as to the when of it: the evening of October 4, 1980, which was not one of your storm-tossed lightning-wrent October nights like Neely has been known for, but was more along the lines of one of your regular tranquil early autumn evenings.

It seems a Smith or a Hayes could not find any matches to light his cigarette and woke up a Darden to get some. But the Darden, who could not recollect if it was a Smith or a Hayes that woke him up, did not have anything but a striker himself, so whoever it was that had woke up the Darden in the first place gave up on the notion of matches altogether and proceeded to light his cigarette off the back burner of the electric range in the upstairs hallway. I suppose he was so taken with his resourcefulness that he neglected to switch off the range eye once he'd lit up his cigarette without singeing his nose appreciably, and this particular Smith or Hayes went off to wherever it was he was going and left the burner to glow unattended for awhile. Of course the hallway got exceedingly warm presently, especially the stovetop, and a halfroll of papertowels laying longways up against the oven switch turned a little brown and then began to smoke some and at length burst into legitimate flames and sent fiery ashes all across the hallway floor. Apparently even by the time they settled down several of the ashes still had enough glow to them to touch off the wallpaper which was old and brittle and made a respectable kindling for the lathing strips which set the rafters and the joists afire, or anyway that's how Mr. Pipkin figured it once he'd stirred up the rubble to his satisfaction.

Naturally, people were far too busy avoiding the Pettigrew house to notice it was on fire straightaway, so by the time Mr. Wily Gant happened onto the catastrophe and ran down the boulevard to the Omega firehouse to spread the news, smoke and flames were already boiling out some of the upper windows and an assortment of Smiths and Hayeses and McKinneys and Dardens along with a lone Parham had climbed out onto the portico roof and were making highly animated requests for assistance. The fire whistle brought the most of Neely outdoors and we all chased the sirens down the boulevard to Miss Pettigrew's house where the firemen were trying to make a path for themselves through the front yard, which was littered all roundabout with various vehicles and all manner of near hysterical tenants. The Smiths and Hayeses and McKinneys and Dardens and Parhams on the ground were waving their arms and screaming and generally attempting to impress upon Chief Pipkin and his men the gravity of the predicament of the Smiths and Hayeses and McKinneys and Dardens and Parham up on the portico roof who themselves were growing more animated by the minute. Chief Pipkin, never a man at a loss in a grave predicament, responded almost immediately by waving in the hook and ladder which he was bound and determined to use for something besides reindeer, but no matter how Mr. Myrick at the front end and Mr. Bridger at the backend manuevered the unit they could not seem to put it where it would serve anything but a decorative purpose. So two otherwise unengaged firefighters fetched an extension ladder off the pump truck and ran it up to the portico roof.

However, even once the Smiths and Hayes and McKinneys and Dardens and Parham on the portico roof had been reunited with the Smiths and Hayes and McKinneys and Dardens and Parhams on the ground, nobody could say for certain whether or not the house was entirely empty. I mean of course Sheriff Burton ordered a head count and from it he determined there was a full complement of Otts and Moffets and Linleys and McKinneys and Dardens and Parhams but he could not be certain as to the sum total of Hayes and Smiths since even the Hayes and Smiths were not certain as to their sum total themselves. So Chief Pipkin sent a half dozen of his men on into the flames to hunt up any malingerers and though they did not discover a single Smith or a solitary Hayes, they did carry a Gresham out in the horizontal and laid him on the front lawn. The firefighters studied him and poked at him, and Chief Pipkin and Sheriff Burton stooped over him and studied him too, and from out in the street where we were we tried to see him but couldn't really so we discussed him and speculated as to his circumstances and decided fairly unanimously that things were probably pretty much up with that Gresham. We figured the flames or the smoke had taken him in his sleep and Mrs. Phillip J. King blessed his everlasting soul, but she reversed herself soon thereafter when two of the firemen picked Mr. Gresham up onto his feet and leaned him against a Pontiac. It seems it had not been flames and had not been smoke either but had instead been two and a half quarts of Wild Irish Rose.

With the rescue of Mr. Gresham behind them, the firemen decided they'd best go ahead and put some water on the house since it had become all wrapped up in what Daddy called a full-fledged conflagration. I recollect everything was on fire but the brick chimneys and the concrete front steps by the time Mr. Bridger and Mr. Myrick took ahold of a hose together and ran on into the front yard with it. And though they yelled and hollered and hooted and said they were ready for the water, I guess they weren't actually ready for it when it finally came because Mr. Myrick slipped down in the grass and the hose got away from Mr. Bridger and went off across the lawn by itself. It bolted and squirmed and darted throughout the whole of the front yard and then jumped nozzle-first all over the cotton mill Ott's Chevrolet and nobody managed to close down the hydrant until that hose had squirted near about every squirtable item in the vicinity except for the house, which was roasting away in a most glorious fashion. In fact, the fire was such a success that Chief Pipkin gave up on Miss Pettigrew's house almost before his men could douse it down any, and instead he directed water to be concentrated on the surrounding trees and onto the roof of Mrs. Tullock's outbuilding across the alleyway as a precautionary measure, and Daddy said it was his experience that if the fire department could get to a thing before it started burning they could usually put it out. So Miss Pettigrew's trees got saved and Mrs. Tullock's outbuilding survived also, but Miss Pettigrew's newly painted, freshly rented house burnt to the ground, and we all watched it go, watched it late into the night and with some melancholy and regret I suppose, but the most of us marveled at the smoke and the flames like maybe we had set the thing ourselves. And in the morning we came to watch it smoulder a little, though there was not much left to smoulder but for a pile of ashes and charred wood which the chimneys had collapsed onto. There was not much else to see really. The tenants' cars had been moved out into the alleyway and the tenants themselves had gone wherever it is those sorts of people go while the trucks and firemen and firefighting paraphernalia had returned to the stationhouse. Only Mr. Pipkin and Sheriff Burton had remained behind to poke around in the rubble, so we watched them do their poking and then even they left and we had nothing to look at but the blackened wood and the jagged hunks of chimney and the miraculous concrete front steps which had remained uncluttered and unbroken and led up off the front walk to nowhere at all.

iii

THE LADIES of the Neely Garden Society desired to purchase the property, not straightaway but once the city had cleared it of all the rubbish and cinders, everything that is except for the concrete front steps which nobody seemed to have the means to lift or the truck to put it on. The ladies intended to erect, build, and cultivate a Pettigrew memorial park complete with a wide and exotic assortment of trumpet flowers, a selection of blossoming bushes, a vine-covered lattice arbor, and a gazebo, and since they meant to pay dearly for what they called the accoutrements of the place, they did not wish to pay dearly at all for the place itself and so in a formal letter they petitioned Mr. P. Merriman Bledsoe of Stokesdale to seek out the charitable corner of his heart and let the property go for what Daddy said was not even a song but more like two stanzas and a refrain. I suppose Mr. P. Merriman Bledsoe sought and sought, but he came up empty in the end and gave the ladies what amounted to a symphonic price which they simply could not begin to pay. So the Garden Society went back to tending its rose bushes at the water tower and the sewage plant and Mr.

P. Merriman Bledsoe let it be known through Mr. Ellersby that
he would entertain most any reasonable offer, would even consider negotiating with the garden club ladies if they would seek
out the sensible corner of their hearts.

Of course, since Mr. P. Merriman Bledsoe did not live in
Neely he did not much care who bought the property or what
he put on it be it an exotic memorial garden or a stagnant pond.
If Mr. P. Merriman Bledsoe showed any preference whatsoever
I guess it was towards franchises, especially franchised restau-
rants, and when word got out from Mr. Ellersby the city council
immediately commenced to search all local ordinances and find
out if the Pettigrew property wasn't somehow or another zoned
against hamburgers and batter-dipped chicken. We did not suspect it was however, but refused to panic nonetheless since we
already had a Burger Chef three blocks south and a fairly new
Hardee's just below the Holiday Inn on the bypass. Now the
Burger Chef had not ever done anything in the way of steady
business because it had not ever served anything in the way of
edible food, and as for the Hardee's, it seemed to us in town
that the bypass was a considerable distance to go for a hamburger, even a charco-broiled one. But that was before Mr.
Ellersby let it be known what Mr. Bledsoe intended to do with
Miss Pettigrew's property. The news altered our outlook extrav-
agantly. We had never before realized the true extent of our
loyalty to the Burger Chef and whenever we had a prominent
opportunity we took to praising their hamburgers and cheese-
burgers and fish filet sandwiches and we were outright raptur-
ous over the french fries. We could hardly ever contain ourselves
when Mr. Ellersby was around and some people even went so
far as to eat at the Burger Chef by way of active illustration.
Of course the Hardee's became exceedingly convenient for us,
and of a sudden we discovered it was on the way to everywhere
and we could not begin to prevent ourselves from stopping in
for a biscuit or a milkshake or a turnover or especially one of
those delicious broiled hamburgers. We had discovered nothing
was so satisfying as grilled meat. And our patronage to the
Hardee's was as utterly unshakable as our patronage to the
Burger Chef and we told Mr. Ellersby as much, told him he'd
best leave off fishing for a franchise buyer, told him we could
not even contemplate the purchase of a competing burger. So
Mr. Ellersby suggested chicken and we found we had some

very strong and near about violent opinions on assorted pieces in buckets and dinners in boxes also. The very idea seemed a profanation to us.

The surveyor from McDonald's came to town in the middle of November and sized up the Pettigrew property with his surveyor's contraption, but somehow or another the lot did not suit him and did not suit his employers, so Mr. Ellersby turned to the Burger King instead but they did not seem much interested in the place either. He negotiated with two representatives from a chicken outfit for awhile but could not entice them into a deal and he had some contact with the manager of Captain Mulligan's Fish House in Greensboro where the waitresses wore black patches over their eyes and red bandannas around their heads and looked for all the world to be a cross between Blackbeard and Aunt Jemima. But the manager complained that the Pettigrew lot was a little scant to the leeward and considerably shy to the windward also which made him reluctant to drop anchor on it, so he shoved off and took his excessively nautical self on back to Greensboro on the wings of a southeaster. Consequently, come Christmastime of 1980, which was this past Christmastime, Mr. P. Merriman Bledsoe had not succeeded in relieving himself of the Pettigrew property and Mr. Ellersby had not succeeded in disposing of it for him, so throughout the holiday season the mayor and Miss Pettigrew's grassy lot sat unbought and unlooked at and entirely unoccupied except for the concrete front steps, which the city was apparently attempting to move through the sheer force of good intentions. The holidays themselves were unexceptional enough. I do not recollect that the fire department got Santa and his sleigh and his reindeer onto the courthouse roof with any sort of remarkable velocity, and I do believe the Methodist Christmas pageant was fairly much of an unblemished success except for a brief interruption when one of the shepherds tending his flock by night got tangled up in the hem of his raiments and fell onto the crooked end of his staff which took his breath temporarily but did not cause any lasting injury. On Christmas morning I gave Momma a new sugar bowl and gave Daddy a hat and Daddy gave Momma a green skirt and a new book to read in February and Momma and Daddy gave me a wristwatch and a pair of shoes and then Momma gave Daddy a little box wrapped in foil paper with a ribbon around it and Daddy untied the ribbon and tore off the paper and opened the box to find a clear plastic Zippo lighter with an orange baitfly in the tank of it. I expected him to be delighted and I suppose Momma expected him to be delighted also but Daddy was not delighted, could not even bring himself to pretend to be delighted, and I do believe at the very moment he flipped open the top and touched off the first flame Daddy's enthusiasm for tobacco began to wear away.

By the second week in January there was talk all roundabout town of a branch bank on the Pettigrew property. Some people said it would be First Citizen's and some people said it would be Northwestern and most people said it would be Wachovia, but in February when the two men came in the green pickup truck they erected just inside the wrought iron fence a sizeable wooden sign which announced that the property that had gone from Pettigrew to Pettigrew to Bledsoe had subsequently come into the hands of the South Atlantic Finance Corporation, which Daddy said was not the same thing as a bank exactly, was not the same thing as a bank at all. So we waited for the South Atlantic Finance Corporation to stake out their office and pour their footings, but construction did not commence in February or March or April or May or June or all throughout the rest of the summer and on into September, and the city kept the property up from month to month, mowed the lawn, trimmed around the sign, sheered the shrubbery, and continued to intend to move the concrete front steps.

Along about the middle of October, with the Pettigrew property still uncultivated and unerected and unbuilt upon our anticipation had died away to a considerable degree and so we were easily distracted by the news of a package that the depot was holding for a Mrs. Willa Ross Bristow. It had arrived in the underbelly of a Greyhound bus out of Charlotte, and according to Mr. Lanchester Petree of the Lawsonville Avenue Petrees who had gone to the terminal to fetch his wife's sister's husband off the same bus and who had seen the item for himself, it was not one of your regular negro to negro packages but was instead a stenciled crate that appeared to have originated with some official arm of the very governing body of these United States, Mr. Lancaster Petree put it. But before we could even commence any sort of earnest calculations as to just what official arm of the very governing body of these United States, we found out for certain from a fat hairy Simpson who went by A.E. or O.I. or U.A., two vowels anyway, and who had driven Aunt Willa to the Heavenly Rest in his Blue Bird cab. The double-voweled Simpson said it was a zoo box, said he had read the stencil and figured out it was a zoo box for himself even though it did not say zoo or box either anywhere on it but said instead zoological park from which the double-voweled Simpson had precipitated and distillated zoo box. Daddy said you could hardly hope to put anything past a Simpson.

At first, the double-voweled Simpson had not especially objected to carrying a zoo box to wherever it was a negro might want to carry one, but he had planned upon carrying it in the trunk of his Blue Bird cab and not in the backseat, which is where he ended up carrying it, and he did not object straightaway because he did not smell anything straightaway but presently the aroma of the zoo box impressed itself upon the double-voweled Simpson and he attempted utterly unsuccessfully to get shed of Aunt Willa and get shed of her boxed up aroma, but at length wisdom came to him and he drove Aunt Willa to the Heavenly Rest with the most of his head laying out the side window which itself attracted some considerable attention even before anybody discovered it was Aunt Willa in the backseat with the late Mr. Britches in a crate beside her.

The commander had agreed to a burial, had been paid for a burial, had actually been paid for a burial and a chapel service, but psychologically he was not prepared to receive a monkey corpse only a scant two years after he'd agreed to receive one. After all, the commander had figured the zoo would not send it to him anyway, had figured they would throw it in a hole down around Ashboro and cover it up, but they did send it to him inside of a plastic bag inside of a wooden crate and even then the aroma drove the commander and Mr. Tally and Mr. Dunn and the double-voweled Simpson and Aunt Willa out of the parlor and onto the shaded front porch and Mrs. Ida Joyce Hinkle, who stayed behind for a viewing, would probably have been killed by the stench if she had not been dead already. Of course the commander was bound and obligated to see to the monkey's disposal; he had made an agreement and Aunt Willa still owned the receipt. And though not eager, the commander was willing to hold up his end of the bargain and would have too if not for the local uproar which set in once folks found

out what manner of creature the commander was intending to
hold services for. People generally did not want a chimpanzee
eulogized where their mommas and daddies had been eulogized
and where they themselves expected to be eulogized in the
distant future. Of course the commander held that his was a
nondenominational air-cooled chapel, but most people felt
strongly that a monkey did not even qualify for nondenomi-
nationality, especially this monkey since it had not been in any
way a Christian creature but had instead been a vile and excessively urinary animal, had in fact been a flat out pagan beast,
Mrs. Phillip J. King called it, and there was serious talk that
a chimpanzee service in the nondenominational air-cooled chapel
would probably be the final service ever held there. So the
commander found himself in a tight spot with some specifications of the deceased on the one hand and a gracious degree
of public outrage on the other, and after only a brief period of
consultation and review, since the aroma was not in any way
diminishing, the commander went ahead and yielded to the
public outrage. The deceased had been dead near about two
years, so her specifications did not hold the sway they had
previously.

The commander had been instructed to lay Mr. Britches
away in a finely appointed child's coffin, but for what he said
were health reasons he cremated the monkey instead and filled
up a ceramic jug with his ashes. Then the commander made
the appropriate arrangements with the only man he could have
made arrangements with, and the morning after Mr. Britches
had arrived at the Heavenly Rest inside a plastic bag inside a
wooden crate he traveled to Casper Epps's Holy Jesus Chapel
inside a ceramic jug inside a black Cadillac limousine. The
service was to be held at two o'clock on the afternoon of
October 17, 1981, which was a Saturday, and since word of
the proceedings did not get much broadcast roundabout from
the commander and from the commander's employees and from
the great preponderance of decent and God-fearing local people
me and Daddy and Mr. Russell Newberry and Mr. Phillip J.
King near about missed the funeral. In fact, by the time we
got to the Holy Jesus Chapel all the chairs were taken and there
was not much leaning space left either. Daddy said everybody
who is nobody was there, and I guess that's pretty much the
truth of it. There weren't any Benbows or Singletarys or Fra-

ziers or Tullocks, not any white Tullocks anyway, but there was a scandalous load of everything else, and even with Casper Epps's chapel expansion and renovation due to the stove explosion of the spring of 1970 elbow room among the mourners was passably scant.

I do not believe Casper Epps had ever played to a full house before. I do not believe he had ever presided over any sort of official function either. But once he came out from a room off the kitchen in what looked like a white linen bathrobe, Casper Epps did not appear the least bit worked up on account of the genuine throng or on account of the special duty. Previously he had taken out what part of the wall between the kitchen and the living room the stove had not taken out for him, and before he passed directly off the linoleum and onto the hardwood he raised his finger and blessed that assortment of mourners who were leaning against the kitchen counter. Then he proceeded straightaway to the altar, which was nothing but an oak tressel table with a Bible and the bottled up monkey on top of it, and he waved his finger at the rest of us and blessed us also. Casper Epps had set aside his Uncle Bill Collier's upholstered chair for the family, but Aunt Willa, who apparently had not held the monkey very dear, was not present at the Holy Jesus Chapel, so Casper Epps waved Mrs. Pearl Betts towards the upholstered chair and welcomed her to set her phlebitis down in it. However, Mrs. Pearl Betts, who was one of your more lowly Bettses, did not much appreciate all the commotion stirred up by a monkey in a jug, and as she made her way across the living room she gave Casper Epps a piece of her mind, told him he should worry himself with healing the sick and leave dead monkeys out of it, told him there was plenty enough suffering among regular people to keep him occupied from now on, told him she was in some considerable misery herself, told him he'd best toss that jugged up monkey on out the window and see to it, told him she had a son, Claude Laurance Betts jr., who'd come straight over and kick Casper Epps holy butt if he didn't get back to his regular line of work, and then she sat down in the late Uncle Bill Collier's upholstered chair and Casper Epps raised his finger and blessed her.

Shortly thereafter the funeral commenced, or anyway I guess that's what it was since the ceramic jugful of monkey ashes seemed to figure into the proceedings every now and again, but it was not one of your more clearcut ceremonies. I mean it was not all shot through with sobriety and Godliness like the funerals the commander usually put on at his air-cooled chapel. Actually there was very little about the monkey to it, and mostly the eulogy hit upon the highlights of Casper Epps life in preaching and briefly examined several of the more notable and miraculous episodes. We sang once that I recollect, but I do not believe I ever knew what it was we were singing, and we prayed any number of times, mediated mostly with some ecstatic shrieks thrown in every now and again for effect. And then towards the end, when we were all a little worn out and near about done in, Casper Epps raised his finger and said, "Bless this beast among the creatures that crawl and those that fly," and he scooped up the jug in his arms, crossed the living room, and went out the front door with it. We had not been invited to follow him, had not been in the leastways encouraged to, but curiosity got the better of us and everybody except for Mrs. Pearl Betts and her phlebitis and Mr. Raymond Duggins, who had the excema on his forearms, followed Casper Epps out the front door and around the house to the sideyard. Two little Broadnaxes had been paid fifty cents to dig a hole and by the time Casper Epps got to it along with the rest of us there was still about twenty-nine cents worth to go, so me and Daddy and Mr. Russell Newberry and Mr. Phillip J. King and Mr. Wiley Gant leaned up against the late Bill Collier's clapboard and Mr. Russell Newberry and Mr. Phillip J. King smoked Mr. Wiley Gant's cigarettes while Daddy and me chewed gum. And once the hole was sufficiently wide and sufficiently deep to accommodate the jugful of monkey ashes, we all gathered at the graveside and listened to Casper Epps's benediction, which was a wild and wholly incomprehensible animal itself, and then we watched him set the jug into the hole and kick some dirt in on top of it.

Momma did not want to hear anything of the monkey's funeral. She would not let Daddy speak of it at supper, would not let him speak of it in the house at all, so after we ate me and Daddy took to the porch and he sat on the glider and I sat on the front steps and we talked about the monkey and talked about Casper Epps and talked about the mayor and, at last, talked about Miss Pettigrew.

"She's gone two years now," Daddy said. "Doesn't hardly seem like it."

"No sir," I told him. "It surely doesn't."

"She was an odd creature, that one," Daddy said, "an odd creature."

"I suppose so, Daddy," I told him and picked at the top step with a stick.

"I don't guess she was made for this world," Daddy said.

"I suppose not, Daddy," I told him.

"It just never seemed to suit her, never seemed to suit her at all," Daddy said.

And I scratched at the step and did not bother to suppose one way or the other.

"I mean, Louis, you have to bend some," Daddy said, "you have to sway a little every now and again, don't you know."

And still I did not bother to do any supposing.

"I mean, Louis, the world isn't ever the same place it used to be. It's a disagreeable and unfortunate fact, but Louis," Daddy told me, "it is a fact."

"Yes sir," I said, "I suppose it is."

And I guess that's the truth of it. I don't know. Anymore we hardly ever talk about Miss Pettigrew or the mayor, don't ever talk about the monkey, and rarely have a word to say on the property since the city is still only intending to move the concrete steps and the South Atlantic Finance Corporation has yet to erect anything more lasting and permanent than a wooden sign. We do not worry much about Pettigrews at all anymore. Momma says there is no cause to dally in the past. Momma says we should forge ahead, break new ground, look to the horizon. Lately she is ever making the bravest sort of noise. Daddy figures it's the fire and the monkey and the prospect of winter working on Momma all at once and together. He says she's just whistling as loud as she can. But Momma has never much excelled in brave noises, and Neely is cold now and lifeless and near about at the end of another year. We have emptied the gutters and cleaned out the crepe myrtles and stacked all the screens in the cellar, and anymore when me and Daddy walk off our supper to the boulevard and back we wear our lined coats and our gloves and our fuzzy wool hats because the evening air is sharp and painfully cold and sometimes when the moon is out and the clouds blow free of the stars it seems to me you could swing a hammer against the night sky and shatter the whole business.

State College-Raleigh 1981–1983

About the Author

T. R. Pearson was born in Winston-Salem, North Carolina, in 1956 and now lives in Fuquay-Varina, North Carolina. A SHORT HISTORY OF A SMALL PLACE is his first novel. His subsequent novels in the Neely, North Carolina, saga are OFF FOR THE SWEET HEREAFTER and THE LAST OF HOW IT WAS.

The Undisputed Masters of Contemporary Fiction